# MARCUS
# THE INTREPID
# VILLAGE BOY

\* \* \*

*Victor Waldron*

Best Wishes
VH

HANSIB

First published in Great Britain by Hansib Publications in 2019

Hansib Publications Limited
P.O. Box 226, Hertford, SG14 3WY

info@hansibpublications.com
www.hansibpublications.com

ISBN 978-1-912662-01-2

A CIP catalogue record for this book
is available from the British Library

Design & Production by Hansib Publications Ltd

Printed in Great Britain

# DEDICATION

I am truly grateful for the fact that I have been relatively healthy over the eight decades that I have lived. More especially, the fact that I have retained my faculties over this period cannot be overstated. Equally as important is the family structure around me which I regard as priceless.

My daughters, Karen and Claire, have been foremost in giving me the encouragement needed to apply myself to the task of pursuing my objective. My dear wife, Gloria, has also been steadfast in her support, and never allowing me to lose interest.

Colin, my son, grandson, Kamal, and son-in-laws, Derek and Ron, provide the vital ingredients necessary for my general welfare and help to keep me grounded. My ten-year-old grandson, Tyrese, whose potential for the game of golf stimulates my interest, and regularly walking the course keeps me relatively fit.

What cannot be discounted is the contribution from my brother-in-law, Keith Gordon. He has given me support and guidance every step of the way. Without the input from all of you, this book may never have materialised. My eternal gratitude goes out to you all.

# PREFACE

I have the greatest regard for the men and women who delight and impress us with the written word. They stimulate the mind and create lasting memories, especially for those of us who find reading a fulfilling and relaxing pastime. This art form has given so much to our world and provides so much pleasure to many.

I have always had an active mind and a vision of things that I find noteworthy. I, therefore, decided to add my own composition to this wonderful medium.

Having written and published my first book and autobiography in 2007, which covered the period of my life between Guyana, my birthplace, and London, I decided to embark upon a project far more challenging. I chose to continue the theme of Guyana and London because they are both integral parts of my life.

While my own contribution to this amazing industry is modest, I hope that my effort has a degree of merit and that it is appreciated by others.

This story of zeal, restlessness and ambition is set in the post-war era, and tells of a young man's dreams of attaining the love of his life. Trying desperately to escape from his humble beginnings, his greatest wish was to become a soldier in the British Army. But he was faced with the task of breaking down barriers at a time when society's stringent rules dictated otherwise.

Having accomplished his initial objective, was this going to be enough to win the heart of the woman of his dreams?

VICTOR WALDRON

# MARCUS

It was 6.30 pm and the sun was setting. The magnificent splendour of it, alas, was short lived by nightfall, which with equal impressiveness, spread its dark cloak with rapid urgency, obscuring what was left of the fleeting red cloud that accompanied the once golden sun.

Marcus Gullant had seen this phenomenon of nature's glorious exchange on countless occasions as a young lad growing up in his native British Guiana. But now, the magnitude of this spectacle had become a sight to behold. He smiled, thinking how this great act of nature had been taken for granted as a boy, yet as an adult, he was able to appreciate this moment as if seeing it for the first time.

The nightfall brought with it a strong southerly breeze, enough to make the SS *Aracassa* somewhat unsteady on its keel. The darkness was now total, as he looked out onto the vast volume of water and paid tribute to man's own ingenious ability to navigate such wide expanses with so much success.

The fierce wind blew aggressively across the bow of this huge liner, with more than enough chill to prompt him to take corrective action in order to keep warm. He began buttoning his shirt right up to his neck for ample protection. He was now alone; a cursory glance around indicated that the multitude of passengers only a short time ago that were enjoying the idyllic conditions had now scampered away to a warmer sanctuary. He stared into the blackness of the night and felt his nose to see if it was still intact against the fierce wind. The tropical climate of home had now long since gone.

His thoughts were set on London. This time there was no sense of joy or jubilation that once stirred his imagination. He fully appreciated that the circumstances were far different from the last journey he made to his beloved homeland. The memory of that visit loomed largely in his mind. How different can one journey be from another? Then, it was the ultimate period of his life. He was returning to London with his beautiful wife to be, with expectations of unending ecstasy. Then, life had a completely new meaning to it. It was purposeful, consummate and seamless. So much so, it was difficult for his over joyous mind to fully appreciate it all.

Yes, he was overwhelmingly smitten by this serenely wonderful woman, who was soon to become his wife and naturally he had envisaged a life of eternal bliss.

The *SS Aracassa* was taking a battering. The elements had changed rapidly and were now in a mode of belligerence. Apart from the ship's hands, who were attending their tasks, no one else but Marcus was willing to face the howling winds and driving rain that danced merrily around this vast vessel. He held firmly to the rails determined to pursue his thoughts in the face of such inclement conditions.

It all started so many years ago in a little village where he was born. It was a lovely place with very simple rules. It was a colonially structured village, where accepting the local culture was paramount. In other words, know your place in society and life would bode well. The village had a texture of severity about it. In that context it was disproportionate. The assumption that if you were born poor, accepting the criteria of poverty without murmur or fuss was considered a given. It was a way of life and as a result, it was not to be questioned. In the minds of many, that philosophy was how it was meant to be.

Being no ordinary villager, he was a dreamer of immense proportions. But foremost, he was a young man with visions of grandeur, sustained by an unwavering belief in himself. His certainty of reaching his goal, finding success and making it big was his primary objective. In his mind that was almost inevitable.

How or when, he could not say, but his positive attitude, his determination and his desire to succeed were undoubtedly the qualities that propelled him forward.

His family's poverty would not act as a deterrent and his reticent manner belied his positive attitude and determination surprisingly, many of the rank and file villagers regarded him as being eccentric and even insubordinate.

His flight of fantasy placed him beyond the scope of normality. In the village, the philosophy of knowing who you are, and accepting your poverty with a degree of contentment, did not fit well on his youthful shoulders. His approach to life differed almost exclusively from that of his contemporaries, making him less compatible with those around him, often creating discordant conditions and non-acceptance within the group. While others would be content with the considered norm, Marcus would happily sit on the walls of the seafront in glorious isolation, looking far into the horizon and pondering about the great unknown, where he imagined, life would have a new meaning, where hope lives, where ambitions are achieved and aspirations are obtained. He was well aware of his status and bothered very little about comments made about him.

If nothing else, he was comfortable in his own skin and was never unhappy about the process of his thinking. Dreaming big lifted him out of the ordinary and helped him to cope with the humdrum existence that he was part of. Nevertheless, he was always of good grace and remained calm, polite and courteous as best he could. The unkind and unnecessary suggestions that he did not belong and that he was different mattered very little. Marcus knew only too well he was a good villager and made great effort to function within the boundaries of this place he called home.

Marcus loved and adored his mother Mama G. She was a woman of thrift, energy and wisdom. She was always at the forefront of everything connected to their very existence. Her role was not only crucial, but it was also thoroughly essential to the otherwise smooth running of the household. Mama G accepted life the way it was. She was a great believer and contended that it was God's will and guidance that kept her strong. Her temperament and her pursuit to maintain a degree of adequacy for the family was an overall success.

His father, Albert, a carpenter by trade, was blighted by ill health and was never able to fulfil his obligations in the fullest of ways. Nevertheless, his support level depended largely on his ability to function adequately and consistently due to factors largely beyond his control. Although he could not be considered as weak or unreliable, Albert tacitly conceded he was no match for a wife such as Mama G. Her natural survival instincts and her ability to solve difficult problems left him in awe of her. In the Gullant family, Mama G was undoubtedly the boss.

Robert, his eldest brother who was a policeman, provided prestige to their family's name in the small village community. Adel, his only sister was forever a thorn in his side. Although she was only two years older, would never allow him to forget it. As a result, they bickered constantly and the harmony that should have been apparent in the relationship suffered immeasurably.

Marcus was quite clever at school, although he was intelligent and resourceful; he was convinced that he would never be able to reach the optimum of his ability, mainly because of his parent's economic situation. He was aware that there were serious constraints on finance, thereby radically reducing his chances of higher education. Even as a young man, he was far-reaching in his ideas. His greatest wish was to be in uniform, not as a policeman, but as a soldier in the British Army. However, as far as dreams go, the most illustrious of them all was to have Teresa Malison's love and affection and hopefully one day making her his bride.

There was no one on God's earth, outside of his mother, that he cared for more than Teresa. From the first moment he saw her, he was captivated by her beauty. He would lay in bed looking up into the dark ceiling, creating and recreating wonderful scenarios about her. She happened to be in his every existence. But he was aware of the fact that although they were villagers and living in close proximity of each other, she never consciously appeared to notice him once. Marcus really hoped and wished that one day that would change. As he watched her grow up, he realised that the possibility of his dream becoming a reality was simply an illusion.

# VILLAGE PROTOCOL

The Malison family were the village elite. They were seen in the highest of esteem by all and sundry. Every important occasion or matters of interest were represented by a Malison, making them undoubtedly the most revered family around. The respect that was shown by the village community for them was not out of place. Their social skills, their academic prowess and their subsequent success, were part and parcel of a well-achieving family. The parents, Malcolm and Edith Malison, studied in the USA. They were, in fact, the first couple in the village to have done so. Malcolm was a headmaster, his wife a top civil servant, his son Eric a lawyer and his eldest daughter Alice an accountant. It was that kind of social divide that separated their two families. In the grand scheme of things, Marcus knew the chances of ever becoming remotely close to Teresa, much less to form a relationship, was virtually impossible. He was by now certain of the fact, that his love for her would never diminish. He can only hope for a miracle and miracles just did not happen in the village.

Next door to where he lived was his mother's best friend Nanny May. The bad news was she happened to be his Godmother, who paid far greater attention to his spiritual endowment than his own mother did. She was once someone of normal attributes and generally speaking a rank and file villager of no particular persuasion. That all changed miraculously and in an instant when she was faced with serious life challenges. That change saw her gravitate from one extreme to another. Suddenly and without warning, she became a devout Christian woman of immense stature.

Nanny May's entire strategy left a sinister connotation to it. Ever since her husband left never to return – he went prospecting for gold – she was adamant that her life would not be held up for ridicule. In a village where nothing goes unnoticed, she was determined to find a niche. Her opportunity to establish herself as someone of merit came under Father Gull, a white priest of English origin. The good clergyman was suitably impressed by her relentless pursuit in gaining his attention as regards to matters of the church; thereby she was able to transform herself from a common busybody to a conscientious and loyal trustee of the establishment. Her efforts and her energy were enough to win over the sceptics and fainthearted, who once saw her as a figure of fun.

Even at a tender age, Marcus could not be swayed by his Godmother's conversion and he remained convinced, although tacitly, that she was not the genuine article. Doing God's work was clearly her new mantra and Marcus, a most reluctant recruit, was forced to do her bidding, regardless. He fully realised he was unable to complain. After all, in many ways, she was one and the same with his mother, regarding matters of the church. In fact, Mama G was a willing participant in allowing Nanny May the freedom of helping her son to acquire his proper Christian fulfilment, which she believed could only be to his benefit. What was not to Marcus's satisfaction, however, was to be under the yoke of someone whose interest in him was negligible and one who in the final analysis, was feathering her own nest, at the expense of all else. In the village, especially with regards to matters of the church, everyone with few exceptions, fervently believed that they were heading straight to heaven.

Another couple of interesting personalities in the village were Harry Sidwell and his new bride, Mertle. Harry was a retired engineer; he was seventy years old and a widower, who wasted no time to re-engage in marriage. Mertle was half his age and was full of life and energy. The chasm between them was enormous and it was plain to see the oddity of it. Marcus was always uncomfortable about this connection and considered it most distasteful. Harry was cheerful and of a pleasant demeanour, against his robust and fun seeking wife who loved dancing, enjoyed the company of other men and never showed fear or discretion in her activities, most of which Marcus believed to be void of principle or conducive to common decency. Witnessing this spectacle left a major imprint on his young mind.

Being young in a village where the normal criteria apply – kids must be seen and not heard – he readily assumed that the woman was a product of unwholesome habits and of a licentious kind which he thoroughly abhorred. At the other end of the spectrum, was cheerful Harry, ever pleasant and showing no signs of worry or discontent. Rather like the old man river, he just kept rolling on. It was left to Marcus to ponder in his own youthful way, why in a village of such moral fortitude, the villagers were so indulgent to Mertle's effervescent and non-conformist ways.

Marcus simply loathed Mertle for the way she behaved and as time went by, that loathing increased. It was out of that relationship that a decision emerged. He made a solemn oath never to marry anyone more than five years younger than himself. That became a creed. He always felt sorry for Harry. He believed Harry was the victim of unfair play. That odd couple managed to shape his thinking in a massive way. In his mind, that principle would remain valid and consistent without fail.

Another interesting character in the village was Martin Jules, a free-spirited young man. He was not a villager and showed a degree of discomfort being there. Martin was a breath of fresh air to Marcus. He was knowledgeable, stimulating and very inspirational. Compatibility between them was simply a matter of course. 'Martin the Mouth', as he was generally known, was a description that was false and inappropriate. Because of his talkative nature, many regarded him as a braggart. As a result, his popularity in the community suffered severely. His parents were city people and were less liked because of their son's supposedly overactive mind. However, he was high on the popularity stakes as far as Marcus was concerned. He found

Martin most refreshing and in many ways akin to his way of thinking. Martin was a happy fellow and certainly not a "stick in the mud" individual, like so many around.

Sundays in the village followed a normal pattern. Usually, it was a holy day and the churches predominated. This gave Mama G the opportunity to appear smartly attired and along with Nanny May, their solemnity was second to none. They would martial the troops and collectively parade through the village to the church. Well – there was one exception, Albert Gullant, his father, who showed stubborn resistance to this rolling bandwagon, using every trick he could muster, including his illness to rid himself of this rigorous routine. There were those who deemed him ungodly and questioned his sincerity, but no one was brave enough to challenge or confront him.

The Malisons were no exception to this carefully organised programme of church attendance. It was by tradition that they occupied pews at the front end of the church for themselves and family. In descending order, were the Gorndis family and the Bannians. These three families were regarded as the most important ones in the village structure and accordingly, they automatically occupied the pews immediately behind the Malisons.

Marcus saw that as errant. In a place where God lives such exclusiveness should not be tolerated in his estimation. Render your heart and not your social status was his motto. These village practices as he saw them were not in the interest of good Christian behaviour. However, it was an accepted fact of village life. It was the kind that seemed to be set in stone.

Set in stone also, were the village habits especially at weekends. The magnet of Saturday nights undoubtedly ignited everyone's interest, all with the exception of Marcus. As far as he was concerned, the village activities had a particular inevitability about it. Because of the profile of sameness, he, unfortunately, found it less stimulating. This, however, was not consistent with the average villager, whose participation and involvement belied the lacklustre attitude of Marcus.

Debro's cake shop was regarded as a fitting meeting place and indeed a convenient stop for refreshments of every description. Debro's place was by no means the only venue of interest but attracted by far the greater numbers for what he was offering. He was renowned for his famous mauby and pastries which made him and his cake shop very popular. The attraction of the village was totally lost on the young man merely for its unbending nature. It was the repetition of a most monotonous kind that never ever seemed to waver.

For example, Taff, Duce and friends were in their customary positions playing dominoes. Mido was a champion player of draughts. His supremacy was meritorious for someone who was alleged to be illiterate. He defied anyone to beat him and was open to any challengers, such was his confidence. In the end and to the best of his recollection, Marcus could not remember anyone taking his crown. Then there was old Makay, strumming his guitar far more enthusiastically on a Saturday night, fully aware of the attention he attracted.

Adjacent to the shop was Boysi's peanut stall. He was a true character who always had a reputation for being the best in the business. Never short of a word or two especially about peanuts, which he claimed were the best this side of heaven. Not too many disagreed, since the common consensus of rank and file agreed that his nuts were almost always perfect.

Marcus's general outlook to this humdrum establishment left him bored and unsatisfied, although he could not deny that for some unknown reason, Debro's mauby and cakes seemed to taste better at weekends. What was undoubtedly the enterprising and uplifting part of the evening for him was the presence of Martin Jules. Armed with a glass of mauby, or a bottle of lemonade, a pine tart or a salara, Martin Jules came into his own. He commanded a great deal of attention with his knowledge of things exquisite. He expounded about Ethiopia and Haile Selassie, he talked about the pyramids, about Marcus Garvey and topics of which few of the villagers were aware. Some regarded him as erudite; others dismissed him as a lunatic with a big mouth – a windbag – to which he paid minimum attention. He was someone who was always in the know and cared very little about negative opinions. He was always ready and welcomed a good debate.

The Second World War was now a year old and the quiet trend of the village was very often shattered by rumours of one kind or another. Invasions among other things were mentioned. The Germans were coming. It was also alleged that ships were being torpedoed at sea and the general fear of sailors was manifested everywhere.

Martin's friendship with Marcus became beneficial and productive when he alerted him of a recruitment drive that was imminently taking place for crews to man merchant vessels across the ocean. The German U-boats that were prevalent on the high seas and causing great havoc discouraged hardened sailors from accepting the challenge. One man's meat is another man's poison was as true an adage most befitting of Marcus's circumstances. For him, this was a chance of a lifetime, a chance to finally escape village life. It was a golden opportunity for him to accomplish hidden dreams and to experience true adventure. It was also the moment he had been waiting for to exchange this slow and monotonous village life for something more tangible and exciting. In many ways, his time had come.

The news that Marcus was leaving the village was difficult for his parents to accept. Mama G and his sister Adel could not hide their grief. How could someone so young, be willing to accept such a massive undertaking in the light of so much danger on the high seas? They both begged him to reconsider but Marcus was now ready. His plans were quite clear, he would voyage to England, jump ship and be conscripted into the British Army. His vision of a fighting man in the armed forces, confronting the enemy and becoming a national hero was beginning to gain momentum. Adel – a strong woman – besieged her younger brother to think again.

Albert, his father, was now on his last legs and Mama G could not cope with the stress of it all, but Marcus knew that destiny called and nothing could now sway his mind. His tactical intentions were already in place. In the interest of creating peace of mind to his immediate relatives, who cared dearly for him, he decided to remain tacit in regards to his ultimate plans. Marcus was driven by the unrelenting desire to become a frontline soldier. He imagined becoming a real fighting man and one who thrived on combat. Such was his courage and determination. He regarded the opportunity a watershed moment, a chance in a lifetime. To reveal his true intentions to his loved ones would only accelerate the grief that was already predominant, as a result, it was prudent not to divulge his innermost thoughts to them. He was about to live his dream in a world that was full of possibilities.

He was now a very muscular young man, eighteen years old, six foot three inches and full of confidence, especially after his affray with big Wally, the village bully. That, more than anything else, gave him the courage to move on. His Godmother Nanny May's remarks about him keeping bad company and living with the devil may have influenced him even more. In the great scheme of things, however, this was certainly the opportunity he was hoping for and, come what may, he was about to grab this wonderful moment with both hands.

# BRITISH BARRACKS

Three months had elapsed since Marcus' arrival in England. His ability to rapidly adjust to both people and the elements challenged him to the fullest. It was diametrically opposite to what he had left behind. The slow snail's pace was replaced by this vast fast and rapid moving environment, compounded by fog, smog, sleet, snow, chill and damp. Obviously, these were serious obstacles to overcome. If the elements were not bad enough to deal with, his communication with people was by far more problematic. Very often he was met with mind-boggling indifference, amazing curiosity and at times extreme contempt, but in a strange way, these were all factored into his thinking. He craved a new life and was more than prepared to endure any setbacks that came his way. The fact that he was now in uniform, a member of the King's Army, gave him a sense of exhilaration that preceded all else. He had accomplished much in a short time. His vision of things to come was still intact. As far as he was concerned optimism ruled.

His first day in the British Army gave him a foretaste of things to follow. The wretched weather, the armies culture, the shouting of instructions, the ability to get it right, the alertness that was required, the endurance and patience, the snares and name calling, were the ultimate experience and with a background such as his, if he was to succeed, his village mentality needed a swift revision. He genuinely knew that being out of step with this new environment would be counterproductive to his ultimate ambitions. Being well aware that his world had turned upside down; this was now real and not imaginary. It was, without doubt, something he craved and it was obvious that whatever was thrown at him, he would ensure he succeeded.

Being a part of a regiment, wearing the King's uniform, fighting a war for the Mother Country, was far and beyond his wildest dreams. It was reality in its absolute form. He certainly was not afraid of hard work, although he imagined the wintry months would prove a great test of his endurance; however, it was a challenge he was prepared to confront. At the back of his mind being the optimist that he was, when the struggle had finally rescinded, he would ultimately become a hero, especially on his return to his homeland. In the village, he would be master of his domain, king of the land. Martin Jules and his contemporaries would have to stop and listen to the main man from England, who wore the King's uniform and fought the good fight for peace and freedom. Just imagine what impression that would make on his beloved Teresa. To that end, whatever he had to endure would be well worth it.

Marcus felt he was the focus of much attention. His skin colour made him stand out, especially amid the great multitude of white folks; he was some kind of a spectacle. He remembered that Martin Jules had told him that white folks thought that black people had tails. He was astounded that such a view could ever be perceived by rational people.

However, as the days and weeks passed, he began to think that there was an element of truth in Martin's ludicrous anecdote. His first night in barracks proved to be a unique experience. It was late evening and the camp was hurriedly preparing for bed. Undressing, Marcus could not help but notice several members of the unit paying undue interest in his activities. He was again the focus of attention. A young soldier was observing Marcus's every movement and then called out to his mate. "Terry! Terry! Look, this black geezer is carrying his tail in front of him, and not behind." Marcus didn't know whether to laugh or cry. The soldier's mission of discovery was evidence enough that black men were, in fact, very different. Marcus was fully entrenched in a cold, damp barracks in Norfolk, surrounded on every side by people whose behaviour and attitude he could barely comprehend.

His departure from the village was as wide as the ocean itself. Never in a million years would he have believed what was happening to him. It was all so new. He swallowed hard as if to take it all in because this was for real and nothing, but nothing could alter it now. Yet in a very strange way, he felt a tinge of excitement running through his veins. He was totally relieved moving out of an environment that was stifling him to death. He had sprung the trap and was heading in the direction he craved. He fully understood that this new experience would be comparatively difficult, but in a most curious way, he welcomed it. Marcus settled himself in the camp bed wishing things were more ideal but was ready to accept the reality of the situation. He looked around the camp furtively assuming that he was the only person of colour among the jabbering, vociferous men severely encroaching on the silence of the night.

Charlie McBean seemed to set the tone for the rest to follow. Charlie was egotistical, with language so colourful, only rats in a sewer would be inspired by it. His antics and mannerisms matched his personality; crude and unattractive. Without a doubt, he was Kingmaker and commanded – even compelled a strange kind of response and respect from the others. So absorbed was Marcus by the newness of it all, he totally overlooked the only other African in his midst. He was Roland Buckley. Roland was short and tubby. Hence his nickname: 'short ass'. Nevertheless, he was truly a welcome sight to behold.

In many ways Roland's presence was a tremendous boost to his spirit, knowing he now had company. Unfortunately Roland was not a new recruit; in fact, he was the only person of colour before Marcus arrived in the regiment. Being quiet and polite was certainly not to his advantage. In fact, Roland was the butt of every soldier in camp. The pranks that were played on him were simply diabolical. Charlie being the chief instigator, always whipping up support wherever and whenever he could, somehow Roland managed to withstand it all. Marcus, on the other hand, was rarely picked upon; he was six foot three inches tall with a muscular physique. He seemed older than his years would suggest and as a result commanded respect from everyone, perhaps more for his stature than anything else.

Roland responded well to Marcus but was always careful to fight his own battles. Not that he did it well, but was always afraid to get anyone else involved. He simply absorbed the antics and behaviour of the other soldiers with quiet dignity and never complained. It was obvious he factored these difficulties in as a way of life and was more than prepared to accept them – no matter how hard it got. Marcus indicated to Roland that he should fight back; do something to stop the abuse, but he seemed quietly prepared to put such matters behind him. In reality, he was ready to live with it. Much of the verbal degradation unnerved Marcus. The daily diet of being called 'nig-nog', 'darky', 'jungle boy', 'midnight', 'cannibal' and the rest, was becoming intolerable, but Marcus kept his cool. He was sure of one thing: if there was any trouble, he was almost certain he could not rely on Roland for support. It, therefore, made good sense to pretend that all was well.

The overriding theme, firmly embedded into his subconscious, was that when things were bad; when life offers little hope; when difficulties prevail, he would wrap himself into his world of fantasy, a world where nothing could distract him. Romanticising about Teresa Malison, gave him the strength to endure all things. This was a place where all his dreams came true.

There were times when reality would kick in – when the possibility of having that dream fulfilled seemed remote, but he would simply dismiss it and not be deterred. In his mind hope springs eternal he would assume and as always he was a super optimist. Marcus would read and re-read Mama G's letters constantly, always with a hope of seeing some mention of the Malisons. Mama G was not a gossip, but she reported everything that occurred in the village: births, deaths, marriages, etc. Never was anything said about the Malisons. Was that intentional?

Could it be that they were deliberately excluded from her news? No one knows. Whatever it was, he held the view that no news was good news. One thing was absolutely certain until he heard anything to the contrary; he would continue to live his dreams and hope.

He recalled quite vividly that evening that was to have changed his life completely. The smile on his face became wider until his entire features were engulfed in it. He arrived at the barracks despondent, wet and weary. The evening was sullen and miserable, matching the mood of the day. His assignment of moving heavy stock from one place to another with a task force that offered little by way of help or cooperation made the experience ghastly and unwholesome. There were occasions when the work conditions degenerated to a degree of sheer drudgery. Lesser mortals would have buckled under this pressure.

Yet not to be deterred, he carried on manfully, constantly reminding himself that those in the front line were in far worse situations than he. Very conscious of the fact also, that he was a visible minority surrounded on every side by people who saw him differently and behaving in an abstract manner towards him, which was obviously what he expected. He fully realised that charity was not on the agenda and quite frankly he expected none. He was Marcus the interminable and was prepared to remain that way. Trusting in the law of averages and hoping for a change of direction, which undoubtedly would have been better than the existing one that had prevailed. The mood of the barracks was far from normal. The sniggering and muted whispering gave the game away. He was aware that something was certainly afoot. Whatever it was, Marcus had very little time for it. More than anything else all he wanted was a night of uninterrupted rest.

# HONOUR AND PRIDE

Marcus tucked himself in for a quiet evening when all hell broke loose. The barracks residents were in absolute glee, falling over themselves with laughter as Roland kept hopping around in distress. Someone decided it would be amusing to up-side a bucket of water all over his bed, which drenched him in the process. This was a stupid and unnecessary prank, merely to facilitate a cheap laugh. Apart from the fact that it was hardly a night for it, it was by any standard a ghastly thing to do. For the first time Roland showed annoyance, but as usual, he reverted to his normal stance quickly. Instinctively Marcus intervened. He sprung out of bed, his fury so intense, it was enough to make the jabbering laughing idiots take notice. In an amazing turnaround, there was a sudden hush all around. His instinctive reaction took them all by surprise.

"Which one of you did this?" Marcus fumed. "Tell me who's done it so I can knock the living shit out of them?" The silence was deafening. No one expected an outburst of such magnitude. Even Marcus surprised himself by this sudden show of strength. Rightly or wrongly, he was now committed to facing the situation head-on. What was, in fact, a defence of Roland initially had swiftly moved on. The entire dynamic had changed. He was now forced to defend his honour, so come hell or high water that moment had come. As he looked around the camp, he realised the inevitable was imminent.

All eyes were fixed firmly on big Charlie McBean who quickly and readily accepted the challenge. Charlie was the camp's boxing contender at light heavy. His credentials were regarded by many as merely run of the mill, yet he commanded huge popularity in the camp mainly due to his bragging and attention seeking attitude. His tough determined quality in the ring was his greatest asset. Charlie, however, had an elevated opinion of himself. His ego was much larger than any talent that he ever possessed. Nevertheless, he saw this as a wonderful opportunity to showcase his ability against this black upstart.

He ambled over to face Marcus square on. With eyes set deeply in a head which projected square jaws, with an out of shape nose that was showing obvious signs of being hit too often, he was ready. His smile betrayed his intention to flatten the 'darky', who had the temerity to challenge him. Rubbing his right fist into his left palm like an excited schoolboy, Charlie was now within striking distance of his opponent.

"If you want to knock the shit out of someone, try me!" He grinned, twisting his body in mock imitation of someone being hurt, creating fresh humour for his supporters.

Marcus cared very little for violence or confrontation. His general upbringing and excellent discipline moulded him into someone who was sound of temperament and attitude. Nevertheless, he was always ready to face adversities of any kind with a degree of quiet confidence. Charlie's words made him remember a character defining moment in his youth several years ago. He recalled when he was confronted by a threat far greater than this. It involved Wally Green, the village bully. A man feared by everyone; something big Wally enjoyed immensely. Marcus was very careful to keep out of his way. After all, why should he want to tangle with a brute like Wally? To avoid him at all cost was a principal objective of his. However, in a small village, incidents do happen and it was one such incident that caused Marcus to come face to face with this dreaded demon.

Sandra Marrow, the village belle, and a natural flirt was, of course, the principal architect of that conflict. Sandra was both bold and confident. She almost always got what she wanted. She was not blessed with extreme beauty but made up for it with a body that was both stunning and alluring. Fully aware of her assets, she used her attractiveness with great skill and cunning. She was forever giving false hope to many of the villagers, all competing with one another to gain her attention and friendship. All with the exception of Marcus, who was not attracted to her in any particular way. As Marcus was never in the race for her attention, she felt utterly rejected.

Hell hath no fury like a woman scorned holds true in this regard. Out of spite and for the benefit of revenge, she cosied up to big Wally and pleaded with him to warn Marcus off. Her manufactured tale of not being able to take his pestering any longer was indeed all big Wally needed to commence battle. In fact, it was sweet music to his ears. This was a task he welcomed with both hands. To him, it was a noble gesture and in his eyes, it was his duty to defend the young lady's honour. Very soon the news was out and as usual Martin Jules was the first to know about her feelings for Marcus.

Martin confided in Marcus about Sandra's intentions and begged him to be nice to her, but Marcus showed indifference to the whole idea and never gave it much thought. The circulation in the village was immediate. Big Wally was on the lookout for Marcus. His objective was obvious; he was about to rearrange the poor young man's face. Wally Green was an immense hulk of a man. He was six foot four inches of solid muscle. He used his fists like a jack-hammer to get his way – all bullies do – he towered over Marcus who was then only five foot, eleven inches and growing.

It was a normal quiet afternoon in Debro's cake shop. Old man Johnson was slowly sipping a bottle of coke; Taff and Duce were playing a game of dominoes. Old Mackay was in his usual place strumming his guitar. A strong breeze was gusting, helping in a very pleasant way in cooling the otherwise sticky heat that prevailed. Marcus was sipping a glass of Debro's mauby and merely observing the flickering birds playing hide and seek, as the high winds commanded the trees to sway in gay abandon, against a cloudless sky and a sun that was now almost ready to expire. Suddenly the otherwise quiet repose of the village was shattered by a din which became louder until it developed into a thunderous crescendo.

Marcus peered through the fading light, only to behold the silhouette of this mighty giant being followed by a multitude of people, moving swiftly towards him. The scene reminded him of the Pied Piper. Out of the semi-darkness emerged Wally and instinctively Marcus suspected imminent danger, as this man mountain duly encroached on space that was once his. Wally was now his usual self. Always comfortable about things of this nature, his eyes wild with excitement and dripping perspiration, he was now within hitting distance of his adversary. Marcus, totally perplexed by this sudden intrusion, tried to retreat but Wally was having none of it. Backed up into a corner Marcus was now positive that he was in serious trouble as Wally towered over him. His chest heaving like a blacksmith's bellows, prodding Marcus with fingers which looked like huge sausages, he angrily remarked. "I hear you've been pestering my woman."

Marcus was not totally oblivious of the charge, but he was both surprised and aggrieved by this travesty that had befallen him. He was surprised by the viciousness of Sandra to exact revenge for something so scurrilous. Angry also, that he paid little attention to Martin's warning and totally unhappy to be trapped in the web of this violent hulk of a man with nowhere to run. Wally was a man who derived the greatest of pleasure cracking skulls and crushing bones of others, just for the sheer fun of it. "Who am I supposed to have pestered?" Marcus asked innocently.

"Don't play innocent with me." Wally barked impatiently, still prodding him and spilling what was left of his drink. Marcus placed his glass on the counter and decided to move away from this menacing obstacle that straddled his path, an action that infuriated this massive beast of a man even more.

"Don't you walk away from me if you know what's good for you," Wally shouted; the crowd behind him becoming more and more vociferous and embroiled.

"What is my crime?" Marcus pleaded. "What have I done?"

"You've molested my girl Sandra – as if you don't know," Wally announced still prodding Marcus in the chest.

The frantic crowd, some still braying for blood, were encouraged by Wally's action, persistently spurring him on.

It was a well-known fact in the village, that Marcus was a man of peace, a gentle person. It was often assumed he did not possess one contentious bone in his body. As a growing lad, he was blessed with a fine physique, but this was undoubtedly no match for this giant rugged man that was Wally. Yet here he was confronted by a threat of enormous proportions, many believed it was beyond his ability to handle. Wally, on the other hand, was a human battering ram. He thoroughly enjoyed beating up on folks just for the delight of it. As it happened, Marcus was no exception. For Wally, it was just another episode to be dealt with quickly and efficiently.

Marcus turned to face his adversary, knowing there was no escaping his impending doom. It was decision time, he knew in terms of percentages, his chances of successful combat were slim to zero; he was now prepared to deliver the first blow come what may. He would then have the justification of knowing that Wally did not have things all his own way. The fear he felt for this mountain of a man, soon dissipated – replaced by a sudden adrenaline flow that surged through his body. He took his one chance before he was blown away and mustering every bit of energy, he struck Wally with a solid blow flush to the chin. The reaction was not immediate. The impact seemed to have taken ages before the dismantling process began.

All of a sudden this huge man's contorted face mirrored pain and surprise in equal measure, he began to wobble, his legs behaving like a newborn giraffe trying to find its balance, his legs crumbled under him as he fell in a massive heap on the ground. Silence befell the once braying crowd. Astonishment prevailed. No one could believe that this mighty bully could be demolished by one single blow. For a brief moment, Wally's massive frame lay motionless on the ground.

"You killed him." Someone shouted, finding their voice eventually. Just then the big man stirred and out of sheer pride he attempted to get to his feet, but his legs totally disobeyed instructions. His every effort was in vain. This mighty unit of a man was thoroughly humiliated.

"End of an era." Someone yelled. "Good on you Marcus." Another continued. Eventually, Wally got to his feet shakily, dusted himself off and ambled away into the night. The dispersing crowd could not believe their eyes. Wally was eating humble pie for once in his life in the village where he reigned supreme. News that he was seeking revenge never materialised. He subsequently remained a silent and almost remote figure; it was a major change that was welcomed by many. So much so, that the summary topic of that experience was echoed constantly around the village in a symbolic way, as a source of good against evil.

Mama G and the rest of the family were totally overjoyed by the fact that her son had defended himself adequately and was not beaten to a pulp by someone she regarded as evil. She tacitly disagreed with Nanny May's opinion of Marcus, who she accused of keeping bad company and recommend he goes to church and confess his sins for contaminating his soul. The incident was naturally a huge turning point in the young man's life. The confidence he obtained from big Wally's subjugation made him both self-assured and determined. His peaceful demeanour was still very much intact, but it gave him the added belief in his own ability, to face adversity of any kind without fear or apprehension. Sandra, on the other hand, did not win many friends by her action. She was regarded as untrustworthy. Perhaps that more than anything else hastened her eventual exit from the community.

Here, in the barracks, he was once again knee deep in trouble, in an environment totally different from the experience he had in the village. This time it was of his own making. Although this was essentially in the defence of Roland, he instinctively knew it was not what Roland would have wanted. Nevertheless, in his own mind's eye, Marcus was defending something far more substantial than mere provocation.

He was fighting for honour and respect which was abundantly absent in the camp. Realising the gravity of the situation, after all, this was the British Army, misbehaving, carries a very severe punishment, but the penalty for refusing to confront big Charlie McBean and his mob, not to mention the ignominy of it all, would be too much to bear.

Charlie advanced a little closer, prompting a backward step from Marcus, a move that Charlie found amusing.

"What's up, nigger boy, do I smell?" He took a whiff of his armpits and bursting out laughing, he turned to his ardent followers and declared mockingly: "Oh, it's not me that smells, it's the black boy!"

This encouraged more laughter from his supporters. Stepping back gave Marcus the leverage that he wanted. Whatever resulted from this fracas one thing was most definite, Marcus wanted the first crack at his antagonist. With every fibre of his being and with every sinew at his disposal, he let rip, connecting flush on the target he aimed for. Big Charlie's eyes rolled in his head like a pinball machine. His body quivered as if hit by a truck. His face showed serious distress and hurt as he crashed to the floor in an untidy heap. Stunned silence in the camp. The impossible had just occurred. The Army's light heavyweight prospect was knocked out with one ferocious punch.

Sergeant Grimes was right on cue to see McBean in a horizontal position, with Marcus hovering over him like an eagle conquering his prey. The sergeant's appearance sent everyone scuttling back to their respective places, leaving Marcus and McBean as visible evidence of what had happened just seconds ago. What the sergeant witnessed hardly seemed real. He had a look of disbelief written all over his face. The regiment's best boxing prospect knocked to the ground in front of everyone in the camp. How was that possible? McBean somehow managed to find his feet and remained vertical in the presence of his commanding officer.

"What the hell's going on here?" Grimes asked observing McBean's unsteady posture.

"It's him, sir, causing problems," McBean spluttered.

The sergeant turned to Marcus. "Is that true?"

"No sir, I was only defending myself, sir," Marcus replied calmly.

The sergeant observed both men, still in the consternation of what he saw. He slowly walked over to Marcus, standing as close as was possible to him he murmured. "You are in serious shit private." He paused. "This is the British Army; you will learn to respect it and what it stands for. You will learn how to behave like a civilised human being, black boy!"

He waited for a reaction; none was forthcoming. "We do not allow riff-raff to wear this uniform."

He continued. "When I'm done with you nigger boy, you will wish you were never born." Still standing close to Marcus he smiled faintly then stepped back. "Now get some sleep private, because tomorrow your ass belongs to me."

That night, Marcus twisted and turned in bed pondering over the incident and feeling a sense of remorse for what had happened. It was never meant to be so. He realised it was naive of him to take on someone else's quarrel, especially since it was never going to be appreciated. He always considered himself to be a decent, upright young man with impeccable credentials. He had now lost the moral high ground, something he always held in the highest esteem; now he must face a reality check that was both stark and unyielding. He loved the Army, enjoyed wearing the uniform, the very idea of him getting kicked out was a thought not worth bearing; however he must now be prepared for the consequences of his actions, whatever that difficulty might be.

Lieutenant 'Hard as Nails' Carter was perhaps the sternest and most unfriendly individual Marcus was ever likely to confront. A quintessential Englishman, he was a soldier first and foremost, cared little for any kind of sentimentality or compassion. He was vehemently opposed to foreign personnel.

They were, in his opinion, infiltrating into a uniquely British institution. The British Army was for British boys; they understood the system, flew the flag with great pride and were trusted patriots.

Those were his strong and consistent principles, both lasting and enduring. He harboured no time for emotional hogwash. A proud and intelligent force must not be hindered by all and sundry. He was convinced of the oath the Army should pursue and the credentials it should possess. Moving from that stated path hinders its progress and subsequently reduces the moral correctness of its status. He was also fearful of diluting the forces with men whose mental capacity, devalues the uniqueness of what the British Army stands for. Nothing can be gained by this action. The benefits can only be considered as negligible. These facts gave the lieutenant absolutely no joy whatever.

However, here for once in his life, he was confronted by a huge and very unpleasant dilemma. Behind that solid and unbending exterior, was a man with a chink in his otherwise puritanical armoury. He was an avid boxing enthusiast. He cherished the dream of having someone in his battalion with the quality and ability to be the best there is in the profession. Observing this fine robust specimen of a man in front of him, he began conjuring up notions of grandeur. This lad could be useful. Perhaps he will be the next light heavyweight champion in the country or beyond. What was more, it would be under his watch.

Carter knew Charlie McBean, a tough and aggressive fighter, hardly a world-beater, but no one could fault his drive, stamina and commitment in the ring. To be knocked senseless with one punch was unbelievable, almost unimaginable. With the right training and guidance, who knows what this young man could attain. He frowned at the thought of making such an important compromise in his life but found it expedient to do so and wax lyrical at the very idea of success. How gain-worthy that would be watching him develop. A strange glow took hold of this hard uncompromising man. Such emotion was hardly the preserve of the lieutenant, but for once he was prepared to break with

VICTOR WALDRON

tradition merely to see what this young man was made of. The news that was orchestrated around the camp was chilling indeed. McBean was knocked cold with one single punch. That was unbelievable stuff. Anyone knowing this tough extravagant human being could hardly comprehend such a thought. Yet that was the reality of the situation that everyone was left to imbibe.

Lieutenant Carter finally acknowledged the man in front of him in salute. His piercing blue eyes seemed almost invasive as he scrutinised Marcus in great detail. Whatever else he might have thought of Marcus, he was quick to realise this was a fine specimen of a man.

"What is your name private?" The lieutenant asked.

"Marcus Gullant sir," He replied.

"And where are you from?"

"Guiana sir – British Guiana," Marcus replied briskly.

"Is that some part of Africa?" The lieutenant enquired.

"No sir, South America sir," Marcus responded, surprised to realise that a man in such an exalted position did not know his geography as much as Marcus expected him to. The lieutenant looked almost impatient as he continued his observation of the man in front of him. He was positive he had never heard of such a place, however, being British gave the whole idea some sense of respectability. It was good that the British were able to take these backwater places and give the natives civic upliftment, something he was always in favour of. After all, Britain is the very embodiment of excellence. It is the only country capable of bringing light to these backward and desolate places.

"Where did you learn to speak English?" The lieutenant enquired.

"In my own country sir. It's the only English-speaking country in South America." Marcus replied. "We fly the Union Jack and sing the national anthem, sir."

"If you were brought up under British rule, then you should know how to behave. You understand what discipline means don't you?" The lieutenant asked.

"Yes sir, I was properly brought up sir."

"Then you should know something about good manners? This is not a scouts' jamboree in your native backyard, wherever that is. This is the British Army, the finest institution in the world, and as long as you wear that uniform, you will learn how to respect it."

"Yes sir, I will do my best, sir," Marcus said.

The lieutenant shifted restlessly in his chair, more out of exasperation than discomfort. His fixed gaze upon the man in front of him was penetrating. "What I find most disconcerting above anything else, is that the powers that be in their conventional wisdom succeeded in placing people like you in our midst, who seem incapable of functioning in a civilised manner. That, of course, makes our job of work all the more difficult." He stopped briefly and with a heavy sigh, he continued.

"However duty dictates that we are obliged to bring you in line with what is needed in our Army and by hook or by crook it is our job to make certain that you do not stray from the principles of what we stand for. Do you understand?"

"Yes, I do understand sir," Marcus responded.

The lieutenant began writing and then stopped to look at the young soldier. "Now tell me, what was the disturbance about?" He enquired.

"No disturbance sir. It was merely a disagreement."

The lieutenant sighed heavily. "So you hit Private McBean because he disagreed with you?"

"Only in self-defence sir," Marcus retorted.

"It is not satisfactory that you go about thumping people because they disagree with you. That is bad behaviour to the very extreme." The lieutenant advised somewhat impatiently.

"In this instance, it was necessary sir," Marcus replied.

The lieutenant began writing again. Finally, he looked up at the young man, frustration written across his face. "You have given me no satisfactory reason why you should not be severely punished. It is not the done thing to go around knocking people about because they disagree with you." Replied Carter, with his piercing blue eyes still penetrating Marcus's defences.

VICTOR WALDRON

Marcus knew the lieutenant was not the benevolent kind and as a result expected the worst. He was never prepared to tell more than he needed to whatever the outcome.

The lieutenant, on the other hand, was ready to throw the book at the young soldier but was mindful of the fact that Marcus was an opportunity that he could not afford to overlook. It was his chance to gain glory; a once in a lifetime moment to savour. Perhaps the biggest dream of his life would be fulfilled. The great dilemma was, he needed to show the ruthless side of his nature, but by the same token, did not want Marcus to be crushed to the point of uselessness. The lieutenant knew Sergeant Grimes' modus operandi. Left to him, he would tear the black upstart from limb to limb without breaking a sweat. However, his strict instructions were to test the young man's resilience to the very maximum, without any physical damage. He needed to know if Marcus had the strength and durability to make him a formidable champion.

Ten days had elapsed since the unfortunate incident. Those days seemed more like an eternity for Marcus. Sergeant Grimes was administering his version of punishment that was both cruel and inhumane. The sergeant had the ability of a hangman. His natural disposition was that of a sadist. He wanted blood. Nothing would give him greater pleasure than to see the young soldier squirm. However, his terms of reference were abundantly clear. No physical harm must come to Marcus. Nevertheless, Grimes applied pressure so extreme, lesser mortals would easily have succumbed to the vile nature of such abuse. Digging ditches and refilling them; sleepless nights; press-ups; climbing hills; breaking bricks and everything else that would humble most men. Somehow Marcus found the depth and inner strength to withstand the horrors of Grimes' acts of brutality. Marcus simply refused to bend. He was not prepared to give the sergeant his desired wish, nor the pleasure he craved. At the end of this enormous experiment he was as near to breaking as he could possibly get, but he simply defied the odds and in the end, it became a moral victory over adversity. Marcus felt in his own mind, this was a battle half won.

The real problem now rests with the lieutenant. His natural contempt for foreigners was very much in evidence. Thinking back, he wondered if his act of defiance in refusing to wilt under pressure from Sergeant Grimes' brutal punishment would be counterproductive to his cause, allowing Grimes to inflict further punishment. He was now ready to meet with destiny. The outcome of which would decide his future whatever that may be. He cursed himself for his indiscretions in taking on someone else's problem and making it his own. A fault line he vowed never to repeat as long as life lasts. His cherished hope of being a soldier could now come to an ignoble end because of one act of folly.

Marcus was very proud of his Army status. He was a happy member of this British institution. Loved his uniform and was now ready to accept any further punishment other than being discharged. His ultimate hope was to return to his village in sartorial splendour as a member of the British Army. Much kudos would be gained by such an exercise, enhancing every possibility of winning the heart of the adorable and most desirable Teresa Malison.

Sergeant Grimes' report to the management was one of great astonishment. He marvelled at the quality of Marcus's endurance and his natural ability to absorb punishment. "This one is not ordinary sir. He is strong as an ox, stubborn as a mule and there were times when I felt he was not human. I am simply amazed at the man's strength and powers of recuperation sir."

Lieutenant Carter listened to his sergeant's assessment of the young soldier and expressed no surprise over Grimes' report. All of what he said was consistent with his own mindset about Africans. All that he has read and to the best of his ability, he was convinced that black men were strong physically and sexually, but were incapable intellectually. Marcus was hardly an exception. What he was seeking, was a fighting man and Marcus fitted the bill. If he was capable of destroying McBean with one punch, he was more than capable of being a fighting machine. The report Grimes gave to him renewed his enthusiasm for the future. Marcus was now his trump card for the success he sought. As of now, he must be treated with due care and attention.

# TURN AROUND

Three months had elapsed and there was no explanation for the sudden change of status that Marcus was given; no more back-breaking work. He was duly summoned to see Lieutenant Carter and was given the option of working as a storeman or part of the engineering department where he once brought heavy-duty machinery to be repaired. He chose the latter. It was an opportunity to work with Sergeant Ronald Pearson. He was a man who regularly greeted him with a degree of courtesy and was always pleasant. Sergeant Pearson's father was a Naval Officer who subsequently worked with the Government as an Advisor on Foreign Affairs. As a result of his extensive travel to Africa and the Caribbean, Walter Pearson always spoke favourably of the people he met on his travels. His experience of working and meeting with black folks was always a great source of delight and he never failed to express those sentiments to his family. Ronald benefited from his father's experience and was readily prepared to show politeness to black folks whenever possible.

Walter Pearson was someone who was enriched by his extensive travel. That made him to be a person who saw the world differently. That knowledge gave him reason to understand the nature and attitude of Africans with a far more sympathetic outlook than most of his peers. Walter articulated his experience to anyone that cared to listen, expanding his education to those whose thinking was contrary to his. Especially the kindness and generosity he received from his expeditions around the world. His son Ronald was duly impressed by what was often expressed to him and as a result, conducted himself in a manner that was both courteous and civil to anyone of a different culture. Marcus fell amply into that category.

In addition, Marcus was assigned to the gym, under Sergeant Custard. This amazing turnaround, so far as the young soldier was concerned, only happened in the world of fiction. It was a fairytale conclusion for him, causing him to ponder why his luck had changed so dramatically. He was well aware that Lieutenant Carter was never one for charity or pity. He was a hard clinical human being. This new found change of heart astonished him comprehensively. It was diametrically opposed to anything that he was likely to expect or anticipate. Not that he was complaining; this new existence of his was certainly beyond his wildest expectations. He naturally expected further punishment for his act of indiscretion towards McBean, like being thrown to the wolves. Instead, he was enjoying a life of comparative leisure and fulfilment and wondered momentarily, if misbehaving was so amply compensated in the Army. Perhaps if he should commit another act of misconduct or anything diabolical, he may be promoted to a corporal or even a sergeant. Cognisant of the fact that such a thought was totally naïve and lacked constructive value, he soon dismissed it comprehensively and utterly from his mind. This new found position, however, had a serious drawback. He was now answerable to Sergeant Custard, the boxing coach. Custard was not very far removed, as far as temperament goes from that of Carter. He was both mean-spirited and unyielding, with a personality to match. Marcus instinctively knew that the sergeant cared very little for him. However, Custard was a solid soldier and his orders were to train Marcus to the optimum of his ability. He nevertheless had ideas of his own.

McBean was very much under his tutelage and in his opinion doing quite nicely. Now he was given this black boy who he felt unjustifiably was stealing McBean's thunder; which he believed must be seriously addressed. Revenge in some form or another would make the sergeant a happy man indeed and would satisfy him immensely. Marcus' training began to take shape. As always he was diligent as in all things that he embarked upon. Boxing was no exception. It was not a sport that he was prepared to participate in willingly because it was not an automatic choice. Since that was the case, Marcus readily deduced that this was imposed upon him from the highest echelon of the unit. That person undoubtedly would be Lieutenant Carter. It became obvious to the young soldier that someone had observed that he had the potential to develop, therefore he was duty bound to do his best to please. He was cognisant of the fact also, that this was a form of exploitation. No one asked him if he wanted to fight nor did he give consent. He understood completely that it was foisted upon him. However, his growing confidence in his own ability and the experience of his past made him ready to meet this new challenge with utmost confidence and weighing up the percentages, he fully realised this was a happy place to be.

Sergeant Custard worked Marcus most vigorously and very often excessively. It was the sergeant's way to frustrate the young man of ever wanting to be a fighter. Above everything else, Marcus saw this excess as an advantage; he wanted to be in the best shape possible in order to do battle in a sport he concluded to be both dangerous and very often perilous. Fully realising the enormity of the task, he needed to be at the optimum of his fitness and knowledge of the game, in order to meet these new and exciting challenges ahead. Looming largely in his thoughts also, was the natural and explosive gift he possessed – a punch that was capable of unhinging anyone – what was now needed was the skills necessary to make him an accomplished fighting machine. Sergeant Custard, like Carter, quickly observed that Marcus was not run of the mill. He was supremely confident, strong and a very quick learner. His ability to absorb and execute information was simply uncanny.

Six months of solid training and four fights later – all bouts were stopped in Marcus's favour – which was solid evidence. That was when Custard decided to put his evil plan into operation; by arranging for Marcus to fight against the Army's champion Gerrard Wince; who was a man far superior in the art of boxing. If ever there was a mismatch this certainly was it. Marcus was a work in progress, plying his trade as best he could. Wince was an accomplished and vastly experienced champion, with good enough skills to upset anyone. Therefore this was commonly seen by everyone as the most disparate match ever made; to everyone except Custard. In this vast ocean of indifference and hostility, Marcus was certain that there was at least one man who was fighting his corner. That person was undoubtedly Sergeant Pearson. His assignment with the sergeant was to a very large extent successful. Pearson was the only one that showed extreme patience, great kindness and guidance which benefited Marcus enormously. Pearson's love for engines was considerable and Marcus mirrored this.

Not only did Marcus show promise, his fulsome enthusiasm for all things mechanical convinced him that at long last he had found what he was seeking. Without a doubt he had discovered his true vocation. Sergeant Pearson understood the enormity of the situation young Marcus was experiencing being matched against Gerrard Wince. Sergeant Custard deliberately placed Marcus in a calamitous position. He was being exploited by someone with a secret desire by matching a fighter of repute against a relative novice. Because of his sheer dislike for the young soldier, he was willing to see him slaughtered for his own personal gratification. In other words, Marcus was simply a piece of meat between two slices of ego and unfortunately, he was unable to do anything about the situation. Everyone, including Sergeant Custard, knew that Marcus was not ready.

The time of the fight was rapidly approaching and Marcus was most reticent and nervous, traits that were not a common factor in his general make up. Pressure was now the order of the day and the young man was feeling every inch of it.

"How bad is it?" Sergeant Pearson asked looking directly at the young soldier, noting that Marcus was not displaying his usual calm temperament. "You're showing lots of tension lately, is this fight getting to you?"

Marcus nodded in the affirmative. His attempted smile never developed into much. He was not aware that he was giving so much away by his disposition and realised his attempt to put a brave face on the ensuing encounter failed miserably. That was largely as a result of the incessant remarks and negative comments of so many observers, expecting imminent slaughter, which made him quite uneasy. "Yes, I am a bit worried," Marcus replied taking a deep breath. "Everyone thinks I'm a disaster waiting to happen."

The sergeant smiled sarcastically and waved his hand as though swatting a fly. "Tosh." He chuckled. "The lad has a pair of hands and feet just like you." Sergeant Pearson retorted. "He is a good fighter; no escaping that fact, but he can be beaten." Sergeant Pearson looked long and hard at Marcus before he spoke again. "Look here Marcus, you have something that cannot be created in a gym. You were born with it." The sergeant raised his right hand and made a fist. "That is what you have, dynamite in that fist of yours, you were born with it and you can put anyone away with it. Do not let anyone take that away from you."

Marcus smiled pleasantly. It was something of an encouragement to hold onto more than anything else. Even though he knew that he could not rely on power alone.

"Your punch is so explosive you can destroy anyone with it, do you believe that?"

Marcus nodded agreement but remained tacit.

"You are the underdog. No one expects you to win; so go in there and believe in your own ability. Be positive, nothing else matters." The sergeant continued.

The advice given by Sergeant Pearson resonated in the young man's head like fine wine. In a certain way, this was the tonic he needed to fulfil the task ahead. It was an emotional surge so effective it boosted his confidence and helped to restore his belief in his own ability. It also helped to calm his anxiety.

# FIGHT NIGHT

At last, it was fight night and the arena was filled to capacity. There was an almighty buzz of excitement radiating around the hall, creating an electric atmosphere. This huge mass had assembled merely to see the total annihilation of this young black boy who dared to cross swords with someone that was massively superior in every department of the game. Put into proper context, it was a fight between man and boy.

Marcus entered the ring with jeers and boos ringing in his ears, and it was clear that he would have no support from this hostile crowd. He did, however, gain confidence from those he knew were on his side: Sergeant Pearson, Lieutenant Carter and Roland. The enthusiastic crowd had come mostly to see him slaughtered. Sergeant Pearson was prominent in the first row and gave him the thumbs up. Not far away was Lieutenant Carter, looking pensive and unsure. In the opposite corner was the formidable Gerrard Wince, brimming with confidence.

Marcus knew he needed a strategy to neutralise the force and power of Wince. A plan of survival was necessary in order to withstand the fury of his opponent. His first option was to keep Wince at arm's length; that meant jabbing and getting away, and for the first minute that ploy proved successful. Unfortunately, Wince had other ideas. Not only had he caught up with Marcus but he was now throwing punches from all directions. Facing a flurry of blows, Marcus was now in danger and his initial strategy was failing. Wince was proving to be far stronger and more dextrous than anticipated.

Wince threw a right that grazed Marcus's temple. Fortunately for the young man, he was moving backward, eliminating the full impact of the blow; he still felt a weakness in the knees and grabbed hold of Wince to avoid further punches and to gather his senses.

The bell rang out ending the first round, but Marcus already felt beaten. Wince was getting the better of him. As he sat in the corner he looked across and saw Sergeant Pearson waving his fist in the air, indicating to Marcus to use his power. So animated was the sergeant, a normally reserved and laid back individual, it brought a new sense of spirit to him. Custard, on the other hand, had a smile on his face that gave the game away. His general demeanour forecasted the disaster he anticipated. The sight of the seemingly contented Custard was almost too much for the young soldier to bear. But the encouragement of Sergeant Pearson stirred Marcus from within as the seconds ticked by. Before the start of the second round, it occurred to Marcus that there was a serious deficit of positive thinking on his behalf. The two minutes of the first round can only be described as lacking in purpose on his part which diminished his thought process considerably. His own ability to inflict pressure on his opponent totally eluded him. A new initiative was now necessary. After all, he was capable of delivering power of his own and he felt the time was appropriate to execute.

The bell rang for the second round, which if anything started very much like the first. Wince in command and showing aggressive intent. He threw a punch, hitting Marcus on the side of his face, engendering pain, but for the moment self-preservation was far more important than the pain he was suffering. This battle had to be won and in all probability, it appeared that the advantage was clearly not on his side. Suddenly he felt an imperative need to change the situation before it was too late. It was abundantly clear that urgency of action was required. After much bobbing and weaving, trying his best not to become an obvious target, the bell rang to end the round. Marcus sighed with relief for the good fortune that had

VICTOR WALDRON

prevailed, but recognising, however, that this was a temporary condition in this epic encounter, but more importantly, the punch that he received during that round had become excruciatingly more painful. It had now become a do or die situation and one that needed immediate attention in order for him to survive.

Marcus felt daunted, overwhelmed and dispirited as he trekked back to his corner. He needed inspiration of some kind to bolster his flagging confidence as the seconds ticked away and he needed it now. The excited crowd was being treated to a spectacle in which they had gathered to witness much to their utter delight. What was conspicuous in those dwindling seconds, before the start of the final round and what caught his attention was the smugness of Sergeant Custard, pleased that his plan was bearing fruit. However, the actions of Sergeant Pearson had a significant impact on Marcus. This cultured and generally laid-back man was remonstrating in a way that Marcus did not know he was capable of. The sergeant was completely on his side, giving his full support. His waving fists and his aggressive manner of encouragement was indeed the catalyst Marcus needed to face the challenge he was up against. He instinctively knew that aggression was the only path to success, a do or die attitude was necessary and as the bell rang for that final round, he remembered his encounter with big Wally Green, the man mountain he was able to dismantle in his village. If he was capable of upsetting someone of such magnitude, he was positive he could repeat that feat against Wince. Encouraged by the confidence of Pearson, Marcus was now ready for war. The round started with Wince showing obvious signs of over-confidence. He hit Marcus on the side of his face with a degree of venom about it, enough to wake the young fighter from the fear and complacency that previously engulfed him.

His own ability to inflict punishment had eluded him, after all, he was capable of devastating power of his own and the time was now appropriate to deliver. Marcus's reaction was spontaneous. His surprisingly positive approach shocked his opponent, who least expected Marcus to be so aggressive. The fury of the young soldier dismantled Wince's progression and momentarily stalled this rampant adversary in his path. The sudden change of gear brought a wry smile to Wince's face. No more must he go looking for Marcus as he was now ready to stand his ground. His job would be much easier if this black upstart was prepared to give away the only advantage he had of running for all he was worth, in order to escape danger.

Paradoxically, Marcus had ideas of his own. Trying to be elusive was not a successful ploy. Wince was now ready to raise his game and was confident that Marcus was heading for a total eclipse. He threw a flurry of punches, some missed, but Marcus was caught by a punch that resonated right down to his toes. Fortunately for him, it was slightly off target. That punch removed any inhibitions that were inherent in his system. This enraged him enough to retaliate with a vengeance. Throwing caution to the wind, Marcus threw a right, it was not a perfect punch, but it was enough to let his opponent know he too was in battle. Wince blinked, backed off somewhat and began adjusting his headgear. That was a serious error of judgement because it gave Marcus another opportunity to land another haymaker; this time with serious repercussions. The blow landed flush on the nose of his adversary. It was a punch of real savagery, enough to put an end to a contest that seemed most unlikely to end in Marcus's favour. Unable to breathe, Wince went down on one knee. His blood-splattered face was evidence of a man in serious trouble. His nose was smashed and so also was his spirit to continue. The hush was deafening.

The expectation of this widely animated and exuberant audience dashed. The visible astonishment around the arena was almost palpable. Marcus came face to face with destiny. This was the hardest day of his life. Luck or good fortune was undoubtedly on his side in this instance. The victory, however, did two important things for Marcus, it gave him a massive boost of confidence and raised his self-esteem to its very optimum and giving him the belief that nothing was impossible to achieve. The fact that Marcus was mandated to fight meant he was obliged to do so. It was the experience that changed his entire perspective as far as boxing was concerned. Nevertheless, he was proud of his achievement, bragging rights were now exclusively his. But he needed to be calm and collected. He must carry this victory over Wince with dignity, never allowing himself to appear pompous or triumphant.

The weeks and months moved rapidly along and Marcus began to notice a sea change in the manner and behaviour of many who were otherwise hostile towards him. He was acquiring respect – very often grudgingly – from quarters that cared very little for his good health. Needless to say, it was welcome and very much appreciated. Custard, however, felt enraged by the result of the encounter with Wince but was compelled to carry on training Marcus regardless. His hands were forced; as anything less would have been counter-productive to the plans of Lieutenant Carter who saw Marcus as a potential champion in the making.

He was obviously conscious of the fact also, that it was the direct result of his fighting spirit and his ability as a warrior. He was quite aware that his demeanour and his good conduct constituted immensely to that end. Those months saw Marcus pursuing with great interest the option of acquiring skills necessary to become an engineer. Sergeant Pearson contributed largely to assist in that endeavour. The bond that developed between the two men gathered pace. In the end, it was obvious that friendship was inevitable. The trust that Marcus felt for the sergeant was well and truly reciprocal. Pearson continued to give Marcus every help possible and was surprised how quickly he responded to tasks that were most complex and difficult. Marcus, on the other hand, felt for the first time in his life that engineering should be his vocation. It was what he really wanted to do. His confidence matched his ability as the weeks and months slipped by, giving him a completely new lease of life.

# SETBACK

Rumours began to emerge that the war was taking on a new dimension. The Russians surviving the massive onslaught that had beset them were now beginning to retaliate. The news circulated the camp like wildfire, creating exuberance of incredible proportions, prompting high hopes and heralding huge expectations that the fighting was coming to a conclusion. What should have been a state of ecstasy, turned sour in an instant. Fate was instrumental in dealing Sergeant Pearson an unfortunate hand in what was to become a most surreal experience. The sergeant was doing his customary duty of inspecting the heavy machinery that came and went when suddenly there was a loud bang. The explosion was both unexpected and disconcerting, immediately changing the mood of the workshop.

To the consternation of Marcus and others, the sergeant was trapped under heavy machinery which broke away from its otherwise secure position, pinning Sergeant Pearson underneath. Marcus's reaction was immediate. He grabbed a steel bar and beckoned to the others to assist in levering the sergeant to safety. The task was monumentally difficult and required every ounce of energy and manpower to prise him from under heavy metal. Finally and at long last they succeeded, exposing the severely crushed and blood splattered leg of the sergeant. The horror of it all was most devastating to everyone, but more especially to Marcus. Pearson had become not only a tutor but also a trusted friend and confidant. As the sergeant was rushed to the hospital, Marcus prayed that the injury that his friend had sustained was not as serious as first thought. To lose a friend of such dimension would no doubt be a crushing blow to the young man's morale.

The news that Pearson would lose his leg was not what anyone wanted to hear. Fortunately, the doctors miraculously managed to save the sergeant's limb. It required a great deal of reconstruction and as a result, rehabilitation was required, which was a long and arduous requisite to his eventual recovery. Whatever was necessary to restore the sergeant's good health was made possible for him and like a true soldier, he worked assiduously to that end. Marcus paid remarkable attention to Pearson's recovery. Every available moment he was able to muster was inserted towards helping his friend's restoration. Pearson was quick to acknowledge the sincerity of his young friend and showed appreciation enough to ensure the bond that was already there, was now more than ever apparent.

The war in Europe was also coming to an end. The news lifted the spirits of everyone as the Germans were repelled and the shape of a new dawn beckoned. Marcus paid his usual visit to his friend and found him in high spirits. He was sitting on the bed and beckoned Marcus to sit beside him.

"Good news all around my friend." The sergeant said. "In a week or so I'll be walking out of here a totally new man."

That information brought a huge smile to the young man's face. "What do you plan to do with your life now?" Marcus asked.

The sergeant laughed, picking up his stick and waving it in the air. "This is my new partner now; in fact, it's my bodyguard. Everywhere I go it'll be beside me." Pearson got up and walked around the bed leaning heavily on his stick. Still grinning he asked. "What about you Marcus, are you about to become the next light heavyweight champion of the world?"

Marcus's rather thin smile broadened into a cheeky grin. "What do you think? I want your expert opinion?"

The sergeant reverted to his sitting posture keeping his stare resolutely on Marcus as if he was studying the young man's character. "Do you have it in you to be a champion?"

Still smiling; Marcus rose to his feet slowly. He already knew what the answer would be, but he wanted an answer from his friend and was determined to get it.

"I'm still waiting for your opinion." Marcus retorted.

Pearson sighed heavily, still looking steadfastly at his young friend. "You have something many professionals would die for." The sergeant made a fist with his right hand and thrust it into his left hand. "You have dynamite in that fist of yours Marcus. You also have a good degree of other skills, but do you want it enough? Do you have the drive, the desire, or the ambition to be a champion?"

Marcus sat next to his friend once more, his smile broadened appreciably. "Thank you for being honest and you are right, I simply do not have the desire or ambition for the game, but I am grateful for the help you have given me to become an engineer. All I want now is a decent job and to get on with my life."

The sergeant placed his hand on the young man's shoulder and smiled. "Don't worry Marcus you will find a job and no thanks to me. You are a smart and intelligent young man. You have picked up the skills in a remarkable way. If anyone should be thankful, it should be me. I thought I was a gonna when that lump of steel fell on me. I would certainly recommend you in dispatches for your alertness."

"Thank you," Marcus replied. "You are a very kind man."

Pearson shook his head negatively. "I don't know about that. What I do know is that you'll have to face the lieutenant about your decision not to be his star fighter."

Marcus instantly felt a sense of guilt about the entire episode of fighting for a living. So far as grand designs go, he had no desire to be a boxer. He did it out of pure expediency. It gave him a life of relative ease and more so, it gave him the opportunity of becoming an engineer, something he was very proud of. One fact he was completely certain of; in the Army, you follow orders and he did that implicitly. Now the fighting was coming to its conclusion, he was now prepared to perform on his terms and no amount of persuasion would change his mind as regards to fighting for a living.

He was positive that soon he would be free to do as he so desired. Trying to look as relaxed as can be he remarked. "Well! As far as I know, I made no pledge to the lieutenant and I do not know what he expects of me, but I simply do not want a career in boxing."

The sergeant shook his head vigorously "I'm well aware of what you're saying, but the lieutenant has set his sights so high and so far as you are concerned the sky is the very limit."

Marcus wore a smile more out of sarcasm than real but did not respond and for a brief moment, both men merely stared at each other. Pearson, at last, broke the silence. "Well, I think you should know that he's connected to a syndicate that is looking for perspective champions. You have become a golden nugget in his eyes. Believe me when I say he will do anything in his power to make you a champion of some sort."

"Well, in that case, I do hope the war finishes in weeks rather than months because I do not want to be a fighter." The young man retorted.

"I do understand," Pearson replied. "Whatever he offers and be sure he would, just say no and be resolute."

The ward was full of soldiers with ailments of one kind or another. Marcus observed with interest the overwhelming degree of patients curiously leering almost maliciously at the two men as they conversed. It suddenly occurred to him that he was conspicuously different amongst so many white men who were perhaps wondering how Marcus was able to strike up such a grand relationship with the Army sergeant. Pearson was not entirely oblivious of the attention being paid to them, but being the man he was, he was not inclined to take that seriously. In any case, he owed so much to the young man who had the presence of mind to act with great efficiency in order to save him from further disaster. Pearson smiled broadly. "So what if you are the centre of attraction? Do you realise that some of these men have never seen a black man before?"

A puzzled Marcus simply nodded in the affirmative. "So tell me." Pearson continued. "What do you plan to do when this wretched war is over?"

"I intend to find a job on civvy street," Marcus answered wearing a huge smile across his face.

Pearson looked at him quizzically. "You mean you're not going back to your sunny Guiana?"

"I intend to go back, but only for a short while." He announced. "England is now my home. There are lots of things that I'm attracted to about this place."

"You mean like snow, fog, cold, damp and the rest?" The sergeant asked with more than a little sarcasm. "You know Marcus, the average Englishman dreams of living in the tropics, enjoying the beach, the sunshine and the wonderful climatic conditions, yet here you are, telling me you would exchange all of that for a heavy dose of winter and smog?"

Of course, the sergeant was correct. Weather-wise, no comparison could be made, but steadfast in the mind of Marcus was the village he left behind, a place that gave nothing away, a place where opportunities were as terminal as many of the soldiers in the hospital with little hope of recovery.

"You are absolutely right about the weather, but I need more than sunshine. I want to be able to achieve things in my life and I can only do that if I stay here in England."

Pearson nodded in agreement. He knew Marcus was ambitious. He was aware that he had the personality to pursue any venture in the Army that he attempted; he was clever and very adaptable. These were qualities that were very conducive to an excellent future.

"You are right about your future Marcus. Happiness is wherever you can find it. However, it is in my opinion that wherever you go, or whatever you do, you will make a complete success of it."

Marcus was extremely pleased to hear such fine compliments coming from his friend. It was most certainly a boost to his ego to have someone with whom he regarded so highly uttering such words of encouragement. Marcus as ever the diplomat turned to confront his friend; smiling broadly he asked. "Enough about me. What do you plan to do when you leave here?"

The sergeant paused momentarily and for a while, he almost looked a troubled man. "As you know Marcus this war is over as far as I am concerned and as for the future? Well, that's another matter altogether." He sighed heavily and offered a pretentious smile. "As you can see, young man I do not have much of a future. As of now, I shall just drift away into oblivion and leave the stage for young ones like you."

Marcus having known the sergeant for a considerable time had never before seen him in this light. Pearson welcomed him with open arms right from the inception. He showed an incredible degree of tolerance throughout their association and mentored him as though he was obliged to do so. The range of highly specialised skills that Marcus developed were due entirely to the kindness and dedication of Pearson over a considerable period of time. The sustaining fact that was self-evident and could not be ignored was the sergeant's attitude towards him. He was the only European who didn't take a disparaging outlook towards him. As a result, he felt a sense of trust that he hoped would continue to develop long after the war was over and beyond. He needed a friend, someone to whom he could relate; someone he could trust in times of need. What was extraordinary and very novel about this relationship was perhaps for the first time in his entire life, Marcus was seeking friendship with someone. The irony of it loomed large in his thoughts. His natural disposition allied by his covert tendency did not encourage friendship as a young man, back in the village he was a loner and very comfortable being so. Perhaps the only person that came close to befriend him was Martin Jules. He was of the opinion that Martin was something of a visionary. He gleaned information from every corner and expounded things relevant and enlightening to everyone who cared to listen. As things stood, times were very different now.

This was a new place, many miles from the village and expeditiously planning ahead was now a serious imperative, especially since he now considered Britain to be his new home. Marcus understood the difficulties ahead, with the war coming to its conclusion and with everyone on civvy street; would the sergeant have it in his heart to have a man of colour in a social capacity as a friend? He pondered that thought for a while and concluded that one way or another he was determined to make London his new home.

The sergeant's help would be very much appreciated. It would serve as a life jacket to keep him afloat in an ocean of indifference, which was a normal trend to what he has already experienced since his arrival in the country. The sergeant was the only exception to that rule. Marcus watched Sergeant Pearson doing his rehabilitation routine; stepping off and walking unaided; striving to keep his equilibrium; pain and determination in equal measure etched on his face, as he defied life's adversities which he resolutely intended to overcome. Returning to his bed, he flopped down heavily showing serious evidence of stress. He sighed and tried to replace the grimace on his face with a smile for the benefit of Marcus. "No pain no gain as the saying goes." The sergeant announced.

Marcus nodded in the affirmative. "I can see you will be a very fit man before long."

"Well!" The sergeant contended. "They tell me my recovery would very much depend on me. If that's the case I can assure you I will give it my best shot."

Marcus nodded agreeably. The sergeant was easily one to be admired; he was a strong resolute man who was capable of overcoming adversities of any kind that he may encounter. Thinking back, only a few short months ago of the enormous injury he endured, the kind that would have broken lesser men and to observe his rapid recovery was almost breathtaking.

"I'm sure your family will be glad to have you back now that you are on the mend." Marcus hinted as the sergeant continued to do his leg flexing exercises. Pearson stopped immediately and for the first time his expression became sombre, showing emotions that Marcus would never have associated with this stoic and most remarkable man. With moist eyes and trembling lips he murmured. "It would have been nice to go home to my wife – she was a wonderful woman, but unfortunately she passed away six months ago."

The silence between the two men was only brief, but somehow to Marcus, it seemed like an eternity. The shock of knowing this gentle man's misfortune resonated throughout Marcus's entire body. It was all the more staggering that there was never a time when he showed signs of distress for so huge a loss. His expression hardly changed as he continued. "My wife died of tuberculosis." The sergeant stopped and stared into open space, doing his utmost to keep his composure. He then turned his gaze towards Marcus. "She was a fine woman in every way. When she became a Matron at the hospital, I figured she would have been safe, you know; just giving orders, but not my Mary, that was never her way. She was an extremely hands-on person, never shirked responsibilities. She worked in a TB hospital and even though I warned her to be careful- she would always say what will be will be. Two years ago she contracted the disease but that did not stop her. She just thought she had to do God's will."

"I'm sorry to hear that." Marcus heard himself say, thinking of the sheer bad luck for him to have lost his wife at such a crucial time in his life, especially when he himself needed help. The sergeant stood up and for the first time, his expression became less sombre. He engaged Marcus with a faint smile. "You know Marcus; we are not in this world forever. That's what the loss of my wife has taught me."

Marcus nodded in the affirmative, realising the resilient qualities that his friend possessed and wondered if he could ever emulate such a person.

"What would you do now?" Marcus enquired.

"Live the best way I can." Pearson retorted. "I have a beautiful home in London that someone looks after and when all of this is behind us I will invite you to visit."

He looked at Marcus inquisitively. "Have you ever been to London?"

"Yes, I have in a roundabout sort of way." Marcus indicated.

"Well! This will be a fine opportunity for you to see the city." The sergeant explained. "My rehab is very much on course. I am sure by the time you see me in London I will be right as rain."

"I have no doubt that you will be fit as a fiddle very soon." Marcus agreed as the two men parted company.

It was late evening as he left the hospital and even though the weather was bleak and rainy, Marcus's mood contrasted sharply with the surroundings. He felt a tingle of delight – a sense of exhilaration from the good news he received. At long last, his friend was making a rapid and astonishing recovery, coupled with the unexpected but welcomed invitation he received to visit this great city of London. It had been, in fact, a secret ambition of his to one day visit the city.

Reading in his *West Indian Reader* at school, he had learned about the history of the Mother Country and about the people and places of repute. The power and might which he imbibed over the years and which left a mental imprint so strong, it was impossible not to fire his imagination, in anticipation of seeing the city (of this Great Empire) in all its glory. The sights of great interest to him were London Bridge, Buckingham Palace, Trafalgar Square and more. To add to his delight Marcus felt there was no one more capable of showing him the sights of London other than the sergeant himself. So far as he was concerned this was worth its weight in gold. This was an amazing prospect in the making. However, he needed to keep, matters in perspective. Fully aware of the fact that the war was not over yet and what was more, he was still obligated to the lieutenant whose expectations of him of becoming a professional fighter was still to be fulfilled. In fact, this had become a dilemma for him.

He was fully aware of the fact he did not choose to be a fighter that decision was made for him, nevertheless, he discovered in the grand scheme of things he possessed a talent for this particular art form. A latent ability which had served him well. He was also utterly aware of the fact that to be a fighting machine – a real warrior – you need the qualities of ruthlessness and a sense of devilment which he had a serious deficit of as a human being.

His natural disposition as a docile and mild-mannered person did not lend itself to the rugged brutal and often bloody game of boxing. What obviously reinforced that decision more than anything else, was the contest he had with Wince; who incidentally was a whisper away from gaining victory over him. Wince threw a punch that landed fractionally short of the mark only because Marcus was retreating backwards. Nevertheless, the impact was enough to temporarily dismantle his entire nervous system. So severe it was, he felt his head spinning like a top and that sensation travelled to his legs, which for a brief moment felt like he was walking on stilts. He, fortunately, recovered enough to land a punch of his own to end the fight. The message he received from that experience was enough to indicate that fighting for a living was simply not what he wanted to do.

Uppermost in his mind also was the discussion he had with Sergeant Pearson who took him aside and told him about the lieutenant's secret plans. He admitted to being in partnership with a syndicate who was convinced beyond any doubt that Marcus was heading for the very top and nothing would prevent them from exploiting him to the very limit. "Be prepared for the unexpected." Sergeant Pearson indicated.

"But I did not promise them anything!" Marcus pleaded.

"Well! They are prepared to move heaven and earth to achieve their aim; so it is very much up to you to avoid being suckered in their plans." Sergeant Pearson said.

Marcus felt the weight of obligation that was put on him was hardly fair. In the eyes of the syndicate, however, he was the golden nugget and they were prepared to make him an offer he could not refuse. He thought seriously about what the sergeant said and smiled warmly after he congratulated him on winning, realising how heavily the odds were stacked against him.

"Putting you in with Wince was suicidal. Grimes was definitely up to no good letting you fight him." He gave Marcus a pleasing look. "But you're good, damn good. You have what it takes to be a champion."

Marcus pondered contentedly. He knew how much Grimes hated him. His racist intent was enough to see him get pummelled even though he knew that this was a definite mismatch. A different result would not have been to Grimes advantage, but he was prepared to live the lie that he felt Marcus was ready. The result only compounded Grime's resentment even more; a very good reason why Marcus was only too keen to rid himself of this evil individual. What kept repeating in his head over and over was the advice given to him by the sergeant. "You can be the best there is if you believe. If not, do what your heart tells you. Fulfil your ambitions, not someone else's."

He realised it was just a matter of time before all this could be behind him, but for now and until the fighting comes to an end, his decision to decline boxing for a living must be a well-kept secret. Knowledge of his intentions could only be detrimental to his ultimate plans.

Still very prominent in his thinking also was the recent past, when he was ensnared in the working situation which was nothing short of hellish. He realised the horrors of the truck and heavy machinery that he endured. The back-breaking efforts he experienced; the indifference of the men he worked with and the serious and painful calluses he endured, as a result of the winter that was so cold, it attempted to break his spirit. Those were the dark days of the past. A past he was very certain he would never again want to revisit.

# END OF WAR

It was liberation time, the war was finally over. The Germans capitulated under the severe onslaught of the combined forces, bringing to an end this tragic confrontation and the entire country was able to breathe a huge sigh of relief. It was victory in Europe and for very good reasons, it was not before time. This was a period of unimaginable glee. It was as if someone had taken the lid off a volcano. There was an eruption of emotions that was difficult to subdue. Everyone, everywhere, was expressing maximum relief that at last the burden of this conflict had finally subsided.

This was very much a new horizon and everyone was reacting accordingly; the hope that this era of comparative peace and contentment would continue. Marcus was particularly pleased for multiple reasons. He was awarded a medal for the prompt action he took in averting further damage to Sergeant Pearson. He was promoted to a position of corporal for his sterling efforts in his place of work and finally, he was now a free man having liberated himself from the Army. Moreover, he was now able to make decisions that were in his best interest.

His initial meeting with the lieutenant was blunt and to the point in spite of the fame and glory that was dangled as the prize for his skills. He was adamant that fighting for a living was simply not what he sought. The Army taught him a useful lesson. The controlled environment that he was part of for the past four years, taking orders, adhering to instructions and never free to make plans of his own was an experience he never regretted, but that was more than enough in his lifetime. To enter into an obligation as a professional fighter, placed him in a position of control by others, who may see him merely as an object for exploitation. Lastly, it would remove him from his alternative plans. He was returning to the village with his handsome features intact; this would allow him the best opportunity of achieving his goal and hopefully winning the heart of Teresa.

The lieutenant showed a sense of dismay hearing the unfortunate news that Marcus was negative to the idea of achieving great rewards as a fighter. Never ever did anyone impress him more than this young black fellow, who with a professional team around him, could easily turn into a wonderful fighting machine. The ability and natural poise he showed, especially against Wince more than convinced him that this young man was top draw. He showed ability far beyond his years and stopping Wince when everyone was expecting him to capitulate, was something to behold. The lieutenant imagined that taking Marcus to the very top of the boxing profession was as obvious as it was inevitable.

What was more, he would be right there to see the finished article. He could not believe that Marcus would say no. Marcus' refusal spurred him into action. The syndicate which he was associated with was quick to respond. Like the lieutenant, they saw potential in abundance and they were quite prepared to exploit it to its very limit. It was readily agreed that the matter needed urgent attention. Hence collectively it was decided to grant Marcus an offer to which he simply couldn't ignore. He was given a thousand pounds to use on whatever he wished. This was a gift pure and simple. He was also given an option of an additional thousand pounds if he signed within one calendar year. That was before he laced a pair of gloves on his hands.

The entire package, however, was designed specifically to create maximum impact on Marcus, with the promise of unparalleled fame and fortune. This was a magnitude he could never have imagined. The temptation of accepting this amazing offer coupled with the chance of being famous was far less easy to reject and so became a litmus test to the young man's resolve.

However a decision was made in his heart and nothing, no matter how extraordinary things were, could change that. Marcus wanted out.

The train journey to London was as special as it was memorable. The high expectations of Marcus were very much intact. Although there was standing room only in the packed train, no one was complaining. Amity was the order of the day. It was as if nature had rekindled life's glorious pleasures of communication once more. Everyone on board exuded friendship and conviviality long forgotten in the mire of a war that did no favours to anyone. The lid of that particular era had at last lifted and no one regretted seeing the end of it. Reflecting on those past years, Marcus smiled wryly. He fully realised that it was time to look ahead to a future that was worthwhile and fast approaching.

He admired the rolling hills, the delightful landscape of the countryside; the cultivated fields and the array of animals grazing contentedly. He knew he was in territory where he wanted to be. A sense of eager anticipation consumed him. Very soon he would be in the city of London but most importantly, meeting up with his friend the sergeant.

It was several months since their last meeting, although they corresponded regularly. Nevertheless, seeing him in the flesh would be a welcomed treat. He was fascinated with the thought of being a Londoner and felt soon he would be able to establish his own footprint in this new environment. He was now convinced beyond doubt that his time had arrived. The sequence of events that he experienced, the success that followed so consistently gave him a sense of assurance that nothing he set out to achieve could not be attained if he remained positive.

# CITY LIFE

London was everything he expected and more. The pace of the city was something to behold. The haste and the hurly-burly did not bode well for him, initially. If anything he was completely out of step with his surroundings and needed to amend his ways quickly. It was his first experience of urban living. Something he was forced to come to terms with. A rapid response was needed to alter his negative ways. Fortunately, help was readily at hand from his teacher and best friend Sergeant Pearson. The capable sergeant was predominant in smoothing the path for the young man and helping him to adjust into a society that he did not find straightforward to settle comfortably into. He regarded highly and was most appreciative of the diligence and scrupulous attention the sergeant paid to him.

In fact, he was the father that Marcus never really had. Albert, his father, was a pleasant but very reticent individual. His natural demeanour was calm and controlled. He was known to be someone who would never say a word out of place. In the context of the village he was always regarded as the quiet one and although he may have been approachable, no one took the opportunity of finding out, hence the lines of communication was somewhat non-existent.

Conversely, the sergeant was always ready to render help where necessary. However, Marcus was hell-bent on exercising independence of his own. He showed remarkable initiative in finding a job and accommodation without the help of anyone. He knew that if help was needed his friend and mentor was always available to assist. Highbury was the first choice of residence and it was where he met Hardy Lamble, a young man of mixed heritage. Hardy was someone with a tremendous sense of humour and with a personality to match. Like Marcus, he was an ex-soldier, but he also played the saxophone and, therefore, spent most of his service as a musician.

According to him, because of his talent as a musician, he was able to live the life of Riley in the forces and was very happy to do so. As a result, they became pals very quickly. Hardy was very much in demand for his music and being a Londoner, he took Marcus wherever he was performing. Apart from the fun aspect of it, it gave Marcus a wonderful insight into this huge and varied city which was more than invaluable to him.

It was a bright and sunny day as the two men were enjoying a glass of wine when the good sergeant dropped a bombshell. "So what are your plans, Marcus? Are you still heading for home?"

"Of course." Replied Marcus. "My plans have not altered, but first I must obtain a home."

Sergeant Pearson was well aware of the financial status of Marcus, who was quick to confide in him on matters of such nature. What the sergeant was unsure of, was whether Marcus was ever tempted to accept the offer of the syndicate that was still available to him.

"So what is it to be? Are you heading for stardom or just a humdrum existence?"

Marcus puckered his lips and gave a wry smile. "No I am not tempted, I am positive of what I want out of life. If the lady of my dreams says yes, I'll be the happiest man on this side of the planet."

For a while, the sergeant studied his young companion and smiled pleasantly. "You know Marcus; you are an incredible young man. You certainly know what you want out of life and I applaud you for that." He stopped briefly still giving Marcus his full focus as he continued. "I cannot think of too many people who would have given up the opportunity of fame, popularity and the bright lights, for this quiet life you seek. Who knows –

perhaps with a bit of determination you could easily be a formidable fighter, maybe even a world champion."

Marcus laughed heartily. "You make it sound so very easy." He paused for a while to think. "The truth is; even though I was tempted, I came to the conclusion that fighting was not the life I would choose. I do have a dream, but it is not getting my head knocked off in the ring. I want to be in charge of my own destiny and that's the way it's going to be."

The sergeant inhaled sharply and with a smile still present on his face, he shook his head affirmatively. "That's just what I mean Marcus. Nothing or no one can entice or influence your chosen path. That is why I admire you so much, you are an extraordinary young man."

Marcus visibly blushed at the remark of the sergeant, displaying emotions rarely seen by the young man. It was always in his thoughts that fate had played its part inevitably in forging a friendship which was profound and true, one that he was able to derive dividends of enormous proportions from and of which he would never be able to repay.

Recounting his good fortune, he realised that although the two men were paradoxically different and indeed worlds apart historically and culturally, the friendship they acquired benefited mainly from the common human spirit of decency, respect and regard for each other. It was far removed from past experiences of hostility, negative reaction and racist taunts of which he was a victim. Those were the norms of which he got a daily diet from the inception before their friendship developed. The sergeant took a positive interest in his welfare becoming mentor, guardian and caretaker, relative to his present position. He knew, without doubt, this relationship was a case of a friend in need is a friend indeed. Marcus was fortunate to have met such a person.

The sergeant was still suffering from the effects of the injury and showed signs of discomfort which Marcus noticed but remained tacit about. It was obvious the recovery that was expected did not materialise and he now felt duty bound to take an interest. "How is that leg of yours? It seems to be giving you a lot of bother."

The sergeant's retort was swift. "Never mind about my leg young man, that's immaterial. I'm fortunate to have the use of it more than anything else. Let's concentrate on you. You have an unbelievable talent that most men would be happy to exploit. Yet you turn it down, flat."

Marcus scratched his head and smiled wistfully. "As much as I was tempted to go for the big times, I just know I am not cut out for such things." Running his fingers across his face, he continued. "Besides, I want to retain my good looks for as long as possible."

The sergeant nodded in agreement. He was positive his young friend had a stubborn streak and was not open to changing his mind. "I understand that Marcus; what I cannot contemplate, is why you would want to remain in England; forsaking the tropics and all that glorious weather for this cold and grim climate."

Marcus laughed out loud. "You know at the back of my mind I always wanted to be here, I read so much about this country that has fascinated me; I know it was only a matter of time before I got here. My next ambition is to find a home, return to Guiana, marry the woman of my dreams and live happily ever after."

"That sounds good to me, you certainly deserve it." The sergeant suggested. "A wife I certainly cannot help you with, but I can surely assist in finding you a home." The sergeant paused briefly to observe Marcus, knowing the supreme shock he was about to deliver. "This place can be yours and you have first option of acquiring it. I know you have the resource, so what do you say?"

Marcus was thrown into a state of bewilderment and shock but was trying his best to remain composed. Finally, he responded. "Yes, yes, yes, but why do you want to sell? Or is this some kind of a joke?"

"It's as real as I'm sitting here." The sergeant uttered. "You are right about my leg. I am having serious issues with it. The advice from my doctor is quite straightforward, if my leg is to improve in any substantial way, I need to find some place warm. So I have decided reluctantly to join my elder brother in Australia." He chuckled amusingly. "It's ironical is it not? Here I am rushing off to find the sunshine and you are running away from it."

Marcus nodded in the affirmative, still totally overwhelmed as the sergeant continued. "The truth is, my brother, emigrated to Australia many years ago. He always had a farmer's mentality. He started as a sheep-shearer and eventually worked his way to the very top. Like you; he was always ambitious, always enthusiastic, never a backward step. Now he owns the farm. Like everything else, he's getting on in life and wants someone to do the books for him, so I've decided to sell up and go. I guess my life can do with a change now, especially since this wretched war is over and the Mrs is no more."

The news, sudden as it was, made it all seem so surreal to the young man. Things were happening so quickly he was beginning to imagine it was an illusion.

This new episode was so breathtaking, it was somewhat difficult to believe and as far as Marcus was concerned it was the very pinnacle of everything he had wished for and was now confident given the opportunity, he could walk on water, such was his good fortune. As far as his aspirations went, this exceeded all expectations. Such was the emotions running through his veins, he was now of the belief, he was standing on the threshold of life and nothing was beyond his scope of accomplishment. The dynamics were stacked so spectacularly in his favour, he was now of the belief, that all things were possible. The final piece in the jigsaw, making Teresa his Queen seemed totally realistic. It was a notion he constantly felt was impossible in the past, now it seemed very achievable. All that has happened to him in the recent past was favourable to the very extreme, bringing unbridled joy to him.

He had conquered all his inhibitions and had become a person of repute in the largest Metropolis in the world. His considerable advancement, moving from a naive kid in a remote village to becoming a solid citizen in an advanced society such as

England was regarded as a great accomplishment. However, he was now going back to the village of his birth, hoping for a minor miracle. It was a place where things had remained unchanged for generations. If there were any reservations in his mind, it was how to break through these barriers. Conscious of the fact that those in the upper echelon of the village society who would easily regard him as an upstart. Marcus was also aware that his quest to attain respectability in some circles was a quantum leap into the unknown.

Those who knew of his past – someone who was considered relatively insignificant with no positive pedigree – would hardly be willing to forget his background and treat him as their equal. He knew that he was returning with a stripe on his sleeve and a medal on his chest. This would hardly be qualifications that merit promotion worthy of recognition. Somehow, however, he was totally unfazed by this new challenge and was prepared as best he could, to remove any obstacles that might emerge if he was to accomplish his ultimate aim. In his mind, it was undoubtedly a necessary imperative that was worth fighting for.

# GOING HOME

The ship heading towards the Caribbean Sea was one of great significance as far as the soldiers on board were concerned. Men were returning to their homeland after serving gallantly in the British Armed Forces, after five difficult years of warfare. The spirit of friendship on board and general relief were all too apparent as they journeyed homeward. Men who were prepared to risk life and limb for what was imagined to be a worthy cause, fighting the great fight for Mother Country England. The banter and general good humour was in fact easy compensation for men who were now relieved from the stresses of years of fighting, of misunderstanding and difficulties that they endured throughout their experiences of war. It was something of a battle of survival as much as recognition in a variety of ways. The repressive conditions, for one, were pretty standard fare. Much of what they suffered was considered normal. Rejection and scant respect were constant in their daily existence.

The changes of the environment – moving from tropical to a more demanding, temperate climate – were factors not to be dismissed lightly. Most noticeable among many of the men, however, were the condescending attitude that was displayed towards them, mainly as a result of cultural difference and the instilled belief that people of colour were different. This stereotypical notion was cultivated over a period of time and deeply entrenched in the most negative of ways. Therefore, it was believed that Africans were sub-human, simplistic and stupid. For many of the lads, this was a fight for survival in itself. The war was now over, but an element of mental scars were very much in existence and very often considerable. It was the equivalent of post-war fatigue.

Going home was a relief of great magnitude for many of the soldiers. In spite of the many difficulties that ensued, these proud men were in high spirits and remained that way throughout. Marcus was by far the most popular of the lot. His ability to rise above adversities was remarkable. Helped by the good fortune of his own ability, the amazing coincidence of a lieutenant whose fetish for the game of boxing and the absolute good grace of connecting with Sergeant Pearson who was someone he regarded in high esteem. Without them, he most certainly would not be in the position he now held.

Confident also of the fact that his upliftment was one of fairytale proportions of which he was very proud. His was the kind of success you read in books. The news of his prowess circulated far and wide which was also very encouraging. Marcus was nicknamed 'The Warrior', a name he was deeply proud of. There were some amongst his colleagues who thought he was unwise not to go the full distance where boxing was concerned. However, that was not a concern to him.

His agenda was different in many ways. His homecoming was temporary, hopeful of finding the love of his life and returning to London was his primary objective. Marcus was well aware of the challenges he faced in the village, a place where old habits remained static, and a place where barriers are built so high, it would take a monumental effort to put a dent in it. So resolute and unchanging were the folks, it would take a miracle to alter the habits of the place where he was born. A daunting task if ever there was one. However, it was a matter that could not be avoided and must be confronted head-on. He was bringing to the village a degree of confidence and success way beyond anything the villagers could have anticipated, yet he knew that convincing them of his new status would be a most difficult feat to accomplish. The cynics and sceptics would hardly be impressed by someone who had suddenly become larger than life; whose ambition some would say exceeds his ability. After all, it was only a few short years ago that many remembered him as a shy and somewhat introverted and insignificant member of the community, an image that would be almost impossible to dispel or overlook.

All the negatives were in place for a huge fight, one he considered to be inevitable. If at all he was to achieve his grand desire, he needed good fortune on his side. One small chink of light at the end of the tunnel however and which was a redeeming feature in the grand scheme of things, were his credentials. Being a member of the British Armed Forces was a most impressive and an absolute bonus in his favour, especially since he was known as the great warrior. A name that placed him high in the esteem of many who saw him as someone brave enough to succeed in the ring and also fighting in a war for Mother Country, England, among other things.

The throng of people that gathered at the wharf to meet the returning soldiers were both spectacular and overwhelming. The enthusiasm of the huge gathering to witness the return of these fighting men was somewhat unexpected but most welcome. The colonial leaders; the press and the radio station were all complicit in making the homecoming a monumental and impressive success. Celebrations were elaborate and of the highest standards, matched only by the respect that was given to the soldiers for their duty to society. Civic activities were too many to mention, but the biggest banquet of all was reserved for Marcus. His village participated in a magnificent homecoming that anyone could have imagined. The village school he attended was adorned with bunting and flags of every description and even with a fresh coat of paint, which made it simply delightful and aesthetically pleasing to the eyes. The school hall was packed with every important village personnel available, not to mention the local villagers who were frantic and eager to get a piece of their war hero.

Marcus was beginning to imagine, based on the welcome he received, his path of overcoming the sceptics would be made much easier. Remembering he left the village as a youth abruptly and unheralded. He was now returning to his home triumphant and held in the highest regard by the multitude, which was indeed a moment to savour, but in his thoughts he more than understood the philosophy of one's existence, he was aware that life is woven into the fabric of objectivity; sometimes you win and sometimes you lose and although he was riding on the crest of a wave, he always understood or believed in the law of average; nothing remains the same forever.

The evening was certainly the most amazing in his entire life. It was all the more remarkable because it was in acknowledgement of his efforts in the British Armed Forces. In his wildest dreams, he never could have imagined his homecoming would have stirred so much enthusiasm and high excitement; on the rostrum where he sat with his proud mother Mama G. Most, if not all, of the village elite were present. A gathering so impressive it sent a tingle through the spine of the young soldier. Before the proceedings commenced, he noticed an empty chair two paces away and wondered which of the dignitaries failed to attend.

His curiosity was soon rewarded when suddenly appearing in the distance and heading towards the rostrum was the most curvaceous figure imaginable. She was the personification of absolute beauty. Her charm seemed to exceed all expectations. She looked stunning in green. Her well-fitted dress accentuating her every curve. It was poetry in motion, a perfect fusion of human perfection. There was a sudden hush that enveloped the otherwise packed and noisy school hall. It was as if she commanded special attention. As she approached she bowed politely to Marcus and his mother and smiled, exposing rows of beautiful white teeth and leaving behind a dainty and delicate fragrance in her wake. She was undoubtedly the woman of his dreams and in his eyes, she was a Goddess in every majestic detail. He was now experiencing joy beyond compare. That person was Teresa Malison.

There was an element of exaggeration in the comments made by some of the speakers. Remarks that were exceedingly out of touch with actuality, superlatives that were way off beam with the truth, giving the impression that he was a front-line soldier, that he was in enemy territory combating the Germans and although the sentiments may have impressed Teresa and others, it made him cringe with embarrassment and guilt. Being someone of integrity and honesty he felt ill at ease. He leaned over to Mama G and whispered. "Mama G, I cannot let them carry on like this, I was never a frontline soldier."

Mama G smiled and took her son's hand into hers. "Son." She replied. "If you interrupt or tell them the truth you'll only belittle them. After all, who is to know what you did in the war."

"But Mama G." Marcus insisted. "It's not the truth. I do not want to live a lie."

Mama G, still smiling, concluded. "My dear son, who is to know – just let it be."

Observing his mother's calm demeanour, he acceded to her wisdom. After all, she may be correct. Who is to know what he did or did not do in a war that was now history. In the interim, the evening was a huge success. Marcus meddled with old friends and villagers who simply wanted to know more about England and how he survived the vicious onslaught of the enemy. His medal and the stripe he wore on his sleeve was more than enough proof of his bravery. However, his preoccupation was clearly elsewhere. His attention was fixed on Teresa hoping against hope that she did not just vanish into the night.

As the evening wore on, Marcus availed himself with every opportunity to meet and also make acquaintance with the village functionaries, knowing it was appropriate to do so and especially since he was the centre of attraction. Standing tall and looking eminently handsome in his uniform, which was undoubtedly a charm offensive to the ladies, he was becoming fully aware of his prime importance in a village environment that is impervious to change. With raised ego, he imagined this was indeed the moment to impress and reinforce the notion that he had crossed the social barrier and equality was now assured.

VICTOR WALDRON

The climax of the evening was undoubtedly remarkable. Marcus was overwhelmed with having his first dance with the woman of his dreams. This was the moment of a lifetime. It was a moment to savour for all eternity. His pounding heart and dry lips were evidence that he was now in the presence of someone who was the embodiment of everything he had hoped and prayed for. The reality of this day compounded his belief that all things are possible.

The band played and as she moved to the rhythm of the music, he felt he was in paradise. Her soft alluring aroma consumed him, her hair fresh as the summer's breeze, her skin smooth as silk, he concluded in his own mind that nature was exceedingly kind to her, she was indeed perfection personified.

Teresa looked up at Marcus and offered a smile as bright as the morning sunshine. Her lovely hazel eyes flickered in concert with the warmth of her radiant features. She emitted a sensuality that blew Marcus away and rendered him speechless.

"So you are the brave villager everyone is excited about?" Teresa asked with a dainty smile. Marcus did not attempt to reply mainly because he was unsure of what to say. The evening was dotted with inaccuracies and he did not want to commit to a lie. He smiled pleasantly in response to the question but remained tacit.

"Are you as brave as they make you out to be?" She persisted.

"Well you have to have the courage to be in uniform, but I am not what they are making me..." Teresa interrupted by putting her finger to his lips. "Modesty becomes you." She informed. "Soldiers are a special breed of people."

"I guess you are right." He uttered.

"So now you are back? What do you intend to do in this sleepy village of ours?" Marcus, still in a state of awe was now beginning to relax. Teresa's personality was so disarming; he was starting to feel at ease in her company.

The fact that she saw the village as a drab and uninteresting place was a complete surprise to him. She unlike him had the privilege of the high superior status of her family and her unlimited scope for opportunities and freedom around town. Unlike his own existence; before he left was at best staid, irrelevant and lacking momentum or real purpose.

"I'm afraid I'm only here for a short stay before I return to London. You can say I have important business to settle which I hope I can achieve." Marcus admitted.

"London eh?" She remarked. "That's interesting! I thought you were back here to settle."

"No! No! London is now my home. All my main interests are there."

Teresa studied Marcus momentarily. "If I may ask; what kind of interest would that be?"

"I have a great deal of unfinished business to attend to," Marcus replied.

"Oh! That's interesting. You sound like a man in a hurry. Why the big urgency?" Teresa responded.

"Well." He smiled. "I have a very good job that requires my attention. I own a lovely home that I need to run, so you see time is of the essence."

"You own your own home in London?" She inquired.

"Yes." He announced. "Newly acquired and I'm very proud of it."

"You have not been away that long. Tell me, soldier, does money grow on trees in London?"

The remark brought giggles to the young soldier and gave him a sense of ease, being in the company of someone so illustrious. Her interest in him was remarkable and knowing the calibre of the lady, he wondered if it was just conversational, or whether she had a genuine concern for his achievements. Whatever it was, however, it opened a door and gave him the opportunity to, express his virtues and hoped it would gainfully advance his position.

"And without being interfering, could I ask what business are you proposing here?" Teresa asked with more than a hint of interest.

"Not at all!" He retorted. "After I left the Army, I realised that I could never return to this country to live. It's far too humdrum for me; London gave me opportunities I would never have had here. It's a very exciting place; lots to do and now that I own my own home and have a decent job, I merely want to settle down and perhaps raise a family."

"And what is your job if I may ask?" Teresa enquired.

"I'm an engineer; I work for a very large company. I was trained in the Army and I think I'm good at what I do."

Teresa seemed very impressed by what she heard and it was as if Marcus had injected a powerful and positive interest in her thinking about countries such as England. He was away for only a comparatively short span of time. Furthermore, he was able to secure so much in such a brief period was ample evidence of what could happen in a large or developed country. Not that Teresa was unaware of that fact, as her brother Bertie, a lawyer and her elder sister Myola, an accountant, were both qualified in the USA and were subjected to the most unfortunate experience of coping with their Aunt Beryl who lives in New York. Residing with her was the nearest thing to hell. Her general demeanour was that of a dragon. After her husband's demise, she was transformed from a gentle and sincere being to something of an ogre. Showing consideration only for her two cats and the organ she played in her church with majestic dexterity. Her harsh conduct and extreme discipline was, unfortunately, her hallmark. These were qualities that rendered them never to return to dear Aunt Beryl again.

"So no more village life for you as far as I can see?" She mused wondering if Marcus was overstating the case for England.

"You are so correct. If ever you are fortunate enough to go to a city like London, I guarantee you will not want to live here anymore."

"Then it might be the perfect opportunity to do what I have always wanted to do, which is to become an architect. My parents are dead set against me doing such a thing." She offered.

"Well, London is definitely the place you'll want to be as there are several learning institutes that can give you exactly what you are looking for instantly."

Teresa gave him a meaningful smile. "Well mister soldier boy; it is worth thinking about, I will keep that very much in mind." She said flirtatiously, with a slight twinkle in her eye.

# SUNDAY THANKSGIVING

The Sunday service was as great an attraction as the evening before. The usually healthy attendance was undoubtedly enhanced by the announcement made that it would be a special day of prayers to honour the return of the young villager from the most dangerous mission of war. Fully aware that he was the focus of attention, Marcus needed to grab this final opportunity to create the maximum impression in his quest to appeal to all ranks and classes, especially Teresa whose easy charm and infectious personality the previous evening assisted not only in creating a glorious experience but also gave him a reason to hope. He looked sartorially immaculate in his best uniform as he entered the church, fully aware of the fact that he was now playing for high stakes and wanted nothing to jeopardise his plans, however, central in his thoughts, were the issue which haunted him since he was a child and which he considered counterproductive to the principles of the church.

Acknowledging that he was embarking on dangerous ground, he nevertheless felt compelled to break the long-standing tradition that persisted of allowing the three most important families – the Malisons, the Gorindis and the Bannians – their apparent dominance in a place of worship. It was taken for granted that these families, based on their social pedigree, reserved the pews on an exclusive basis, at the front of the church as a given right. Only if invited were any of the villagers permitted to share or be accommodated by the respective families. No one dared to challenge this order of what was now considered an accepted village custom.

The Bannian family generally encouraged folks to sit with them; a strategy they deemed as good for business since they owned most of the shops in the area. Marcus always resented this improper behaviour as an act of vanity which should be broken and this was indeed a golden opportunity to do just that. He certainly had no qualms about the enormity of the situation and the risks involved, but propelled by his own conviction that this was a tradition too far, he felt obliged to break it. This was his moment anyway. He was undoubtedly the focal point in this instant and with his ego intact, he felt he was entitled to one indiscretion and hoped to be absolved by the congregation should it go pear-shaped.

Marcus entered the church slowly and deliberately, knowing the impact his very action would create, but never for one single moment was he prepared to change course. His awareness that he was totally in the spotlight was unmistakable. He approached the front end of the church and as he reached the Gorindis family, he bowed courteously and proceeded to join them without an invitation. His action provoked a ripple across the length and breadth of the church, especially among the older members of the congregation, who were not accustomed to such behaviour. This move was simply unprecedented and would in the normal way create turbulence of considerable proportions, however, the family showed remarkable resilience of recovery and welcomed the young soldier, especially since he was the celebrated personality that so many came to see and admire.

Nevertheless, surprise was the order of the day and although there were no visible protests due mainly to the Gorindis' courtesy and goodwill, his Godmother Nanny May was incandescent with rage. In her estimation, this was an act of provocation and to a very large extent disrespectful to the Gorindis family. She considered it a grave transgression that should not go unpunished. His action, however, was given a stamp of approval by at least one member of the congregation. Teresa smiled and nodded at the young man's sense of daring;

VICTOR WALDRON

that sense of approval, however, did not go down well with her mother, who found the action of Marcus most distasteful.

It was now mid-morning and there was still a lingering crowd of well-wishers in the churchyard, inquisitively hanging around merely to press the flesh or ask questions of one kind or another, but as they gradually dispersed, Marcus felt relieved that the opportunity had finally come to rekindle an old habit of finding his favourite spot on the sea wall. It was a wall that prevented the tide from washing the village away. As he sat on the wall and stared at the vast ocean, Marcus smiled contentedly. As a young man, this place was a sanctuary. A place where he felt safe and unburdened; where all his dreams were crystallised, where his imagination knew no bounds; where he held the entire world in his hands. In that world all things were possible. But by far the greatest wish of all was always to capture the love and affection of Teresa Malison, making her his wife and living a life of perpetual bliss. On reflection much of what he hoped for had been achieved. He felt his progress so far had been remarkable. He agreed his attainment over such a short period of time was nothing short of spectacular.

The overwhelming approval of the villagers in his estimation had exceeded all expectations. So much of this seemed stranger than fiction, only a few hours ago he was holding his greatest prize, Teresa Malison; her seemingly pure and unadulterated charm; her effervescent personality still haunted him. In a manner of speaking, this was the perfect storm. He was living the dream. His sigh was one of great satisfaction, thinking not without merit, his journey had been extraordinary. His newly acquired status was totally and relevantly earned, but more importantly, the community – a place where changes are not always acceptable, has given him a sense of approval for his efforts and position borne out of ambition and hard work.

Marcus started off in quiet contemplation as he strolled through the village, observing the local village activities which he found most interesting. He could not help but notice the unique village environment, which was full of activity of varying capacity and hue. For example, the kiskadees' consistent chirping on rooftops, domestic flies flickering around with vigorous energy, dogs barking, ducks fluttering in a lively fashion in the trenches, bees extracting pollen from the flowers with sumptuous enthusiasm, hawks seeking out whatever they can find, blackbirds flying in formation as if trained to perform, trees dancing and swaying merrily, obeying the command of the sea breeze blowing with compelling force. The midday sun standing loftily in the cloudless sky, emitted rays of energy in an indulgent manner as if to facilitate animals, birds, insects and vegetation to perform an act of village soap opera. Much of this typical display intrigued Marcus which almost always went unnoticed by those who live there. He smiled wistfully at the significance of it all. Only a few years ago, all this was very much a part of his existence, which he prudently substituted for what he now considered to be a better way.

As he approached his destination he saw a large bit of real estate with what appeared to be a shack in the middle of it. In front of the shack was someone sitting in a stooped position chopping wood. Careful scrutiny revealed the unmistakable figure of big Wally. He was crouched in an almost uncomfortable posture, doing a job of work hardly appropriate for this once awesome and aggressive individual. Big Wally was chopping wood for his coal pot, a facility used for cooking his meals. In front of the yard was a small stream with a rickety bridge to gain access. The yard itself was sparse with fading grass which showed signs of fatigue, having the sun beating down on it constantly. Wally looked so meek and submissive, it was difficult to imagine someone who was once so powerful and abrasive could be reduced to the status of a pussycat. As he sat there doing his task, Marcus could not help wondering where the might and power of this colossal man had gone. The venom of this once fearful giant had almost evaporated.

Skipping across the shallow stream, avoiding the rickety bridge, Marcus was now in touching distance of Wally who never wavered from his task. He was fully aware of the fact that the big man was completely conscious of his presence. Wally was wearing a tatty vest that had more holes than a golf course; equally, his pants seemed smaller than the required fit, giving the distinct impression that it was hardly a thing of comfort. It was obvious that he had fallen on hard times. Marcus studied him for some moments, but the big man carried on regardless. It was as if he was not there.

"Hello, Wally," Marcus called out. He got no response. "Do you know who I am?" Marcus enquired. Wally looked up briefly and half nodded in the affirmative. "Are you keeping well?" Marcus asked.

No response again from Wally. Marcus wondered if his former adversary was still carrying a grudge after all those years; perhaps thinking that he might still be 'king of the jungle' had it not been for the abrupt way in which Marcus ended his reign. Marcus dug deep into his pocket and produced a hefty amount of dollars and waved it in Wally's direction. "Take this Wally – get yourself something nice."

Gradually the chopping stopped, Wally placed the axe down gently and for the first time, he actually looked at Marcus. Slowly big Wally stretched his massive hand out to receive what was on offer. Putting the cash away, big Wally resumed his task of chopping. Marcus gave Wally a substantial amount of cash, the kind that he would not have seen before and although the big man did not show emotions of any kind, Marcus was positive that he would have appreciated the gesture. By all intents and purposes, big Wally became a recluse after the collapse of his reign as the tough guy.

The massive gale force that was once this powerhouse of a man had now rescinded. The fact that he did not engage in conversation was in part due to the overwhelming embarrassment he was subjected to on that unfortunate evening. Not only did he lose the battle, but he also lost every drop of confidence he ever possessed, sending him into a state of complete oblivion.

Marcus hopped across the stream once more, avoiding the bridge that seemed even more vulnerable than big Wally himself;

as he carried on his journey, he was still somewhat perplexed by Wally's behaviour. He looked back to see the big man staring intently at him until he was completely out of sight. Fate or destiny, whatever it was, brought him face to face with someone like Wally. The end result was amazing. That gave him the strength and confidence to face the world and expose the hidden talent that would have remained latent, had it not been for the big man. It also gave Marcus great satisfaction that he was able to give Wally something back in return. For Marcus, this was a gratifying experience.

His mind was now firmly fixed on Mama G's home cooking. She promised him a feast for a king and this was the moment for her to deliver. She loved cooking and her culinary skills were exemplary. She was renowned for her fine hand in the kitchen and he was convinced many of the villagers kept her company mainly for the chance to benefit from her sumptuous and delightful meals. She slaughtered a pig, several ducks and fowls for this occasion, convinced and rightly so that he did not benefit from these wonderful treats whilst residing in London. Mama G was determined to put on a spread that he was not likely to forget. Added to her cooking, she presented items such as Jamoon and rice wine; the likes that would not usually see the light of day before Christmas or New Year's Day, the traditional time of year when luxuries of such nature ever emerged.

However, this was no ordinary occasion, this was a proud mother preparing for a son who came from the dangerous mission of fighting for King and country, for freedom and moreover as a national hero. As he reached the neighbourhood, his sense of smell picked up the exotic aroma coming from Mama G's kitchen. Her wonderful cuisine was making its presence felt. A contented smile spread quickly across his face; as he rubbed his hands in gleeful anticipation. If there was one thing that Marcus missed most of all, it was his mother's wonderful meals. He entered the house to a sensational welcome. Families, friends, invited guests and well-wishers were all enthusiastic in their greetings for the young soldier. To him, it was a fitting climax to all that had happened before.

Nanny May was conspicuous by her absence which was most unusual. Nanny May was always in the forefront of everything that happened in the Gullant household. In fact, as a young man growing up; Marcus felt his mother had the patience of a saint for putting up with her constant unnecessary meddling. For a brief moment, he wondered why she was not in attendance and immediately came to a ready-made conclusion that it was his intrusion in church that caused her distress. She was not one for dismissing such behaviour lightly. He was positive also that he would be rebuked for such arrogance and smiled pleasantly to himself, knowing his Godmother would not forgive him for such a brash act of disrespect. Marcus quickly devised a cunning plan to combat the wrath of this woman, which to his mind was inevitable.

# TERESA

The afternoon moved rapidly into the evening, such was the delight of Mama G's meals which were exceptional. Robert, Marcus's brother, who was normally reticent by nature, felt intrigued by his younger brother's attention to Teresa and naturally, aided and abetted by Mama G's home-brew felt light-headed enough to tease Marcus on his performance the evening before.

"I see you could not get enough of the village queen last night?" Robert mused. "It's not often you see the ladies doing things locally. I can't help thinking she was slumming."

Aware of his brother's reference to Teresa, Marcus smiled softly. "The young lady was very good company, I found her most interesting." He retorted.

Adel, his sister, hissed her teeth, her face carrying a frown of sheer hostility. "You're talking about miss high and mighty. I don't imagine the likes of her go to the toilet like we do."

"Why the attitude?" Marcus asked. "Is she public enemy number one?"

Robert giggled at his brother's remark. "No she's not; it's just that she has no idea that people like us even exist."

"That's not the impression she gave me. As a matter of fact, I found her most stimulating." He intimated. Marcus turned to look at his mother, she was wearing a stern – almost worried look and although she did not engage in the conversation, he was sure she carried the exact sentiments of Robert and Adel. Marcus did not initiate this topic of conversation, but the tone was enough to suggest that Teresa's name was far from popular in the family household. That raised a level of concern that was most unwelcome since his entire plan of action was everything to do with smoothing the path for a relationship he hoped would healthily come to the fore. The attitude from his family seemed hardly helpful.

"I'm getting the impression that the young lady's name is taboo around here," Marcus remarked.

"That depends," Robert retorted. "I have nothing against the young lady, but as far as I can see if you're not a lawyer; or a doctor; or somebody with an equally grand profession; she would not give you the time of day..."

"Look," Adel butted in. "Why would you want to be nice to her anyway? That woman is nothing more than a stuck-up git."

Marcus sighed heavily. His suspicions were now vindicated. He realised Teresa was the equivalent of a red rag to a bull. All of this negative attention towards her left a bad taste in his mouth.

After enjoying the sapid extravagances of Mama G's home delights, this was tantamount to swallowing a bitter pill. It was clearly not what Marcus had hoped for. His optimism, based on all the positives that were in place, seemed to be coming to an abrupt conclusion. To compound the situation even more, much of the resistance was coming from within. This ran contrary to his ultimate plan. However, despite this unexpected obstacle, Marcus was most determined to pursue his objective. Having attained such dizzy heights, it seemed inconceivable not to continue. The histrionics coming from his siblings were in his opinion, an irrelevance he was determined to overlook. In this instance failure was not an option. The lull which lasted less than a minute seemed an eternity, moving the otherwise convivial atmosphere, which was apparent throughout, to suddenly becoming unfriendly.

Mama G was quick to observe the tension that emerged and with a huge smile and a wave of the hand she declared. "Come on folks, live and let live. We cannot all be the same. Don't forget why we are all here. Let us concentrate on having a wonderful evening."

Mama G was just being diplomatic. She noticed that Marcus was far from happy with remarks made by Adel and Robert and readily decided to douche the fire that was beginning to rage. Positive that she did not want a confrontation, but by the same token she was eager to know her son's intention with regards to Teresa.

Marcus took a sip of his mother's home-brew and pondered momentarily, feeling a sense of disappointment which otherwise blighted a most successful evening. Still smiling Mama G got up, took Marcus by the hand and pointed to the bedroom. He was quick to respond, this was as good an opportunity to discuss a matter that was top of his agenda and most critical to his future wellbeing which also meant so much to him.

As they entered the room, Mama G put her back to the door as if to avoid intruders. Marcus sat on the bed with a look of grim expectation on his face. Mama G smiled infectiously, Marcus tried his utmost to return the compliment. "First of all my son, I must thank God for keeping you safe and sound. I can't tell you how happy I am to have you back in one piece."

"Well, Mum, I was part of the war, but not part of the fighting."

Mama G was not quite sure what her son meant but shook her head affirmatively. "During that terrible war, I kept praying for your safety. When your dad died – God bless his soul – I kept wondering if I would lose two of the men in my family."

"God took care of me Mum; you can say that I'm blessed."

Mama G walked over to the bed and took her son's hands in hers. "So now you're here, what are your plans for the future?"

"Well!" He smiled. "I shall be going back to London as soon as I find myself a wife, but not before I consume a lot more of that fine food you gave me today."

"Son!" She replied. "If you stay in the country you will get all the food you want. You know your mother is always willing to please."

"Thank you Mama G, I know that, but right now I am on a mission."

She looked deep into his eyes as if to study what was in her son's heart. His focus which was once weak and yielding as a child now seemed so totally different. "So why do you want to leave us again for a place you don't even know that well?"

Marcus smiled contentedly. "I know a lot of London mother, believe me. I'm happy there and I would invite you to come and live with me."

Mama G laughed out loud. "Son, nothing but nothing would remove me from this village and when I die I just want to be buried with your father." She paused momentarily as if to let that digest. "I was born in this village and the Lord was good to me. He allowed me to bring up a family to which I am very proud of. Why should I want to leave? Thanks but no thanks."

"If that is your wish, Mama, I will not get in your way."

Mama G persisted after a gentle pause. "My dear son there is something I would ask of you as a favour. Please help your sister if you can, to make the journey to England. God knows I would miss her, but it would give her a chance to make something of her life."

"That is not a problem Mama." He replied.

"Thank you, son, at least your big sister will be able to keep an eye on you, she is a good girl and she will take care of you."

Marcus giggled loftily at his mother's comment. "Mama G; I have been away for many years now, I have a job in London, I also have a home there. Believe me, I am very comfortable, I don't need looking after. I am here to find me a wife which would go a long way to complete my happiness."

Mama G looked somewhat puzzled. "You have all those things already? Tell me son does money grow on trees over there?"

Marcus could hardly contain himself with laughter. "That's very funny. Teresa asked me that very question only last night. The answer to that question is no. Money does not grow on trees there. You could say I was fortunate to have succeeded in a place like that. London can be very tough."

"God takes care of his own son – you are a wonderful young man and you deserve your good fortune." Mama G added as she sat on the bed adjacent to her son, still with a puzzled look on her face. "About this young lady, what is going on?"

"Teresa you mean, her name is Teresa Mama G. I get the impression that her name does not sit easily in this household."

"Okay, Teresa." His mother retorted. "What is the story with this girl?"

"The truth is, Mum, I am very passionate about her." He announced softly.

"But son, you don't even know the young lady. How could you be so interested in such a short time?"

Marcus remained quiet for a moment before turning to face his mother squarely. "Mama I know this will sound odd, but I saw Teresa when I was about ten years old and from that day on, I have not stopped thinking about her. Every living day of my life I see her in everything I do. At first, I thought it was some kind of crush or fantasy and when I left the village for England I imagined that feeling would subside. If anything it became stronger. I wish that it was not so, but it is."

Mama G smiled and tried to make light of the subject. "My son you now look so much like your father." She stopped and stared into space as if to make a vivid recollection of that moment. "When I met him for the first time, I told myself no way do I want him for my man. Do you know why?"

Marcus puckered his lips in quiet expectation. "Come on Mum don't keep me in suspense, I know you will tell me."

"It was because of his good looks? He was such a handsome man and I thought to myself, a man like that would have all the girls running after him. The truth is I was afraid to take that risk." She placed her hand on her son's shoulder. "Son, with your good looks you will have no problem finding a nice young lady to be your bride and there are so many to choose from."

"That may well be so Mama, but the way I feel about Teresa is so different, so intense and so captivating, I simply can't help the way I feel."

Mama G clasped her hands as if in prayer. "My boy, I do love you. I am very proud of you and believe me when I say I would not want you to make a serious mistake in your young life. I know these people. The Malisons would not accept you for their daughter. They will think you have ideas above your station. They would feel you are trying to marry someone who is superior to you. In other words, they will simply reject you."

That remark made Marcus cringe. "Well Mum I can see where you're coming from, but unfortunately I do not buy such hogwash. I grew up in this village and for most of my life, I simply could not agree with the philosophy of this place. That is why I had to get out. Because you are poor and the Malisons are better off; you for some unknown reason, believe they are superior to you? What kind of thinking is that?"

"My child we always give these people the respect they deserve. This is a small village and things work better that way."

Marcus shook his head vigorously. "No Mama G; respect them by all means, but what you and others accept is that being poor equals being inferior and that is a ridiculous attitude."

Mama G was prepared to remain resolute. "I don't want to change your views my son, but we get on fine the way we are. All I'm trying to do is stop you from making a mistake that could affect you for the rest of your life. Whatever you say, Marcus, that young lady will not see you as her equal. In their eyes, socially you are at the other end of the scale."

"Well Mum; Teresa and I had a very interesting conversation last night and quite frankly she did not give me the impression that I was beneath her."

"Most of the people in the village would condemn such a relationship." His mother replied swiftly. "Can't you see Marcus? This – this is not going to work." She emphasised.

Marcus felt slightly enraged. "Everything and nothing seems to change in this village. I'm sorry to say this Mum, you and the rest of the people here are stuck in a time warp. It is about time you move on and take a reality check." He suggested impatiently. "It would do you all a power of good."

"Son, in my eyes you are an inspiration. What you have done in such a short time is outstanding. Believe me, it's nothing short of a miracle; yet – for all of that; there are folks who would only see your past. You left the village a poor struggling boy who is now trying to promote himself as someone who he is not. All in all, unfortunately, this is the way so many people think."

Marcus sniggered scornfully. "Well then, all we have to do and I'm talking about people like myself, is stop trying; find a little corner and go hide yourself. Life becomes meaningless. Can't you see the folly of such a conclusion? No one should strive for progress or attempt to better themselves if that is the case. Come on my dear mother; where is the intelligence in that?"

"There is none." Mama G replied. "But that is the way folks around here think. All I'm doing son is trying to stop you from falling into a situation you may live to regret." Mama G was now experiencing mixed emotions about Marcus. Although she was sympathetic about his feelings towards Teresa, she was equally annoyed he was not prepared to take heed of what she considered was good advice. "Son, England has certainly changed you. You are not the same boy we have grown to love and respect." Mama G conceded.

"You are absolutely right about that." Marcus retaliated. "England has changed me. I left these shores a boy and soon had to make a rapid change in order to survive. I had to contend with the food which I hated, the culture I did not understand, the environment, the negative attitude, the insults which I got a daily dose of and I survived it all. I took it on the chin when it mattered most. Mum, you have no idea what it is like to be cold, upset, frustrated and miserable all at once. To have people talking down to you as if you are rubbish. Experiences you can never forget. I was fighting a war as much as I was in one."

Mama G was now beginning to realise the difficulties her son had endured. She was adamant however that the proposed relationship would be a natural shipwreck. She felt duty bound to create an awareness which she honestly believed would have serious and negative repercussions on her beloved son's future. It was therefore imperative to fully point out his error of judgement. She tried to change the tempo by applying the charm offensive. Smiling broadly she placed her hands on her son's even broader shoulders. "My child, your father and I were in love, but in our case, we had the same social background, the same conditions, it was a level playing field and very easy to work through, all we needed to contend with was how much we cared for each other. In your case, it is not so. You may not accept it but you are stepping out of your class. However you may think about them, those folks will never see you as their equal. My dear son – all that glitters is not gold."

Marcus gave an ironic grin. "I beg to differ Mama G; I just came back from another world; a big country. I see people marrying from totally different backgrounds. I am talking about a developed country with no time for silly class structures or social attitudes. In the Army, for instance, you are rubbing shoulders with people of different classes, the rich, the not so rich and the very poor. It is sometimes difficult to distinguish one from the other. Over there you work hard, you achieve and you get on with life. It is not uncommon for a headmaster to marry a housemaid, providing they love each other. Professionals marry people completely out of their status. We simply have to stop being so petty. What we are talking about here is a family that is not better than us; they are of course people with good jobs; more opportunities and privileges; but so what!"

Listening intently Mama G remained relatively composed. "All I am asking you, my boy, is not to let your heart rule your head. I'm your mother; I may not be as clever as you son, but I see danger ahead and as a good parent I feel I should bring it to your attention. Marriage is not only about love, you also need many more things to work in order for love to benefit. That young lady is a high maintenance sort of person; she needs material things to keep her contented. Can you continue to give satisfaction on that level forever?"

"I care enough to try," Marcus replied obstinately. "You need to understand that is my choice and I have to live with it. I really thought if anyone would understand it would be you."

Mama G was now fully aware of the seriousness of her son's intentions, but she felt it was necessary for some home truths. "My boy, take it from me, I watched that young lady grow up. Her attitude is one of indifference. You need lots of ingredients in a stew to make it palatable. Love is not all it's cracked up to be. I have nothing against the young woman, other than to say, she has; in my opinion, an all-consuming nature, it's all about herself, her charm is her greatest asset, which she uses as a kind of weapon. It's a flaw which I'm sorry to say, will not bode well should you enter into a relationship with her. She regards men as trophies and I would not want my son to suffer that fate."

Marcus studied his mother's expression. It was one of sadness. He was absolutely sure she meant well but based upon his years and the experience he derived from a large country and more to the point, doing as well as he did, it was time to take decisions conducive to furthering his own interests. Teresa was obviously his ultimate goal and whatever was necessary to obtain her favour, he was determined to achieve it. In essence, he realised he was fighting his corner against very serious hostility.

"I know you have my best interest at heart Mum, but I beg of you to understand the way I feel about the young lady and I'm prepared to take my chances."

Mama G observed her son with sadness. "My boy, sometimes we cross the line without knowing it until it is too late."

"Mama G, for what it is worth I am prepared to take the risk. I spent the last six years working shoulder to shoulder with white folks fighting a war; I have experienced things that would make many brave men shudder. What I have endured helped make me the man I am today. I have invested an amazing amount of effort and energy to be where I am now. I have become a qualified engineer which I received from the British Army. Do you know why I'm called a warrior?" He raised his hands to make a pair of formidable fists. "I was a boxer in the Army, I fought the best that they could find and I won. Whatever I do in my life I intend to win. Mama G, I am under no illusion of who I am. Mine was a case of blood, sweat and tears. I'm not at all fazed by people anymore. I feel I am equal to anyone. As for the Malisons, to me, they are just people very much like you and myself."

Mama G sighed heavily, she was now certain she could not break her son's will. She got up slowly from beside him, held his hands and pulled him up to his full height. Looking up at her son, she offered a faint smile. "London and that war you talked about has made you both a stubborn and determined child."

"You are absolutely right Mother. If you want to get on in a big city like London, you need those qualities."

She shook her head affirmatively. "Marcus, listening to you would make any mother proud to know they have a son like you. You've done so well over these past years, I believe you have everything to make any woman in this world happy. That is why I want you to consider this matter carefully. Someone once said to me that there are things in life that you see but cannot get. Unfortunately, I'm afraid that that is the way of the world. Are you prepared to risk everything for someone who may not want you in that way?"

"Mama G I have felt this way about Teresa for a long time. It's not as if I want her because she's a Malison, I came back hoping that perhaps that possibility might exist, I really do care about her."

His mother saw in her son's eyes how sincere and caring he felt for someone who did not merit his attention. However, Marcus was a confident and successful young man. Someone who was prepared to go that extra mile to achieve his aims, as a result, she was forced to concede that nothing would get in the way of his quest for the woman he loved.

"Tell me, son, does Teresa know how you feel about her?"

"Not yet." He replied briskly. "But I promise you I will do everything I can to gain her affection."

"Well son, whatever you do, you will get all the support your mother can give you. You have my full blessing. I hope the good Lord will take good care of you."

Mama G knew that this was an argument she could not win. Reluctant as she was, she quite understood that her son was not about to change his mind. Before she left the room, she took a long hard look at her son. It was a look of great sadness, which she felt ultimately, would not be in the best interest of someone she loved so dearly. She knew in her heart of hearts that Teresa was not a good fit for him.

Conversely, Marcus felt differently. He was emboldened and very much encouraged by the positive responses he received from Teresa. He believed that fate had dealt him a golden hand. One he needed to accept, come what may. This long-awaited dream of his was now within reach. In view of that fact, he felt it necessary to pursue that opportunity in spite of fierce opposition. After all, this was his call and no one else's.

"I do not know what your father would have made of this." Mama G whispered mournfully.

"Don't worry Mum. I will visit him in the cemetery and let him know exactly how I feel about her and I hope to get his full approval." Marcus responded gently, he felt that he had won the battle of words.

# NANNY MAY'S WRATH

As Marcus and his mother left the bedroom, it was noticeable that Nanny May was still nowhere to be seen. That was all the more conspicuous because her presence in all things that occur in the Gullant household, usually get her stamp of approval. In a word, she was considered family. Her motto of "God will provide" was taken literally by all, since she had the uncanny sense of timing of being present at mealtime. Her constant appearance and general meddling with matters that were totally out of her orbit constituted no unnecessary inconvenience to her best friend Mama G, who was always seen as someone with the patience of Job, not to mention her tolerance and generosity which was boundless. However, there were times when Adel would take objections to her meddling, but the calming effect of her mother almost always won the day. Mama G was fully aware of Nanny May's financial condition and made allowances for it. She would always say that giving someone something to eat was the natural thing to do and anyway, she liked her friend Nanny May in spite of her idiosyncratic ways, which at times bordered on the bizarre. Their shining moments were perhaps on Sunday mornings, clad in their best attire, joyfully walking to morning mass for their blessings. For them, it was a hallmark of theirs and one they fully appreciated.

Marcus's normally placid demeanour was severely tested by his mother's disapproval regarding his proposed relationship with Teresa. The general rank and file consensus in the household against her did nothing to enhance his prowess in that direction. He was saddened and very disappointed with the outcome and attributed it to the proverbial village curse, which was still very much in place. The changes that he had anticipated remained as elusive as ever; where attitudes were constant and steadfast; where barriers simply could not be breached; where the status quo remained solidly unaltered. He was hopeful that his return as a rising star; a true son of the village who had achieved much would have mattered. As a result, it was a setback he did not care for, but he continued to be determined and committed to his task of wooing the lady (Teresa) for all it was worth.

Mama G came in with a beaming smile and placed a huge cake on the table. "This one was made especially for you my son." She announced knowing Marcus was extremely partial to her delicious fruit cakes and beckoned to him to participate. "Come on my son help yourself." She urged Marcus as he rubbed his hands in gleeful anticipation, when suddenly Nanny May finally appeared, sweating profusely. Her untimely intervention surprised Mama G since it was totally unusual to see her friend in any kind of haste. Her punctuality was second to none, especially at dinnertime, but haste was never her call.

Nanny May was wearing a scowl reminiscent of his Sunday school days, when an infringement of any kind, regardless of its quality, brought a rebuke or a clout or both, by the lady who did not accommodate anything less than absolute focus, especially when dealing with matters relating to her bible lessons. Nanny May indicated privacy and just like his mother, pointed to the bedroom. Marcus instinctively knew what was on the agenda and was not in the mood for further stress, especially after his mother's indifferent attitude to his future plans. His general inclination was to avoid confrontation of any kind whatsoever. However he was mindful of the fact that the church incident was enough to suggest that a reprimand was imminent from his Godmother who prided herself as a guardian of the village culture, thus it was imperative that the good lady must have her say, to put any wrong to rights.

It was incumbent on him to hatch a plan in order to negate any wrath or verbal pasting that she was about to impart. He entered the bedroom for a second time in quick succession for an audience with his Godmother, which he expected and it was self-evident that his mood was far more bullish than his prior visit. He resented the very idea that he should be admonished for something so trivial. Marcus was still scarred by his mother's total rejection for his choice of woman which was Teresa and his natural compulsion to retaliate aggressively to Nanny May gained traction. However, as if by magic that emotion rescinded as quickly as it developed. It was replaced by a strange sense of calmness as he entered the room. For whatever reason, Marcus was now consumed by a degree of sheer compassion for the woman in front of him and felt that being calm and collected was of greater merit than anger. In the grand scheme of things, Marcus had a deep-seated fondness for Nanny May, despite her intolerance of him.

In spite of her rabid obsession and her undeniable focus of trying to mould him into something he did not want to be, Marcus was clear in his mind that there was no other reason to dislike his mother's best friend. He felt that she was in many ways misunderstood. She was someone whose life had an amazing amount of knocks but in spite of her problems he was convinced that Nanny May was a woman of resilience and that she deserved to be treated respectfully. Her husband, who was at one time a crane operator, decided to make a career change and went prospecting for gold. It was a period when men were returning with rich pickings from the gold field, prompting others to do the same. Unfortunately for him and indeed Nanny May, a decade and a half later, he had not returned. No word from her husband had created nothing but distress; heartache; uncertainty and disappointment. Much of her general demeanour was a manifestation of someone who had experienced a great loss. In a small village, as it was, rumours circulated wildly in terms of what had happened to him. Speculation was rife about his whereabouts. The most feasible being, he had met someone else and simply absconded, leaving poor Nanny May to her own devices.

This was the first occasion of seeing his Godmother at close range since his return and knowing her as a young man growing up in the village, he was startled by her general appearance. As he remembered her she was always one for neatness and expressed a certain sense of glamour especially on Sunday mornings. It was not as if she was commanding attention of any kind, it was just her natural tendency of being immaculate especially on church days. Mama G matched her in every detail and although nothing was mentioned, everyone was of the opinion that they were trying to outdo each other in the fashion stakes. It was a contest borne purely out of a tacit but friendly rivalry between friends and for once, the thought of rendering your heart and not your garment was essentially overlooked.

Far removed from those happy times, when all things were in place and circumstances were different, Nanny May now looked extremely haggard. It was a serious case of falling standards. For someone who usually took pride in her appearance and demanded the best in everyone, her present demeanour was certainly a departure from the norm. Buttons were missing from the blouse she was wearing, her skirt was well worn and ill-fitting and her shoes were scuffed and had seen better days. It had left no doubt in the mind of Marcus that his Godmother had fallen on hard times. In reality, she was no longer 'in vogue'.

As he entered the bedroom and closed the door behind him, Marcus was absolutely sure about his strategy. Placing his back to the door he smiled broadly. However, it was a smile that did nothing to calm a situation in which Nanny May considered to be serious. If anything, his action merely proceeded to exasperate the problem to a greater degree. Nanny May's frown became more extravagant, but before she could react, Marcus raised his left hand like a traffic policeman would do, stopping her in her tracks and with his right hand he withdrew a fistful of dollars, making it as conspicuous as possible. It was a tidy sum, the likes of which his Godmother would not have seen for an exceedingly long time.

"I was about to offer you a present, but I guess it can wait," Marcus announced with that fixed smile still in place, he gave the indication that he was about to replace the cash into his pocket. Nanny May was taken completely by surprise. Whatever was in her thoughts was for now purely irrelevant. By far the greater priority was to accept the gift that was now on offer. The scowl she was wearing rapidly changed to delight and just as rapidly, she crossed the floor to whisk the intended gift from the grasp of the young man and put in a very safe place; it rested securely in the sanctity of her bosom. Still, in a state of wonderment, she embraced her Godson. Marcus did not mind Nanny May's embrace, what surprised him was the strength and vigour of someone perceived to be so delicate. She looked up at the young soldier and offered a weak smile.

"Thank you, my boy, this was a gift from the Almighty. I always say God works in mysterious ways." Still looking up at Marcus tears and sweat running down her cheeks, she smiled cheerfully. "Marcus I hope you trust in the Lord as I do. He can work miracles as he did for me today."

Marcus nodded in the affirmative; he may have achieved victory by his cunning plan, but now considered it hollow against the backdrop of a woman like Nanny May. Not only was she emotionally moved by his amazing gift, but she also demonstrated her conviction to her faith and the unswerving belief of that commitment to prayer. This was undoubtedly the almighty answering her call in her hour of need and it was, without doubt, a glorious moment in her life. Marcus still with arms around his Godmother could not help feeling humble. He fully understood her doctrine and knowing her as he did, he was convinced that it was all that mattered to her, as far as events went, all else was completely irrelevant. Marcus gave a huge sigh of relief. At least, for now, this episode was over. "Well." He uttered. "Since our business here is finished, shall we go and join the others? Mama G's cake looks so inviting, let's go and have some before it's all gone."

Mama G was both surprised and relieved by the briefness of the meeting and judging by the smile on their faces, it was obvious that the matter was sorted out amicably.

# CLOSE CONTACT

In spite of events that had passed Marcus was now setting his thoughts on his main objective, which was turning on the charm offensive to Teresa regardless of all opposition. He sat in eager anticipation for the arrival of the woman he aspired to be with. This was their first social meeting, a chance to express the things that mattered and which he believed his future depended on. In that interim period, so much of what he hoped and prayed for had at last become a reality. He was aware of the fact that it was an opportunity that should not be wasted. He was also mindful of the massive hurdles he needed to cross if ever success were to be achieved, accepting that in order for any positive results, it was imperative that he managed his expectations to the best of his ability in the hope of winning the heart of Teresa. Success in his estimation would not come easily.

Teresa finally arrived, appearing as stunning and impeccable as ever and wearing a smile as bright as the midday sun. Marcus was temporarily spellbound by her poise and beauty but managed to restore a sense of calm as she sat down beside him. Teresa's fragrance matched her beauty, both subtle and alluring and there was no mistaking the fact that she was a unique and exquisite work of art. His focus on her was totally engaging.

"Thank you for coming." He uttered. "I imagine you are someone whose time is of a premium. I hope you did not break any rules?"

Teresa smiled politely. "Marcus as far as rules are concerned, I make up my own."

Teresa herself felt that this meeting was of mutual benefit. She needed to learn more about this wonderful place called England and was willing to venture out, leaving far behind a country that she felt was stifling her progression. Marcus was prepared to advance a favourable impression about himself, about London and all the advantages that such an undertaking would allow her. He was also ready to accept to a very large extent her way, which he was positive would create a huge measure of encouragement for her. He knew full well that such an opportunity would only be to his detriment. However, this was no ordinary lady, success depended largely on how best he was able to gain her favour and if a measure of subordination was required for his ultimate gain, it would be a price he was prepared to pay. He was very much aware of his good fortune, to acquire any kind of genuine attention from Teresa. She, on the other hand, showed acute interest in the possibilities of what he was able to offer and the advantages she could derive from it. Teresa was sure there was no physical attraction towards him; this was a situation that appeared to be made more out of expediency rather than genuine affection. She looked at her companion and smiled bewitchingly, her hazel eyes flickering mischievously, accentuating her natural charm and beauty. It was a combination he found irresistible, the kind that sent a shiver down the young man's spine. Teresa was undoubtedly someone of immense attraction, something she was very conscious of and she used it to full effect.

They sat and talked freely. It was a getting to know one another sort of evening. Marcus was quick to relate the things about London he felt would impress Teresa. Suggesting to her the advantages and prospects that could be to her merit. Equally, Teresa did not hesitate to impart the obvious. She indicated to him that she was a woman of status in her present environment, which offered her a great deal of privilege. Although she found much of what he offered was appealing, she was careful to remind him of her excellent and exulted standing in the community and she was not prepared to compromise any of it should she decide to accept his invitation and follow him to London. At this stage, he would do anything to gain her favour.

After much reflection and discussion, Teresa asked. "Again I ask Marcus, why should I leave all of this to go with you to London?" She quietly enquired.

"I am confident that London has so much to offer you. But that apart, you would be fulfilling three things at once – living in a large city, achieving your dreams of becoming an architect and last but not least having someone like me; a loyal and dedicated person to take care of you."

She pondered over his words and still smiling pleasantly she asked. "What is that meant to be? Is that a proposal you're making to me Marcus?"

"Yes," Marcus replied. "I would dearly want you someday to be my wife."

Teresa sniggered. "Proposals; proposals! Everyone wants to see me tied down. I've had as many proposals as there is sand on the seashore. So far I've managed to resist the temptation; tell me, Marcus, what makes you so different?"

"I would like to believe that I am honest in what I do and I cannot see you regretting in any way the opportunities that you can derive from coming to London."

Still smiling, Teresa looked directly at Marcus. "Your intentions may be good, but there are things you need to know that may not meet with your approval." Teresa's smile was now a thing of the past and she became very serious. "Marcus, my parents have given me a life of luxury. Something I am very content with, I am not prepared to settle for anything less. What is more, I am by nature a free-spirited individual and I would not want anyone or anything to get in the way of that."

He was now certain that Teresa was a seriously difficult hurdle to cross and he needed to assure her of the realities of life without causing her too much distress. It was therefore imperative that he proceeded with caution.

"Look, I really do not want to undermine your lifestyle, but there are options you have to take in life. Going to London

VICTOR WALDRON

would give you all the opportunities you need to realise your dreams and accomplish your ambitions. There is no greater joy than that, believe me."

Teresa pondered momentarily. "I guess you're right. It's funny I can study in the USA. My Mum's sister resides in New York, but the problem with that is she is something of a tyrant. 'Rules, rules and more rules is her motto and that would not suit me one little bit."

"Then the best choice you have is London." He stopped as if to let it sink in. "Look at me; I'm the perfect example of someone who's made it by going abroad. Those short years that I have spent in England, elevated me to be where I am today. I have a beautiful home, a decent job and what is more, I am relatively comfortable financially. Can you imagine what would have happened to me if I had decided to remain in this God-forsaken place?"

She nodded approvingly. "Well! The prospect seems good. The only difficulty lies with my parents. They would most certainly object to anything of that nature and to be honest, I'm not sure how best I would be able to convince them."

"I know how difficult it would be," Marcus replied. "My folks may not all be in agreement with what I do, but if you have an objective, you have to pursue it. There is no greater satisfaction in life than to know that you have an end product that you are proud of. I have attained what I set out to achieve, it is really up to you to do the same."

Teresa thought about what Marcus said and with almost a grimace she replied. "You have left me with a huge but exciting problem. What you're offering appeals to me, so much so I will give it my fullest consideration." Her smile was one of great satisfaction and intrigue. It was the first time she was offered a gift of such dimension. In spite of all the pleasures and opportunities that she was accustomed to; the excellent quality of life that she was generally a part of; the luxuries that she enjoyed; she felt she was yet to attain the zenith of her well-being regardless of her good fortune. She firmly believed that something far more meaningful was somewhere on the horizon still to be fulfilled. Her restless nature rendered her as someone who seemed incapable of finding true happiness.

Teresa acknowledged that her present position, allowing her the freedom to express herself and the manner in doing so was priceless. However, she truly felt that there were things in life that remained out of reach; things she felt passionate about; matters that would elevate her life and give her a true sense of contentment. Above everything else, she loved and adored her parents and was always grateful to have such a wonderful family around her, but her parents' preoccupation of wanting her settled in marriage, was indeed a heavy load to bear and one she gave very little consideration to. In terms of men, Carlo Banal came closest to what she would desire in a person. He was handsome, he had prestige and beside those qualities, she was certain her lifestyle would be enhanced immeasurably. Unfortunately, she would be trapped in a condition she feared most; being a wife.

Teresa treasured her freedom the most and would not want to become a victim of an existence that was based on routine. That brings her back to Marcus. Here was a man who had been away for only a comparatively short time and had achieved more than seemed possible. In a massive way, he was the perfect example of what could be attained in a large Metropolis. It was clear in her mind that he may have exaggerated his position, in order to give a grand impression, but that was not her major concern. On the contrary, the motivation she got from listening to him was extraordinary. She was convinced Marcus did nothing for her by way of physical attraction, not that he was short of charm and good looks, but he was genuinely giving her an opportunity to spread her wings in a way she always wanted and to create an interest of her own making. This was a chance to advance her position and to exploit Marcus's offer for all it was worth. She was adamant that she had all the aces and was willing to use them accordingly.

Teresa was positive that Marcus was bowled over by her charm and charisma and felt certain he could easily be manipulated. His adoration for her was fairly obvious. Twisting him around her finger would hardly pose a problem. Of greater concern to her at least for now, was breaking the news to her parents. That confrontation was an obstacle she did not relish, especially her father. In his eyes, Marcus would be no more than a gardener or a caretaker. The ignominy of this news would be palpable to them. It would also have the same effect on her mother and she was sure it would render to them the darkest day of their lives. In no uncertain terms, not even remotely, would Marcus be considered fit to have an association with Teresa. But weighing up the pros and cons, Teresa fell on the side of self. This opportunity of a lifetime to roam freely and unhindered; to do all the things that mattered; to follow her dreams and to be her own woman was more than appealing to her. She felt that this was her moment and was prepared to grasp it for all it was worth.

# ALTERCATION

It was late evening when Teresa arrived home. Her mother was having supper on her own. Malcolm, her father, was out, as usual, doing his customary duties as a dependable servant of the community. It was an ideal and most appropriate opportunity for Teresa to raise the subject with her Mum, which she was more than confident, would be met with stern opposition. This was an explosive bombshell, a bone in the throat that would not be swallowed easily. It was, however, necessary, as far as Teresa was concerned, to broach this matter merely to see her mother's reaction, without the input of her father.

Edith was very fond of Carlo Banal as her future son-in-law and it was generally accepted by her parents, that this was a foregone conclusion – a done deal. As parents, they were aware of Teresa's intransigent qualities. As a result, they adopted the strategy which appeared never to persuade or over commit her to anything. Teresa's reaction would almost certainly be opposite to their wishes. In view of that general tendency, careful application was always vital. However, the idea of leaving for London with someone they regarded as well below par was something of an apparition to disturb their consummate plan such as this and would obviously be for them, a bridge too far.

Carlo's interest in Teresa was undeniable. He was a man who executed great tolerance and patience but became somewhat frustrated by her delaying tactics, however, to sit steadfastly and wait until the lady was good and ready became his general intention. Edith looked up and half smiled at her daughter as she entered the room. "You're rather late young lady, I thought you would be back for supper."

"I'm not particularly hungry Mum; I had a lovely lunch with Marcus."

Edith almost choked on her last mouthful. "Marcus? You mean that soldier boy?"

She nodded in the affirmative as she sat adjacent to her mother as if to study her reaction.

"Yes, Mum, the soldier and he made me a proposition that I find most attractive. He wants to take me to England."

The shock of Teresa's statement left Edith in a state of bewilderment. She stared at her daughter in utter disbelief before normality resumed. What she heard was simply outrageous and for once she thought Teresa had lost her senses.

Edith exploded furiously. "What on earth are you talking about child? Have you gone completely out of your head? You have a perfectly healthy relationship with someone who is absolutely crazy about you and wants you to accept his undying love and you are prepared to throw it all away? Are you out of your tiny little mind?"

"No Mother I am not mad, I'm just thinking about my future. I want to do things while I'm still young and able to do so, – is that so bad?"

Edith was far too furious to carry on. "Teresa, this matter is closed. We will continue this discussion when your father gets home."

Teresa contemplated for a while. "Mum this is a conversation between you and me; that is what I want. Please understand my position."

"Teresa! I'm not prepared to listen to this most absurd and ridiculous tripe that is coming from you. Have you suddenly become a fool? What you're saying makes absolutely no sense whatsoever, so stop now, I do not want to hear any more of your nonsense."

Edith was inconsolable, waiting impatiently for Malcolm. The shock of her daughter's revelation was to her mind nothing short of foolhardiness. Malcolm was equally pained by Teresa's sudden change of heart and did all he could to comfort his wife from her moment of distress. He gently took her in his arms and embraced her. "Darling, Teresa would not do anything as foolish as that, she's probably having a bit of fun with you."

Edith looked up at her husband as she wiped the tears from her eyes. "The trouble with you Malcolm is that you do not know your own daughter. Teresa is not the kind of person that says something that she doesn't mean. The girl is as serious as I've ever seen her. She took the opportunity of telling me that when you were not here."

"Are you saying that she wants to leave a life of comfort to go to London? Is she prepared to give up what she has here? To ditch Carlo; someone of status and professionalism; someone who would make her a very happy woman? What would she gain by that?"

"Teresa will do what Teresa wants, you should know that. We have given that child too much of her own way. Now I'm afraid it has come back to haunt us for the rest of our lives."

"Okay, Edith," Malcolm replied ruefully. "Stop upsetting yourself more than you need to. Tomorrow she will come to her senses. Mark my word, I will have a very serious discussion with her; stop fretting and go to bed."

Malcolm was up earlier than usual after a turbulent night's rest. It was the end result of what he had been told the night before by his wife Edith. The news that Teresa was thinking of leaving home for London with Marcus, left him in a state of devastation that was difficult to overcome. Was Teresa just being mischievous? Was this a practical joke played on her Mum merely for the benefit of fun? Or was she serious? To his mind, it was inconceivable that his daughter, someone of good breeding, someone of distinction and superior quality would condescend to a level that was far below her status for any good reason that he could imagine. Lowering the family's good name for something so irresponsible would break the very foundation that their reputation was built on. Not to mention the obligation that was owed to Carlo and the reaction that such an unfortunate act would carry. Malcolm was also mindful of his social standing to the villagers and others and the high regard and respect that he received over the years, would be immeasurably damaged.

Such a thought would be difficult to contemplate. Edith, his wife, carried the same sentiments. For both of them, this was a moment of impending disaster. It was a catastrophe of enormous proportions. It was a fault line that needed urgent correction. After all, making bad choices at this crucial time in her life must be averted, more especially since the road ahead, as far as her parents were concerned are paved with gold. This matter was very simple, all Teresa needed to do was to accept Carlo's proposal of marriage and this problematic situation would automatically vanish. It cannot be overstated that the Malisons were a proud and respectable family and were naturally eager to protect their cherished status.

Teresa's sudden and very unexpected idea of jumping ship and heading off to London would obviously do nothing to enhance their good name. The fact that they would have to explain to this young Doctor, Teresa's rapid change of direction would not only be an embarrassment, but it would also certainly deflate their position in the eyes of everyone. Malcolm's approach to this matter required a measure of extreme caution, in view of his daughter's intractable disposition. A confrontation was the last thing he would ever want. Smiling broadly he nodded to his daughter.

"Good morning Teresa."

Teresa's calmness and completely unruffled nature were difficult to understand, but she responded with a smile of her own.

"Good morning Dad."

Malcolm was baffled by her poise and relaxed manner, knowing that there were questions to be answered, regarding her sensational pronouncement to her mother the night before.

"What's this I hear from your mother that you want to go to London?" He enquired, trying the best he could to match his daughter's calmness.

"Yes, Dad! I told Mother that I was thinking of going to London to study."

"Why the sudden change of heart? And tell me, why London?" He enquired with a grimace.

"Well, it occurred to me that I need to do something more tangible with my life, now that I am young and able to do so." She retorted.

"But tell me, why London? You don't even know anyone there."

Teresa smiled positively. "Marcus the young soldier was telling me about London and from what I gather it's most interesting..."

"Marcus?" He railed. "What do you know of this young man? And why should you be talking about him? Teresa, listen to me. You have commitments here. Have you suddenly forgotten that Carlo is waiting patiently for you to be his wife? Are you prepared to chuck this wonderful opportunity away?"

Teresa sighed heavily. "Dad, Carlo is a very nice person, but I'm not sure I want to marry him, not now anyway."

"You cannot be serious, young lady. That man is the best chance you'll ever have going forward. He is in an ideal position to give you everything you require. I am very sure of that."

Teresa shook her head vigorously in the negative. "Dad! That chance you refer to is exactly what I want for myself. I have objectives and I want to fulfil them."

"And going to London with this boy is going to do that for you?"

"In an odd sort of way it will." Teresa stopped briefly as if to study her father. "Dad, what Marcus wants to do is to help me get ahead, to enable me to achieve my aims."

Malcolm was now becoming somewhat intemperate with his daughter. Her obstinate behaviour was getting the better of him. "Teresa – stop being so stubborn and listen to reason. Your mother and I are only trying to guide you in the best possible way we can. Believe me; it is in your best interest to listen."

"That is the whole problem." She responded. "It would appear that neither of us is listening. What I am saying is very simple. It is my aim to fulfil my own ambition. I want to feel self-satisfied. I want to do something tangible with my life. Is that too much to ask of myself?"

"No, but going to London with that lad is doing nothing for you. It would be lowering the tone of your background. Can you be satisfied that is what you want?"

"Certainly not." She snapped angrily. "But I can also end up being a doctor's wife and nothing more. Is that the sum total of what I am seeking in life? I don't think so."

Malcolm looked long and hard at his daughter. It was as if he was staring at a stranger or someone different. She was a woman who suddenly became bereft of reason – a complete oddball. He needed to restrain his emotions and in doing so he may ultimately win her over.

"Teresa, you are heading in the wrong direction. If you want to study, we will back you. Just go to your Aunt in the United States and we will definitely take care of the rest."

"Here we go again." She fumed. "You're imposing your wishes on me. When do you think I will be able to figure things out for myself? Look, Dad, you and Mum have been excellent parents, I simply cannot fault you in any way, but you must relent and give me a chance to make decisions for myself. I am of age to do so. Why are you not listening to me? As for my Aunt in New York, she is very controlling and that would be the last place I would want to be."

"Teresa you are wrong. You are making twisted decisions, the kind that may come back to haunt you. In simple terms that is what we are trying to prevent." Malcolm announced wearily.

"What you are basically saying Dad, is that I'm incapable of using my brain cells to work out what I need. I am an intelligent young woman, you both should know that; you sent me to the best schools, does that really count for nothing?"

Malcolm was now totally irate – his patience running thin. "Not in my book, if you are prepared to go to London with a half-wit, with no credible background. Only a short time ago that boy was walking around the village with his backside hanging out behaving like a complete nonentity, fighting on the street and making a total spectacle of himself. Now, all of a sudden you want to give respectability to him? What's the attraction? Are you one of those people who gets excited by his uniform?"

Teresa was not impressed by her father's reaction. "I'm not excited about his uniform at all. But yes, I'm attracted by his ability to do so well in such a short space of time. That half-wit now owns a beautiful home in London, a beautiful car; he has acquired excellent qualifications as an engineer and is now working in a well-established company there. It only goes to show how different things can be given the opportunity. That is what motivates me Dad, not his uniform."

"Now we are getting to the bottom of it. Believe me when I say you are a huge disappointment. Your ambition is to have someone come home with grease under his fingernails and smelling like an oil drum full of petrol? How on earth would that be of any comfort to you?"

Edith entered into the fray eventually. It was not that she showed a lack of interest, she was keeping a respectful distance, with the hope that Malcolm was persuasive enough for Teresa to see the folly of her ways. She felt totally distressed by her daughter's sudden change of heart and it was clearly evident by her manner. Looking Teresa straight in the eyes, tears visibly apparent, she sat beside her daughter. "What is going on in your head Teresa? Why this sudden fixation about London? Have you finally lost your marbles, child?"

"No Mother, I am the same young lady that I was yesterday and hopefully I'll be the same tomorrow," Teresa explained resolutely.

Edith shook her head vigorously. "Not from where I'm sitting. Your entire attitude has changed in an instant. You are behaving like a headless chicken. Are you trying to bring shame to this family? Do you want us to look like people without principle?"

"Why should I want to do that?" Teresa protested angrily. "You two are highly respected servants of the society. Folks everywhere have nothing but the highest regard for you both, so why should that change? Mum and Dad, my situation is of a simple equation. I have seen the possibility of a life changing experience and I am prepared to take it. It may never come my way again. Why can't you both be happy for me?"

"Well young lady, it's because what you are proposing to do displeases us comprehensively. This sudden notion of yours defies logic. What do you know about this young man? He could be telling you a pack of lies merely to impress you." Edith screamed. "Tell me honestly, how do you know he is sincere?"

Teresa was flushed with anger. "You folks are not listening to me. This is not about Marcus, this is about me. It is about fulfilling my potential and it is imperative that I do it now."

Malcolm was livid; his attempt to win the argument with his daughter was hopelessly and utterly ineffective. Her unwavering and intransigent manner was manifestly clear. His attempt to induce a degree of aggression and mild intimidation into the argument was his final resort. "Teresa you are certainly not the child that your Mum and I have cultivated over the years. We have given you the best that money can buy; we have inculcated a sense of value in you, not to mention impeccable good manners and for what? So that you can turn it around and tell us that what we did meant nothing? This new you has developed a philosophy of self-aggrandisement at the expense of all else. Nothing or no one else matters. Is that how it should be?"

"No Dad, I do not wish to be ungracious, you have both given me a good life and I am thankful for it, but I have been brought up to think independently. Believe me, I am no fool, I want to test the calibre of my thinking; I want to exercise my own ability and come up with answers. If that is a crime then I am as guilty as sin.

Malcolm is now totally enraged. "Should you take the decision to go to London Teresa, you will certainly not get our support. I am emphatic about that. You go and you are very much on your own. I will not give you one red cent to assist you in doing so, nor will I raise a finger to help you if you are in distress. This matter is now in your own hands."

Teresa stood up to face her father. The fear that he was expecting in his daughter's eyes was not forthcoming. She was as unperturbed as ever. "I hardly believe my parents would hold me to ransom for wanting to better myself. If that is the case, so be it." She swiftly turned on her heels and left the room.

# EXPECTATIONS

Marcus's eagerness to see Teresa once more was overwhelming. She, on the other hand, was not in a good frame of mind, not by a long shot. Her father's anger and frustration over her negative verdict; placed her on a downward spiral and for the first time, she felt downhearted. Marcus observing her appearance smiled broadly, in his own mind he did not expect matters to go smoothly.

"What is the problem? You do not look your usual sparkling self. Are you worried about something?"

"You can say that." She revealed. "My dad believes that going to London would be the worst decision I have ever contemplated. He believes life is a bed of roses here and that I should learn to appreciate it."

Marcus sighed heavily. "And what do you think?"

"Right now, I really do not know what to think. I am in a very bad place at the moment. My mind is in turmoil." She mourned.

"Well, it's a difficult decision to make and you must be clear in your mind about what you want to do. However, I'm firmly of the opinion that your life should take on new meaning. If you go to London it would be a completely fantastic experience. One you will never regret."

"Why are you so sure Marcus?" She enquired.

"Because I made that move myself and it has paid dividends for me. I have become the person I want to be. I took the risk and it was definitely worth taking."

Teresa studied Marcus long and hard before she spoke. "Are you asking me to give up everything I have here for London? I have a very good life already. How can it be improved by going to London?"

"It can in many ways, none greater than being in command of your own destiny." He explained. "Look, I came home to find someone who would make my life complete in London. If I'm fortunate enough to have you as that person, I would be the happiest man on this planet." He smiled wryly. "Let me say this; I would endeavour to make your life equally happy too."

"Why does everyone want to marry me? She echoed. "That's just the problem; I really do not want to be tied to anything that would bind me, nor do I want to be answerable to anyone. Right now I need a sense of purpose, a totally different direction."

"Well, that's exactly what you'll get from me. I do not intend to hold you down; you could be the most liberated wife ever. Look, Teresa, I know what you want and I'm prepared to help you get it. You cannot imagine what it was like to be an underdog in a large country like England, where everything was set against you. You cannot comprehend what I endured in an environment that was both hostile and unfriendly. Fortunately for me, however, the Army gave me a survival kit, which I used with great efficiency, combating the culture; racism, the climate, the food, the people, the lack of any kind of respect and much more. But I overcame it. So I do not intend to hamper that spirit of adventure you seem to possess. In fact, I will nurture it. So come with me and give yourself an opportunity which can only be to your advantage."

Teresa took a deep breath and smiled pleasantly. "That was quite a mouthful. If that is a promise Marcus Gullant, I very much intend to hold you to it."

Marcus laughed out loud. "You're dead right, I have made a pledge to you and I have no intention of breaking it."

Teresa looked slightly puzzled. "If what you say about England is true, why then do you want to live there? Surely all those negative things that you've mentioned cannot be to anyone's advantage."

"As cynical as it might seem, I want to live there because it offers me possibilities that I could only dream about when I was here."

"It's quite odd." She remarked. "You think so much about the place and yet the impression I get is that it's not a very pleasant country to be in."

"In the beginning, it was not for many of us." He laughed out loud. "I've experienced things that would make the hairs on the back of your neck stand up."

"Like what for instance?" She enquired.

"Well, for one, the natives thought we all swung on trees. We were all monkeys from that Dark Continent and we were regarded as uncivilised and unintelligent. It took them a while to understand otherwise. Many still believe we are carrying tails. As a result, we were open to insults and derision of every description. They would stop and stare as though we were creatures from Mars. They had strange concepts of us. It was assumed if you touch a black man it would bring you luck. In a very small way, we've managed to reverse some of their beliefs. When I told them I came from Guiana, they would laugh and correct me. You mean Ghana, they would say."

He hesitated before continuing. "In fact, that was the general thinking, that we were all idiots. They did not know that Guiana existed as a country. We were that insignificant. It was really difficult to work through all that baggage to be where we are today. All in all, I would say with some confidence it was worth it."

"Wow, you must be a man of great tolerance to withstand all of that." She whispered.

"Yes, it was a heavy load to carry, but in the back of my mind, I knew what I wanted and in the end, I was very sure I made the right choice."

She hesitated momentarily. "I must give it to you. You are very convincing, but I have serious doubts about leaving my home. I know what I have here and would certainly not want to leave it for anything less."

Marcus was now beginning to understand the complexity of what he was faced with. The hurdles although not insurmountable, still carried huge obstacles that needed to be crossed. His awareness in terms of his own family network, whose resistance to Teresa was clearly obvious. It was also a factor that Mama G all but forbids such a union. Teresa, on the other hand, was faced with opposition far more robust than she would care to admit. What was in no doubt was her desire to see the world and what Marcus was offering, was indeed a gold-plated opportunity for her to do so. However, her conditions at home were extremely favourable and she was mindful of the fact that changing the dynamic of something that worked, for a mere promise was somewhat foolhardy. It was that kind of a situation that confronted the young man. He had come thus far, almost the journey of a lifetime, it would hardly be appropriate to tumble at the final fence.

Life's good fortune had propelled him to this point; failure as far as he was concerned was not an option. He took a long look at Teresa who showed signs of wavering and smiled nervously. "I was watching a tugboat bringing in a vast liner to dock recently and it made me think. That tugboat was doing a very important job, but in a strange way, once it navigated that liner safely, the importance of that little tug was over. There are some things that a tugboat would never be able to do. That's really the way of the world. The progress of that tugboat is very limited."

Teresa looked perplexed. "What on earth are we talking about? If you are trying to lose me you have succeeded handsomely."

"Well." He uttered. "When I lived in the village, it was the equivalent of being that tugboat, I felt suffocated and totally restricted. So I transferred to that massive ship with all the room and space it offered me, not to mention the latitude and boy oh boy what an amazing difference it made. It opened new doors and gave me perspectives that were stifled before. So tell me do you want to be nailed to a routine forever? I don't think so."

Teresa shook her head affirmatively. "I can see your point." She said.

"Imagine going to a city and seeing Buckingham Palace, the Queen's residence, London Bridge, what a structure that is, the Tower of London, Trafalgar Square and Nelson's Column, trains that run underground and a rich variety of other amazing things that elevate your mind. Believe me, Teresa, you cannot help but be inspired." He announced.

Teresa smiled pleasantly; she could not help being impressed by her companion's narrative. "You are quite an articulate young man." She chuckled. "For someone who was walking around the village with his backside hanging out, you are certainly not doing badly."

"Is that how you see me?" He enquired.

"Ah, forget it. It was just something I heard."

"Well, going to England has made me the person I am and I'm sure it would do the same for you."

Teresa looked at Marcus long and hard. "Something is bothering me Marcus; it is the haste in which you are moving. You hardly know me and yet, you seem hell-bent on putting a ring on my finger – why? Do you realise it could be the worst decision you have ever made?"

"Perhaps, but we should not try to predict the future. It is not in our gift to do so."

"But why me?" She enquired.

Marcus swallowed hard. "I need to explain to you a simple truth. I was an innocent young boy when I first saw you and from that moment on I was smitten. When I left the village I thought that feeling would go away but I was wrong. In fact, it grew stronger; you have motivated much of what I did. Every success I had somehow had a large degree of you in mind. I must say fate has been good to me in a wonderful way. When I returned home and found that you were still unmarried, I felt it was beyond my wildest expectations. Perhaps asking you to come to London was meant to be."

"That is most extraordinary." Teresa murmured. "It seems so unreal; I guess I have to accept your honesty in telling me.

"They say honesty is the best policy," Marcus replied.

"Perhaps, perhaps. If we are going to be honest with each other, you should know that I don't cook; I am not a maid in any shape or form. I have a generous existence at the moment, but most importantly I do not want babies."

That remark made Marcus cringe. In his humble opinion, he felt marriage carried an important obligation. For instance, having children was something he yearned for and felt it was a natural progression in the scheme of things.

"Well, you are definitely different. Most women I know really look forward to having kids. They say it gives marriage a certain sanctity."

"That's just it," Teresa responded with some urgency. "Right now I'm not prepared to be shackled in any way or form. I need my freedom to do as I please. I'm not sure I'm the kind of woman that every man would want. So if that is your wish, then I'm not the person that you seek."

"Teresa, let's not jump the gun. Like I said before you have my word. I certainly do not intend to hold you captive. You have my promise on that."

Teresa studied Marcus momentarily and smiled. She was now convinced that the young man was a man of integrity; someone who could be trusted. After all that she heard, the prospects seemed very healthy. It was a generous and attractive proposal that he was offering. She felt it was now necessary to give it urgent consideration. "You have convinced me that going abroad is my best solution – what you need to do now is convince my parents." She said with a degree of sadness.

"That's just it; I can quite understand your problem. Your parents will be none too happy to have you gone. You have benefitted from them all along, but your life and your wishes are still to be fulfilled. This is an opportunity for you to reach out and find yourself."

Teresa knew Marcus was correct about where she wanted to be. It was still an extremely difficult road ahead and it projected a challenge beyond anything that she had ever attempted. However, the idea to travel gained rapid momentum and readily appealed to her otherwise placid and carefree nature. "Are you sure that what you are suggesting would work?"

"Of course it would," Marcus replied. "You would be realising your life's ambition and with any luck, I would have the most cherished woman in the whole of Guiana beside me, nothing but nothing would give me greater happiness."

The extraordinary bluntness of Teresa however, created a measure of discomfort and unease for Marcus, especially her reasons and her lack of desire for kids. Being a firm believer of marriage and the natural consequences of it, Teresa's remarks were totally unexpected. In his mind, he felt it was a violation of the normal rules as they apply. Be that as it may, as matters went he was especially hopeful for compromises of some kind subsequently. To oppose her wishes now, would border on the suicidal. Since rejection was not what he wanted to receive from her, it was, therefore, expedient to park any notion he may have about that to the contrary and in a quiet place of rest. What he needed most was Teresa's approval and even though he realised he was somewhat reckless with his promises, he knew it was a matter of necessity. This was nothing more than a damage limitation exercise and he was well aware of it.

Teresa smiled pleasantly. "Marcus I can only conclude that you are a super optimistic man who is fighting against tremendous odds."

Marcus shrugged his shoulders in a carefree manner. "In life, you have to be. I've always taken my chances and more often than not I've succeeded."

# RETURNING TO LONDON

A new beginning had dawned. This was a completely novel chapter which was now in place and happiness was predominantly in the ascendancy. After the procrastination; the humbugs; the hostilities and the general raw emotions that preceded the difficulties they endured, Marcus had finally attained his objective. He was now back home in London with Teresa by his side. Needless to say, this was a victory of enormous proportions and endless possibilities. He was not alone in his thinking, as this larger than life city motivated a sense of wonderment also for his companion Teresa. Her boundless curiosity was manifest, as was her desire to exploit this place for all it was worth.

This was a triumph for Marcus. Defying all the odds of bringing Teresa away from her creature comforts and the lifestyle she experienced in her homeland. It was far and beyond his wildest dreams. This feat was simply greater and more complex than he may have wanted, the trail of misery and distress especially from the Malisons; the objections that were raised and general disapproval from Mama G, Adel and the rest, marred the situation and left a bitter taste in the mouth of both participants. The effect wore heavily on Marcus initially and to some extent created a degree of circumspection in its wake.

Teresa's anguish was also quite evident. The acrimonious fallout over her decision to leave, from her parents, was all too apparent. Her father insisted should she leave, she no longer had the right to be called a Malison. He stated in his opinion the fact that she was leaving a thoroughbred, which was Carlo, for a farmyard mule who disgraced himself and family fighting in the streets, was far too difficult for him to comprehend. Choosing someone who had ambitions above his station and who lacked social etiquette. He cautioned her also that she would lose her inheritance and any entitlement belonging to her forever. These were comments that may have easily damaged a lesser mortal, but not Teresa. No sooner did she step aboard the *Varnessa* heading for London, her worries and most of her problems seemingly disappeared – vanished into thin air. It was as if she had undergone a complete metamorphosis. Her rapid mood change startled Marcus who found such actions difficult to fathom.

The chilling turn around could easily be described as the actions of a chameleon; leaving him to ponder about Teresa's balanced state of mind and general well being. Was she something of an enigma? Was she someone so superficial with an inflated ego; who would allow nothing to cause her pain? Or was she merely acting out a soap opera for the benefit of pleasing him? Whatever it was, he was obliged to acknowledge this completely new scenario and take it in his stride. After all, in essence, she was the ultimate prize he sought, and this was a direct result of his tenacity and patience.

Teresa was the woman of his dreams and there was no escaping that fact. However, in achieving his success, he may have been guilty of inadvertently promoting London as if it was a package holiday, rather than a serious proposition of marriage as he had intended. Teresa on the other hand seemingly perceived it as such, as an adventure into the unknown. For instance, he made two huge promises which undoubtedly turned the tide in his favour. Should she feel uncomfortable or unhappy about her trip and her new place of abode, he would return her to the village and to her parents unscathed. Aboard the liner, *Varnessa*, he enjoyed a blissful existence, although holding to his second pledge that no physical interaction would ensue until she was relatively satisfied with her new environment. He realised that he may have over-committed on his promises, but it was a conundrum of his own making and one he hoped he would be able to resolve eventually.

Teresa settled in London quicker than most. In fact, she took to her new environment like a duck to water and proceeded immediately in setting up programmes conducive to her general development. Two months had elapsed and with a great degree of satisfaction in place, Teresa decided the time was appropriate to concede to the wishes of Marcus. For him to have Teresa as his bride was indeed a journey fulfilled – his eureka moment. The elation he experienced was so uplifting, nothing could bear comparison. He remembered his boyhood days, sitting on the village sea wall, being at one with nature, where all his dreams were born. He remembered looking in the vast expanse of the ocean, wistfully hoping that one day he would be transported to a far land and that all his wishes would be realised. Where hope would spring eternal; this was that moment. Teresa's acceptance was indeed the zenith of all his aspirations.

One year had passed and things were beginning to gradually develop. Marcus was relatively satisfied with the progress made. In the interim, many things were occurring simultaneously. Hardy, the musician, had moved to Balham, in south London, where he acquired his first home. Even though it was good to have his friend in close proximity, it raised issues that to some extent were nothing more than problematic. Marcus responding to his mother's request, decided to honour his pledge to Mama G in bringing his sister Adel to London. He was sure in his heart it was a dangerous risk to take. Adel was no shrinking violet. She was someone who could easily be described as abrasive or worst and being fully aware of his sister's attitude toward Teresa, no attempt was made to connect one to the other. Hardy was the natural foil to an otherwise delicate situation. Not only did he accommodate Adel in his home, but he also found her extremely attractive. His fascination grew and very soon a rapid association ensued. Ultimately, they became an item and their relationship readily prospered.

VICTOR WALDRON

Extraordinarily however and bizarre as it may seem, Adel felt that she had a sense of duty to perform towards her brother, as directed by Mama G.

"Take care of your little brother." Was the firm message and as a result, she felt a certain compulsion to do so. Not only did he persuade Hardy to keep his sister away from Teresa, but he also discouraged any kind of home visits from her. It was no secret that Adel despised Teresa; her beef was many because she felt her sister-in-law was pompous and arrogant. More so, she firmly believed that the marriage was one of exploitation and that her brother was simply a victim of a relationship that was not working in his favour.

Teresa, on the other hand, never saw Adel as someone she wanted to know back in the village since her friends and associates were by and large considered refined and sophisticated. Adel in her eyes was in a word, invisible. The chasm between the two parties was huge and in many ways unbridgeable. This was a solid case of the irresistible force meeting the immovable object. Nevertheless, Marcus's obligation to Mama G regarding his sister was strictly adhered to. Being aware of Adel's disdain towards Teresa played heavily on his mind, but a promise is simply that, he brought her to London and regardless of the circumstances, he felt compelled to act accordingly. He realised it was a fragile situation, the kind that needed tact and a massive degree of patience and how right was he!

Adel soon found work with London Transport and swiftly became an assistant cook in the Works canteen. Access to free passage on the underground, gave her license to visit Marcus which was not always appreciated. It was obvious and very much without doubt that her brother was subordinated to every task there was domestically. Adel reproached him constantly for being soft and allowing Teresa to treat his home as if it were a holiday let. Teresa's contribution was negligible and even though Marcus was always ready and willing to carry on, the novelty of his wife's lack of effort around the home was beginning to have a negative effect on him.

Adel's visitations and observations almost always had the same narrative. "What are you?" She would ask. "Some kind of slave? Why are you allowing that woman to treat your home like a hotel?"

"What I do in my home is none of your business. I will not tolerate you coming here to make trouble." He snarled.

"But that posh bitch of yours is riding you like a donkey."

Her brother's patience was wearing thin. "Adel, if you can't behave when you come here, I would advise you not to visit. You are nothing more than a pest and I am not prepared to put up with your nonsense, so zip it or I will have you out of here right now." He snapped angrily.

"I have a right to be here, Mama G told me to look after you and that's exactly what I intend to do."

A livid Marcus turned sharply to confront his sister. "Young lady, don't make me laugh. I gave you an opportunity to come here to make something of your life and you want to do what? Do I look like I need looking after?"

"You do Marcus," Adel replied. "That wife of yours is behaving as if you are a hired hand. You have to get a grip."

"I've heard enough of your silliness; now go before I throw you out," Marcus responded furiously.

As always Adel exited very quickly leaving her brother in a lather and spitting fire. He was fully aware that Adel may be correct, but such comments did absolutely nothing for a man's self-esteem. Meanwhile, Teresa dedicated her attention earnestly to study for her degree. Her persistence drew admiration from Marcus; who in his estimation regarded her efforts as considerable and commendable, and it was certainly not wasted. Her dedication and single-mindedness were exemplary. He felt it was fair to allow her the latitude to carry on in an effort of becoming an architect. However, in the passage of time, after four years of the marriage, there was a gradual process of deterioration that became obvious. If anything, there was a distinct erosion. They were heading down a slippery slope that appeared to have a profile of its own.

That was the year that manifested the biggest obstacle in their relationship. Teresa became pregnant and that was definitely not written in the script. It was clear to Teresa that Marcus had broken a solemn pledge, which she found most unforgivable. In all her futuristic endeavours, children were not part of her reckoning. Not that she hated the idea of kids; it was simply that she did not want any. It was clearly not in her psyche. She felt she had not the quality or desire to develop maternal instincts of any kind and as such, she regarded Marcus as the villain of the peace. This, without doubt, brought about a noticeable cooling off of the relationship.

Peter was a handsome baby boy, the kind that any parent would be proud of, with the exception of Teresa. Her entire attitude towards Peter, her son, was strange and completely unattached; in her estimation, Peter was a stumbling block. He was something that got in the way of progress, rather than someone who should be loved and cared for. Quite unlike Marcus, whose love and dedication for his son was second to none.

Teresa's behaviour stiffened and her unaltered objective of self-aggrandisement placed added strain on an already topsy-turvy relationship and although Marcus kept his head down and powered on; his general assessment of Teresa as a clinical and cold-hearted mother gained prominence. That, however, in no way changed his feelings towards her and his love for the lady remained constant.

They limped along with habits that were unsustainable from Teresa, whose general regard for harmonious accord was simply not in evidence. Progressively, her natural mood filtered away, giving Marcus cause for concern. He realised his agenda right from the outset was a dismal failure. His lack of defined rules or functions were never in place, giving Teresa free range to disregard marriage as if it was just another irrelevance, which was an almighty mistake on his part. The arrival of Peter, which should have made a huge difference, unfortunately only succeeded in widening the gap. A gap that was negative in design and gradually gaining momentum in the wrong direction. Their marriage was now an empty shell and bereft of any serious affection on her part. It was hanging on by a thread when disaster number two came along.

Teresa became pregnant once more. That, in fact, was the final straw. Not only was the pregnancy an error of judgement, but it was also most disconcerting for Teresa who was working feverishly, to complete her studies of becoming an architect. Sara was an addition she did not want or catered for. It was the final nail in the coffin. As a result, it was the end of any cohabitation that may have occurred between the couple. The relationship was now in serious demise. In fact, in Teresa's estimation, she felt it was an act of sabotage, one based on spite and as a consequence, she decided to vacate the matrimonial bedroom once and for all. Sara was a child of good fortune. On the day she was born, Marcus became a lucky punter on the pools, winning one hundred pounds. That win convinced Marcus that Sara was a child of destiny and named her accordingly. He aptly named her Sara Fortune Gullant.

Teresa, as with Peter, showed minimal interest, especially towards her newborn. Her maternal instincts were conspicuously absent, amplifying the dying embers of what was left of the marriage. Paradoxically, as Teresa's affection waned, Marcus kept matters going regardless, heaping massive love and devotion to his children, in compensation for what was missing from a mother whose natural instincts remained unfathomable.

Somehow, the process continued and miraculously survived another four years. It was a period when many things were happening simultaneously. Through those years, Teresa had managed to become a qualified architect; applied for a job with a large company, who saw the tremendous potential she possessed and gave her employment. Accordingly, she wasted no time in moving up the ladder of progress and began to structure her life to complement these changes. Her first acquisition was a brand new car which she felt befitted her new status and with frenzied haste, gathered friends which naturally set the trend for her new lifestyle. As her popularity grew, she became noticeable, doing the rounds with her four friends which Adel labelled as the Teresa's 'Posse'; they were seen everywhere; parties; clubs; theatres and other forums. There were four girls and one boy. It was as if they were tied together by a single cord. The young man in their midst was Jonny Bellaw. He was European. No one knew to whom Jonny was attached, other than to say that he was always present among the ladies.

In the interim, news from the village indicated that serious problems had arisen with Teresa's father Malcolm. He was in bad shape, hospitalised with a massive heart attack from which unfortunately he did not recover. Teresa's reaction to her father's demise was simply astonishing. She displayed no visible signs of grief in any way, as if void of feeling and carried on in her usual way, as though it was a matter of minor importance, totally refusing to travel or attend her father's funeral. Marcus's disillusionment was paramount; his was one of utter disbelief. He wondered how anyone could show such callous indifference to someone so close. How sad it was that she was incapable of showing even the mildest of sorrow for someone so dear. More to the point, why did she not want to support her mother and the rest of her family in their hour of need? Was she emotionally bankrupt? Was she suffering from a condition that mired her sense of feeling? No one would ever know. However, he could not help feeling compassion for the woman he loved so dearly in spite of her state of mind.

While Teresa's popularity grew amongst her friends, Marcus retreated into himself and adopted a stance that was regarded as both negative and unproductive. Convinced that Sara was a child of destiny especially since his lucky win on the day she was born, he embarked upon a plan that seemed defeatist to everyone bar himself. Acknowledging tacitly, that matters had spiralled out of control and his ability to retrieve lost ground was highly improbable as regards to Teresa. He, therefore, concluded that a rapid solution was needed. Hence, in his estimation, winning a large sum of money was the only way forward.

That period saw a massive decay of conditions, both in the marriage and in his behaviour, exacerbated by Teresa's selfish actions which made Adel incandescent with rage. Her worry was transmitted solely by Teresa's attitude of doing whatever she wanted come what may and without proper care or consideration for Marcus. Buying a brand new car was a typical example of this new behaviour. Strutting around with friends across the city as if there was no tomorrow, was indeed another example. Her self-indulgent pomposity was based on an artificial premise of independence and superiority, which she considered above all else. That gave Adel more reason to believe that her sister-in-law was nothing more than an egotistical snob, who used her good looks and charm to gain an advantage over others; displaying actions tantamount to a diva out of control, which was most disconcerting to her, especially since Teresa was a married woman with responsibilities.

That was an opinion that Adel firmly held even when they were back in the village. Teresa's actions were made worse by the fact that Marcus was on the receiving end of this utterly bad experience. She felt he was a man that deserved better. He was someone whose loyalty, decency and caring personality were seen to be trampled upon. In spite of the fact that his good nature helped Teresa to achieve her ambitions and which she took for granted, the kindness was never reciprocated. Her action was one of ingratitude. What was worst, it was as if behaving badly was okay. Adel was in no doubt that her brother's undying love for Teresa in this farce of a marriage, kept him going. His strength of mind to hold on in the face of adversity and to what many would see as a lost cause, amplified his steely nature and his sense of purpose. In fact, he was never a man to give up. What also kept him going to a very large extent were his beloved children.

That was all the more reason for Adel to badger her brother about her suspicions of Jonny Bellaw. It was magnified by the fact that he was always there in the mix. Her repeated reference of Jonny did not make a single ripple to her brother's disposition.

Teresa, as far as Marcus was concerned, was entitled to her friends and her space as anyone else. As a result, it was not gossip he was willing or ready to accommodate. He fully understood the situation and felt there was no great advantage in trying to change what was now seen as irreversible. As always he was determined to keep the home fires burning however low the flames were.

The fear of ending this marriage with the scenario of 'I told you so' ringing in his ears from all and sundry was quite real. He did not doubt the fact that he was dealing with someone of a mercurial personality; of that, he was sure. She happened to be someone who did not show enough regard for others in the pursuit of her own objectives. She was someone who built walls metaphorically to keep out the realities of life, which in her own strange way; she considered to be normal, showing a complete lack of remorse, sadness or humility, especially in view of her father's demise. However, in spite of the existing failures on her part, he was not in a particular hurry to remove the last vestige of their union. Being a supreme optimist he was forever hoping that change would come, advancing the notion that age and maturity can repair what he concluded as a dismal and unfortunate experience, which one day could possibly alter for the better.

Marcus thought long and hard about the moment and wondered if the downward spiral could have been avoided. The motto "Be careful what you wish for" kept constantly resonating in his mind. It was love at first sight from the moment he laid eyes on Teresa, as a young man in the village. Her beauty; her easy charm and her poise captivated him. That fascination grew to tangible proportions, occupying his soul and every second of his waking life. It was Teresa that inspired him to reach heights that he never imagined.

Everything he did was motivated by that single dream to attain her affections. Even now with all her imperfections and the negative aspects of their marriage, he felt the effort to keep it together was wholly justified. In his book, half a penny was better than none at all. That did not stop Adel's persistence informing her brother at every given opportunity about Teresa's flirtatious manner with Jonny. Reference was also made to him by Hardy his musician friend, who occasionally noticed the 'posse' as it was called, having fun with Jonny forever present. However, it was Adel who was most vociferous. Harping constantly about the company Teresa kept. "Why are you allowing that woman to treat you like something she stepped on? Are you blind? Can't you see she has no damn respect for you?"

"I would advise you to let people get on with their lives without you interfering. What Teresa does is absolutely none of your business." He responded trying his best to conceal his emotions.

"Wake up to what your wife is doing to you." She blurted in frustration. "Don't just sit there and mess about with coupons. You need to behave as if you have a life. That pompous git of yours is trampling you into the dirt. Be a man and do something about it. Come on my brother, have some balls."

Marcus became totally exhausted with the prying attitude of Adel and decided he was having no more of it. He felt aggrieved at her insinuation that Teresa had gone astray. He felt casting spurious aspersions and vicious innuendos about his wife were seriously offensive. He was getting to the very end of his tether with Adel and wished for once he had not succumbed to his mother's wishes in bringing his troublesome sister to London, who was hell-bent on making his life as miserable as possible.

"Adel I do not want to hear any more of your nonsense. Now get out of here and do not come back unless you can behave." Marcus uttered finally.

Adel turned to leave but could not help irritating her brother once more. "Marcus Gullant, you will wake up when that wife of yours ends up with that white man. Don't say I did not warn you."

That, unfortunately, was the scenario that Marcus was faced with. His sister's robust; constant and most aggressive attempts to find evidence that would prove Teresa was abjectly in default of standards that were required in fulfilling her status as a trusted wife and mother. In Adel's view, Teresa's manner and behaviour fell short of the mark, as far as decency was concerned. Hence her vigilant efforts in alerting her brother on matters she felt he should be aware of. Marcus remained unimpressed and totally untroubled by what he regarded as tittle-tattle. Knowing his sister as he did, he was convinced she was behaving abominably and with an agenda all her own. She was always spilling vicious accusations towards Teresa for her own sordid ends. Teresa may be many things, but in his own mind, she was not one for certain excesses, especially amorous ones. Based on the years they have spent together he did not experience any extreme zeal or any description that was worthy of such rebuke.

Teresa by nature did not exhibit a high degree of romantic verve towards him throughout their relationship. Given that fact it was a logical conclusion to perceive that Jonny was not in any way connected romantically to her. He may be part of the company she kept, but in his humble estimation, the idea of an affair was completely out of the equation. Marcus's perception of his wife was based on a spurious notion that his faithfulness and loyalty to their marriage was a typical example to follow. He saw no good reason why she would deviate from the principle of that commitment. What he failed to factor into that theory was the vulnerability of the flesh and more so in the eleven years that had expired, despondency was now the order of the day.

The growing disaffection between Teresa and himself was now a cause for serious concern. He was fully aware of the sea change that transpired over the years and of the steady erosion. Redressing the balance, although not impossible, now seemed highly improbable. He was conscious of his shortcomings and knew positive changes were now a matter of urgency. In the grand scheme of things, apart from the first three years, most of the ensuing years in the marriage could only be regarded as ordinary. Teresa was never motivated by the very idea of togetherness and as a result, destroyed the process of what a happy union could be. Her uncaring behaviour cast a shadow on proceedings which ultimately killed a golden opportunity that could easily have existed.

The zest and enthusiasm that he managed to generate were met with robust rejection, especially after Sara his second child was born. Teresa now perceived him to be the villain of the peace. It was inconceivable to him that her two beautiful kids were the greatest barrier between them. One that got greater as time passed. His own commitment to winning the pools was a huge mistake and only compounded the situation in a massive way. He was sure he needed a more constructive approach to stem the tide of woes that was undoubtedly evident.

To add to his pain was Adel's rampant charge against Teresa. Her innuendos and blatant accusations were enough to test his inexhaustible resolve to the very limit. He was absolutely certain he needed a miracle in order to face the challenges ahead. He also needed continuity in abundance for obvious reasons. In spite of her frailties, her general attitude and her stringent disregard for her family, he was still helplessly in love with the woman he called his wife. That in no uncertain manner was the crux of the situation. Marcus realised it was not the ideal scenario to be a part of, but there was still a modicum of life left in the marriage and, come what may, he needed it to be sustained, if only for the great and lasting affection he felt for her.

Extracting from his past experiences and his amazing quality of resilience, he would not be deterred from keeping the home fires burning even though they were all but extinguished. Drawing from his resources, he firmly believed in the process of recovery. His natural tendency as always was to look ahead for better times. He regarded and equally remained committed to the very ideals of positive thinking and to his credit, he always found remarkable success accentuating confidence and hope as a way of life.

# FADING RELATIONSHIP

It was just after Christmas and all the flurry and excitement of the season had subsided. Life was slowly replaced by post-holiday calmness once more. It was late Saturday afternoon but it was no ordinary one for many obvious reasons. It was stormy, cold, damp and very bleak. Altogether it was simply a wretched evening. It was the kind of weather that would deter even the bravest from venturing out. Most if not all would be prepared to take sanctuary in the comfort of their homes. Extraordinarily as it may seem, Teresa was the exception to that golden rule. She was prepared to defy the elements for her customary night out. This was an action that defied logic. Her departure left Marcus sad and deflated. He wondered why anyone would be foolhardy enough to brave such inclement conditions for the sake of having a bit of fun. Yet it was largely these extreme weather conditions that worked admirably in his favour.

That evening brought him a change of good fortune. Routinely checking his pools coupon, he found he was a winner. The pools had paid out the second best prize and although it was not enough to make him rich, it was more than an adequate amount to make him substantially and financially potent. Marcus was in ecstasy. His moment had arrived. His undiminished joy was matchless, an experience that was in the capacity of equalling anything before or after, especially since it could alter the course of events for his immediate future. He felt it was time to recompose his thoughts and to take advantage of this moment; to do what he felt was necessary to regain lost ground which obviously would benefit his marriage in the long term. He was positive he understood Teresa's appetite for material aggrandisement and was now ready to fund it for all it was worth.

In a word, he would spend, spend, spend, if that's what it would take to regain her favour. His conclusion which he perceived to be valid, gave him reason to believe that it was not his charm, his persona nor his enchanting qualities that influenced her decision to travel to London; it was largely expedient to her own needs. As a result, a new strategy was imperative. He needed one that was full of glitz and glamour. Charm would be replaced with the power of money. He was positive she could not resist the offer of fabulous hotels, magnificent shows, extravagant holidays, elaborate clothes and other accessories relevant to her exquisite taste and her refined personality. Confident of the fact that he had a recipe for success, he smiled contentedly, a smile that had a mark of satisfaction written all over it.

As the wind rushed against the window and the cold frosty chill prevailed, Marcus could not help his feeling of upliftment. It was as if life had given him a completely new purpose. He was happy also in the knowledge that he had reached a point which by virtue of his new financial status, things could only get better. His exuberance was uncontainable, and rightly so. In view of this highly charged feeling which consumed him, he decided it would be appropriate to furnish this wonderful news to Teresa on her return home. With that in mind, he made himself as comfortable as possible and with a bottle of wine, some of his best music, his radiogram and heaps of beautiful thoughts for the future, he patiently waited. The time moved slowly, it was two o'clock and going, then three, then four. Even in a positive frame of mind and his over-eagerness to convey this good news to Teresa, he felt she was well overdue.

Just after four o'clock, there was still no sign of Teresa and a degree of agitation crept in to nullify his mood. It was almost five o'clock when Teresa finally entered the house. She immediately observed activities of one kind or another that was in evidence.

Her reaction to that was one of hostility. In her mind, this was a vigil she did not care for and considered it somewhat intrusive. In normal parlance, this was a red flag to a bull. She slowly opened the door and peered into the living room, only to find Marcus fully awake; a glass of wine in hand and a welcoming smile. That smile was not reciprocated. "I thought you had forgotten where you lived," Marcus uttered trying to maintain his natural poise.

Teresa's response was one of anger. "What is this supposed to mean?" She interjected.

"Well, I thought you were never coming home." He remarked.

Teresa stopped him in his tracks. "What is this? Why the interrogation? Have you joined with your silly sister in spying on me? Is that what you've reduced to?"

"Spying?" He retorted. "Why the hell should I spy on you? I simply waited up to give you some good news. I actually won money on the pools and I wanted you to be the first to know."

"Marcus I do not want to know about your winnings. It has nothing to do with me." She responded. "What I do want to know is why you are listening to that woman and her slander, which you seem to enjoy for some unknown reason."

Marcus could not help being peeved by her remarks. "What on earth are you talking about? Do you think I'm one for listening to gossip?"

"Yes." She retorted. "I have heard her on several occasions spitting her vile poison and what's more you seem to encourage it. They say if you sleep with dogs you end up with fleas. For the life of me, I do not know why I did not listen to my parents."

"Teresa it's no good behaving like the spoilt brat you are. For once you are totally out of bounds. It's about time you grew up."

"I live the life I want to live." She uttered being unimpressed by her husband's action of waiting up for her. "You must know by now that I'm not bothered by jealous or undesirable people who can't mind their own business and I most certainly do not intend to condescend to their level."

Marcus was overcome by this sudden blast. It was not meant to be this way. He needed to change the complexion of this discourse. Raising a faint smile he explained. "Teresa, please listen! All I wanted to do is give you news that would help us to be better people. I'm only too willing to change my life so we can have a bright and fulfilled future. Please understand me; we can prosper if we try."

Teresa was in no mood to compromise. "You can keep your good news and everything else that goes with it to yourself. I've had enough of you and your stupid sister. Give her the good news for me. Tell her that as of today I intend to sever all links with the Gullant family and good riddance."

She slammed the door behind her and hurried away to her room; leaving a bewildered and shaken Marcus in her wake. This was certainly not written in the script. What should have been a new beginning was now a huge catastrophe; a totally unmitigated disaster. The entire episode had left him in a sombre state of mind. Digesting this macabre and totally unreal scenario tested his resolve to the limit.

In the stillness of the morning, he could hear the raindrops beating down on the window pane, as if in sympathy with the way he felt in this dark hour of despair and grief. As he sat in puzzled contemplation, the plot thickened. Teresa returned moments later accompanied by a small grip which she set down by the doorway. She walked over to the table where she placed her rings. This was a different Teresa to the woman he remembered. This woman was as hard as nails, astringent and very determined. It was obvious by her manner; she had decided to dissolve the relationship once and for all. "These are yours to do whatever you wish to do with them. They are of no interest to me anymore."

A puzzled and rattled Marcus offered a weak reply. "Don't be silly Teresa, the rings are yours. Please consider carefully that you are not making a huge mistake by walking out on us, it may be something you regret."

Teresa walked slowly and deliberately to the door, picked up her grip and as if she was most certain of what she was doing, she turned to face Marcus. "No Marcus, the mistake of which I have regretted, was wasting my life with you."

"Don't say that, Teresa, you're trying to hurt me for some unknown reason. I simply do not know what your agenda is but I do not deserve this."

Teresa smiled sarcastically. "That is a matter of opinion. All these years of procrastination; watching and putting up with people who cannot elevate their minds to a level of decency and respectability. I have endured your sister and her slanderous behaviour for far too long, and for what? Were you man enough to put a stop to her nonsense? No, I think you've encouraged it. That money that you say you've won; why not take it and help her to be a better person and stop being the low life she presently is. I am going because I can take no more of it. As for regret that's a laugh. I really don't think so. You have failed in your promise to me and you have no idea how much I loathe you for it. I did not want children and you gave me two of them. If I regret anything it's meeting up with you."

She turned and departed into the early morning mist and rain, leaving behind a trail of grief and turmoil beyond comprehension. This was unexpected and extremely harsh for the young man. In fact, it was nothing less than a Tsunami moment for him.

As Teresa drove away, she was in no doubt that a conspiracy or one kind or another had taken place. Adel contributed largely to that theory. However, conspiracy or not, she felt it was time to liberate herself from a situation she could no longer tolerate. Deep in her mind and in her heart, she knew that Adel was correct. Her preoccupation with Jonny had taken on a new meaning. She was beginning to experience a genuine attachment, which she found irresistible and did nothing to alter. Her general feeling for her co-worker had become tangible, a feeling that was mutual in every respect and since there was no reward of being trapped in a relationship that was now completely stagnated, she knew it was time to move on. It was also true that for the first time in her entire life she had begun to experience genuine affection for someone, even though her existence was one of numerous flirtations, none was ever taken seriously, this was enough to pursue with care and tenderness. If the truth be told, Teresa was captivated by the charm of Jonny Bellaw and was falling in love with him.

Marcus knew the pitfalls of life but refused to be daunted. Being a supreme optimist, he was prepared to carry on regardless. However if ever there was a period in his life where hope seemed to fade and doom reigned, it was now. His despair was augmented by Peter and Sara's persistent questions about their mother, which evidently had now become conspicuous.

Teresa was never a hands-on parent, but it was obvious by her absence that a rapid transformation had taken place. It was evident that her presence, even though it was never in abundance was now completely extinct. The only chink of light that was apparent happened to be the things that she most treasured, her prized possessions; most of her personal effects were still very much intact. Marcus was in no doubt that it was only a matter of time before she would return to collect items that were very important in enhancing her natural vanity and materialistic zeal. Teresa was also the mother of two wonderful children, Marcus believed it hardly seemed conceivable, that she would not return to say goodbye to them. A simple act that would set her apart from being seen as callous, hard-hearted, and unworthy to be called a mother.

Days ran into weeks and still no sign of Teresa. The expectations which Marcus held began to evaporate along with the faintest of hope that existed. He vividly remembered Mama G's prophecy. "My son, do not marry that girl. It would not work. All that glitters is not gold."

It was empathically true and without doubt words of wisdom. Teresa was a face of extreme beauty, but with a heart of stone. It was clear in his mind that the situation had reached a tipping point. He needed it to be decisive if only for his own peace of mind. What was necessary and most important now was to confront her once and for all, to know if this was the final call.

The desk clerk was a charming young lady. She smiled pleasantly as Marcus approached. "How can I help?" She enquired politely.

"I wonder if it's possible to speak with Mrs Gullant?" He asked tentatively.

"And what is your business?" She asked still smiling.

"She happens to be my wife and I need to speak with her urgently."

"Very well Mr Gullant I will get her to see you shortly."

The clerk pointed to the seats behind him. "Please make yourself comfortable, she will not be long."

It was the first time Marcus felt it necessary to visit Teresa's workplace. It was an imposing building, the kind that fits her personality admirably. However, the anxious moments of waiting began to take its toll. The duration was lengthy which made him believe negatively that Teresa would not approve of his visit, an instinct that proved to be absolutely correct. She finally approached and it was pretty obvious that his presence there was far from welcomed. She appeared ashen-faced and with an attitude of reluctance that immediately gave the game away. "What do you want Marcus? Why on earth did you come here?" Her behaviour gave the impression that she was embarrassed by him. Realising that he was now between a rock and a hard place, it was necessary for him to make an extreme effort to be calm.

"Teresa, I am here because I think it is important that we have a serious discussion on how we can go about mending fences."

"I would have no such discussion with you." She retorted. "Get it in your thick cranium Marcus, this marriage is at an end."

"Look!" He reasoned. "Our marriage can be saved if we try a little harder. Teresa, there is so much at stake. Besides the kids are missing you, they want you at home. We all want you back home."

Teresa was now showing impatience of a very high degree, responded angrily. "Marcus I told you repeatedly, they are your children not mine. They are your problem, you deal with them."

Marcus flushed with anger and frustration was now at his wit's end. "Teresa, why are you behaving so despicable? I really do not think I deserve this. I think I have been a good husband to you. Is this what I get for all my efforts?"

"You get what you deserve." She replied. She reached into her pocket and produced a bunch of keys. It was obvious by her actions that she had predetermined her husband's visit at some point. "These are yours; I will not be needing them any longer."

Marcus was reluctant to accept them. "For heaven sake Teresa please stop behaving like a juvenile. Let's try to settle this matter like grown-ups once and for all."

"There is nothing more to discuss." She blurted out, looking at her watch anxiously. "I have a job of work to do and I would very much like you to leave."

Marcus sighed heavily. "What about your belongings? What am I supposed to do with them?"

"Do whatever you wish." She retorted aggressively. "Burn them for all I care."

She turned her back and slowly began walking away, then stopped, turned to face her husband once more and as if to rub salt in the wounds. "Please, Marcus do not ever come back here again."

He watched her go and felt like a dark cloud had descended on him. It was a gloom that had the stench of permanence, which if encouraged could be detrimental to the depths of his soul.

# JESSICA

As the wind buffeted the young soldier, he simply could not help remembering the journey he made to London for the very first time with Teresa by his side; the overwhelming joy he envisaged; his hope that this eternal bliss would be unbroken for as long as life lasts. Those images are still as fresh and alive as if it was only yesterday. Her beauty still reigns supreme in his thoughts. Her fragrance still radiates warmth around him, lingering legacies of happier times. Sadly it was now behind him and it was time, difficult as it seemed, to put those protracted thoughts to bed. He was going back to London a free man, a bachelor and now must endeavour to reconstruct his life to extinguish thoughts or memories that belong to yesterday.

He also needed to take stock of the prevailing conditions around him that had suddenly deteriorated. The fierce wind by now had graduated to a storm with the might and power of overwhelming authority. So much so, that the majestic and well-constructed vessel the SS *Aracassa* seemed to be in total subordination to natures aggressive command. Forcing the giant ship to dance and sway merrily to its ferocious dictates. Marcus knew it was now time to take leave of this inclemency around him for a more favourable environment. He needed a stiff drink to clear his mind from what he considered to be no more than a blip in his otherwise successful existence. He was in no doubt that matters of the heart pose greater difficulties to overcome than anything else he had ever experienced thus far.

However, dwelling in the past was most certainly not the path to follow. He needed to embrace new concepts and to remain optimistic about the challenges ahead. He was also satisfied his children Sara and Peter were now in good hands. Taking them home to Mama G was undoubtedly the most sensible outcome. It was delightful to see the love and affection they received from their Grandmother, which incidentally was truly reciprocal.

His yearning for a drink or two to drown his sorrows was most compelling. He also needed to remove the chill that had penetrated his defences as he reminisced on things that had gone before him. On his approach to the bar, something in his peripheral vision caught his attention. It was someone who in his opinion merited assistance of one kind or another. She was young, very tall, angular and in some difficulties. His immediate instinct was one of indifference. She was a stranger with problems which was none of his business; however, curiosity took the better of him and a compelling urge transpired; enough for him to discover the reason for such distress. He moved closer to the individual only to realise that her plight was worse than he first thought. She was wearing a dress that was at least a size too large for her delicate frame, accentuating her slimness to a greater degree. Tears streaming liberally down her cheeks, her eyes cherry red and bulging, her quivering body racked with emotions, which gave the impression of someone in desperation and obviously in need of solace. She was wiping tears from her eyes with a handkerchief so saturated; it was at the point of redundancy. This stranger needed help and quickly.

The SS Aracassa was at the mercy of Mother Nature and was now in roller coaster mode, making equilibrium for everyone very challenging to maintain. There were many onboard that were feeling the effects of this mighty onslaught. It may have been this new experience that created a state of panic for someone so young, or being in an environment she was unable to comprehend. Either way, Marcus felt sympathy for this stranger and a compulsion to assist. As a result, he decided to invest an interest in her well-being, which he felt was a natural or common human act of kindness to perform.

"Young lady – you seem to be in some kind of distress. Can I help in any way?"

The stranger looked up and seeing Marcus there, tried to bring some degree of poise to her otherwise frantic behaviour. Still dabbing her cheeks with a handkerchief that had clearly lost its usefulness, she bowed her head without responding.

"If you think I'm interfering, just say so and I'll be gone?" Marcus indicated, still observing the troubled stranger and waited for a response.

Once more she looked up. It was slow and deliberate. She sighed heavily, trying to prevent her delicate chest from heaving up and down, giving the impression of someone having an attack of hiccups. "Thank you for your interest sir, I guess I am in a bit of a state but I should be okay."

The *SS Aracassa* was still being pounded by waves of savage enormity. It was difficult to ignore the feeling of discomfort such a journey entails. Furtive glances indicated that many of the passengers were reacting unfavourably to an experience that was undoubtedly unpleasant.

"I guess all this is a bit too much for you," Marcus said. "I don't know of anyone who enjoys this kind of weather."

There was still no response. It was quite clear this tall stranger was hardly in any mood for general conversation. Her cheeks were still wet from the trickle of tears coming from the corners of her eyes and although she was not responsive, he was positive she needed time to restore her composure. He handed her his handkerchief. "Take this and dry your eyes. Whatever it is it's never as bad as it seems."

It was some moments before she accepted the offer of his handkerchief. Moments of reluctance that did not sit well with him. He hoped his small act of kindness was not being misconstrued in any shape or form, but nonetheless, he was willing to remain patient with someone as young as she appeared. She was definitely in need of help.

Gradually the stranger looked up again and nodded appreciably. Her demeanour had taken on a different and almost complete transformation. It was as if an opportunity had come her way suddenly, one she felt compelled to acknowledge. Out of the mire that she was very much a part of, comes this certain element of change that was most comforting. Her distress and pain that anchored so heavily around her, was now subsiding and clearly making way for something more tangible.

Her assessment of Marcus was now beginning to take shape. His maturity perhaps gave her reason to feel at ease in his presence, which was of comfort to her. Burdened with the process which was acid and destructive in one moment, she was able to find a degree of contentment in the next. All this was due in no uncertain terms to this stranger who offered his assistance in time of need. She felt that this was an opportunity to savour. It was something out of nothing and a glorious chance to accept friendship of one way or another; if only for her own peace of mind.

"Unfortunately my current predicament is getting the better of me. It is something of a nightmare, but hopefully, I will be able to manage." The young stranger said.

"I do hope so." He assured her. "But whatever it is, I am sure you will be able to deal with it adequately."

She smiled faintly. "I guess we all have our cross to bear and deal with it we must."

Marcus smiled. "Well, there is no time like the present, to deal with your problems. Let me know if I can help in any way?"

"My parents believed this was the best thing for me to do but I'm not so sure."

Marcus chuckled. "Parents always think they know best and invariably they do. But not always; I don't want to scare you, but this journey and all it stands for is not for the fainthearted.

"You can say that again." She responded.

He looked at her quizzically. "So what is your story if I may be bold enough to ask?"

The pause that resulted from that question told Marcus that he was fishing in very deep waters. The stranger was obviously not prepared to answer questions of such a delicate nature.

Especially with someone she had just met. Yet she knew it would be un-diplomatic not to respond.

"It's a very long tale to tell and I am not sure you would understand."

Marcus grinned boyishly. "You are so right. I am very sorry to be asking you about matters that do not concern me. But whatever it is, I do hope you can come to terms with it."

The stranger responded with a faint smile. "Anyway, I am glad you are so sympathetic to my cause."

A slow thaw was now evident, producing a pleasing change of heart, which made her much more amiable. Her smile seemed to be both of a friendly and responsive nature as she attempted to return the soiled handkerchief. "I am very grateful for your assistance, thank you very much. I feel so much better now."

Marcus declined the handkerchief. He was very relieved that his efforts to help were not entirely wasted. "Keep the handkerchief, I have plenty and think nothing of it." He responded. "In my opinion, it was the only decent thing to do."

The stranger nodded in agreement.

"Look!" Marcus continued. "I am a little concerned about you. Are you old enough to be making a journey like this on your own? I hazard a guess that you are not much older than fifteen or sixteen or are you with someone?"

There was another pause of considerable length. It was long enough to give Marcus the impression that his observation was out of step. The stranger smiled displaying a wonderful array of gleaming white teeth and rendering a softer more pleasant side to her personality, the kind that was massively overshadowed by her emotional upheaval.

"I am nineteen years old and therefore yes; I am making this journey on my own."

"Well!" A surprised Marcus replied. "You don't look a day over fifteen and that was my main concern."

"There are some things that I find difficult to cope with. This entire business is driving me crazy!" She uttered.

Marcus studied her briefly. Convinced that part of her problem was travelling abroad to a destination she was unfamiliar with. "Were you told that going to London at such a delicate age was not a walk in the park?" He enquired. "I get the impression that you are not quite ready for this venture. It can be rigorous."

"No, I was not told anything. It was kind of a rush." The stranger suggested.

"Well little lady," Marcus remarked grinning visibly. "You are no more a damsel in distress. If you let me, I will be your knight in shining armour. I will endeavour to transport you safely to your destination. Once you are there I will be satisfied that I have done a good deed for a deserving young lady."

"That sounds so wonderful." She responded. "The truth is, I was not exactly enjoying the prospect of doing this journey on my own."

"Now that we have settled that little problem; I'm off to get myself a stiff drink. Do you care to join me?"

The stranger somewhat reluctantly conceded, accompanying Marcus to the lower deck. Moving unsteadily as she did so. "Perhaps a small glass of white wine would be fine." She eventually responded.

He gave her another quizzical look. "I still think you don't seem old enough to be having any kind of alcohol."

"Do you want to see my birth certificate?" She asked.

"No, I will have to take your word for it." He mused.

Down below, things were very lively. The bar was full and relatively noisy. Some of the passengers were dancing to a tuneful band, even though the liner was being subjected to a battering, whipped up by the turbulent waves which dictated its movements. There were others that were merely making the best of a situation that could hardly be considered as ideal.

Marcus returned to where his new companion sat, showing imaginative skills in balancing in order to remain upright and not spill the drinks. He chuckled loudly as he sat beside her.

"What must you be thinking of me? I guess my manners have deserted me. My name is Marcus Gullant. Not the most exciting name you would have heard, but it will do for now."

"And I'm Jessica Wiss. Pleased to meet you." She replied.

They shook hands and Marcus remarked spontaneously as he raised his glass.

"Well, Jessica I sincerely Wiss this friendship would not falter."

"You have a good sense of humour, "She grinned. "You should be on stage."

Marcus chuckled heartily. "To be on stage you need a special kind of talent, the kind I lack completely."

Jessica nodded approvingly as she sipped her wine. It was obvious to Marcus, observing his young companion, that she was displaying signs of extreme fatigue.

"Whereabouts in England are you going if I may ask?"

"London, I'm going to London actually," Jessica replied.

"Well! Like I said before." He informed. "This trip will not be easy for you, especially for one so young."

Jessica smiled warmly. "I'm aware of that, but I'm sure with a little bit of help I should be able to manage."

Marcus nodded approvingly. "That's the spirit young lady, always remain positive."

"You sound as though you have knowledge of travelling. Have you been to London before?" She enquired.

"I'm an old soldier." He informed. "This is my third trip to the Mother Country."

"That makes a huge difference. No wonder you look so confident and assured." She replied.

"I'm not sure about confidence, but London is now my home. I took a sabbatical in order to take my kids to stay with their Grandmother. I wanted them to experience the kind of upbringing I once had. It's a worthwhile venture in my opinion and so far, no regrets. You should see how wonderfully they interact with their granny. It's so amazing to see." He informed Jessica with a smile of contentment.

"Obviously you seem a very proud father. I take it you're a married man, so where is your wife?" She asked inquisitively.

"That's a very good question." He sighed heavily. "I imagine she's somewhere in Canada now. Anyway, our marriage has ended. It collapsed after almost twelve years."

Jessica observed the huge disappointment in his reaction and immediately felt it was appropriate to render a touch of humour merely to lighten the mood.

"I'm so sorry to hear that, but I wonder why she should leave a handsome and considerate man like you?"

Marcus smiled pleasantly. "Thank you for your compliment, but we were hardly a match made in heaven. What she wanted out of our union and what I wanted were completely different things. The bottom line is; I did not win the argument." His voice cracked and it was plain to see that he was still hurting from this horrid experience.

"I'm afraid that's not good news." She echoed. "But life throws up unfortunate circumstances."

"Yes it does," Marcus replied, still wearing a grim look, which he tried to conceal. "But that's the nature of the beast. You can't win them all as they say."

Jessica, still trying to make light of the situation, smiled broadly. "You're so right, but you're still alive and kicking. I can't imagine a man like you would have difficulty finding another woman if you so desire."

Marcus looked at the young woman long and hard. "My dear, a woman is the very last thing on my mind at this time. I have nothing against them I can assure you, but right now it is not my overwhelming priority. Anyway, that's enough about me. Let's concentrate a little on you. Where about in London would you be residing?"

"A place called Highbury. That's where my cousin lives. Are you familiar with it?"

"Familiar?" He boasted. "I lived there for a while after I left the Army."

"Oh good!" Jessica replied with a degree of excitement. "At least that is half of my problem solved. My next worry is recognising him."

"Whatever do you mean by that? Don't you know him well?" Marcus enquired.

"I do and it should not be a problem, but he's been gone for almost six years, he may have changed in all that time."

"Don't let that be a problem, Jessica. Once you see family, you will always recognise them."

Jessica nodded affirmatively. It was somewhat amazing how relaxed she felt in the company of someone she hardly knew. However his approach and general demeanour gave her every confidence to trust his honesty. She was well aware that all was not well with him and there were issues to tackle and probably overcome in order for him to regain his sense of purpose once more. It seemed a foregone conclusion that he was strong-willed and possessed the qualities necessary to bounce back from any eventuality.

Marcus glanced at her empty glass and judging by her appearance, he was certain it was her last drink. He rose to his feet half-heartedly. "Can I get you another drink?"

"Not for me thanks. This journey is quite upsetting. I'm not sure how much more of this I can take." She admitted.

The ships unsteady path was a major factor in Jessica's ill feeling. It was undoubtedly a rough passage and there were many who shared that sentiment.

"Then let me escort you to your cabin." He suggested.

Jessica had no reason to disagree. The journey had become a challenge thus far. She got to her feet in an unsteady manner, simply in response to the ship's erratic movements and gave Marcus a faint smile.

"I'm not tipsy; it's just this silly boat behaving quite badly."

"You're right dear," Marcus replied. "The *Aracassa* is taking a bit of a bashing."

"Bashing?" Jessica enquired curiously.

"Yes, you know." He indicated by moving his hands up and down to illustrate the ship's motion.

"Oh, I see." She replied cautiously.

He quickly realised the word was unfamiliar with his young companion and chuckled loudly. "Oh, I can see you are puzzled.

You're not used to the word bashing. Well, we often use words in Britain that can be very strange to a West Indian – you know, words like bloke meaning a man; ta, meaning thanks; things that will appear strange to you at first but you will soon get used to them."

"Ta, for this wonderful information." She smirked, seeing the funny side of what was said. "And ta for your patience too."

"You see?" He announced jovially. "You're halfway to becoming one of us already."

The journey to her cabin had become a trudge. He was surprised to find it a long and tedious path, deep in the bowels of this vast liner. It was a far cry from his own accommodation which was first class. At last Jessica stopped and pointed to her cabin. "Well, I've reached my destination." She announced showing marked signs of fatigue.

"Okay Jessica the rest will do you good and tomorrow, we can resume where we left off."

"It's a small world and you are good company, so I'm sure we'll be seeing each other." She remarked.

"How right you are." He retorted. "This ship is our world for another twenty days unless one of us decides to jump off."

Jessica smiled limply. "Well, that won't be me. I may have been thinking suicidal thoughts earlier, but I'm alright now."

"That's the spirit young lady. Tomorrow is another day." He turned swiftly waving goodbye as he departed.

The following morning Marcus felt somewhat energised. After breakfast, he decided to resume unfinished business, which was to renew his acquaintance with his otherwise susceptible new friend, Jessica. Mindful of her frailties of both mind and body, he felt his was a mission unfulfilled. Nevertheless, it was one of significant importance and one that must be handled with sensitivity and care. Recalling her emotional outburst and her extreme grief, he felt it would have been less than human not to rescue her from such an unfortunate abyss. That he was able to achieve a measure of success, he felt it was now incumbent on him to follow through to its final conclusion. He was confident that he did not engender any motives towards his young companion, regarding her as someone whose vulnerability which was at a point of desperation, needed protection from the fears and uncertainties that consumed her. In an extraordinarily strange way, connecting with Jessica was something of a distraction for Marcus. In his summary, however, he considered it a very welcomed one. Still plagued and tormented by his own broken marriage, the absence of his children, who were many miles away in the custody of their Grandmother, but most importantly the notion that he may never see his estranged wife ever again, were difficult problems that created a lingering propensity that he found difficult to digest or forget. Jessica was the antidote that he needed to distract himself from his own misery.

There was something about his young companion that was quite refreshing. She possessed an alluring aura. She was extremely charming with an engaging outlook that merited attention. What he considered as an act of compassion, swiftly elevated to one of amity, which he was only too happy to accommodate. This was not a journey which he contemplated with any type of enthusiasm, but it was now emerging to be something that was both enterprising and gratifying. It was now a prospect that brought him a modicum of satisfaction.

# JENNY

The breakfast room was filled to capacity, but there was no sign of Jessica. It was not entirely surprising to him since when he last saw her she lacked sparkle and was not brimful of good health the night before. However, being missing at lunchtime gave him reason for concern. In view of her absence, he decided it was time to investigate. Making the journey to her cabin, he was fortunate enough to see someone entering as he approached.

"One moment please." He called out. The young woman stopped at the door and turned to face Marcus with a strange degree of admiration and exuding antics that made her strikingly conspicuous. Her hair was short and shiny which gave the impression that it was plastered to her scalp. She was short, but made an effort to seem taller than her five foot three inches. She had lively eyes and a wicked smile.

"I believe there is a girl named Jessica in there. Could you ask her to come out and see me for a moment? My name is Marcus."

The young lady looked him over amorously and without replying, disappeared behind the closed door. Moments passed, long enough for Marcus to realise that he was in an environment that was somewhat prohibitive. The corridor was alive with activity, women moving to and fro, all of them giving the indication that he was the centre of attraction. Some were snaring, some giggling, others whispering in disgust at his presence. In a flash, it occurred to him that he was trespassing on territory that was exclusive to the opposite sex. Those moments of waiting began to multiply to a high degree of discomfort when the door suddenly opened once again and the young woman poked her head out. She looked at Marcus dispassionately. "She said she's not well enough to see you, but if you like you can come in for a minute."

Marcus was glad to see the young woman's face if only to remove himself from what he considered to be a hostile place. As he entered the room the young lady began to make her exit.

"Wait!" He announced as he unconsciously held her hand. "Please wait until I'm ready to leave. I will not be very long." He assured her as he released her hand.

Jessica was lying in bed as he entered; she was far from well but managed a weak smile.

"Hello Jessica, what is the matter with you?" He questioned.

Jessica sighed heavily. "I really don't know. Since I saw you last, I have been feeling awful and these wretched conditions are not very helpful."

"Well, he assured her, the first two days are always the worst. Very soon you will forget you are on a floating vessel."

Jessica forced a feeble smile. "I hope you're right Marcus, this is an experience I never want to have again."

"I have some tablets which I'm sure will help. I'm certain they wouldn't half make you feel better."

"Wouldn't half make me feel better?" She quizzed.

"Oh, it's just another of those English terms which you'll hear from time to time."

She nodded in agreement. "No doubt I'll be hearing a lot more of them before I get to London."

Marcus chuckled politely as he turned to face the young woman. "Would you be so kind as to bring these tablets back here? I would hate to run the gauntlet as I did not so long ago." Gesticulating about the experience he encountered on his way in. The young woman still in some degree of admiration towards Marcus smiled warmly.

"Yes, I will do that favour for you."

A relieved Marcus turned to Jessica. "If you're not better by tomorrow, I'll have the ship's doctor look in on you." Marcus was out in a flash, the young woman right behind him.

"You're not supposed to be down here you know. This is the girl's dormitory." She giggled blissfully.

"No wonder I have been getting so many stares. But don't worry yourself I won't be repeating this trip in a hurry." He explained.

At last, they were out of harm's way with the young woman keeping pace. Her attention for the young soldier was still undiminished.

"My name is Jenny. Is she your girlfriend?" She enquired.

"No, not at all." He assured. "Jessica is her name, she seems a nice young lady and all I'm doing is giving her a helping hand."

"What happens when your wife finds out you've had a little bit on the side?" Jenny asked.

"With a bit of luck, she will never find out," Marcus announced mockingly.

Still ogling him with a high degree of adoration, she announced. "You are a very handsome man, do you know that?"

Marcus smiled coyly. "Steady on young lady, but the last time I checked that was far from the truth."

They arrived at an area of the ship that was a world apart from the dormitory that they left behind. The upper deck had a splendour of its own, something that did not escape the attention of Jenny. Marcus sat her down and hurried off to his quarters, arriving back as quickly as he could. Jenny Still, in awe of the surroundings Jenny exclaimed.

"How come you are up here? Are you rich or something?"

"No I'm not rich but I like a bit of comfort." He was quick to explain.

Still not happy with the answer she received she carried on.

"You don't fool me; you are some kind of a big shot. Not many black people travel like this."

"I agree." He replied. "But that does not make me a big shot as you put it."

"That woman that you're so keen on ..."

"Jessica, you mean?" He interrupted.

"Yes, Jessica! Are you positive she's not your bit on the side?"

"Absolutely not. The young lady needs help and that's what I'm doing, helping."

Jenny threw him another amorous look. "Would you have done the same for me?"

"Sure thing!" He answered. "If you were in the same situation, I would gladly assist, I'm a good person."

She chuckled. "Men are really funny. That Jessica is nothing but a bag of bones. If you're after a real woman take a look at me." She began with a slow twirl, as she gyrated her ample torso rhythmically, accentuating her natural assets to a maximum degree. Turning full circle as she did so, finishing with a big slap of her posterior. A demonstration that was as conspicuous in its display and one which was designed to excite the young soldier.

"Now that's what you call a woman and you can take me for a drink anytime." Jenny fawned.

Naturally, the exhibition did nothing to whet his appetite. If anything, it caused him to cringe with embarrassment, however, he was mindful of the young lady's sensitivity and did his utmost to show appreciation for her efforts.

Smiling impishly he declared. "Wow! You're quite a woman and I would bear that invitation in mind."

Marcus held her hand and placed the tablets in her grasp. "Now, be a nice young lady and take these tablets to poor Jessica and I promise I will not forget your offer."

Jenny smirked and gave a gracious bow as she sauntered off to do her errand, convinced of the fact that she had made an indelible mark on Marcus. Jenny departed and was almost out of sight when, as a reminder of her intentions, she further demonstrated with a significant swagger, designed primarily to emphasise her enormously prominent rump. But more especially; it was to create maximum impact on the young man. The kind he was hardly likely to forget. It was obvious that Jenny had an eye for adventure and Marcus seemed the ideal man for her exploits.

Travelling to the other side of the world, she was ready to make the journey as active, exciting and productive as she possibly could. She was convinced she had more to offer than Jessica, who she regarded as inferior in physical terms and was far less robust than she was. An advantage she hoped Marcus was willing to consider, and one she intended to pursue. He chuckled merrily to himself as Jenny disappeared around the bending corridor. Although far from impressed by her remarkable display – flaunting her assets in such a conspicuous manner – he nevertheless, appreciated her vanity and spunk for advancing her case so effectively. He fully realised it would not be an easy task to dissuade Jenny's advances, especially in an environment that was so restrictive. However, the Jenny's of this world never succeeded in the past. He was confident that he was more than capable of fending off any imminent challenges that Jenny may pose as far as romance was concerned. Jessica, on the other hand, demonstrated a totally different set of problems. Unlike Jenny, her situation required a measure of subtlety and patience. Being of a vulnerable disposition and very unsure about her future, he regarded his task towards her as something of a crusade. It was a mission that he felt obliged to pursue. This was an act of kindness that was capable of bringing great satisfaction, both to himself and to a very sensitive young woman who he was positive needed every ounce of assistance possible. That was exactly his only motive. As far as any other end product was concerned, there was none.

It was breakfast time and, as usual, everyone was preoccupied with the idea of filling their stomachs accordingly. The hive of activity was for once not of immediate importance to Marcus. He was primarily concerned for Jessica who he felt needed to be up and running for her own sake. Her frail and lanky physique was desperately in need of sustenance and he was prepared as best he could to give adequate attention to her needs, in the light of what he saw the night before.

# EMBARRASSING MOMENTS

The *SS Aracassa* was cruising in calmer waters now. The storm had subsided and the sun was shining brightly. Scanning the multitude of hungry travellers all rapidly moving towards the food hall, he at long last spotted Jessica. She was dressed in pink, an outfit that fitted her elegantly. Moving unhurriedly against the natural tide of people, she carried herself with a degree of poise that trickled graciously through her delicate frame. It was obvious she was a woman of resilience; in spite of her frailties, she was also able to show remarkable self-assurance. Marcus rushed down to meet her with a smile as bright as the morning sunshine.

"Good morning. I see you've recovered after all."

Jessica affected a warm smile, far less radiant than her companion's. "Yes, I'm still in the land of the living. At least I am still breathing."

He beckoned to her to follow him, a gesture that somehow did not appeal to her better judgment.

"We are going up. It's better for you upstairs." He hinted.

Jessica followed Marcus with some apprehension. Her best instincts told her she was heading in the direction of danger, but Marcus being who he was, someone who was strong, confident and very motivated, a person who easily inspired self-assurance, she decided very much against her will to heed his instructions. They sat in a quiet part of the upper hall, far removed from the jostle and commotion of those in the main hall below that accommodated the folks of a lower class. Jessica was wearing a look of timidity as she sat opposite Marcus, scanning the otherwise quiet and orderly surroundings with a furrowed brow. It immediately transpired to him that his companion was ill at ease and decided to put her worries to rest with a broad grin.

"Relax my dear; you are in very good hands."

Jessica merely stared at Marcus as if he was speaking a language she did not understand.

"What a change has come over you. Yesterday was a complete washout and today you look a million dollars." He intimated.

Jessica looked relatively uncomfortable but tried her best to be at ease. Marcus noticed this change in her body language. Her grey eyes had a touch of sparkle in them that complemented her exquisite features. She was not a vision of loveliness, but there was no mistaking the fact that her potential for being so could hardly have been missed. Her innocent and simplistic nature made her curiously appealing. She was a pleasantly amiable young woman with admirable traits. Even though the relationship was relatively brief, Marcus was convinced that there was an element of symmetry between them.

That in his mind could only be to the benefit of them both. Realising his remark was meant to be no more than flattery, Jessica shook her head negatively.

"I do not feel a million dollars at the moment, but I cannot deny I'm feeling a lot better today."

"Guess I was right after all," Marcus replied. "It was nothing more than a touch of sea sickness. As I said, the first two days are always the worst."

"Whatever it was I'm still grateful for your help." She answered.

"Think nothing of it." He replied looking around impatiently for breakfast, which seemed long in coming. "I'm starving at the moment and I hope you feel the same. I'm sure eating a bit of food would do you a power of good." He hinted.

"Well, I'm not really hungry, but I guess I need to eat something, if only for my health." She muttered.

Suddenly the waiter arrived accompanied by a steward. It was obvious that their attention was directed towards Jessica and

Marcus. Reaching the couple, they stopped abruptly. "Excuse me sir, but do you have upper deck booking?" The steward asked in a somewhat stringent manner.

Marcus looked up. "Yes, if you must know, I am a first class passenger."

Still somewhat impatient, the steward directed his attention to Jessica. "And you madam, have you the same?"

Jessica was flushed with embarrassment, especially since the dining hall was now full and the stares were many. This was not what she wanted; although she anticipated her move to the upper deck was most likely to prove problematic. Recalling the unfortunate trauma she had experienced only a few short hours ago, saved only by the patient and caring nature of Marcus, she was once more in a predicament of a different kind, it was nonetheless equally humiliating. She half rose to leave but was gently and firmly persuaded to be seated by Marcus.

He swiftly got to his feet. "Any questions you require to be answered would be done by me. Ask me what you want, but leave the young lady alone. Do you understand?" He raged.

"The young lady can speak for herself." The steward persisted. "Allow me to do my job, if you don't mind"

"And I'm telling you to address your questions to me." Marcus snapped.

"Look! I am trying to establish why the young lady is not where she should be." He gestured pointing to the lower deck.

Marcus looked about him quickly and then redirected his attention towards the two men. "Tell me." He blurted out. "Why did you pick on us? Are we that conspicuous? Or do you think that black folks should not be up here? Have you a personal agenda or something?"

"No." The steward replied impatiently. "But my job is to see that everyone is in their right place."

"Then get on with what you have to do and leave decent people alone." Marcus retorted.

"I cannot do that. I must be allowed to do what I'm paid to do." The steward responded in frustration. "Which means you'll leave me no choice, and I will be forced to call my superior." He turned his back and disappeared out of sight.

This was not a golden moment for Jessica. Her shame was now total. She could not look up for fear that her presence was causing tension she did not consider necessary. She knew instantly she was the centre of attention and was now convinced this environment carried a degree of hostility she was not sure she could handle. However, this was her companion's call and it was in her best interest to give him support. The moments passed slowly, the buzz around the hall was distinct. This was enough to give Jessica food for thought that she was on the wrong side of this particular argument.

She looked up only to observe the young waiter and steward returning with their supervisor, moving briskly and somewhat confidently to pursue further confrontation, the kind she did not feel Marcus had the faintest chance of winning. Alongside them was the chief steward, a clean cut bespectacled man, with a smile that appeared more theatrical than real and a manner that can only be developed through the process of dealing with problematic matters. Suddenly he stopped and bowed gently. "What seems to be the problem?"

Marcus's anger was clearly apparent. "Are you really telling me, having been brought here by your colleagues you don't know what the problem is?"

The chief steward fixed his gaze on Marcus. He delayed his reply long enough to give breathing space to this delicate situation and chuckled politely.

"Okay, you're right." He conceded. "It was not appropriate for me to ask since I already knew what the matter was. Let's just see how best we can approach this problem and try to solve it."

"Look! I told your people I'm a first class passenger. A facility I'm prepared to abandon for the sake of my friend here. As you can see; the young lady is far from well, so I invited her here to get away from that hurly burly situation, which in my opinion she could not cope with. That did not appear to meet with the approval of your colleagues. Apparently, we were too conspicuous to miss. So far as they were concerned, they showed absolutely no consideration towards us whatsoever, even though I tried to explain."

The chief steward turned his gaze towards Jessica and nodded again." I agree; your friend does not seem very well, but you must understand our position, we are trying to run a tight ship and we need a degree of discipline in order to do so."

"Don't preach to me about discipline." Marcus raged. "I've spent many years as a soldier and I know what discipline is all about."

The chief steward smiled pleasantly. "Oh good! Then we can have a civilised conversation. The way I see it; this matter is not unsolvable. Like you, I was also a soldier. Let us proceed in a sensible manner and try to knock this silly problem on its head."

Marcus could not help being impressed by the way the situation was handled by the steward. He looked at the man in front of him long and hard before exhaling. "Look it's plain to see what I'm trying to do here. I'm trying to help someone who needs assistance. You seem reasonable enough for me to say this; my friend has been going through a torrid time. I only met her yesterday. As you can see, she's quite young and very much out of her depth. I'm only out to fulfil a humanitarian purpose. This is a novel experience for her. She cannot withstand the hustle and bustle of those folks downstairs because of her condition."

"That was an excellent gesture on your part, but you have to give consideration to my people, who are trying to do what they are paid to do."

"I certainly have no problem with that." Marcus frowned. "What I very much resent was their attitude."

The steward looked at the young waiter seriously. "You have to give a bit of latitude to the young. Very often they suffer from over-exuberance."

He studied the situation for a while before he spoke again. "Since you are a first class passenger and your heart seems to be in the right place; I'm prepared to make a decision that I hope both of you will be satisfied with."

He pointed to a quieter area of the deck. "Will you follow me please?"

Reaching an appropriate section of the diner he stopped, giving Jessica his fullest attention.

"Young lady, I brought you here because I wanted you to be away from prying eyes. Will this accommodation suit you?"

Jessica's eyes lit up. This was, without doubt, a triumph for her. "Yes, yes this is just fine."

The steward then turned to Marcus. "And would this be convenient for you and your companion for the rest of the journey sir?"

"If the lady is happy, then I guess I am too." A more relaxed Marcus replied.

"You must understand sir; this is not something I'm prepared to do every day of the week. However, I'm making an exception for the sake of good relations. I'm happy we can solve this matter amicably." He bowed gently and with a swift arc, he beckoned the others to follow.

Marcus, still aggrieved, slowly descended into his seat. The strain of the situation overwhelmed Jessica to the point of tears. Marcus reached over and touched her hand in a reassuring manner.

"Come on Jessie it's not as bad as all that, it's just a storm in a teacup."

"It may not be for you but I'm not used to all this fuss." She whispered.

"This is nothing to upset yourself about. The only reason why I was so mad was simply because of the attitude of those guys. They showed us absolutely no respect."

Jessica sighed heavily and wiped the tears away. "It's all my fault. Since I met you I've been nothing but trouble for you. I'm so sorry for all the unnecessary stress."

"Nonsense." He remarked. "Those men were trying to throw their weight about and I'm just not prepared to let that happen."

"I can't blame them; they're only trying to do their jobs." She reasoned.

"What about trying to do it properly? Anyway, it's all history now." He concluded.

Jessica nodded approvingly.

The morning passed without any further histrionics. Marcus ate sumptuously, Jessica less so. Marcus smiled broadly. "That was good." He muttered. "A pity you're not a glutton like me."

"I'm fine with food. It's just that I have not been eating well lately." Jessica announced.

"I do hope your appetite will return soon." He looked her up and down. "Your body could do with some filling out."

"I was not always like this," Jessica remarked. "I have lost a lot of weight lately. It's all to do with these issues I have with my father."

"Well! I'm not one for prying." Smiling faintly as he said so. "But if you want a shoulder to cry on, I'm always here."

Jessica beamed broadly. "I believe that you have done more than your fair share since we have met, don't you think?"

"Nothing is ever enough. What I'm trying to do, is to give you the benefit of my experience, which incidentally comes freely." He insisted.

"Then you must be a glutton for punishment, but I'll bear it in mind." She concluded.

Marcus shook Jessica's hand. "Well okay, we'll have a contract on that."

# HEADING HOME

Eight days into the journey had simply slipped away. The giant ship, the *SS Aracassa* was heading towards its destination with rapid efficiency and appeared to be right on schedule. It was a fine day. Passengers were out in force to make use of the conditions that were ideal in all its splendour. The sun was shining with great purpose. White clouds drifting slowly across a brilliant blue sky, accompanied by a soft and gentle breeze. This was as fine as nature intended. Looking at the far horizon, however, it was easy to be deceived by the lowness of the sky. It was as if large chunks of it would fall into the vast ocean and disappear into oblivion. But alas it was nothing more than an optical illusion that intrigues the mind and fires the imagination. This was a fine exhibition of the planets gift to mankind.

Sitting on the deck alongside Marcus, Jessica felt a degree of delight. It was if she was responding to the wonderful atmosphere that engulfed them. She was experiencing a sense of relative ease, an indication of the difference she felt now, against the backdrop of situations that were far from ideal, not so long ago. That brought a wry smile to her face. It was one of contentment over adversity, which threatened her very existence in a considerable way, episodes that now seem to be in the distant past. She cringed at the thought of the nightmare that almost decimated her life and brought her to a place of destruction and grief. Remembering Marcus; who was her saving grace which brought her comfort. She was fully aware that he made this day possible. The overwhelming change that turned her life around was none other than this stranger that was sitting down beside her. That person was Marcus Gullant. His strength of purpose, his thoughtfulness and his humanity in helping her, exceeded any description possible. What was unique above everything else was his willingness to assist with no hidden agenda. All of which seemed stranger than fiction to her.

It was now time to process what was in store for her and her new task ahead. She was heading for a place which held a degree of fear for her. It was larger than life and an existence that was way outside of her scope of thought. However, this was reality and it needed urgent consideration. Her new found spirit and self-confidence was undoubtedly a result of meeting this complete stranger, giving her a new perspective, the kind that can only be to her best advantage. So far as priority goes, Jessica had long acknowledged that the friendship between Marcus and herself could only gather momentum. She was positive she needed it and although it was comparatively new, she was not about to question the quality of it. Was he genuine? Was he worthy of her trust? That answer was in her estimation very positive. So far as she was concerned, he was the epitome of excellence. Her vision and reflection were now on Cleveland, her cousin. Much depended on his outlook, but more importantly his attitude towards her. A thought that gave her jitters, considering they had not met for a number of years. Would he possess the patience and resourcefulness that was equal to Marcus? Only time would tell and she was hardly in the mood to speculate what the future would hold.

The calm but compelling vista that clearly dominated the day induced more than a degree of fascination for Jessica. She looked around in quiet contemplation, observing the joy and happiness of so many who were benefiting from the grandeur of the moment that only nature can provide. "Isn't this a most amazing day Marcus? Can we not have this forever?" She uttered.

"If only." He responded. "But reality tells us that we can only accept those gifts of nature with gratitude and move on."

"And leave all this behind?" She announced, spreading her arms as if to encompass the general surroundings.

Marcus chuckled warmly. "It's such a wonderful day, but we should not overindulge."

"Whatever do you mean?" She echoed amusingly. "Why can we not have a touch of the good things in life forever?"

"I wish I knew the answer to that, but as you know nothing in our world is static."

"That's true." She conceded. "Which brings me to another question; I know it's none of my business, but can I ask you something personal?"

Marcus assumed a quizzical expression. "I guess you can, but do not make it too difficult."

"Are you a man of means?" She enquired.

"Oh no, whatever gave you that impression?" A surprised Marcus asked.

"Well, you are a First Class passenger. You must be able to afford that."

"Look! I would be lying to you if I say I'm broke, the simple truth is, when I took my kids home, I went First Class; I wanted them to be comfortable; so it's only natural that I return the same way."

"Jenny told me that you are rich. She was boasting how you made promises to her. She thinks you are Prince Charming."

Marcus giggled mirthfully. "Are you kidding; that young lady is amusing. I guess she fancies herself a bit."

"I really don't know, but she kept on about you wanting to take her for a drink. She definitely has eyes for you."

"Jessie." Replied Marcus still amused. "Jenny is just looking for a bit of fun. Unfortunately, I am not in the business of messing about with young ladies. If I'm to be truthful, I'm a rather peculiar man when it comes to the opposite sex. I do have a strict and abiding principle and girls of that age really do not interest me. She's way too young anyhow."

Jessica swallowed hard. Jenny was older than her by far and it was strange for him to have made such a distinction.

"I understand that, but it's hardly fair to make promises you cannot keep."

VICTOR WALDRON

He looked at her pensively. "In my village, there is a saying: 'Easy lesson is good for a dunce'."

"So tell me this dear sir; why is your attitude towards women so stringent? I cannot pretend that I know a lot about you, but the way you express yourself about the opposite sex has me very puzzled."

Marcus's scowl was very obvious. "Jessica! Let me make it very clear. I do have a lot of time for women. However, I'm not sure this is the time to discuss the pros and cons of it." He insisted.

"Forgive me for being so intrusive," Jessica replied apologetically, fearing she may have upset present company. She smiled indulgently. Marcus's response was less so. A lull ensued, enough to make Jessica rather uncomfortable. Deciding to break the impasse, she stood up and gazed into the vast ocean. "There's water, water everywhere and not a drop to drink."

Indeed, that is so true." He announced. "We are now in the serious business of getting to the other end of the pond."

"This is a world of its own. It's like nothing I've ever experienced."

Marcus agreed. "How right you are. We are in the middle of nowhere."

Jessica looked at Marcus meaningfully. "Would I be right in saying you are a very brave man?"

"What on earth brought that on?" He enquired.

"Well the way you tackled those men that morning, it must have taken a lot of courage to confront them."

"Oh, that was no problem. Actually, you learn to live with these little upheavals; it becomes second nature like most other things."

She emitted a nervous giggle. "You must be something of an enigma. One minute you were in conflict with them, the next minute it was like it never happened. How do you explain that?"

"Because it was nothing more than what it was, run of the mill. The reason why I bollocked those men was because of their attitude. They deserve to show respect, especially to folk like us."

"You can't blame them, Marcus, they were doing what they were paid to do." She reminded him.

Marcus gave her a serious look. "My dear, now that you are going to live in London, it will not take you long to find out that being black in a world of white folks is not an advantage. I'm an old soldier – believe me, I know what I'm talking about."

"Well that's all very new to me; I'm not accustomed to such things."

"I guess not." He declared. "But my advice to you is to get used to such matters very quickly. Living in a big city is so different from what you know. It's not picking cherries. You would have to face up to and defend yourself if you want to survive."

"You make it sound as though London is a war zone." She remarked timidly.

"No it's not, but it is not your typical country lane either. Life is different, attitudes change, it's a lesson you should learn and quickly." Marcus offered readily.

"Are you sure Marcus that you're not trying to make me very nervous?"

"That is not my intention Jessica. I simply want you to be aware of what to expect. If you cannot change or stand strong in defence of your own interest, then you might as well ask the captain to put you off at the next port so you can get back home."

Jessica did not reply, she merely stared into the vast ocean wearing a look of apprehension.

"Look, Jessie, I'm not trying to scare you, I just want you to know London is no bed of roses. Anyway, you are going to family. That's half the battle won. He will make sure you are well looked after."

"I sincerely hope so." She replied cheerfully.

"By the way, what is the name of your cousin?" He enquired.

"His name is Cleveland Darnel."

"And what is he doing in London? Do you know?"

"Cleveland is studying dentistry." She responded positively.

"In that case, providing he's studying, he should be near the end of his discipline by now. It does not take six years to become a dentist."

Jessica was quite stunned by the remark. Cleveland was considered the brightest spark in the family. He was an excellent student and someone who had shown early ambition to succeed. It would be utterly unimaginable to think that the opposite was the case, especially since his father was constantly giving positive updates on his son's progress. "Whatever do you mean by that remark? Cleveland is a very intelligent young man. I simply cannot see him being less than the successful person that he's striving to be. He's ambitious and extremely serious about life."

Marcus was slow in replying. Almost reluctant to pursue the point he was trying to make. Fearing his young companion may misconstrue its proper meaning. Being an old hand in a city that was very often most unforgiving to newcomers, more especially people of colour, he was only demonstrating to her the real problems that could arise. A quick glance told him everything he needed to know. Jessica's frown was one of surprised anger.

"Jessica! I mean no disrespect to your cousin, but very often, ambitious people find London an exacting and very tough city to make genuine progress. That is the unfortunate truth."

"You seem to have made it. Why do you think others can't?"

"I would be the very last person to cast aspersions on anyone. I simply was not built that way. What I was trying to illustrate to you was the simple fact that London is a tough nut to crack and many people with good intentions have fallen by the wayside. As for me – making it – mine was a combination of grit and absolutely good fortune. Not everyone gets a winning hand like I did."

"Well, you are wrong about Cleveland. I know him well. He is definitely someone with the ability and the will to succeed."

"Well, with that being the case," Marcus responded. "I will be the first to congratulate the young man for his efforts if at all we meet. Tell me." Marcus continued. "Did you communicate with Cleveland to let him know you were coming? I know it may seem a silly question to ask."

"I'm afraid not. I did not have the time to do that. It was my dad who arranged it." She answered. "Left to me, I would not be on this ship."

"It sounds to me as though all of this was done in haste."

Jessica did not respond. Her furrowed brow depicted stress that Marcus was consciously or otherwise, eliciting on her. It was obvious also that Jessica was not a hardy type of individual, so he decided a lighter vain of conversation should suffice.

"Life is not always black and white and very often we misunderstand how this thing works. Take yours truly, for instance, I came to England at the most dangerous time you could imagine. It was said that the Germans were sinking ships in the Caribbean Sea, a time when brave men lost their nerve to man these ships, but I did it." He paused for a moment. "The strangest thing about it was that I ignored the perils of that experience and the only thoughts I had in mind then, was where I wanted to be. For me, the British Army beckoned and my objective was to become a soldier come what may. I left my country Guiana full of purpose and determination and nothing or no one was going to stand in my way."

"So you are Guianese; I wondered where you came from."

Marcus offered a broad smile. "Right first time Jessie, I am from Guiana." He paused momentarily. "You know what was funny? When I landed in England, no one knew where Georgetown, the Garden City was. I would say, 'I am Guianese' to the natives and they would respond, 'you mean Ghana?' It was not easy to convince people that such a place existed."

Jessica giggled heartily. "Are you kidding? Everyone knows where Trinidad is."

"That's correct and everyone should know where Georgetown is. Unfortunately, it's not always the case."

"You have been away from your country for quite a while. So do you miss it?" She enquired.

"Of course I do. It's a part of me. There are some things I long for, however, I see myself as a Londoner now. It has given me everything that I wanted." He stopped briefly and smiled. "With one exception; I miss my mother's excellent cooking. If only I could transport her to London, I would do it without any hesitation."

"Well, why don't you?" She asked.

"Young lady! No crane is big enough to move my mother away from the village. Anyway, she's doing a wonderful job caring for my two angels. She's a very proud Grandmother, going to church on a Sunday morning with her two adoring grandchildren. Take it from me; it's really wonderful to see."

Jessica paused momentarily. "Your children obviously mean a lot to you don't they?"

"They are the only good thing I have from a broken marriage and I intend to give them my undivided attention." He uttered solemnly.

Jessica, observing her older companion, smiled wistfully. "Marcus I do not know anything about you, but from what I can see, you appear to be a very remarkable person. You seem so sure of yourself. It's a fine quality. If only I was as strong as you are. I would love to possess your confidence."

"Well." He uttered ruefully. "The people around me when I was growing up were disciplinarians, especially my parents who were very strict. Then there was my Godmother Nanny May, who ruled with an iron fist, but I'm not complaining. So when I joined the Army, it helped me a great deal to withstand the pressures which I experienced from the very outset. The truth is I have learned how to be tough."

"You know Marcus," Jessica explained, chuckling to herself. "You made a fine assessment of me. My life has been a very sheltered one. I guess I have a lot to learn. I came straight out of college and into the teaching profession, now this."

"Never mind." He responded amusingly. "You have lots in your favour. You are young, intelligent and attractive. With a little bit of help and some experience, the sky could be the limit."

She offered a weak smile. "Marcus you continue to amaze me for the short time that I've known you, there seems to be different sides to you.

Marcus shook his head in agreement. "I guess I'm a bit unpredictable. That is the impression I give, but why should I be a robot? I am what I am and that will always be the case."

"So where do you live in London? Is it far away from Highbury where I'm going?"

"It is far enough if you do not drive. He declared. "For me, it would be less than an hour on wheels."

Jessica studied her companion momentarily. "You see Marcus, that's the mystery. I'm of the opinion you have your own home; you drive a car; you travel First Class; you can hardly be considered as ordinary and yet you deny that you are not well off."

"I hate to shatter your illusion about me." He replied giggling heartily. "But I can assure you I am not anywhere close to what you think."

"Well I would never accuse you of lying, but there are things that do not add up. For instance, you have everything a man could desire. On top of that, you are handsome, honest, generous and you are extremely confident. I dare say you could have any amount of women falling at your feet and yet you give me the impression that women are taboo. How do you explain that?"

"Thank you for the superlatives, but mine is simply a case of once bitten twice shy."

"Would I be correct in saying that your marriage was a bad experience?"

"It was in a word disastrous." He uttered. "But it was not for the want of trying on my part."

"I'm so sorry to hear that, but it is often said you should not dwell on things that give you pain." Jessica intoned in a conciliatory manner.

"That is so easy to say and so difficult to do." He retorted.

"Well, you are a very resilient man. I cannot imagine any problem is insurmountable to you."

"High praise indeed." He replied sarcastically. "I can see that you're using your skills as a teacher on me. But there are problems even Marcus Gullant is incapable of solving."

"Coming from you, I find that hard to believe." She intimated.

Marcus turned slowly to face his young companion. "Have you ever had the pleasure of being in love?"

This time it was Jessica's turn to be reticent. It was a question she was not prepared to give a total or conclusive answer to, for fear that it may jeopardise her at some future point. It was therefore expedient to be as economical with the truth as much as possible, merely to be on the safe side of this discussion. After all, it was love that got her into her present predicament. It all began with her rapid and profound friendship with local boy Alan Bray. He was a young and very handsome man with a notorious reputation and an avid appetite for the opposite sex. Alan was a slick operator, with silky skills and an infectious charm, coupled with an appealing but compelling personality. It was obvious to Jessica that the friendship was fraught with danger.

Since the general perception that circulated far and wide indicated clearly that Alan was a predator. In spite of such information, Jessica, who found Alan irresistible and a breath of fresh air was quite prepared to take the risk. She was also aware that Alan fathered children, with girls that he discarded with impunity. Unfortunately so excited was she about the relationship, his activities did not deter her from keeping his company. Jessica's father Alvin got word that romance was in the air and his daughter was to become a victim of this charismatic playboy, hell bent on seeking new game. Desperate to avoid such a calamitous situation from taking root, Alvin took immediate steps to dispatch Jessica to London where she was to become guest of her cousin Cleveland. That fundamentally was the crux of the situation. Cleveland was hardly regarded as a close relative.

Because of a family feud, which caused a rift in the relationship, he became somewhat remote. As a result, he was less frequent with his visits. Added to the fact that he had been away for a number of years, she figured identifying him could pose something of a challenge. Being uncertain made her less confident in recognising him, as he may have changed in features or appearance. That raised the spectre of fear, panic and confusion. Emotions so acute, it almost brought her to the depths of despair. Here she was, in a position where she was suddenly deprived of love, taking a journey she did not bargain for, finding a cousin she hardly knew and travelling to a large city she felt unable to cope with. These problems that confronted her and which gave her grief were to a large extent undesirable. Fortunately, the timely intervention of Marcus saved her from a place too dark to contemplate. He was in no uncertain terms and according to his own statement, her knight in shining armour. She was therefore nowhere ready to tempt fate or reveal more than she needed to.

"Yes." She informed. "I met someone I cared about, but things did not go according to plan. My dad did not approve."

"What was the matter with him? Too old or was he married?"

"Oh no, he was a young man, but my dad did not think he was suitable."

"Then what was the problem? Was he a ladies' man? Someone who always played the field?"

"I guess you can say so. Lots of girls found him attractive."

"That's exactly what I imagined Jessie. Experience told me when I saw you that evening on board. I figured something was fundamentally wrong. You were in an extreme state of panic. It all pointed in the direction that your departure was done in haste. Would I be correct?"

Jessica took a deep breath before answering. It was rather uncanny how Marcus was able to predict her plight. "That was very much the case. There's hardly any point denying that things were a bit rushed."

Marcus observed immediately that Jessica was uncomfortable with the subject matter and decided to change course. "Well you know what they say; parents always seem to know best. My folks were exactly the same. They were totally against me getting involved with Teresa and I was a fully grown adult. Even though I was supposed to know what I wanted."

"I imagine that they see things that we can't see." She informed.

"A very good point," Marcus assured her. "In view of what happened, I must applaud my mother's wisdom, she was right and I was wrong."

He paused briefly before continuing. "Anyway my circumstances were quite unique. When I went back to my hometown, I was treated like a film star. I was returning just after the war. I believed that I was at the pinnacle of my life; I had achieved great things for myself, I was indeed a man of status; which I acquired in a relatively short number of years. I had a beautiful home, a lovely car, I was a qualified engineer with an excellent job; you can say I was the proverbial self-made man; so when I told my mother of my intentions – you know, wanting to marry Teresa, she almost had a seizure. To her, that woman was taboo."

"But why is that?" Jessica questioned. "Was Teresa not good enough for you?"

"On the contrary, it's quite the opposite." He informed. "She felt I was about to cross that unbridgeable social divide." He paused momentarily to gather his thoughts. "You see Jessica, the village where I came from, I was not regarded highly. We were a poor family, that placed us in the category of the ordinary. What was extraordinary looking back; I have to concede that it was the most unrealistic and ambitious thing that I ever attempted. I fell in love with the daughter of our village elite. I was about twelve years old when I first saw her. Here was I down here and she was up there and it would have been a miracle of all miracles to bring us together. In other words, it was nothing less than pie in the sky. She was totally unreachable. The problem was that the class distinction, according to village views, was too much for me to overcome."

Jessica listened with some fascination. "That's interesting. Wasn't that the woman you got married to?"

Marcus shook his head affirmatively. "Yes, you are correct. That's why I keep insisting that anything is possible."

Jessica giggled impishly. "You know Marcus this all sounds like a fairytale, are you sure you're not making it up?"

"Do I look like that kind of a person?" He answered very seriously.

"No, I don't imagine so." She replied apologetically. "So how did that relationship come together?"

Marcus looked at her positively. "In a way you're right, it was something of a fairytale. Initially, when I left the village, I figured the dream would end. I thought I could get over the fantasy and the feeling would soon subside. Strangely enough; that was not the case. My love for Teresa grew like a healthy flower on a summer's day. She was in my head, in my heart and it was as if she consumed my very soul."

"What are you saying, Marcus? Is anyone's love that real?"

"For me it was; every living day of it. You may find it hard to believe, but that is what I experienced. However, ironically as it may seem, thinking about her as constant as I did drove me on. It gave me the impetus and driving force to achieve things and to be the man I am today."

"That's an incredible story and you are an incredible man, but it cannot be to your advantage to dwell on the past." Jessica reminded him.

Marcus was now in a sombre mood. He shook his head negatively. "It's not what I want and it's certainly not what I worked so hard for. I gave my marriage every bit of my energy just to hold things together, but unfortunately, it failed and by extension so have I."

"Nonsense!" Jessica rebuked. "I do not know a great deal about you, but given what I do know it is not difficult to observe how strong and inspirational you are."

Marcus raised a weak smile. "I cannot quarrel with much of what you say, but losing out on love as I did damages your confidence going forward."

"Look at you." She reminded him. "You're still a young handsome man with everything to live for and whatever failings you may have had in the past, you most certainly have the resilience and the quality to put it behind you."

His smile grew wider than previously. "You have a way with words for someone so young. I guarantee you would have made an excellent career as a school teacher."

That comment brought a slight blush to his young companion. "You are not too bad yourself. Teaching me the language of

London, such as 'not half', 'ta' and 'bollocked', which is quite educational."

Marcus gave a willing smile. "My dear, you're going to cockney land and it's important that you learn the lingo. It will do you a power of good."

They both giggled like kids.

Jessica was most intrigued if not mesmerised by the account of her companions failed marriage, especially someone like Marcus. With him being the primary factor in this compelling saga. In her estimation and as far as she could imagine, he was someone who showed characteristics of immense repute. A man with qualities more in keeping with bringing things together; a man who unites, rather than one who divides. Marriage in her opinion becomes estranged when one or the other transgresses, therefore it was imperative for him to reveal more, even if it was only to satisfy her avid curiosity.

"Why are the kids with you? Isn't it customary for the woman to take them when the relationship dissolves? How come you have them?"

Marcus gave her a forlorn look. "Teresa was a master class when it comes to beauty, but sadly that did not permeate into other areas of business. If truth be told, she was one of the most irresponsible women I have ever met. But most of all she was not maternal."

For the first time, Marcus showed emotions of anger. He delved into his pocket and produced pictures of Sara and Peter and handed them to Jessica.

"Look at these kids, aren't they wonderful?"

Jessica agreed immediately. Without a doubt they were stunning children. "You have beautiful kids Marcus. If it was me I would not exchange them for the world."

"That's what everyone says, yet for her, these children were non-existent. She does not have the instinct of a mother. Forever reminding me that they were my kids and she never let me forget it."

"But who in their right mind would not want to have such cuties; that's absolutely absurd." Jessica expressed.

Marcus was trying his level best to remain calm. "I guess you have to know Teresa to understand her. To be totally frank she did not want children. That essentially was the problem and it was substantially the reason why our marriage collapsed. She maintained that I could not be trusted."

"Judging by what you said, it appears as though you have broken a pledge."

Marcus acknowledged. "Actually I did. It was one promise I did not keep. She was adamant about not wanting kids."

"Then Marcus, you are not entirely without blame," Jessica concluded.

"My dear if only you knew the lengths I took merely to keep this marriage alive. Believe me when I tell you that sacrifices were made, but that was to no avail. In my book, marriages without kids are incomplete."

"Well Marcus I can understand that, but the damage is now done and it's hardly worth you feeling sorry for yourself. What's past is past." Jessica explained readily.

Marcus studied Jessica momentarily. "Do you know something? I have not told anyone the things I have told you. I have conceded more to you than my dear mother."

"That's because you needed someone neutral to talk to; isn't that so?"

"Quite right you are." He paused briefly as if to consider his words. "The fundamental mistake I made was to take myself too seriously. My ego got in the way of common sense. I returned to the village with the perception that I was more important than I actually was. After achieving a great deal in a large city, I believed I was lord of the manor. Socially I imagined I was on par with everyone; I can look anyone in the eye. Why? Because I did it all and I was proud of my achievements. What I did not bargain for was the fact that Teresa was not impressed with anything I did. Remember her folks had everything. They were the cream of the crop and even though I came back a successful soldier, in their eyes; they still regarded me as the little boy with his arse hanging out not so long ago. For them nothing had changed, they felt I was punching above my weight." He lamented.

"But you know how difficult it is to alter attitudes, especially in small communities."

"I understand that now." He responded. "Perhaps I was too confident in myself and ignored the dangers of being over ambitious."

"Do you think that you overstepped the mark?" She questioned.

Marcus chuckled sardonically. "I overlooked the obvious. Teresa's background was vastly different to mine. Her folks had everything and we had nothing. The idea of Teresa and myself getting together as husband and wife was simply impossible to contemplate. However, the fact that I returned from London after the war a relatively successful man and Teresa was still single, I began to nurture this very compelling notion that perhaps this was meant to be; that fate had once again dealt me a winning hand. It was an opportunity I could not resist."

"Without knowing how Teresa felt, how could you be sure she was attracted to you?"

"It would be difficult to say, she did not show the same degree of affection, since it was a period in my life when I felt indestructible! When I believed all things were possible, the truth was, I did not envisage failure of any kind. What I was not paying attention to, was that social divide between us and the massive gulf that existed."

"So when did you become conscious of that?" She questioned.

"It was when I began to make positive advances." He explained. "Teresa had a wide choice of the most eligible men in the community. Her parents favoured her marrying a doctor, something she never wanted to do. Just then, I came along and gave her the chance she needed and without a doubt she used it clinically. This was a case of expediency at its most ruthless. She needed a way out; an escape route and I gave it to her on a platter. What confounded me no end was how she always totally ignored her children. I was aware that she did not want children, but having got them, how could she behave as though they never existed?"

"I cannot answer that question, Marcus. Only Teresa can give you the reasons for that. Maybe she was not ready for kids at the time." She remarked.

"I'm told a woman's affinity grows stronger in every way when it comes to her children, it's such a compelling force that they cannot disregard it. That is why I believed she would return."

Jessica shook her head negatively, she was sure Marcus was not being realistic. In her estimation, this was a clear case of being in denial.

"When I approached her in earnest her folks went absolutely ballistic. Teresa's people thought I was beneath them in status and they believed that interacting with someone like me belittled her. They believed there was a question of social boundaries to cross and in their estimation, I fell short of the mark." Marcus admitted.

"In other words, you were not sophisticated enough or they believed you were lacking in social grace?" She asked with interest.

"Exactly." He responded readily. "However the one thing we had in common was restlessness. She was tired of being confined, which finally took its toll. Her parents got very much in the way of her career prospects. Teresa had ambitions of achieving her goals and not being tied up with marriage. Perhaps it was a question of timing because that's where I came in."

"So are you suggesting you influenced her decision making?" Jessica asked.

"Well, we spoke about lots of issues and I found out she wanted to escape from her present environment to study architecture. I guess I may have fantasised the benefits of going to London and appealed to her better nature to consider my proposal." Marcus confided.

"I guess that was very helpful for her, did you convince her?" She quizzed.

Marcus smiled warmly. "I would say that is a million dollar question. At the very inception, she had her doubts, but I persuaded her to take the opportunity I was offering. My promise to her was substantial. If she married me she would reap the benefits of studying and doing anything else that would make her happy. I assured her I would be a dutiful husband in every conceivable way. She saw it as an opportunity for her, rather than what I would derive from it. Generally, it must have impressed her because she finally succumbed to my wishes."

"So tell me, Marcus, where did you go wrong?" Jessica enquired.

Marcus puffed his cheeks out and exhaled slowly. It was obvious by the expression on his face that Teresa was still very fresh in his thoughts. "Hindsight is a wonderful quality. You see, Jessica, the phrase, 'be careful what you wish for', was appropriate in my situation. I surrendered my life to a prima donna. She was a woman who cared very little for anyone else other than herself. Once she had achieved her objective, she became massively indifferent to all else. She is someone who is motivated only by her own needs. Immediately after qualifying as an architect she found a job, bought a car and the rest was history."

"How so? What do you mean by that?"

"I meant her antics and behaviour were most unbecoming. It was as if there was no tomorrow. She seemed to have forgotten she was a married woman with responsibilities."

He stopped abruptly, stress etched on his face as if it was only yesterday. Moments of complete silence prevailed until he regained his composure. Marcus offered Jessica an ironic chuckle. "Strangely enough I do not see myself as a loser, far from it; I boxed in the Army and I was triumphant. I showed a pedigree of pure excellence, beating everyone who was put in front of me. I was regarded very highly. Folks believed in me; they told me the sky was the limit, yet I lost this battle to little old Jonny Bellaw." He stared blankly into space; his countenance was a grotesque mask of emotions. "I won all of my fights, but ironically I lost to love. Jonny was the guy that my wife fell in love with and he happened to be white."

Jessica was both surprised and moved by the unfortunate course of events. Especially to someone like Marcus, a man she hardly knew yet she was the recipient of extreme kindness and commitment from him. It was not difficult to imagine the lengths he would go to secure the love that he had for Teresa. That investment came to an inglorious end, shattering the hopes and aspirations of a man undeserving of such treatment.

"Oh Marcus, that was awful. It's most unforgivable." She replied sympathetically.

"That's what I thought. At first I imagined that she would come to her senses; that logic would prevail, but apparently, love has no logic."

"I cannot tell you how bad I feel for you." Jessica offered.

Marcus smiled weakly. "I'm afraid the damage is done. I should have taken notice of folks telling me about Teresa, especially my sister Adel. She was telling me repeatedly Teresa was flirting with this white boy. At the time I regarded it as tittle-tattle. I knew how much my sister hated Teresa and I paid no heed to her warnings. However, you live and learn and that is a fact."

Suddenly there was a terrific blast of the ship's horn, creating an unusual degree of excitement on board.

"Why did they do that? Jessica asked startled by the noise.

"I haven't a clue; although I have heard from time to time that folk jump off the ship for a swim." He joked to lighten the mood.

Jessica hesitated for a while, before seeing the funny side of her companion's sense of humour. "That was not very nice." She announced with a giggle.

# GROWING FRIENDSHIP

As the days progressed, Marcus and Jessica shared amicable moments together that welded their friendship in a very tangible way which had commenced more by accident than design. However, it merited from the natural ingredients of respect and admiration for each other. In the grand scheme of things, a more than healthy degree of compatibility existed between them.

For Jessica, the relationship held a greater advantage for her than she could have imagined. It was indeed a saving grace in the light of the situation, moving her from a state of total disarray to a more satisfactory mode of deportment. Her worry of finding her relative in London was no more burdensome, giving her the time to think of other things, such as her lover Alan Bray, who she was forced to depart from hurriedly. Hers was a romance that was beginning to develop and may have blossomed, had it not been for the sudden disruption that occurred.

She was very fond of Alan, despite his wild ways, and wondered if it would have been a success. That, however, was now a matter of speculation and did not merit further consideration, since Alan had never contemplated leaving his homeland for any other place. He was extremely territorial by nature and was very comfortable that way. What was most imperative now and in her best interest was the futuristic outlook to consider and in all probability, her greatest option of making it in this new place rested solely with Marcus. Working on the theory of percentages, she felt more assured of present company.

She fervently believed Marcus was able to give her the necessary assistance required, rather than her cousin, who may not have been in a position to do so. She engaged the practical view, that going to a large Metropolis with all its complexities and other issues that such an experience entails, her interest would be best served and indeed managed, far more adequately, by someone with greater knowledge and know-how, than Cleveland ever could. Marcus had succeeded in lifting the worry and despair that had crystallised in her mind on their first meeting, from her delicate shoulders, giving her self-belief and confidence, of a kind that she clearly did not anticipate. Her gut feeling, therefore, was to stick to her instincts. It was hardly likely that her new friend Marcus would ever let her down. That would be the equivalent of saving someone from drowning, only to throw them in front of a moving bus. If all else fails, she was confident that Marcus would protect her. For Marcus, it was a totally different scenario. His was a mission unfulfilled. He was championing a cause he considered most worthy.

There was a natural affinity – a meeting of minds which impacted instantaneously on both parties, giving it a degree of social upliftment and relevance that was conducive to an enduring and amicable conclusion. In his eyes, Jessica was a young woman of remarkable qualities. She possessed attributes which pleased him immensely. Her intellect and her maturity were far beyond her years, cementing what was now a mutual respect that existed between both individuals. The task he set himself gave him a sense of pride, knowing that this was done for no other reason than for self-gratification. There was no ulterior motive of any kind.

He considered himself a man of principle. Based on his longstanding and passionate belief, which he held as a young man growing up, Jessica's youthfulness exempted her from any romantic or intimate relationship with him whatsoever. His interest in her was based entirely on her development. Nevertheless, her quiet persona and her compelling charm were contagious and relatively irresistible. She was someone who was difficult not to take notice of. There was no doubt in his mind, that she was someone with the ability to prosper in her new environment and given the opportunity, he would see it as a pleasurable opportunity to promote the talent she possessed to its fullest potential.

Unlike Jessica, Marcus remained sceptical about Cleveland's general progress. The post-war experience that encouraged many to travel, for whatever reason, did not always find clear-cut opportunities to succeed and even with the very best intentions, many have found it a major struggle to exist. Issues of one kind or another threw obstructions that sometimes hindered progress. He hoped Cleveland was an exception to that rule. Whatever the situation, one certainty remained; Jessica would not suffer that fate. The wholesome friendship that was in evidence between them, gave her a clear advantage to develop and to make good the assets she possessed. He was well prepared to mentor her, even if it was at the end of a phone.

The hours multiplied into days and like good wine, Marcus realised an excellent journey was now coming to an end. It would also bring to a conclusion the uncertainties of Jessica, whose future depended solely on a family structure which could not be considered as reliable. There was absolutely no doubt in his mind, however, that the friendship was tangible and whatever the outcome, the relationship, although comparatively new, would remain intact. Accident or otherwise, he was certain that they would both benefit from knowing one another, which was excellent, but what was more, being in the company of Jessica enhanced his spirit and gave him a feeling of contentment. That the journey was coming to a climax left a sense of sadness and regret that he could not have imagined possible just a few weeks ago.

# COMING HOME

The sun was shining high in the sky and smiling broadly on Mother Earth, soothing breeze ideally and effectively neutralizing the rays that it emitted. The clouds, moving leisurely in patterned formation against a radiantly blue sky, made the day as consummate as it could ever be. The *SS Aracassa*, powering at high knots towards its destination on a now becalmed ocean, made tracks in this massive volume of water and left ripples that immediately genuflected in its wake. It was a culmination of nature at its finest. He turned to Jessica, an avid reader, and smiled pleasantly. "I hope you are making the most of nature's gift to mankind. The sun is in its element today."

Jessica closed the book and offered a reassuring grin. "It's a fine day alright. Are you hinting that London is short of weather such as this?"

"Far from it." He informed. "London gets its fair share of sunshine, although occasionally you can experience all four seasons in one day."

Jessica nodded her head favourably. "In that case, I had better enjoy present conditions."

"Please do. In another couple of days, all this will be nothing but a memory. When you get to London, you will find a tempo that is fast and furious, quite different from what you are accustomed to. It will take you completely out of your stride; so be prepared." Marcus informed.

"There are times when I think you set out to scare the life out of me," Jessica replied, wearing a serious frown. "You tend to make it sound so dramatic."

"Nothing of the sort," Marcus responded. "What I am doing is giving you an insight of what to expect. Take Teresa for instance, she was a woman who was almost frantic about her movement. She was forever busy, and even she found it difficult to handle."

Jessica studied Marcus for a moment, and although she felt she understood him to a degree, she was still unsure about his state of mind, especially his obsession with Teresa.

"Tell me, Marcus." She quizzed. "Do you think you can achieve happiness with someone else? It is quite obvious you still love your wife."

"She still occupies my thoughts, something I cannot deny." He offered with a degree of reluctance.

"Then tell me this." She asked. "If she comes back tomorrow and asks for forgiveness, would you take her back?"

Marcus studied the question long and hard before sighing heavily. "Do you really want to know the truth?"

"Yes, I do." She eagerly requested.

"If Teresa is truly sorry, in spite of what she has done, and I was convinced that she meant it, I would take her back in a heartbeat."

Jessica looked at her companion with great pity. How could a man she considered to be of the highest calibre, someone of the utmost distinction amongst other qualities, remain so consumed with emotions of the heart and so in love? "You know she is not coming back?" Jessica intoned.

"I may be a romantic, but I am not silly. I know she is not coming back." He retorted without much conviction.

"Then give your life a chance. Do not stagnate or sell yourself short. You deserve better than that."

Marcus looked at Jessica with an intensity that was not there before. Then, with a gradual change of heart, he chuckled. "Thank you, Jessica." He retorted. "I'm happy that someone like you is fighting my corner. However, I am not your ordinary human being. I cannot do what other men are able to do. I do not chop and change. My love for Teresa is what it is and it is something I am trying to come to terms with."

Jessica could not help being in a sympathetic mood towards Marcus. She knew in her heart he still believed in Teresa, although admitting to the contrary. The hard and uncompromising fact remained, while Marcus was living in hope, Teresa was living a life of bliss. It was obvious she had found love and happiness with Jonny and was content to remain that way. While in the interim, he was living in expectation that one day she would return. "Marcus, at some point you have to change your plan, you are a handsome man and any woman, anywhere would want you."

Marcus smiled contentedly. "You know Jessica you are indeed an interesting person. If only you were ten years older, I might have considered you to be the next Mrs Gullant."

They both giggled heartily. "Shall I get out my wedding gown and ask the Captain to marry us? After all, I wouldn't want to miss the chance of a lifetime."

Still smiling he responded calmly. "Some things will always be constant with me. I stand by my principles which will never allow me to get hitched to someone twenty years my junior. That is my sound belief."

"I know Marcus. I can only admire how principled you are." Jessica announced.

# JOURNEY'S END

The last night on board was full of expectations. It was the Captain's ball and almost everyone was consumed with the moment. There were those who were looking forward to the next phase of their journey and others with eager expectations of fulfilling their dreams. However if ever there was an exception to the rule it was Jenny. She took the fun aspect literally, making every minute of her time on board exceptional. Her boundless enthusiasm for enjoyment was evident. Jenny's explosive energy was simply amazing.

Throughout the journey, she behaved as though there was no tomorrow. Her natural flirtatious instincts commanded huge attention, giving her prominence that most folks regarded as immodest or outrageous, but it was not in her DNA to take heed of anyone's opinion. Jenny used the time to her best advantage, deriving maximum benefit throughout. However, there was a snag in her game plan with regards to Marcus. He was the one big fish she wanted to fry, but that did not materialise for one reason only; that reason was Jessica. She scuppered any opportunity that may have been available by her constant presence around him. It was as if they were joined at the hips. What was worst, as Jenny saw it, was the promise he made to her that had clearly not been honoured and one she was not prepared to forgive him for.

Marcus, on the other hand, was very much aware of Jenny's motives and as a result, became extremely evasive throughout the entire trip. In fact, in his own mind, he was totally convinced he had won that battle and was content with his dexterity and his skilful management of avoiding her completely. There was absolutely no intention so far as matters went, to satisfy the whims of Jenny. It was now almost the end of the journey and he felt a sense of triumph avoiding the clutches of someone as excessive and impulsive as she was.

Sitting on deck Jessica felt it was appropriate to have a glass of wine to celebrate the final day on board the *SS Aracassa* and Marcus was only too willing to oblige. Returning with drinks in hand and tacitly recounting the events and experiences of the entire trip; the accidental meeting and indeed the subsequent friendship that developed with Jessica, made him smile with satisfaction. He was also pleasantly caught up with all the extraneous activities around this massive ship, when suddenly, out of the blue and standing in front of him, hands on hips – teapot style, was no other than Jenny. Her full moon features and her withering frown immediately suggested that all was not well. "Hello, 'Mr Unreliable'." She announced aggressively. "Do you remember me? I'm the girl you made a promise to that you did not keep."

Marcus was flabbergasted. Having dodged Jenny throughout the entire journey with huge success, he now found himself trapped and with no place to run. "Hi, Jenny!" He swiftly responded, racking his brain to come up with a tangible explanation. "I really did not forget my promise to you, it's just that you were so busy, it was far too difficult to get your attention."

"You have to be kidding." She countered. "You know I would always make room for someone like you. The truth is; you did not want to know."

"Please don't say that." He protested.

"Of course I'm right." She interrupted. "And you know it. Everywhere I look, I see you in the company of that maga woman and yet you insist she's not your friend. That makes you a liar also."

"No, honestly, it's not like that, believe me! Jessica has a few problems that need ironing out and all I'm doing is trying to help."

VICTOR WALDRON

"Now I know you're a liar." She announced.

"Everywhere I see you, I see her and I'm positive you are not twins or are you?"

"No we are not twins and I can assure you that there is nothing going on between us." He responded unconvincingly.

Jenny looked at Marcus disparagingly and sighed. "Do you know something? I would never be able to understand some men. You get the opportunity to have meat and veg; and what do you settle for? A bag of bones!"

Marcus was inwardly amused but somehow managed to maintain his cool. It was plain to see that she was irritated if not downright upset by his lack of enthusiasm towards her and whatever happened, he was not prepared to give her the impression that such was the case.

"I'm sorry to disappoint you. I didn't think I had a chance with all the boys paying so much attention to you."

"That just proves that other men can see my attraction. You cannot deny that I have sex appeal." She began moving her rotund body rhythmically to prove the point.

Marcus knew all along that Jenny did not lack self-confidence. It was obvious to him that she was somewhat vainglorious. She was someone who knew what she wanted and was forthright about it. In almost every department she did not fit the bill of anyone he may have any attraction to, romantic or otherwise, nevertheless, he was always prepared to show her a degree of respect and to be less judgemental. He was also desperate to get out of this situation without causing harm. Not to get involved was bad enough, but hurting someone's feelings was quite another matter. That said, drastic measures were required in order to ease the situation. Having lied to her once, it would certainly do no harm to commit another. "Look!" He uttered, trying as best he could to be serious. "They'll be other times, after all, we're not dead yet you know. I am positive we'll meet again on dry land." That was an assurance built on straw.

"But we may never see each other again after today." She uttered.

"No problem – give me your address and I will guarantee that I will be seeing you again."

"You mean that?" She asked excitedly. "I will be going to live in Manchester."

"Is that a fact? So am I, so you see we'll be seeing each other again." Marcus said trying his hardest to keep a straight face.

Jenny's reaction was everything. Marcus was what she wanted and here he was, giving her a reason to be happy. She hastily scribbled her address with the pen she took out of his shirt pocket and with a broad smile she replaced both pen and address with a gentle pat on his chest.

"Now whatever you do, don't lose it, it could cost you a lot."

She wiggled conspicuously as she drifted away in obvious contentment.

Marcus was filled with uncontrollable mirth as he crossed the floor to relative safety from the woman he felt obliged to commit a serious transgression, merely for the sake of self-preservation. Relieved and still grinning boyishly he joined Jessica.

"What in the world is the matter?" She enquired. "You seem totally amused."

"Yes, I am. I just came face to face with your roommate Jenny and if anyone can give me the giggles, she surely can."

"Oh yes – she kept telling us about you and the promise you made to her. That girl has taken a fancy to you."

Marcus still amused. "I know she has. She indicated that to me on the first day that we met."

"Then why make promises that you cannot keep?" Jessica demanded.

Marcus, still finding the entire episode humorous. "I lied; it was the only way I could rid myself of her."

"Then why make promises? Wouldn't it be better to tell the young lady you're not interested?"

"Does Jenny look like the kind of person to take no for an answer?" He giggled.

"That's the price you pay for being handsome." She muttered smilingly.

Marcus still grinning heartily. "If you think that was bad, you haven't heard anything yet. In order to get away from her tongue lashing, I told her another fib, the kind that would make your eyes pop. I informed her that our paths would cross in the not too distant future."

"Would that happen?" She asked.

"Of course not; she will be living in Manchester and that's a long way from London."

"Do you think that's fair?" Jessica asked seriously.

"Well! If you're living in my shoes it is. I'll do anything to get away from Jenny and just in case you're beginning to wonder; I rather like the young lady, but she's much more than I can handle."

"I never knew you were a coward." Jessica teased.

"If that is what it takes to be trouble free, then I am." He responded amusingly.

Jessica smiled warmly; she felt a growing sense of fondness towards Marcus, knowing that she had been the recipient of his friendship and good grace throughout the entire journey. Yet, there was so much more to this man than meets the eye. She was certainly mindful of the attention and patience he continually showed her, but in a strange way, she was seeking to know more. Obviously, she felt a deep sense of attraction towards him which was prudently concealed, knowing full well there was a certain mystique about him that needed to be explored further.

"You are definitely not a predictable person Marcus. Here is a young and healthy woman throwing herself at you and you behave as though you are dodging grenades."

He giggled sheepishly. "It's really not as bad as that, but my principles remain steadfast. I do not indulge in short romances and moreover, I most emphatically do not want to get involved with women who are almost half my age. That's just the way I am."

"But Marcus you are still a very young man. Why do you keep persisting that you are old?"

"I'm old enough to know what I want." He insisted. "That is the bottom line and at the moment nothing is going to change that."

Jessica smirked in a rather sarcastic manner. She raised her glass up high. "Let's toast to that. Young women of this world be warned, Marcus Gullant is not interested."

"Don't be hard on me Jessie, it's just one of those things I'm not prepared to change."

Jessica was pleased she did not reveal her innermost feelings. She offered a weak smile. "Marcus I do understand. Don't let me change the way you are."

"That's my girl." He chuckled. "You don't know it, but you give me hope."

# JESSICA'S NEW HOME

The train moved gently towards Victoria Station. This proved to be a journey that tested Jessica to the very limit of her resolve. It was a bleak day in London and everything around took on a less than appealing aspect. The feeble sun meekly surrendered its fight for survival behind the dark and heavy clouds, rendering a gloomy and unwelcome vista.

As the train came to a halt, Jessica began showing nervous anticipation, for the new and sudden experience that was foisted upon her by her father. That more than anything else; left her with a heavy heart. Prior to all this Jessica was beginning to carve out a career for herself in her native Trinidad, as a schoolteacher. One she envisaged to be extremely successful and one she was hoping to derive a great deal of happiness from. That, unfortunately, came to an abrupt end, by the sudden and unforeseen action that altered her life; a life that promised so much. Her problems were compounded by the tragedy of what she considered matters of the heart, losing her lover Alan. So little time was given to her, she was not able to say goodbye to him in the manner she wanted. As a result, she was left empty and broken-hearted. Now all of a sudden she was entering a completely new phase in her life. One she did not cater for and more so was now faced with the prospect of the unknown.

This, undoubtedly, had placed enormous stress and worry on her less than formidable shoulders. She was now pondering on the prospect of finding her cousin that she had not seen for so many years and adapting to the variances of a country she hardly contemplated on ever wanting to visit, never mind making it her new home. She was left with a strange paradox that did not rest easily on her mind. The only redeeming feature was her companion Marcus, who she met more by accident than design. Who showed kindness to her beyond all expectations and was now someone she depended upon to give her direction and stability if all else fails. She glanced at Marcus who sat beside her and wondered how anyone could be so composed at all times. Marcus glanced back with a smile and a wink. "At long last, we are here. This is now your new home."

Finally, the train came to a screeching halt at Victoria and as the doors of the carriages swung open, pandemonium broke loose. The frenzied sound of passengers and luggage disembarking inordinately was colossal. The deafening noise took Jessica by surprise, leaving her with a degree of disorientation. This was not for the fainthearted or the uninitiated. In fact, she was taken completely out of her comfort zone. "Is it always like this?" She enquired timidly.

In the interim Marcus was quite unmoved by the upheaval. He had witnessed it often enough. "Yes, it always gets a bit chaotic when the boat train arrives."

Jessica observed this unusual activity with astonished surprise. "Well, it seems pretty wild to me." She announced.

Marcus chuckled heartily. "Are you ready to join the confusion? He joked.

She nodded her approval, but the expression on her face betrayed her willingness to participate. It was clear that she was extremely overwhelmed.

"Come on, Jessie," Marcus assured her. "It's hardly anything to be worried about, it's only people."

She gestured agreement and moments later, they were part and parcel of this amazing jamboree. Trains coming and going at rapid pace; guards blowing their whistles and waving their flags; folks hugging and kissing with great enthusiasm; luggage falling out of the carriages in rapid succession; people shaking hands, babies crying, porters moving helter-skelter, newcomers looking excitedly for their relatives, screaming folks finding their long-awaited families all merged with one another in brisk and hectic commotion, that has no place for the timid or unsuspecting individual. The volume of traffic markedly restricted their movement, as they wound their way through the barriers. The huge clock signalled nine o'clock as he set the luggage down.

"Have a good look around for Cleveland." He shouted, raising his voice above the din. "When you find him I'll be right here," Marcus said pointing to the clock.

Jessica nodded, it was clear that she was visibly shaken, but acknowledging there was a task to perform, she sighed heavily and very soon she disappeared among the bustling crowd. She was totally bemused by the avalanche of confusion around her, made far worse by people impatiently going about their business, with the zeal and vigour to which they were accustomed. What should have been a simple exercise of finding her cousin, disintegrated into chaos which left her in a state of total bewilderment. This noisy and rampant bustle was alien to her otherwise introverted nature. She was more preoccupied with the activities around her than the main purpose of what was intended. By the time her function level was restored, this vast eruption around her; the stampede that had her stricken, had dwindled to a degree of sanity.

In the meantime what was very clear, she did not observe anyone who looked remotely like Cleveland and felt maybe, in the mad crush he may have done the same. Suddenly, as if by magic, this massive howling, shouting, screaming gathering had subsided. The early disruption that was in evidence only a short while ago had trickled away to manageable proportions. Sanity had once again prevailed. Out of the corner of his eyes, Marcus observed a dejected; crestfallen figure moving towards him. It was Jessica. The thinning crowd revealed what he had suspected all along and Jessica's posture indicated in an instant, that her venture of finding Cleveland did not bear fruit. It was obvious also, that she was baffled by the vitality and sheer force of this novel experience, the kind she had not been subjected to before.

That coupled by the huge disappointment of not finding Cleveland deflated her completely.

Marcus realised immediately that a new strategy was imperative, by all means possible, to help lift her gloom. He was more than convinced that it would not be easy. He was aware that it would require a special kind of charm offensive; an ability of supreme magnitude; a genius moment if necessary; merely to calm her anxiety and generally to ease her distress. "No luck then?" He enquired feebly.

Jessica stood there tacitly and was very tearful. Words were not necessary to indicate her deep disappointment.

"Still, not to worry; you are in good hands." Offered Marcus, smiling broadly and hoping for a response in equal dimension, which was not forthcoming.

"You need to cheer up my good friend. Have I ever let you down?"

As if words were hard to come by, Jessica just shook her head negatively.

"Very well then you have not got a problem," Marcus assured her. "I will guarantee that in no time at all, you and your cousin will be reunited again. You can trust me on that."

Jessica's gloom marginally lifted by the remarks of this confident man, who seemed incapable of being ruffled by anything.

"Thanks." She responded with a heavy sigh.

"Not good enough." He insisted. "Look! I'm offering you my goodwill, all I want in return is for you to be more cheerful." Marcus announced jovially.

Just then, Jessica realised her companion deserved better. With much effort, she was able to generate a meaningful smile. She began to realise that her problems were more imaginary than real. There were issues no doubt; but it was also reasonable to assume that having Marcus as a companion and friend, her fears should be minimal. He was in her estimation a safe pair of hands.

"I'm not like you." Jessica insisted. "Nothing bothers you, you are so strong and I'm quite the opposite."

"Do not devalue yourself. You are stronger than you think." He insisted. "However, let's not waste any more time, let's go find that cousin of yours."

Marcus hailed a taxi and together they set off for Highbury. The traffic outside of the station showed signs of congestion, perhaps as a result of the residual mingling of people, still finding their way from an area that was inundated only a short time ago.

It was a murky afternoon with a fine drizzle that accompanied what was left of a now fading sunset. It was swiftly surrendering to the permanence of the evening gloom. This was the first impression Jessica was having of London and it was evident that she was far from impressed with what she saw. The jaded outlook was stark and unflattering, conditions that did nothing to raise her morale. If anything, the general outlook only succeeded in lowering her expectations in the worst possible way. Consequently, her mind regressed negatively to the point of stress. As the cab manipulated its way towards its destination, Marcus quickly observed Jessica's mood change and to some extent, understood her state of anxiousness. Since he knew it was not easy for a stranger to be experiencing conditions that were alien to a newcomer with issues other than a dark desolate evening.

Marcus felt sympathy for his young companion's state of mind. Realising that nothing she had seen so far had given her any degree of comfort, excitement or satisfaction. He also understood her anxious feelings could only be contained by virtue of a positive outcome in her favour.

Having been forced against her will into a foreign environment by her father, he thought her new beginnings had begun in a most inhospitable manner. It was something that did nothing to enhance her spirit, nor engender confidence. As a result, the indifference she displayed was not out of place. Fully appreciating the circumstances, Marcus knew the task ahead depended largely on him. His solemn promise to her from the very inception of their meeting was to deliver her safely into the custody of her cousin Cleveland. Since that was his priority, he needed to make good that promise come what may. His consideration for Jessica was paramount. In his estimation, she was hardly someone who was able to adapt to the stresses and strains of any negative problems, should they arise. It would, therefore, be up to him to smooth the path of any adversities ahead. Marcus decided tacitly to shield her from any plight that she may encounter, especially if her cousin was unable or incapable of honouring his obligations.

Jessica remained passive throughout the entire journey, apparently stricken by her own fears and showed no interest in her new environment, even though Marcus was by her side, her general manner was one of dissatisfaction and disappointment. For one, Cleveland's non-appearance became a major factor. How could he be so cruel and unkind when so much depended on him? But, more importantly, how would she be able to cope in an environment that functions at such breakneck speed? It was something she was not looking forward to. Those two things did nothing to alleviate her worry and lastly, the inclement weather conditions did not in any way enhance her spirits. For now, the prospects of being in this new place looked very bleak.

Her mind reflected on her homeland, where so much of what she did gave her pleasure, where her heartthrob resided and where peace and tranquillity reigned. How she despised her father for this present predicament. Marcus was cognisant of Jessica's plight. Her expectations were obviously shaken by her cousin's behaviour. He thought of a mood changer and delivered it with great aplomb. He needed to remove negative ideas infiltrating her mind and in some way change the course of events. In his usual assured way, he scanned the address given to him by Jessica.

"I know this street very well." He announced smiling broadly. "Oh yes, it's been some time ago but I still remember..." He stopped to focus on his companion. "Did I tell you I once lived in Highbury?"

Jessica shook her head affirmatively, without responding verbally.

Marcus laughed out loud, throwing his head back as he did so. "I recall a story that still makes me giggle. There was this young lady living in the same house. For some good reason, she would not leave me alone. Apparently, she took a fancy to me and like Jenny would not take no for an answer. She even told her boyfriend that we were lovers and he threatened to do me in."

It was enough to bring a faint smile to Jessica's face. "And what did you do?" She quizzed.

"Not much." He replied, still very much amused. "I merely told him that I was the Army's light heavyweight champion and that was enough to deter him from any further action."

Jessica smiled warmly. "You see, I told you. You'll always get into trouble with a face like yours Marcus. You are a very handsome man and I think you know it."

"Well, at least you're smiling." He responded looking at his watch. "In another few minutes time, we'll know for sure why your cousin did not put in an appearance."

"I cannot forgive him for what he has done." She frowned. "It's awful leaving me to fend for myself in a place like this."

"Look, Jessica, this is the big city now and things happen. There may be lots of reasons why Cleveland did not show up. Believe me, I'm not defending him, but what is important, now that you are here, is that you concentrate on how best you can succeed in this environment. I know it can sometimes be a challenge, but one you can overcome."

Jessica looked at him solemnly. "I'm not sure what I would have done without your help. I owe you so much."

"Nonsense; you owe me nothing. In a civilised world, people help each other. Life is not always straightforward, but things happen. Someone helped me and I'm sure that one day you will also help someone; that's the way of the world."

Jessica shook her head agreeably and offered a warm smile. "In your next life, I'm sure you'll return as a philosopher."

"Why wait that long? I guess I'm one already." He joked. "What I do want is for you to stop worrying. Things will work out just fine." He placed his arm around her delicate shoulder in a comforting manner. It was a gesture Jessica welcomed appreciably.

"Stop fretting my dear, everything will come good in the end."

The taxi weaved its way through the dismal evening traffic, in pursuit of finding Cleveland, the man whose future Jessica now depends. His absence from the station gave her every reason to worry. The initial damage is done; her main concern now was what kind of welcome was she likely to receive. The cab turned right, much to the surprise of Marcus. Knowing the route as extensively as he did, he was certain the driver's grand design was simply to make a relatively short journey a lengthy one, for a few shillings more. "Where do you think you're going, mate?" Marcus asked.

"Highbury innit, mate?" The cab driver responded.

"Yes, but not the long way round. Do me a favour and get us there as quickly as possible. I know Highbury like the back of my hand, so let's not play silly games." Marcus affirmed.

The driver muttered under his breath and obeyed the instructions.

"Is he unhappy with you?" Jessica enquired.

"Perhaps, but that's no big deal. They do try it on from time to time."

# CLEVELAND'S NIGHTMARE

The cab came to a sudden halt; across the way stood a row of terraces that gave the appearance of neglect. It was hardly the kind that lifted the spirits, leaving Jessica staring into the gloom with more than a measure of astonishment.

"Well, here we are," Marcus announced. "Time for some home truths; let's see if Cleveland is just a figment of the imagination!"

"Please do not say that, I know he's very much a real person." Jessica sighed wearing a frown.

"Well, in that case, I'll go and investigate." He touched her shoulders gently. "No need for you to come right now. This inclement condition would not suit you."

Jessica nodded in agreement as she scanned the area. "These houses look so bleak." She observed.

"Yes, but do not forget, London is still recovering from a war." He reminded her.

Marcus briskly exited from the cab, crossed the street and knocked at the door. After some moments, the door was finally opened by a middle-aged woman. A conversation ensued. The discussion though strained, produced a positive outcome. Marcus returned to the taxi feeling triumphant. "Your cousin is in – you are in luck."

He collected her baggage and proceeded upstairs, passing a hallway which was dark and shoddy. The dismal conditions were as evident inside as it was outside. The uncarpeted staircase creaked noisily with every step, like an out of tune accordion. The damp corridor was mimicking the drabness of the evening, with striking accuracy. The pathway of the building, leading up to Cleveland's room, was limp and wary. The paper on the wall had become devoid of purpose for quite some time. It would hardly be an exaggeration to suggest that Jessica's disenchantment was profound. Observing this depressive and equally dilapidated place, brought tears to her eyes. She was in denial that her cousin could be residing in conditions so grim, even though Marcus was positive he had found the person she was looking for. Every step that Jessica took leading up to the room brought a state of bewilderment that was difficult to digest.

The fear and apprehension that consumed her from the commencement of the journey began to escalate into extreme proportions. To be anchored in a place like this, somewhere that was devoid of any prospect was in her estimation worse than hell on earth. For her, this was a living nightmare. It was certainly not what she expected from her cousin Cleveland. He was, as she remembered him, someone who showed so much promise; so much confidence and more so; an extraordinary degree of flair. Residing in this place gave the impression that all his ambitious plans, appeared to have withered on a vine of hopelessness; living in an environment such as this beggar's belief. The situation was far worse than she could ever have imagined. Having left the comfort of her home in the sunshine and in a place of excellence, she was unable and unwilling to be relegated to a state of wretchedness that this place represented. It was, as she observed, a place of woe. A depressive state she could never tolerate.

Her mind quickly reflected on Marcus once more. She recalled when life appeared meaningless and gloom descended upon her; he was there to rescue her. His promise to see her safely in the hands of Cleveland did not falter. As ever, he was true to his word. However, delivering her to a place as squalid as this was a shock. So much of what Marcus did to raise her spirits, was now in danger of unravelling. Could she rely on him once more to get her out of this mire?

The knock on the door was sudden and deliberate. Cleveland's head jerked upwards in surprise. "Who the hell is that?" He whispered to Helen, his female companion.

"Were you expecting someone?" Helen asked.

"No, I certainly was not." He whispered angrily.

"Then if you stay still – perhaps they'll just go away." She suggested.

He knocked again, this time even more forceful than the first. Cleveland allowed his huge torso to slide slowly from on top of his equally naked partner and waited. The knock became more pronounced, accompanied by Marcus shouting out loudly. "Open up Cleveland, your cousin is here."

"Cousin?" Cleveland whispered to Helen. "What cousin?"

He slowly turned his attention to Helen. "What day is it? Holy shit, it must be Jessica. This is absolutely mental, what shall I do?"

He got to his feet hurriedly and pulled his tattered gown on, then proceeded towards the door. As he opened it, he only allowed the luxury of showing part of his face from the limited gap permissible. It was reality staring him in the face; a moment of absolute disaster. There was Jessica with whom he was supposed to have met and indeed welcome to the city of London. Instead, he was left to execute the worst bit of drama of his entire life and embarrassingly so, with no place to hide. For an unhealthy second or two, Cleveland merely stood and stared at Jessica speechless. His cousin equally unimpressed with this ramshackle existence of Cleveland was left mortified. She remembered him as someone with fire in his belly and a spring in his step.

He had flair and ambition in abundance. He was an eager beaver, who wanted to leave his homeland in pursuit of becoming a dentist. Leaving behind no illusion or doubt of his desire to return home as an accomplished and very successful person. That vision suddenly appeared to have died an irreversible death. Standing in front of her was none other than a pathetic individual, living in a substandard state and immersed in absolute humiliation. For a brief moment, no one spoke, it seemed as though time froze. Jessica felt a strange pang of nervousness running through her veins. She remembered Marcus indicating that London could be an unforgiving place and wondered if she could survive in this vast, fast, new environment that had now become her home, or would she become a mere statistic like Cleveland. She tried to dismiss the thought immediately. It was not one she cared to seriously accommodate.

"Hello, cousin. I was expecting you at the station. What went wrong? Have you forgotten me?" Jessica enquired eventually.

Cleveland was someone who was never short of a word or two, merely stared at his cousin as if hypnotised. If ever there was stress in his life, nothing, but nothing could come close to this. Jessica tried to smile but without success. "Did you receive correspondence from home about me coming here?" She asked finally finding her voice in a weak and shaky state.

"Err ... yes, but somehow I got the dates wrong in my head and I'm ever so embarrassed about that."

There was another tacit moment or two before Marcus stepped forward and tried to prize the door a little wider, but was met with stern resistance from Cleveland.

"I really don't want to know your business young man; I merely wanted to see how large your room was," Marcus explained.

Reluctantly, Cleveland relented, exposing his naked partner in an average sized bed and to reveal the contents of the room, which consisted of a sink, stove, a kettle, a small wardrobe and very little else. Charlotte, the landlady, stood firmly at the foot of the stairs watching proceedings. She showed a great degree of displeasure, seeing someone new entering her home without approval. "Cleveland." She bellowed. "I hope she is not thinking of staying here. I most certainly will not have it."

"Shut your bloody mouth woman." Cleveland retorted. "This is none of your business." He shouted angrily.

"It is my business when you bring people into my home and just in case you have that in mind – you can forget it."

Marcus looked at Jessica and offered a weak smile. She did not reciprocate. "Jessica I will leave you to talk to your cousin. Frankly speaking, you cannot stay here. There is hardly any room to swing a kitten, never mind a cat. I will take your stuff back to the taxi and you can meet me outside."

He took her grips and exited from the house, forcing Charlotte to sidestep from the position she held on the stairs. By now, Cleveland had recovered some measure of composure and fittingly attired himself to greet Jessica. That he was totally humiliated was an understatement. Standing outside his room, his back against the door, he depicted a forlorn and sorrowful figure. He attempted a smile of sorts that died as suddenly as it began.

Candidly observing his appearance of meekness, Jessica became conciliatory towards him. He was wearing a beard which she felt was unsuitable. It made him look much older than his years and there was every reason to believe; he had lost his sense of direction; even if it was only temporary.

Back home, he was a source of inspiration to many who admired his confidence and assured ability. He was a young man who was a shining light in his neighbourhood and beyond. To watch someone who possessed so many fine qualities and self-esteem, being humbled in such a way was depressing to say the very least. This was clearly a hole in the ground moment for him.

"I don't know what to say, cousin, other than sorry." He pleaded.

Jessica reached out to embrace him. "It's okay Cleveland, everyone at home sends their love."

"Thank you." He replied as he hugged her closely.

"The folks expect you to be home soon. When do you think that will be possible?" She enquired.

Cleveland sighed heavily. "I'm not quite sure yet. But what you see now is not permanent. I'm just going through a bad patch at the moment." He responded trying to assure his cousin.

"Well! Let's hope so cousin, you are too much of an intelligent and talented person to be in a situation like this."

Cleveland nodded affirmatively. "You are correct, cousin, but don't worry, I'm working on the matter as we speak. This is just an unfortunate period in my life."

"I sure hope so." Jessica echoed, smiling pleasantly.

Cleveland responded this time with more conviction. "Are you going to be alright?" He asked.

"Yes. Marcus is a wonderful person. When I'm settled, I'll come back to see you."

"Sure thing; I'll look forward to that." Replied Cleveland, bashfully.

Jessica reached the bottom of the stairs, where Charlotte the landlady occupied. Their eyes met. Charlotte turned aside, enough to allow Jessica passageway and followed her aggressively to the door. No sooner was Jessica outside, Charlotte slammed the door shut. "Good riddance." Charlotte murmured as she proceeded back to her room.

As she faced the drizzle outside, Jessica was getting the first taste of this new place and felt as gloomy as the conditions that prevailed. So far as experience goes, this for a newcomer was quite surreal. Back in the cab, Jessica fell into her seat like a sack of cement. The meeting and subsequent discussion with her cousin still weighed heavily on her mind.

She looked utterly disorientated, the kind someone gets from a severe shock. However, it was a reaction that was inevitable in the circumstance. Marcus being aware of the situation, decided on prudence. "Are you okay? What is the verdict on Cleveland?" He enquired sympathetically.

"It's difficult to predict." She commented. "He told me he has a game plan and for some reason or other I believe him."

"That's fine by me," Marcus uttered. "I firmly believe this might be a wake-up call for him. With a bit of positive thinking and mental fortitude, I'm sure he can turn it around." Jessica responded with a faint smile.

The destination to the home of Marcus could well have been a non-event. No sooner was Jessica seated, she fell into a deep slumber. It was hardly a day of triumph for her. That, coupled with the variances of the moment was enough to impact body and mind to a state of extreme tardiness. Her delicate frame seemed to have collapsed under the weight of pressure that perpetrated around her.

Marcus was now her only redeeming hope. He was beyond doubt a man of great honesty and dependability. In all the turmoil that was in evidence, he remained her one saving grace. Therefore, in her mind, she had now resigned herself in the knowledge that all this strife and tribulations; good fortune had delivered her in the hands of someone who was trustworthy and truly capable. That was more than enough to appease her unnecessary distress.

They reached the end of their journey and as the taxi pulled up at the gate, Marcus fully realised, based on the conditions that remained unchanged, it would be a challenge of considerable magnitude to restore Jessica to any form of normality. Still rapt inexorably in a deep state of rest, he smiled warmly as his initial efforts completely failed to gain a response of any kind from his sleeping beauty companion. The driver chuckled to himself as he observed the plight of the young soldier. "Looks like you've got a job on your hands there, mate."

Marcus seeing the funny side of it giggled amusingly. "You're sure right mate, she's out of this world and it looks like I will need a sledgehammer to get her out of that place she's presently in."

Trying once more, this time with robust energy, success was finally achieved. Jessica opened her eyes, bemused and disoriented. "What's happened? Where am I?" She enquired anxiously.

"You're now in the land of the living." Marcus echoed. "Welcome back to the real world and the driver would very much like you to get out so he can also get some rest."

Jessica exited the cab somewhat unsteadily, with the kind and considerate assistance of Marcus. She gathered herself enough to be conscious of the surroundings she was to become a significant part of. The neatly compact row of terraces was impressive indeed. It represented a standard and quality that exceeded her expectations and was undoubtedly poles apart from the conditions that prevailed around her cousin Cleveland. It was a chasm she found difficult to evaluate. Was it careful management on one hand against complacency on the other? Or perhaps Cleveland fell prey to a system he could not quite embrace? No one would ever know!

The door was painted bright green, the same as her parent's home, which gave her a, sense of déjà vu. Smiling broadly she pointed to the door.

"This reminds me of home. It's exactly the colour of our house in Trinidad."

Marcus placed the luggage down and with a smug smile, he beckoned her in. "Well in that case, welcome home."

Jessica entered the house and was completely in awe of his stylish abode.

"Wow!" She exclaimed. "This is simply marvellous."

"Do you think so?" Marcus questioned wearing a contented smile.

"Yes; absolutely stunning." Commented Jessica, giving thorough scrutiny to Marcus's well kept and pleasantly maintained home. Jessica turned pointedly to face Marcus as if her suspicions of him were fully realised.

"Jenny was right. She kept insisting you were rich and I'm now convinced she was correct all along.

"Please Jessica; spare me the rich bit. Anyway, I'm surprised someone like Jenny could lead you astray.

"But you are." She argued. "You're just too modest to admit it."

Marcus giggled like a schoolboy. "If you really want to know, I am fairly comfortable and that is a fact. Rich? I most certainly am not."

"Okay, I hear you." She nodded purposefully. "But I'm truly fascinated by your beautiful surroundings."

For a while, he allowed her the luxury of her curiosity, as she scanned the interior of his home with great interest. It was a bit of indulgence he could well have afforded. However, observing her pleasant appearance, she seemed very much at peace with herself. It was as if all her troubles had suddenly melted away. She wore a smile as captivating as anything he had seen before. Her eyes sparkled like a well-cut diamond and it was obvious by her demeanour, she had undergone a complete metamorphosis. Standing in front of him was a woman with a sweet and alluring nature. The kind that can easily set alarm bells ringing. She was rendering to him another side of her that was gloriously appealing and dangerously so. Fortunately for him, an agenda was already set. The relationship from the very beginning was platonic and in his mind, it would always remain that way. He considered himself a man of high ideals and very strong principles. That being the case, he was not about to yield to any rash emotions, nor did he intend any infractions that would otherwise impede what he now regarded as a valued friendship. By contrast, Jessica's desire for Marcus had become extremely uncomfortable. In a strange way even though she was experiencing strong feelings for him, she was prepared to suppress any emotions that would endanger their newfound relationship.

# JESSICA'S JOY

The following morning was a complete contrast to the night before. The sun's aurora filled the sky with overwhelming brightness. The energy of the early dawn seemed to reflect readily on Jessica, whose eagerness to acquaint herself with her new surroundings became quite apparent. Up at the crack of dawn, she immediately began unpacking and getting ready for this exciting episode to come.

Confident in the knowledge also, that the ghost of insecurity was now laid to rest, which was heartening and with her prospect for the future, life appeared quite rosy. Marcus, no doubt had given her every reason to be optimistic. He, on the other hand, never one for much sleep was already doing chores, much to Jessica's surprise.

"Good morning." She announced in a tone as spirited as the morning sunshine.

"Good morning to you." He retorted. "I did not expect to see you up so early. Is the bed not comfortable enough?"

"Did you say comfortable enough? It was excellent. I just wanted to match the mood of the day."

Marcus smiled politely. "I was inclined to think you were more comfortable sleeping in a taxi than a bed."

"Ha ha! Please do not embarrass me. I was simply overcome by the circumstances of the day. I guess I just collapsed under the weight of so many negative things that were happening."

"I think in the light of what happened yesterday, you have done very well. However that is now water under the bridge, a thing of the past, what is required at this moment in time is a fresh approach." Marcus advised.

"I'm well aware of that, but I cannot stop thinking how lucky I am to have met you," Jessica announced wearing a stern look. "I shudder to think how I would have managed on my own without your help."

"Who knows? If you had to deal with the situation alone, there is every possibility you may have coped better than you think." He suggested.

"You are a very positive man with very little time for failure." Jessica expressed in a mood that was more relaxed. "As for me! I am totally different. There is every possibility I would have panicked."

He chuckled philosophically. "Until you're faced with a certain situation, you can never tell what would be the end result. That my dear lady is how life is; we are all guided by destiny. Do you believe in fate?"

"I am inclined to, although there are times when I'm not so sure."

Marcus pointed to his trophies. "You see these? They have paved a bright future for me. It was far beyond anything I could have possibly imagined and yet all this happened by complete accident." He hesitated for a while before bursting into laughter. "You know what is ironic and awfully strange? Teresa has never seen those trophies."

"What do you mean? You just indicated to me that you were very proud of them."

"Well, it's quite a long story. The legacy I left in the village did not do me any credit. As a result, my reputation was somewhat dented by an unfortunate incident which was not of my making. What came of it, gave folks the impression that I was just someone looking for trouble. They said I depended on my fists to do my talking and that I was capable of very little else. That incident left a mark that I was not proud of. So I decided in my best interest to put my trophies out of sight for my own peace of mind. Teresa was never to know that I was a boxer in the Army. I am sure that may have set the seal of disapproval for her and as far as risks go, I was not about to take any."

Jessica was far from impressed. "You hid the things that mattered so much to you out of fear of what she might think? Isn't that unfortunate?"

"In a nutshell, I was leaving nothing to chance. However, as things stood, it was a situation I could have done without. My problem was a popular young lady in the village sent the village bully, a man called Wally, to give me a beating all because I did not give her the attention she sought. What was so ridiculous about all of this was the fact that I saw myself as a man who did not care for any kind of trouble and I ended up being accused of quite the opposite. Anyway, out of some kind of grudge that this young woman may have had, she decided to cause me problems. This guy, something of a man mountain, just loved to beat the pulp out of anyone who dared to upset him. Unfortunately, it was my turn for a thrashing. To say I was afraid of this bully would be an understatement. There were two distinct options open to me, run like hell or stand up and fight. To be regarded as a coward in my village was far worse than getting a beating and since I could not live with the reputation of being a coward, I was left with no alternative but to retaliate. What was definite in my mind was that this man was far too powerful and way too strong to manage. My only option was to hit him first. At least I would have had the benefit of saying I got the first strike. I took the one opportunity available and as they say, the rest was history."

"So what really happened?" Jessica asked curiously, eager to know more.

"I hit him with one punch and he dropped like a sack of cement."

"You knocked him out?" She asked in total surprise.

"Yes! With one punch! It was sensational. It was a miracle to me and everyone else in the village." Marcus confirmed.

"That must have made you very famous." She intimated.

"Well, everyone knew about it." He offered.

"So you would have become everybody's favourite."

"Not exactly, as it happened there were two different points of view. Some folks were relieved to know that Wally got what he deserved. He was a brute that needed to be brought down a peg or two. Others saw it as quite the opposite. Some regarded me as a bad boy and thought that I was mixing with the wrong kind of people. It was a reputation I didn't deserve."

"But that's far from reasonable," Jessica muttered.

"Well, that's how the cookie crumbles. Leading the pack of disapprovers was none other than my own Godmother, Nanny May, who felt I shook hands with the devil."

"But, why, isn't she supposed to be on your side?"

"My dear, you have to know my Godmother to understand what kind of a person you are dealing with. She was something of a moralist; a self-righteous old soul, who was quite happy to designate you to hell at the drop of a hat. She saw everything through the eyes of the bible and nothing else would do."

"So Marcus, how did you see yourself?"

"Well, I did not consider myself the village's favourite son. I didn't always adhere to the golden rules of the place. We were a poor family and very often there were people who expected us to be meek and gentle and to eat humble pie and be content. But that, unfortunately, was not my creed. So you can say I was the proverbial square peg in a round hole type of person."

"I don't understand that Marcus, you don't seem to be a bad person," Jessica replied.

"Look! I knew I was different; I was not content to be just a number. Everyone dreams and you can say for whatever reason, I personally felt a deep sense of hope. There was a compelling urge inside of me that I needed to explore. Perhaps it's called ambition. That in the eyes of many was considered to be dangerous. Some folks thought my attitude was one of indifference, I did not conform to the norms of the place and as a result, I was not seen in the best of light. However, that did not bother me. Why? Because somehow I knew I would find a way to succeed. To prove to myself that dreams can come true. I needed fulfilment and there was no way I could get it in the village."

Jessica smiled warmly. "So by what you say, I can see why you were not well received. You were certainly not a popular person in the village."

Marcus shook his head affirmatively. "For the most part, I kept out of people's way. Let's just say I liked my own company."

"So you were a quiet lad with a restless soul?" Jessica questioned.

"Well put." He countered. "After the fracas with Wally, I gained confidence I did not have before. Not that I intended to use my power, but it was good to know I could look after myself. So, I arrived in England and joined the Army. Perhaps it was the proudest moment of my life. I was in uniform and in a word that was brilliant."

He paused momentarily then added. "Then something happened, totally alien to my nature. I was only a new recruit but I took on someone else's quarrel. He was a West Indian who would not fight back. It was a silly thing to do, but it was more than I could take. So I naively took on a challenge that could have been the end of my Army life. For me, that would have been disastrous. Looking back, it was absolute folly. However, I started it so there was simply no other choice." He paused once more, prompting an anxious Jessica to speak.

"Come on then Marcus, don't leave me in suspense."

"Well, I was confronted by one of the soldiers who knew his way around the ring. He was a boxer who represented the regiment. He was big, strong and stupid. He was also very sure of his ability, so I challenged him and he accepted. He was also a bit of a loud mouth and, in a way, I was glad to shut it for him. I did to him what I did to Wally. I whacked him on his chin, wham."

Jessica looked surprised. "You mean you got into a fight with another soldier?"

"Yes, I smacked him with venom. His knees buckled and he fell like a log."

"That certainly does not sound like you Marcus." Jessica echoed.

"I was severely reprimanded." Marcus giggled. "But I still came out of it smelling of roses. Someone saw that I had raw talent and decided to harness it. So I eventually became a trained fighter."

"You look healthy enough, but were you good at it?" She asked.

"Was I good? I was fantastic. So much so, I was able to extract a great deal of benefit which suited me; hence those trophies."

"So why did you hide them from Teresa? You told me you were very proud of them."

"I guess it's because I desperately wanted her to think of me as a clean-cut person without a blemish. No one wants to carry a stigma of someone who is all brawn and no brains. So I decided it was in my best interest to put my medals out of sight." He paused momentarily, before adding sarcastically. "Do you know something? It's so ironic, those trophies could have been left just where they are and she would not have noticed them. Such was her attitude." He turned and looked at Jessica squarely. "Teresa took me for granted. She used my home and every conceivable thing around here. She concentrated merely on herself and what was expedient to her; nothing else mattered. She was aware of the fact that I cared deeply for her, so I guess that made me a fool in love. I can only conclude that I became a slave to my emotions. If I am to be totally honest I have paid a heavy price for love."

Jessica smiled pleasantly. "Marcus you are a very interesting person. No one can say your life was ever dull."

"Like everyone else, I've had my ups and downs, but I rely on my survival kit to keep me going. My instincts are my guide and I always achieve a positive outcome when I follow them."

"You are extraordinary; I only wish I had your temperament," Jessica remarked. "I can see you are not one for giving up."

"No," Marcus responded. "Life deserves better than that. Never stop trying."

"I hear you; maybe some of your optimism will rub off on me someday."

Marcus smiled broadly. "Look; you have things to do I'm very sure. So get busy and in a little while from now, I will bring you what I consider the elixir of the British people. It is a liquid that they simply cannot do without."

"What can that be, I wonder?" Jessica enquired."

"You don't know?" He grinned. "My dear, everything stops for a cup of tea."

"Are you kidding me?" An amused Jessica quizzed.

"Believe me, it's the living truth. From the highest to the lowest; from the greatest to the very ordinary, all without exception clamour for their favourite brew."

"That is remarkable. Why on earth is a cup of tea so important?"

"Well, it is what it is. Amazing as it seems, it is the nation's most favoured beverage." He broke into a giggle. "It sounds like a strange habit I know, especially to newcomers like us, who have a wide variety of hot drinks that we are accustomed to. However the British believe it is a very important commodity. It has a unique sense of need for the entire population and there are times when it seems like it's the answer to every problem imaginable."

"Come on Marcus." Jessica giggled. "You make it seem so indispensable."

"But it is," Marcus assured her. "If you break a leg or experience bereavement; if your house is on fire or worst; whatever despairing experience you may encounter, it's always the same. It may not be a problem solver and it may not cure your ills, but it will certainly calm your nerves and that is the common view."

"Well it sounds fascinating, too true to believe, but I'll have to take your word for it." Jessica echoed.

"I swear that's the living truth. It's a British tradition and you know what they say, 'When in Rome...'"

Jessica smiled warmly. "I can see where you're coming from."

"Good." He countered. "Later on when you've had your first cuppa I will introduce you to a proper English breakfast."

"Hold on Marcus, I'm almost out of breath. You are going too fast. I can hardly take it all in."

"Get used to it my dear. I will soon be offering you a 'full English breakfast', consisting of bacon, fried eggs, sausages, tomatoes and toast, and then I will continue your education by introducing the country's national dish: fish and chips."

"Well." Jessica giggled. "You just cannot beat that. In only a few short minutes, I've been given a complete history of the culinary habits of the entire nation."

"My dear lady, that's what I'm here for. You can depend on good old Marcus to put you on the right track."

Marcus bowed courteously as Jessica made her departure. Moments later, he returned as promised, proceeded to her room, armed with a teapot, a cup and a bowl of sugar. His footsteps prompted a smile from Jessica, who was diligently establishing order in her room, to make it as delightful and comfortable as possible. The door was ajar and it was obvious by her studious efforts she was actively trying to create an image worthy of her new environment.

# DECEIT

"Knock, knock!" Marcus shouted as he approached. "Be prepared to be dazzled by a taste of pure Englishness: tea! How would you like it, one lump or two?"

Jessica's smile was one of delight, as she welcomed Marcus into the room. Observing him with more than a touch of genuine approval, it was crystal clear that she felt flattered by his charm and could not help considering herself a child of good fortune to have met someone so unique.

"I'm afraid I have a sweet tooth, I'll have three please." She suggested with a cheeky grin.

"Naughty, naughty." He declared. "I consider that bad for your teeth."

Sitting down slowly, Jessica still beaming began sipping her tea approvingly.

"Well? What is the verdict?" He enquired impatiently.

"It's a delightful cup of tea. I can't fault it." She declared.

"Good." He assured her. "Enjoying a good cup of tea is the first step in the right direction. Like I said before, this society can hardly survive without it."

He looked around the room and was duly impressed with the embellishment that was on show. Jessica's personality was already evident. The room she now occupied was blissfully adorned and neatly presented. Sitting on the mantelpiece was a picture that attracted his attention. It was a photograph of Alan. There was a significant likeness in features; especially the eyes and inadvertently, Marcus imagined there was a family connection.

"Who is the young man, your brother?" He asked in total innocence with hardly much thought behind it.

"Err ... no, he is my nephew." She spluttered.

"Well, he's quite a looker." Replied Marcus as he checked his watch. "Let me get to the business of preparing breakfast, which should be ready in about half an hour."

She was more than relieved that Marcus did not dwell on the photograph, which she comprehensively lied about. Doing so was contrary to her very nature. It was an act that left her guilt-ridden and difficult to digest. Somewhere in her mind, however, she felt it was justified. There she was, embarking on a new course of events and did not intend to blow a hole in her plans, especially as they appeared to be so rosy. Concluding that honesty may not be the best policy on this one occasion and although it was not comfortable for her to transgress, she thought ultimately it was regarded as a safe option. She was convinced travelling abroad was never in Alan's plans, except perhaps to the USA. His boast of being home bred and indigenous to Trinidad was enough proof that moving to London was never a grand design of his. He was a true patriot of his homeland and continually expressed his desire to remain so. Therefore, by lying to Marcus as she did, that Alan was her nephew, would never have to be proved.

Her plans to study and achieve a career in nursing were now her prime objective. She was clearly determined, now that the opportunity had presented itself, nothing would get in her way. She thought it was understandable in the circumstances that prevailed, the relationship which existed between Alan and herself could not continue. He was never coming to London and so she reluctantly conceded that the parting of their ways may well have been to her benefit. She assumed the dynamics had altered enough to suggest that realities must be faced. It was clear that Alan, being the man he was, would never have stood on ceremony. His romantic urge would soon be on display. He was a man with great charisma and flamboyance, someone who would only be too happy to pursue his charm offensive with vigour and purpose, in his quest for the good life. Very soon she would be nothing more than a distant memory.

The morning was rounded off with breakfast. It was Jessica's first English meal. However, there was a distinct change of mood, brought about by her lack of honesty with Marcus earlier. It was also compounded by Cleveland's unfortunate plight, which played on her mind. She appeared less buoyant and somewhat distracted throughout the meal; enough to gain the attention of Marcus. "Well, since you ate everything on the plate, it cannot be the food. Care to tell me what's bothering you?" He asked.

"Really it's nothing." She replied, projecting a false smile.

"Come on girl, you were full of beans only a short time ago. What is bothering you?"

Jessica paused before giving an answer. "If you must know, it's about yesterday. I simply can't get it out of my mind. I mean the squalid conditions my cousin is living under. How could he live the way he is? So much was expected of him, what could have gone wrong?"

Marcus let off a huge sigh. "Well, things can happen to people in this large Metropolis, that folks find difficult to explain. Cleveland may well have been a victim of circumstances. I know what you said about him, being clever and all that. But sometimes you need more than ability to survive. A large city like this can easily gobble you up and spit you out in no time at all. Problems can arise that forces you to do things contrary to your expectations." He studiously informed.

"Look!" She explained. "He had informed the family that he was on course to achieve his aims. Where did it all go wrong?"

"It's difficult to say, but you know what? This can be a wake-up call for the young man. He would be far from happy that you were able to see him in that state. It certainly would not do his ego much good. I would wager a bet he will turn things around. Believe me, Jessica, you could not imagine how completely humiliated he was." Marcus indicated.

"I sincerely hope so, it would be talent totally wasted otherwise."

"Worry not. Cleveland would do what is necessary to put things right. Mark my words." Marcus expressed with some assurance.

Jessica rose slowly looking less stressed. "For his sake and for the rest of the family, I do hope you are correct. I guess we must be positive."

"Exactly, it's hardly worth being negative in life. The way I see things, it's quite simple, he can either become anonymous, losing himself among the crowd and become a nobody, or buck up his ideas, especially since you have witnessed his present plight. I can tell you, he would not want that kind of news to filter back home, so he will change his tactics and do what he came here to do. It is my belief, that the latter will be the case. He will definitely want to prove a point." He declared.

"That sounds about right. It would be difficult to argue against that." She expressed candidly, before adding. "You have a feel for these things, so I will leave it to your expert judgement."

Marcus stood up and bowed gracefully. "Let's be optimistic and give him the benefit of the doubt. For myself, I'm very hopeful."

Looking down at the table, he pointed to the plates. "While we are on the subject of judgement, let me digress for a second and ask you for your verdict on your first English breakfast so far?"

Jessica nodded and smiled. "It was excellent and you are a wonderful cook."

Marcus giggled boyishly. "Not for the first time I've been told that."

"And I'm sure you will not let it go to your head." She offered.

They both giggled simultaneously.

"I'm glad you have approved. However your induction into the British way of eating is still not complete; you have yet to get the benefit of a fish and chip supper, not to mention a Sunday roast with Yorkshire pudding." He finished glowingly.

"Sounds very interesting to me and the way I see it there is no better person I would like to discover it with."

Marcus nodded coyly. "I will endeavour to do my best Jessica."

# JESSICA'S ASPIRATIONS

The ensuing years brought about abundant changes and a complete transformation of events, relating to Jessica's general progress. Her period of adjustment was positively heading in the right direction, indicating her real self-worth. Her efforts and her pragmatism were indeed the motivating factors that propelled her forward, in her relentless pursuit in securing her objective. Jessica became a student at a hospital in Brighton, under the auspices of Matron Andress. The Matron was something of an enigma and was very apathetic towards many of the young nurses with whom she felt were incapable of ever being good achievers. Her general approach was aggressive and very often callous. This was a recipe for making enemies and provoking fear. It was an atmosphere that Jessica endured routinely.

Her career was achieved against a backdrop of Matron Andress's sterile behaviour, which would not win prizes for making friends and influencing people. Realising the nature of the situation, Jessica embarked on a strategy that was extraordinary. As if guided by Marcus's policy of positive thinking, she found a solution that worked. Her motto was never to be daunted. She knew what she wanted to be and more so, what she intended to accomplish. As a result, she did her training with that in mind. Jessica could not be riled or intimidated. That, coupled by her excellent personality and a new found flare, she became not only noticeable but very much an inspiration for others to follow. Over time, her status was elevated to a point, where even Matron Andress paid quiet respect to her achievements and often sited Jessica as a very good example to copy.

Those three years passed very quickly and Jessica emerged in no uncertain terms as a formidable and well rounded human being. Having finished her training as a state registered nurse, she immediately enlisted into a London hospital concentrating her attention on becoming a midwife. Her progress in the field of study was excellent, but what was most remarkable was her physical development; which can only be regarded as stunning, to say the very least. Jessica had advanced from a modest introverted woman to an assertive and very assured individual. Gone was the string bean appearance that was once her natural characteristics, to a superbly structured and well proportioned, vivacious and distinctly elegant young woman. Her natural poise, accompanied by her attractiveness, which was her most enhancing feature, gave her a look of immense quality. Yet as a person, she was able to retain a degree of humbleness throughout. Her irresistible charm did not go unnoticed, even to Marcus, who observed her development with great interest and felt a sense of pride since her progress was mainly due to his fine management and unwavering friendship.

Contented by the fact also that this formidable woman was now a far cry from the one he met on SS Aracassa not so very long ago. It was an irrefutable fact that Jessica commanded attention at all levels. Her congenial manner never failed to attract interest. Her winning smile was very much a part of the engaging persona she possessed, rendering her a superb specimen of a woman.

# PRECILLA

Precilla, a young trainee nurse from Dominica, was Jessica's first contact in Brighton and almost immediately, a genuine friendship commenced. Precilla benefited from Jessica's camaraderie in many ways and was also influenced by her positive attitude. She was someone she could relate to, having been outnumbered by other nationalities for some time. It was good to have another Caribbean girl in the mix. She also brought an advantage that Precilla did not have. Jessica had a link with the City of London, giving Precilla an opportunity to visit this larger than life place, which had always been out of bounds to her. The tedium of Brighton was at long last at an end. Although Precilla had relations in England, a brother in Birmingham and an Aunt in Yorkshire, she was hardly inspired by the quiet country existence where she resided. Not knowing anyone in London kept her totally restricted.

Jessica's warmth and friendliness not only made her life more interesting, but it also gave her a chance to see and enjoy city life in all its splendour. Both parties had something to offer one another by way of compatibility, although Precilla's preference for music and dancing was far greater than that of Jessica's, whose love for reading and more of a relaxed existence was her port of call. That aside, there was enough quality in their relationship to make it a rich and enduring one. As a result, it gathered momentum. Precilla never missed an opportunity to visit London, mainly to demonstrate her dancing wizardry and to give satisfaction to her favourite pastime. She was able to visit the Astoria, The Empire and clubs of every description, became a routine feature in her quest for pleasure. It was at the Astoria that she met and quickly befriended Robin Tendis, a handsome Jamaican bus driver. Robin also loved dancing and it was a foregone conclusion that a binding relationship seemed inevitable. Love was truly in the air, enough to subsequently bring them together in courtship.

Robin was a level-headed young man, with ambitions to become a plumber and he pursued that dream with vigour and enthusiasm. Having qualified, he with Precilla's encouragement and assistance acquired a small run down property and turned it into a cosy home. Precilla on finishing her exams as a nurse joined Robin in London and became a co-owner of the property. In the interim, Precilla's friendship with Jessica grew from strength to strength. The loyalty they possessed for one another never wavered. It was a thing of beauty. So much so, Jessica regarded Precilla not only as a friend but as a sister and confidant.

What was of great significance in the grand scheme of things, as the months went by, Jessica could not help listening to the dedication and constant adoration that Marcus heaped on Sara and Peter; his children. He was undoubtedly a devoted father, who felt deprived of their absence and although he was confident they were in good hands and saw great benefits being in the custody of someone he trusted implicitly; his mother, knowing also their interests would be best served by her, he nevertheless missed them massively. He longed to have them back where they belonged, in safekeeping and ultimately in his care.

The breakdown of his marriage had brought about their departure, which in many ways became inevitable. But he was certain, based on his own upbringing, his mother's abilities to inculcate values and respect, were incentives that were bound to impact on his children. For those reasons alone he thought it was one redeeming feature with which he was comfortable. However, what bothered Marcus markedly was the fact that the children may inculcate the belief that they were abandoned. Remembering that their mother paid scant interest in them before her departure and now being some distance away from him, he believed they may develop the notion that they were orphans of one kind or another.

Mindful of those thoughts, Marcus did everything possible to dispel those ideas, by making them as comfortable as they could ever be. He kept instilling in them the knowledge that it was only a matter of time before they would be reunited. Influenced by his constant discussion about them and seeing photographs in every corner, Jessica experienced an urgent need to be involved.

Jessica's interest in Peter and Sara became heightened. So much so, she requested his permission and received quiet acquiescence to communicate with them through written correspondence. What resulted was both surprising and rewarding for her. Letters came and went in such rapid frequency, that it was as if they knew each other all their lives. Aunt Jessica's popularity exceeded all expectations and in the process, Marcus almost became secondary. Gifts and other presents were given with some regularity, culminating in a rich and very worthwhile connection. Jessica grew in personality to an extent that she became privy to things even Marcus was not aware of. Even though he was conscious of her influence, one which had a measure of dominance, he was far from troubled by it, concluding to himself that it was healthy and above board.

Another feature that was well established was Adel's seemingly comfortable relationship with Jessica. It was a situation Marcus thought could have had dire consequences. However, it turned out to have the very opposite effect. Marcus initially sold his sister to Jessica as a somewhat troublesome individual. He felt that her actions were principally responsible for the premature collapse of his marriage. Adel's constant interference and her deliberate aggressive manner ruined what was left of his relationship. At best, she was more bothersome than she needed to be. In his opinion, if she was more accommodating towards Teresa, he felt the marriage could have been saved. Her detestation for Teresa knew no bounds, although it cannot be denied it was reciprocal. Teresa was most apathetic towards Adel and she was not afraid of showing it. In a strange way, she was born thinking everyone was beneath her and her blatant disregard for others came naturally. Adel, on the other hand, thought that the marriage was a complete sham, borne out of opportunism than of love. As a result, she felt justified in accelerating the demise of the marriage for the sake of her brother. She only wanted happiness for her young brother and was more than prepared to fight his corner.

Extraordinarily, however, Adel's attitude towards Jessica appeared remarkably positive. There was nothing to suggest otherwise. She was warm towards her and welcomed her with open arms. What was not obvious to Marcus was his sister's thought process – her general mindset. She wanted happiness for Marcus and although Jessica seemed undernourished and in need of care when she first arrived, she had blossomed into a fine and very attractive individual. It would not have mattered anyway, as far as Adel was concerned, anyone, but anyone would have been acceptable, as long as it wasn't Teresa. Even if she was half human half beast, such was the antipathy of Adel towards her estranged sister-in-law, who she was positive shared the very same sentiments towards her.

It was a late summers evening. The feeble sun, shining weakly in the distant horizon, quickly lost its effective hold on daylight, to the predominant rush of darkness. Jessica checked her watch, as she eagerly anticipated seeing her friend Precilla in her brand new environment. They had reached an agreement not to see each other until it was appropriate to do so.

It was also the first opportunity for Jessica to feast her eyes on the rapid development the couple had made in their effort of transforming a shabby old building into a thing of beauty. Robin's dedicated effort was more than justified, turning this almost uninhabitable wreck into a cosy and very impressively comfortable and well-deserved home.

Precilla opened the door beaming from ear to ear. It was certainly more than a welcome gesture. "Girl...! Am I glad to see you? I missed you so much." Precilla announced eagerly.

They fell into each other's arms in a warm embrace.

"So am I." Jessica echoed. "As you can see, I obeyed instructions not to come until you were good and ready."

"Good on you." Precilla beamed. "I just wanted the old place to be finished before you saw it."

Jessica began her careful scrutiny and appreciated every moment of it. "Girl, you have certainly done wonders to this place. I cannot help but be impressed."

"Me?" Precilla responded. "No credit to me, it was Robin, he turned this old workhorse into a thoroughbred."

"He sure did," Jessica replied.

"And you have not seen the best yet," Precilla said, as she held Jessica by the hand in escort.

"You remember where the toilet was? It was outside the kitchen." She burst out in laughter adding. "My dear, you would freeze your butt off using it, but that's not all, this place did not have a bathroom."

"Are you kidding me?" Jessica asked.

"No, not at all; Robin said the folks that lived here would visit the public baths at weekends. Otherwise, it was a good old fashioned wash in the kitchen sink."

"That's unbelievable. People don't live like that do they?" Jessica asked.

"Apparently it's an old tradition child. It's just a case of what you're used to." Precilla stopped and turned to face her friend. "The other day an English nurse, a very nice young lady, asked me why I washed so frequently. Was it a habit? Or did I want to become like her?

"Whatever did she mean? Do you want to be white?" An astonished Jessica asked.

"Well, that's the way I interpreted the question. So I smiled and said no darling, I merely wash to stay on the right side of good hygiene. I wash to keep clean, don't you?"

Jessica grinned loftily. "And what did she say?"

"Nothing," Precilla replied. "She just stood there and looked totally puzzled."

"Worry not darling; I guess we will continue to be the subject of study for years to come. I just wonder if they'll ever find the answers they are looking for." Jessica mused.

Precilla chucked. "Honey, at this moment, that is not my problem. White folks will always be curious about black folks, so let them. Anyway, there is a lot more for you to see."

Precilla turned to engage her friend in close contact. Her excitement was difficult to conceal. "This is your room when you visit. I want you to be as comfortable here as you are with Marcus."

"What are you saying girl? You don't have to do this and what's more, I won't let you." An astonished Jessica replied.

"My friend, you have no say in this matter. Robin and I have agreed that there will always be a place in our house for you and that is final."

"What have I done to deserve this?" Jessica questioned.

"Look young lady." Precilla countered. "That's what good friends are for. You are the best friend I have ever had. You came to Brighton and changed my life completely. Looking back, I wonder how life would have been without knowing you. Besides; it was you who gave me the opportunity to meet the love of my life. I tell you, girl, you are indispensable."

"I'm nothing of the sort. It was your personality that won the day." Jessica insisted.

Precilla, still with a twinkle in her eyes, smiled sweetly. "That night when you took me to The Astoria, is a night I will never forget. I can remember Robin standing there looking at me and I immediately said to myself, I hope he's not attached because I would simply want him to be my man."

Jessica chuckled. "Robin was admiring you right from the start. He saw an attractive, effervescent woman he simply could not resist."

"Honey, the feeling was mutual." Precilla insisted. "But it was you that took me there and made it all possible."

Jessica studied her friend momentarily. "Precilla, my dear, fate plays an important part in all of our lives and as the saying goes, 'what will be will be'."

VICTOR WALDRON

"I could not agree more," Precilla responded. "But for someone like you, who is not crazy about dancing, you selflessly took me to a place where I found the man of my dreams. How's that for good fortune?"

Jessica giggled. "Come on Precilla, you talked about nothing else. You cannot help prancing about. Dancing is what you love best so I took you there to make you happy."

Precilla nodded affirmatively. "It's funny, isn't it? We are the best of pals, yet we crave different things. You love books, I just love to dance and I'm crazy about music." Replied Precilla as she wriggled her body.

"Hey, steady on girl. I love music and dancing too, but give me a good book any day." Jessica suggested.

"Don't I know that? You are a bookworm, an egghead. Give you a good book and you are in heaven."

"Well, I would not exactly put it that way. But with an interesting book in hand, I can comfortably find a niche in paradise."

"I know. That's exactly how I feel when I'm twirling around to great music. There is nothing better in this whole wide world... except sex."

The two young ladies giggled merrily as they sipped their wine. Precilla turned slowly to confront Jessica. "Are you still writing to the kids or was it just a passing phase?"

Jessica threw her head back in mirth. "Girl, that's a full-time occupation. We have bonded remarkably well. I just love corresponding with them. It's as if I knew them all their lives."

Precilla found the entire situation rather strange. "What does Marcus think about that? You are taking over the children wholesale!"

"He's okay with it. In fact, he finds it fascinating that I'm able to get so much out of them."

"You are an incredible woman," Precilla uttered. "You have that Midas touch that makes things go smoothly, yet you seem unable to transfer that great gift of yours to Marcus."

Jessica nodded agreement. "How right you are, Marcus is not one for changing his mind easily. That is his problem."

Precilla chuckled amusingly. "What are you saying girl? Marcus is a red-blooded man. Are you really telling me he cannot appreciate a pretty woman?"

"I guess he can, but you know the score. We've discussed this a hundred times before. He is not one for change. Look! Marcus isn't looking for an affair and our reputation is based on a solid respect for each other. I imagine that will always remain the case."

"My sweet friend; what will it take for him to observe that you are one hell of a woman? As I recall you have been in love with that man since Noah was building his ark and I am perplexed to understand why he hasn't noticed you as yet. He may not have twenty-twenty vision, but any half blind person would recognise how truly special you are."

Jessica found the remark amusing. "Precilla, give me a break, I'm nothing special, don't give me what I don't deserve."

"But you are and please don't tell me what I'm seeing is false, your problem is you're too gracious to admit it."

"I'm quite adjusted to the way things are with Marcus. You know the old saying what will be will be."

Precilla smiled. "Young lady you are too good to be true. You are one in a million."

The long saga of Jessica's deep feelings for Marcus was discussed repeatedly and in confidence with Precilla with no particular end result. Precilla's advice as far as her friend was concerned, became too obvious and very much to the point. Her ideas were very simple. With Jessica being such an attractive woman with so much natural charm, making Marcus take notice of her, should not be difficult. She had matured well. Long gone was that insipidly angular individual she once was, blossoming into an attractive, vivacious and stunning woman and indeed a great deal more. Infused with other fine enhancing attributes such as poise, elegance and generosity, she was now a woman of irresistible potential. Her gracious smile fitted amicably with the rest of her facial contour. Her manicured bronze complexion was a transformation of extraordinary proportions. Destiny was more than kind to her, rewarding her with gifts reserved only for a tiny few. She had emerged to become a substantial woman, with enough verve to be a challenge for any man including Marcus.

Jessica smiled pleasantly. "That, I'm afraid, is the great irony. I believe Marcus knows how I feel about him, but he is someone who holds true to the things he believes in. As you know, he is a very principled man. In his mind, he is convinced I am too young for him and somewhere in the crevice of his cranium; he still harbours hope of Teresa's return.

"Don't make me laugh child. That man is delusional, listen to me – Teresa is gone forever. What Marcus needs is a reality check. While she has found love, he is hoping for a miracle." Precilla paused for a moment gathering her thoughts. "Tell me; is there any way you can reconnect with Alan?"

Jessica laughed out aloud. "You are not really serious are you?"

"Just checking," Precilla replied. "After all, he was the man that caused you to be here, am I correct?"

"Yes that's true, but I'm afraid for now Alan is very much a lost cause. We have not communicated since I am here in London. Secondly, he's always boasted that he had no interest in coming here. Last but not least, I have lost any kind of real feeling for him since I'm here. The truth is, after a great deal of consideration, Alan is not the kind of man I would want around me anymore. He was never going to be satisfied with one woman. He has roving eyes. Not a good recipe for someone like me." She concluded.

"Well, that sounds sensible." Precilla intimated. "So we can safely dispense with that notion? Let's just say that idea died a natural death."

"That's so correct," Jessica responded. "It's been a long time and I think that is now in the past, although so that I'm not misunderstood, I do think about him occasionally."

Precilla offered a heavy sigh. "Then that brings us back to the subject proper – Mr Marcus."

"Yes, we are back where we started." A smiling Jessica responded.

Precilla placed her glass on the table to focus on her good friend. "Jessie, if you think Marcus is the man for you do whatever you can to help it along. Let's face it; you have the looks, you are a sweet and charming person, you are smart, you have the body most women would die for, if that's the case, do what comes naturally."

"And what would that be?" Jessica enquired.

"Show him you care. Be positive. You can captivate any man alive. You have what it takes. Use your femininity, show him your sexy side and darling, if push comes to shove, just seduce him."

"What?" Jessica retorted.

"You heard me, child, seduce him, and go after what you want."

Jessica's reaction was one of amazement. Never would she have imagined her best friend would advocate such a rash or daring suggestion. In ordinary situations, such actions or ploys may well succeed, but she would never consider herself in that category. Much as she cared deeply for Marcus, she was not prepared to adopt such crude antics to champion her cause. There was too much respect between Marcus and herself which was of a very high standard. As such in her estimation, it should never be breached, whatever the situation. As a result, she was not likely to adopt tactics of the kind that her friend Precilla was offering.

"Precilla! What are you asking me to do?" An astonished Jessica asked.

"I'm merely saying to you to give the man a nudge in the right direction. A little boldness cannot do you any harm."

Jessica giggled nervously. "That may be the correct thing to do if you are ruthless. But you know me well enough to understand the person I am, I'm just not built that way."

Precilla replenished her empty glass and turned to study her friend momentarily. "You know something? I did not expect you to take my advice and you're right; you're just not that type of girl. But sometimes you have to take the bull by the horns. There is certainly no harm in that. I knew what I wanted when I saw Robin and I was prepared to fight like a Trojan to get him, but not everyone can do that, I guess I'm not the template you would like to follow. You are too gentle and sophisticated a woman and you deserve only the best. You are a true lady and I am not."

Jessica blushed visibly. "I know what you're trying to do is in my best interests. You're not someone who would try to cause me grief."

"Right first time." Precilla echoed. "You are too precious to me, to ever imagine hurting you. Sometimes things get the better of me and I say things I shouldn't say, but believe me, I meant no harm."

Jessica smiled broadly. "Okay, okay! Good friends are forever, let's drink to that. Look we cannot solve the world's problems in one go."

Precilla sighed heavily; relieved she did not upset Jessica by her robust suggestion. Sitting opposite her, Jessica was beaming from ear to ear.

"What?" Precilla enquired. "What are you so happy about all of a sudden?"

Jessica was still grinning broadly. "Good news girl; good news."

"Go on then." Precilla insisted. "Don't keep me in suspense."

"Well, I managed to pass my exams and I'm now a fully fledged midwife."

"Wow!" Precilla exclaimed. "That's remarkable. Girl, you have it all: beauty as well as brains. I'm so pleased for you."

"Thanks. I'm so glad it's all over, now I can begin to plan my life accordingly."

"So what are you planning to do? You clever, clever bunny."

"Okay, what I have in mind at the moment is probably not the best news that you would want to hear, but I'm seriously getting the urge to return to my homeland, somehow Trinidad beckons."

"What?" Precilla exclaimed. "For a holiday I hope!"

"Not really. As things stand, I'm beginning to think it's for the best – besides, I would be good company for my Mum, especially since my dad has gone AWOL."

Precilla put her fingers in her ears. "I really don't want to hear this. How can you even think of doing such a thing? How on earth do you expect me to cope without you?"

"Don't mock me, child, you have Robin, he's your pride and joy. I have no doubt he will give you all the happiness you deserve."

Precilla's frown was one of displeasure. "I know I have Robin, but you are my special friend and I shall miss you so very much."

"Likewise," Jessica responded. "I will miss you like crazy. This is not an easy decision to make, if I make it at all. But right now I'm leaning towards the idea – anyway, no matter what, we will still be the best of friends and perhaps you can come and visit, you know you will always be welcomed."

"Don't worry young lady; you have not seen the last of me," Precilla reassured as she placed her glass on the table. She pondered for a while before asking questions she considered to be important. "Do you mind if I pry a little?"

"Fire away," Jessica responded. "I have very few secrets to hide."

"Why have you decided to take such a drastic step all of a sudden? And what about Marcus, are you giving up on him?"

"Well! I received a letter from Peter, telling me that they would be back here in a few months' time. That to me is a signal that it is time to go. Marcus would need a lot of time to bond with his children, which would only be fair."

"I agree," Precilla argued. "But surely, if you really care for the man, you have to let him know how you feel."

"Are you kidding me? Look, I think he knows how I feel about him, after all, he's not blind, but he has a philosophy that will never change and it would be foolish of me to expect anything else. I know him well enough to believe that it would be wishing for a pie in the sky. Believe me Precilla, he's no ordinary man."

Precilla shook her head sadly. "How on earth can a man resist such a beautiful woman like you, it's something I really cannot understand."

VICTOR WALDRON

"I can." Jessica declared confidently. "The whole truth is, Marcus is not seeking an affair. He does respect our friendship, but most importantly, he wants a wife, preferably the one that left him all those years ago and in his head, that's still possible."

"Well, we know that's not going to happen." Precilla reinforced. "The white boy is not about to let her go and the sooner he understands that the better. He must understand she has found love."

Jessica smiled politely. "That may be true, but Marcus is a super optimist. He's one of a kind. He sincerely believes somewhere, somehow, that miracle will happen."

"Maybe." Precilla grinned. "But I have a message for him, pigs do not fly."

"Try telling him that. He has told me time and time again, that what he wishes for invariably comes true."

"Look! Let's deal with reality here. Marcus may be lots of things but there's a limit to wishful thinking." Precilla paused momentarily before adding: "You know something; I think you are too close to Marcus. Why don't you come and live with us and see what comes of it? That might stir him up and besides; you can take your time deciding about what you want to do."

Jessica giggled joyously. "That is the best offer I've had in a long time. You are determined to have me here aren't you?"

"Not at all." Precilla countered. "I'm trying to stop you from making hasty decisions. More to the point, if Marcus sees less of you, he may come to his senses. He will realise what he's missing."

Jessica was somewhat amused. "Precilla, you are a true friend, but like I said before, my mother needs me. My dad, who is in the twilight of his years, has decided to leave my Mum for a younger model. Isn't that the action of a lunatic?"

"It certainly is," Precilla responded. "Your dad is not chasing a young woman, he is merely satisfying his ego. Some men are like that."

"I know," Jessica complained. "My dad has left a good woman for nothing more than cheap pleasures. Anyway, this gives me an opportunity to have some quality time with her and to also do something different with my life. You know, I need a new perspective; something to get my teeth into."

"Sounds like a good idea, but I think you can do that right here. As for your father, he cannot be thinking straight. That reminds me of what my mother always says."

"What might that be? Some pearl of wisdom I guess." Jessica enquired.

"Some men would look for the biggest tree to chop down, even though the axe they are using is as blunt as hell, but that would not stop them from trying."

Jessica chuckled heartily. "You are so right. I guess they enjoy the challenge."

"Or they like to make a complete fool of themselves," Precilla suggested.

Both ladies saw the funny side of the joke. Precilla got up and placed her hand on Jessica's shoulder. "Forgive me for saying this, but don't give up on Marcus just yet. I know how you feel about him and I think you should be patient and see what gives."

"Precilla," Jessica announced. "I'm not about to leave tomorrow, but I'm not sticking around for the sake of it. I'm letting you know what I have in mind so you will not be surprised if or when it happens."

Precilla sprung out of her chair. "I know, I know." She uttered excitedly. "Have you told Marcus the good news about your exams?"

"Not yet. You are the first to know what I have in mind."

"Well, I've got an idea," Precilla announced still excited. "I know a lovely place in Greek Street. Invite him to celebrate your success. It's a fabulous little hideout. Candle lights, champagne, the lot. The ambiance is also excellent, everything you need to bring out the best in anyone."

"You are a right romantic. Do you know that? May I ask how you discovered this place?" Jessica enquired.

"Robin took me there. Girl, this place has an aura all its own. Take him there and if that does not blow him away, nothing will."

"It's that kind of a place is it?" Jessica quizzed.

"It's that and more. Look, it's my treat. I will set it up for you. Mind you, I cannot guarantee success, but I will be truly astonished if you do not capture his heart and soul."

Jessica pondered the idea for a moment. "I don't know Precilla. I really don't want to make a fool of myself."

"Look, young lady, you are a woman of class. You have what most women would sell their back teeth to get. You are gorgeous in every sense of the word. This is your opportunity to show the man your femininity, let him know how much you care. Use your girliness to get the better of him. My dear friend, take it from me, he will not be able to resist you."

Jessica's face grew into a broad smile. "I have to give it to you Precilla, if there's one thing you are not short of, it's confidence."

Precilla tilted her head in one direction as if to study Jessica. "My lovely friend, everyone has a quality that can be used to their advantage. You can knock 'em dead with looks. Little ole me, all I have is the quality to force the issue with enough gusto to get what I want and do you know something? More often than not, it works."

They looked at each other and simultaneously broke into laughter; eventually falling into each other's embrace.

"You are a devil in disguise, do you know that?" Jessica informed.

"I would hardly doubt that, but you know what they say, there is a bit of devil in all of us, so there!!"

Jessica agreed with her friend readily. "Precilla, you may not believe this, but what you've suggested has a certain appeal. I guess it would do no harm giving it a go."

"That's the spirit girl. It's the best news you've given me today. The way I see it, you are certainly onto a winner."

"It had better work, for your sake, or I'll have to come back and kill you."

Precilla laughed out loud. "You'll have to find me first. Anyway let's look at this positively, what can you lose? I always say there is no harm in trying."

They both contemplated the idea momentarily, enough for Jessica to digest what was being hatched by her good friend. Suddenly she broke into a warm smile. "Precilla, you've convinced me that this thing could work, let's do it."

Precilla's eyes glistened with excitement. "Just what I wanted to hear, let's have a drink to that."

They clinked glasses in merriment to celebrate what was now a confident and hopefully successful plan.

# SEDUCTION

Marcus's surprise was real. He wondered if this was some sort of elaborate hoax. Was someone playing a game too complicated for him to fathom? In his mind's eye, this venue and its surroundings did not remotely represent Jessica's normal personality. If it was, then he had totally misjudged her. This place exuded amorous intent. The cosy habitat had a stimulating effect, enough to inject or induce sensual connotations. In its own remarkable way, the atmosphere that predominated lifted his spirits and generated a vibrancy that amply reflected this very pleasant moment.

He did not have to ponder long. Shortly after he settled, Jessica appeared. She looked exquisite. The soft lights enhanced her radiance and tangibly augmented her natural beauty. She displayed profound sensual attraction beyond his expectations. This was in his mind a remarkable transformation.

Jessica was certainly no stranger to Marcus, yet for the first time, he saw a woman of immense quality, a delightfully amazing person he failed to have noticed before, at least not in this manner. He watched her progress from a shy and somewhat introverted woman, into the person she had now become. Woven into the fabric of their relationship, was a deep respect for each other's privacy. Over the years that remained intact for obvious reasons. Her age represented a huge barrier for one and the hope, the very remotest hope that Teresa one day may acknowledge the error of her ways and return home where she belongs. His optimism regarding the latter was now in diminishing proportions, however, the unwritten rule that was established somewhere in his subconscious mind, remained steadfast until now. Similarly, Jessica understood and very much appreciated the situation. Marcus was not one for changing his mind and she was well aware of that.

Totally mindful of Marcus's position and conversant with what he stood for; this bold exploit of hers was completely out of her comfort zone. It was, however, an opportunity to once and for all allow her emotions to surface. Her mission was to boldly go where she had never gone before and to declare her true feelings once and for all. She thought Marcus had laboured long and hard to revive what was imminently irretrievable; his rationale of ever having Teresa again was now an unattainable, pointless and irrelevant. She was a thing of the past, a bad memory that was best forgotten. He needed to escape from that situation. This was a chance to rekindle his sense of joy and happiness. She thought he deserved it and if it was in the realms of possibility to change his mind and to simply offer an alternative, namely herself, she would gladly do so. This was an induced plan; one that had Precilla's influence written all over it. Should it work, it would be the perfect answer to her wishes. It would be a wonderful dream come true; she loved Marcus implicitly. He represented all the good things a man should be and she was prepared to risk whatever it took to obtain her objective. However, she felt it would be prudent to manage expectations in case of disappointment. Failure would be a major setback, which ultimately would leave no other option than to return to her homeland and to make a fresh start.

Jessica smiled daintily. Marcus offered pleasantries in return. His was consumed by the element of this unexpected surprise. "This is most luxurious." He confessed. "I never expected anything so fabulous." Still maintaining her pleasantness, she sat gracefully beside him. "Well, I think you deserve it, don't you?"

"That depends." He responded, still scanning the joint. "You said it was a surprise, but I hardly had anything like this in mind."

Jessica's smile widened. "I hope you approve. I would be very disappointed if you're not impressed."

"How can I fail to be impressed? I'm still baffled to find out why you've gone to such great lengths." He mused.

Jessica's relaxed manner and her quiet confidence lifted her stature immensely. She was at her radiant best. "It's what you would call a little bit of payback. I have been on the receiving end of your hospitality all these years. Don't you think it's fair that I'm able to respond in kind?"

"I cannot argue with that." He confessed. "But you don't have to prove anything to me. What I have done for you was always a great pleasure."

Jessica's grin grew even wider. "Look! When was the last time you had a good night out? I mean an exceptionally good night?" Marcus chuckled loudly. "It must be many, many moons ago. Look – I'm not complaining, it's just that this seems a bit special."

"That's where you come in." She reminded him. "You are a very special person and I think you should be rewarded for that."

"Okay, Jessica. I bow to your wisdom and I'm very grateful." Marcus agreed.

"Good, then I expect you to make the best of a wonderful evening."

The waiter poured wine into their half-filled glasses, as Marcus gleamed at his young companion. "I think this would be an appropriate time to give you some good news of my own." Marcus declared.

"Wonderful." Jessica acknowledged. "I hope it's exciting."

"I think it is. But first, let's hear the good news you have to give to me. After all, it must be very important." He suggested.

"Well! It would be nice if you start the ball rolling by giving me your good news." Jessica urged.

"Ah hah" He chuckled. "No deal, this is your party, remember?" He reminded her.

"Okay if you insist. I've passed my exams with flying colours and I am now a fully qualified midwife." She gushed.

"Oh, that's absolutely wonderful. I'm so pleased for you." He remarked gleefully.

"This calls for a drink, don't you think?" Echoed Jessica, as she picked up her glass and pointed to Marcus to follow suit. This remarkable spirit of cordiality lifted the mood of Marcus appreciably. His comforting smile demonstrated his sense of contentment.

"Are you trying to get me intoxicated?" He quizzed mockingly.

"No, but I'm proud of my success and I can think of no other person with whom I would want to share this moment with, other than you."

Marcus lifted his glass graciously. "That's very generous of you Jessica and congratulations are very much in order. I think you really deserve it."

Jessica bowed gently. "Why thank you, kind sir."

Marcus was still in awe of the situation. "You know what I think? With your intellect, you should do something more challenging, like medicine. Make no mistake, you have what it takes."

"That is high praise indeed. I guess tonight is the night I should be open to flattery." She offered.

"This is no flattery, my dear, you have the ability and you know it."

Jessica nodded politely. "Thank you, Marcus, you are most kind."

"Come on my dear, you know I'm right, all you need is self-belief and you can go the distance. The sky's the limit." Marcus declared.

Jessica's buoyant mood allowed her to giggle freely like a teenager.

"I'm glad someone has that level of confidence in me. You never know! I might even take your advice and go the whole hog; but before I do, would you give me the good news you promised?"

Marcus's smile was as wide as a barn door. "Oh yes, the good news is about my kids. Sara and Peter will be back here in a matter of months. Isn't that wonderful?"

Jessica, wearing a bland look, tried her very best not to give the game away. After all, it was a blue ribbon day for Marcus. The arrival of his children back to London meant a great deal to him and she was quite determined not to spoil his big surprise.

"That's fantastic news; I guess you are beside yourself with joy to see them again."

Still beaming with delight, he nodded affirmatively. "You've got that right. I just cannot wait to welcome them back home."

She paused for a while before delivering the truth. "You know Marcus, without trying to put a damper on things, I do know that the kids will be back soon and I share your happiness."

For a brief moment, Marcus looked puzzled but recovered quickly. "Of course; of course; what is the matter with me? You are so much a part of these kids' lives, I should have known better."

"I hope I did not spoil your big secret," Jessica suggested.

"Not in the least." He responded. "You have been very good to them and I thank you sincerely for that."

"So, this is really a good night to celebrate; both your success and mine." Jessica indicated.

Marcus giggled boyishly. "Not at all, this is your night. It's a great credit to you and your success. Tonight belongs to you, my dear."

"I'm glad you see it that way," Jessica remarked calmly. "But I honestly would want it to be your night also."

Marcus was now visibly relaxed. Bathed in a state of calmness; his otherwise defensive posture swiftly dissipated. The same was true for Jessica, who was now pleasantly tactile. She reached out and took his hands into hers soothingly, lifting his spirits to a higher degree.

"Marcus, may I ask you a serious question?"

"Of course you can." He assured her.

"You are undoubtedly an extremely amazing human being. Why are you living a fantasy?"

Marcus looked quizzical. "I don't quite understand the question."

"Well, apart from your kids that bring you a great deal of joy, you seem to be putting your own happiness on hold. As I see it, you still believe or hope that Teresa would one day return; a hope that can only lead to despair. In reality, you have to accept it is not going to happen."

Marcus's expression altered appreciably. His conscious mind readily acknowledged Jessica's distinctiveness with a degree of deference. It was, if anything, nearer to the truth than he was prepared to accept. Yet somewhere in his mind, he felt committed to this illusion – this hope, slight and remote as it was, that Teresa would come to her senses and return to the fold, if only for the sake of her children.

"No one can predict what the future holds." He stubbornly contested. "It may or may not be, but there is a vision in my head that it can happen. I sincerely believe that all things are possible."

Jessica immediately observed that there was a weakening in his manner, decided to press forward. Holding his hands she began caressing them tenderly.

"Marcus, wishing for something to happen means nothing. You must not delude yourself any longer. Believe me, I'm a woman and I think I'm in a position to say with some authority, that when someone like Teresa finds love, it is forever. You've admitted to me, she fell in love with Jonny. That means she has found her happiness. Let her be. Find a way to release that dream that haunts you. Life is too short to be clutching at straws."

Marcus tried desperately to present a smile, but one was not forthcoming. He scratched his head and took a sip of his wine.

"Perhaps you are right about Teresa. Maybe she has found what she was looking for, but I am much older than you and perhaps not wiser on this particular matter, however, my entire life has been about making the impossible possible. Look, Jessica, where I came from, no one would have given me the faintest chance of achieving the heights that I have managed and yet here I am."

"Yes." Jessica insisted. "I very much agree; you have achieved miracles and heaven knows you've earned it, but you have to remember that lightning does not strike twice in the same place. If anything, you are a sure winner, so move on and continue to champion your cause in the manner that made you the man you are today."

At last Marcus found a smile befitting the occasion. "Can you remember the first time we met on the *Aracassa*? Something about you, even then... and let's face it, you were in a miserable state, yet somehow I instinctively knew you were someone special."

Jessica nodded assent. "I remember alright. Perhaps for the first time in my life, I felt suicidal. I owe you so much. It was an experience I shall never forget."

Marcus giggled briefly. "Well young lady, you have come a long way; from the depths of despair to a successful future career as a midwife."

Jessica's smile was as warm as the summer's evening. And thanks to you I still have my sanity."

Marcus looked at Jessica affectionately. "Believe me, you were merely the victim of fear. You were placed in a position of uncertainty and apprehension. You were overtaken by circumstances beyond your control and with a future, you could not envisage. No one so young should be placed in a situation like that."

Jessica nodded agreement. "You are so right. To say I was confused would be putting it mildly. The fact that you came to my rescue was an eternal blessing."

"Like I said before." Marcus asserted. "Fate has a hand in all things. In a strange way, our meeting was meant to be."

"Then let's make tonight a night to remember." Jessica insisted.

Marcus's reaction was enhanced by Jessica's prevailing persona. She reached forward and with a graceful nudge, kissed his cheek tenderly. Marcus felt an emotional rush that was rapid and immediate. The dryness of his mouth, the racing of his pulse and the pounding of his heart moved this man of steel into a state of complete physical vulnerability. There was no doubt in his mind that a combination of things contributed to this overwhelming situation. The aesthetics for one; the fine wine; the companionship of a delightful woman and the aura of ethereal enormity, placed him in a subliminal state that he rarely ventured before.

Marcus was now functioning in the abstract, where rules do not apply. His heightened presence placed him in a parallel world where all that mattered was the here and now. Although his natural instincts suggested a tinge of imminent danger, his defensive mechanism, strong and sturdy in the past had deserted him comprehensively. As a result, his principles, which were his strongest assets, fell away like dry leaves in a storm. His discipline melted like ice in tropical heat and his willpower, a vital component in that make-up, collapsed like a house in a hurricane. He was now undoubtedly the victim of his own desires. A man immersed in an amazing state of exhilaration that processed smoothly and rapidly forward, like a runaway train.

The evening moved inexorably onwards. Man and woman without inhibition or fear, consumed only by that natural momentum of mutual compatibility of the moment and beyond. In that remarkable process, they made love. It was an inevitable conclusion and merely a page in the chapter of this unique adventure in all its essential glory. Their bodies and souls welded admirably in a splendid collaboration that reached a summit of their aspirations and finished as it began in harmony and magical splendour. It was an evening that was committed to memory. It was the epitome of perfection, one that could not be surpassed.

# A CHANGE OF HEART

It was the following morning and Marcus was awakened by the sound of tweeting birds outside his window. His far from clear mind was still in the process of ingesting events from the past evening. It was undoubtedly moments to savour and by the same token, he relished the full consequence of it. Yet, in his estimation, he realised it was fraught with danger. He was certain it was not a mirage since the body of Jessica lay adjacent to his in deep slumber. Her naked bosom heaving gently upwards and downwards in measured proportions. He recalled the evening with some degree of awe. It was like no other evening that he'd ever experienced. Fantasy more than anything else vividly came to mind. If anything, he was still in a state of ecstasy.

Jessica was clearly central to his thoughts as he pondered events that transpired hours earlier, which was obviously still fresh in his mind. In his estimation, she was a woman transformed in a way that he did not think possible. Her amazing personality shone through like a beacon. That he was captivated by the enormity of her charm was simply inevitable. It was, without doubt, an incredible evening, one that was distinctive in every way possible, culminating naturally and progressively in a passionate and romantic embrace.

Making love to her was the ultimate conclusion and an experience never to be forgotten. Still fresh in his mind also, was Jessica's declaration of love for him, her overwhelming desire to remain committed and her sincere hope that her expressed love would be reciprocated. Although his scale of feeling for her could not be measured in the degree that she expressed, there was hardly any doubt in his own mind that for the first time his affection for her was more than he cared to admit. Aggrieved by his own vulnerability on that particular occasion, he fervently hoped that he did not give rise to any false impression so far as romantic notions were concerned.

Top of his agenda and regarded as his utmost priority was his children returning to London. Nothing but nothing in his opinion should interrupt that. He needed to give his fullest attention to them. Whatever he may have promised in his moment of madness, his children's natural transition would acquire every ounce of his energy, in order for them to adjust to the country they left so long ago. Therefore, constructive planning and a process of recalibration were in order. He needed a strategy, an exit door; he was hoping for something that would not cause undue harm or distress to Jessica's feelings. What was done could not be undone, but it was imperative to create an interim period to ponder matters; a new perspective that would not hurt Jessica's pride in any way.

Jessica came to the breakfast table with a glow of satisfaction written all over her face. Although she showed signs of fatigue, her general disposition was relatively amenable. She pulled her gown around her naked body, eliminating the chill of the moment.

"Good morning." She announced with an engaging smile. "I hope you enjoyed last evening."

Marcus nodded affirmatively. "It was wonderful; much more than I ever anticipated."

Sitting next to Marcus and still glowing, she held his hands, a gesture that required a positive response, but none was forthcoming. Immediately her natural instincts indicated to her that he was reverting to type. Observing Marcus with startled consternation and dismay, her emotions were still actively functional from that extraordinary and most fabulous experience; she could not believe the negative response that was in evidence.

"Marcus! You amaze me. I thought what we enjoyed last evening was most special and completely out of the ordinary. In fact, it was divine. I get the impression that it was not the same for you?" She said.

Marcus mustered an unconvincing smirk. "On the contrary, it was a fabulous evening. Believe me, it was all the things you've mentioned. However, the news of Peter and Sara was somehow getting in the way of what was an unforgettable occasion."

Jessica was quick to summarise the situation. As far as she was concerned it was an open and shut case of what she was to expect. The wall of defensive posture that collapsed and turned to rubble the evening before was being erected once more, brick by brick; instantaneously forecasting a bleak future.

"Oh yes." She agreed. "I almost forgot the kids. There you go Marcus; you must be the happiest man this side of paradise."

Marcus noticed a tinge of sarcasm in her voice and attempted as best he could to steer clear of anything that would mar the harmony he was desperately hoping to achieve. He studied her for some moments, knowing perhaps that the inclusion of his children at this time was somewhat out of place. However, since he imagined it was a vital component in his strategy, he felt it necessary to do so.

"You know Jessica, last night was simply unbelievable and it was out of this world and way beyond anything I can recall in my entire life. I want you always to remember that. The truth is I do need a period of contemplation, to get these kids acclimatised and in readiness for their adult lives. I also need some constructive ideas about where I go from here."

"Well," Jessica replied. "I quite understand. What do you want me to do?"

"I need some time to work things out. As you know, nothing is cut and dried, but I will find some answers."

She gave out a huge sigh. "Perhaps, we crossed the line last evening. Maybe it was a step too far, would you agree?"

"No, no, no. We may try but we cannot predict our tomorrows. Let's take it step by step and hope for a favourable outcome."

She nodded her head in agreement. She thought she understood Marcus well enough for that. Her time spent with him was not wasted. She knew he was not susceptible to change. That was his modus operandi. He was a magnanimous individual; a man of very high principles and impeccable standards also. Above everything else, he was undoubtedly a kind and honest human being. She could easily testify to that, having been on the receiving end of his generous nature from the very inception. That has always been his way, so why change the habit of a lifetime!

His Christian upbringing was indeed another of his strengths. Although he showed no particular love or affection for his Godmother Nanny May; he nevertheless gave high praise to her for her persistence in keeping him on the straight and narrow. Her constant sermon of things righteous and of good virtue had comprehensively left an indelible imprint on his mind. As a result, he remained morally upright and refrained from habits that were in any way licentious.

Jessica had come to realise that Marcus was not ready for a change of direction in his life, nor would he commit to any form of activity that would render him susceptible to ways that would otherwise compromise the natural order of things as he perceived it. She also knew and appreciated the arrival of Peter and Sara was imminent. Nothing consumed him more than his beloved children. The irony was not lost with them being with his mother and with whom he considered the most trusted pair of hands, especially when it comes to care, attention and love. However, the adoration and devotion he craved for them could not be administered from afar. He longed to have them where he thought they belonged.

In that delicate process of reacquainting and bonding which was long overdue, left him no room for distractions of the kind that Jessica may have anticipated. Then there was the question of suitability. Almost twenty years his junior was completely out of line with his stated belief. To alter what was a committed understanding of a lifetime, on a whim, was never a serious

VICTOR WALDRON

consideration in his estimation. He had reiterated often enough on this particular subject and was clearly of the opinion that there was no room for compromise.

Jessica's deep affection for Marcus did not fade as the weeks progressed, however, she came to acknowledge the abyss that needed to be crossed and concluded that it would be utter folly to pursue an objective that was both impractical and unworkable. The reality was very clear; Marcus as she saw it was completely out of reach.

It occurred to her also; that her energies would be best spent concentrating on her own welfare since she thought it was prudent to do so. That focus yielded a plan that accurately suited her purpose. No more was she prepared to wait on decisions that were outside her orbit, especially one that she could not control, therefore, the longstanding idea of her returning to her homeland began to take on greater meaning. Negative circumstances around her appeared bleak, and going back to her roots seemed more appropriate. In truth, it became a very exciting prospect.

She remembered her cousin Cleveland who seemed hopelessly devoid of any future and living a life she despaired on her arrival. He not only turned his life around but he was also a dentist of recognition and an inspiration to others since he returned home. Jessica's mood began to change rapidly. Gone was the weight of worry and uncertainty that substantially clouded her thinking. It was as if a heavy load had been lifted from her shoulders and a new dawn beckoned. She was now certain her feeling of jubilation was not misplaced. Her decision to return home appealed enormously, giving her a positive attitude she did not have before. However, she had an important mission to accomplish.

She would rally around until the arrival of Peter and Sara. Her extensive contact with them made it imperative for her to see them in the flesh. Communicating with them as she did, gave her added incentive to meet them. She thought altogether, it was a very cordial relationship and the mutual respect that had developed between them could not be faulted. As a result, their homecoming was essential in light of what existed between them for so many years. Equally important and what intrigued her most was the ability and maturity they possessed in their letters and general correspondence. Needless to say, the majority of it was of the highest standards. For those reasons alone, she felt compelled to meet them and remained convinced that the time and effort invested in them was well worth it. Once that had been achieved she would politely and discreetly make her departure.

# CHANGING COURSE

Precilla looked shocked and bewildered by Jessica's narrative of events that preceded the evening she spent in the company of Marcus. Having described the night as an overwhelming success, she was forced to admit the truth that, in the final analysis, her hope of winning his attention was dashed in a most spectacular way. In short, Marcus was not inclined to indulge in any kind of relationship other than with his children Sara and Peter. He thought all his time and energy would be well spent around their transition to the U.K.

"But you said it was a brilliant evening and in the same breath you're telling me that Marcus is definitely not interested?" Precilla enquired.

"That's about right," Jessica informed. "The kids will be here shortly and according to him, all his efforts will be needed for them."

"I cannot tell you how sorry I am for encouraging you to do this." Precilla lamented.

"Nonsense," Jessica responded. "I walked into this situation with my eyes wide open. The only thing that I regretted was my pride being hurt. Anyway, this has given me the opportunity to do what I had intended to do all along. What I am about to tell you Precilla will not be to your satisfaction, I know that and I do regret it, but the time has come for me to make bold decisions. I have decided not to live in London any longer, which means I shall be going back home for good."

Precilla was far from happy with the news. A sombre expression written across her face, told the unfortunate truth as she stared at Jessica in utter disbelief. "Are you saying you will be leaving London for good and never coming back?" Precilla questioned with some urgency.

"Yes," Jessica replied. "And you are the first to know of my plans."

"But why Jessie?" Precilla protested. "There is so much for you to achieve right here. You have the intellect to go on to do great things."

Jessica smiled warmly. "I know, Precilla, and what's more I understand how you feel about losing your best friend. I shall miss you just as much, believe me, but it is something that I have thought about long and hard and right now it is what I want to do."

Precilla was still distraught as a result of the news given to her by her friend. "I guess it's all my fault, giving you ideas that were a complete waste of time."

"Oh no," Jessica assured her. "On the contrary; that was an experience I would not have missed for the world. If anything, I should thank you for it. What came out of it was amazing. Let's just say, he rejected what was on offer. It is precisely why I need to change course. I truly need a different incentive and that is my reason for going."

"So what will you tell him?" Precilla asked.

"Oh, that's easy. I will just say I'm going on a holiday and once there, I will write him a beautiful letter, thanking him for all the wonderful things he has done for me."

"Girl, I'm lost for words. This is all so sudden." Precilla remarked. "I'm so sorry things did not work out, but how can a man in his right mind refuse a woman like you?"

Jessica said still smiling. "I would not call it refusal, far from it; and he is certainly not mad. Marcus is a thoroughly decent human being, with an agenda all his own. He does things his way and why not. It has served him well over the years."

"Look, you have it your way, but I'm saying he has to be blind or mental to resist a woman like you. I mean you have the looks, you have a fantastic body, the kind any man would crave; you are irresistible. So tell me, young lady, why is he so different? Why miss such a golden opportunity?"

Jessica sighed heavily and confronted her puzzled friend. "In my head, he was not looking for an opportunity. I think I know him well enough to say he will not alter his ways. That night on board the *Aracassa*, when desperation was the order of the day, when life seemed meaningless, I found a friend who not only saved me from myself, but he gave me a hand to hold on to and a shoulder to cry on. He raised my spirits and gave me a reason to live."

She stopped momentarily as if to allow Precilla to take it all in. "That's why I'm here having this conversation with you. He came as a friend and remained so throughout."

Precilla softened her tone considerably, realising that Marcus's intention was exemplary and not to be taken as a Johnny come lately. "Well now that you've explained it, I can quite understand. You have never revealed that side of him to me."

"No, it is not something I talk about," Jessica uttered with a chuckle. "Girl, you should have seen me. I was like a headless chicken. I was going to a place I didn't know; to a cousin I was never confident of finding. It was a situation which left me totally distraught. So you can just imagine the state of panic I was in. Believe me, child, he saved my life."

Precilla's face showed compassion. For the first time, she was able to get a snapshot of her friend's unfortunate experience.

"Wow." She exclaimed. "That must have been awful; perhaps I was looking at things from a different angle. Believe me, girl, I had no idea."

"There's nothing to be sorry about," Jessica explained. "I merely wanted to put things into proper perspective. I was so vulnerable; he could have done whatever he liked with me. That is why I cared for him so much."

Precilla sighed and offered a weak smile. "Now I can see why you call him a proper gentleman. He's that alright and I can see where you are coming from."

Jessica nodded in agreement. "He's a good man, the kind you seldom meet every day. However, he always reminded me that my age was a barrier to progress."

"What do you mean?" Precilla asked.

"Marcus does not want anyone so young."

"Now I know the facts, I can see why he is determined to keep things as they are," Precilla uttered.

Jessica tacitly agreed with her friend. She was well aware of what may have been the outcome in her pursuit to gain the love and affection of Marcus. It was a leap of fate into the unknown, and one she assumed would have had negative repercussions.

"He did ask me to be patient. I guess he did not want to cause me any grief, but in my heart, I just knew my venture was never going to succeed."

"So why did you attempt it? Knowing you were going down a blind alley?" Precilla enquired almost impatiently.

"That I do not have the answer to. Sometimes you follow your intuition just to see how it turns out. As it happens, it has proved wrong." Jessica assured.

"Well, I guess that's not a bad ploy to attempt, you win some, you lose some."

"Exactly," Jessica responded. "I really got to know Marcus well on our way to London. He really felt strongly about his children being away from him. Even though he knew they were in safe hands. He also explained to me about his wife Teresa who left him for someone else. I cannot begin to tell you, how slavishly he cared for that woman. He was forever hoping she would return, even though deep down, he must know it will never happen. As for me, I knew since I met him, I did not qualify. He repeatedly told me, I was too young to even be considered."

Precilla sniggered. "Darling! That's a bit rich. I don't understand that. When I travelled to this country, the men I met were not asking for your passport or your age, they just wanted to know the colour of your knickers so they could whip them off."

Jessica giggled pleasantly. Being aware of Marcus and his idiosyncratic ways, especially regarding women, she was quite prepared to come to his defences. "I know lots of men who are skirt lifters. But Marcus is not one of them. I can never forget the young lady who shared my cabin. Jenny was her name. She hounded him from pillar to post with one thing in mind. She simply wanted his body. She'd have done anything to get Marcus into bed, but he was not in the least bit interested. He kept dodging her until we docked. That's just his way."

Still puzzled, Precilla continued. "I can well understand that. Some men would not go for any Mary or Jane, but you are different. It is now almost three months since you have had that most memorable evening with him and yet he is behaving like nothing has ever happened between you two. How can that be real?"

Jessica placed her hand on her friend's shoulder with a smile of resignation. "I told you already Precilla; this man in question is different. We started as friends, we respected each other and I am certain he did not want to jeopardise our relationship. Perhaps I tried too hard to change a situation which I knew deep down would not have worked. I figured it would not have been credible."

"I hear you." Precilla declared. "But I'm at my wit's end to really understand his attitude. Like I said, you are Oscar material, irrespective of your age; you would be a prize for any man. It's not as if he's cradle snatching."

"Perhaps he does see me as a child." Jessica hesitated momentarily. "In a strange sort of way, that may be the image he still has of me. When we met I was tall and skinny. He did not believe I was nineteen years old. It needed a lot of convincing before he acknowledged I was telling the truth."

"Darling, I did not know what you looked like then, but what I see in front of me now is a fabulous woman in every sense of the word." Precilla retorted.

Jessica giggled merrily. "You know something? If you keep on like this, I will begin to believe what you say."

"Trust me, girl, you are the real McCoy."

"And you are not so bad yourself," Jessica responded.

The girls laughed heartily as they hugged each other. Jessica sat down quietly in thought. "You know, Precilla, now that I think about it. Marcus treated me like the father I never had. My dad, when he sent me on that journey to London, he exposed me to great danger; the kind that could well have ruined me forever. If Marcus was any other person other than who he was, I would have been exploited to the maximum degree. He instead showed me kindness and consideration I did not get from my biological dad."

"Well, you have to give him that. He is a thoroughly decent human being."

"He certainly is." Jessica countered. "Sometimes in my quiet moments, I wonder what my father was thinking about when he made that ridiculous decision of putting me on that boat. He obviously did it without a thought for my well-being. It was all to do with his own ego and I could have been the victim of his folly."

"Girl, how right you are. Most of the time our parents do what they think is in their own interests and not ours."

Precilla broke into laughter. "Anyway, I got the chance to know and appreciate you and as it turned out, you are the best thing that has happened to me."

"Isn't that the nicest thing to say? However, don't ever repeat that in front of Robin, he would not be happy to hear that."

"But it's the truth," Precilla replied. "If I didn't meet you, what would have been the chance of meeting Robin?"

"Who knows?" Jessica replied, grinning from ear to ear. "Maybe he would have found his way to Brighton General in search of the woman of his life."

"Fat chance of that happening; anyway, it's just as well I have Robin. I could not imagine facing the world without you or him."

"Oh come on Precilla, I don't want you to be a merchant of doom. Anyway, I'm not dead yet you know. I will only be a few thousand miles away and our friendship as far as I'm concerned; will always be as rosy as ever."

"I know, I know. My man Robin is truly a breath of fresh air but I cannot have girly chats with a man can I?"

"I guess not, but we can continue to keep in touch by correspondence, you know how much I love to write letters."

"That's more your department than mine. I love dancing and you love reading and writing."

"Don't worry my friend; you'll soon get into the spirit of things once we start."

Precilla remarked with a huge frown. "That's like hard work to me, I'm not promising anything."

Jessica found her friend most amusing. She chuckled heartily at her reluctance. "Well here is your chance to sharpen your writing skills and before you know it you'll be as good a writer as a dancer."

"No chance of that ever happening my friend, I can assure you."

"Come on Precilla." Jessica urged. "I want you on board, I need all the support I can get, if we are to remain great pals, I need you to do what is necessary. Do not ignore my letters."

"Alright, don't go on about it, I will do it if I have to. But it will be a whole lot better if you remain here in London. That way you'll make my life a lot easier." Precilla replied out of frustration.

"This is something I have to do and you know it," Jessica replied. "Believe me, I have never been more committed and once I'm settled there, you and Robin will be the first ones I would be only too pleased to entertain. How about that."

"That would be absolutely fantastic. I'm sure Robin would be very excited to hear that."

"Right." Jessica expressed happily. "I need to remove my personal belongings gradually, so that when the time comes, Marcus would not be suspicious of me."

"Do whatever pleases you, darling, you know I'm on your side. I appreciate this is what you want and I'm never going to get in your way."

Precilla showed marked constraint in view of Jessica's action. "Tell me Jessica; don't you think it will appear a bit ungrateful on your part if you leave unceremoniously? After all, he has been good to you for such a long period of time."

"I thought about that and realised that there may be a tinge of ingratitude on my part, but let's face it, I have given myself to Marcus and what did he do? He rebuffed me. That, as you know, is a sacrifice women do not make easily. He knows full well how I feel about him, I've expressed my inner soul to him and what did I get? A very polite snub. If truth be told, I was always conscious of the fact that our proposed plan was unworkable, buried deep in that man's psyche is a woman called Teresa. Someone he simply cannot get rid of. It has become a hindrance of major proportions and until he wakes up to that realisation, it will remain an obstacle he must overcome. He will continue to dream the impossible dream. Now I know my venture has failed, I feel free to indulge in other things. Believe me girl; I have absolutely no qualms about going back. In fact, it is a quiet triumph for me. My cousin, the one who was supposedly giving me shelter, was the one who inspired me most. He had a vapid existence when I arrived. You would not have given a penny for him. The house he lived in was a complete shambles, with living accommodation which was as squalid as I have ever seen. He looked a desperate man with little if any future. I felt a sense of desperation for him when I saw it. Fortunately for me, Marcus saved me from a most disastrous experience. That is why I regard him so highly. Anyway, the shock of me seeing my cousin that way and the encouragement I gave him, changed his attitude in an extraordinary way. Today, Cleveland is living a sumptuous life back home. It is that sort of thing that gives me hope. I want to be a part of that. I would not question Marcus's integrity for one single moment. He made me no promises and rightly so. What I see for myself now is an emerging sense of purpose. I need to develop in a way that gives me satisfaction and I intend to pursue that desire."

Precilla, wearing a look of admiration for her friend, smiled warmly. "Girl, you give clarity to everything. You are the lucky one, no doubt. You have quality in spades, both in looks and grey matter. I do admire that."

"That's why we are such good friends. I most certainly feel the same way about you." Jessica remarked.

Precilla nodded approval. "So as far as I can see it's a done deal. Do you know exactly what you hope to do?"

"I have plans, but first things first; once I'm settled, I intend to write Marcus a beautiful letter of thanks, after all, I do not want to be remembered as somebody who did not appreciate his selfless acts of kindness. He has given me lots to be proud of and he deserves to know the truth."

Precilla puckered her lips playfully. "Don't tell me you're not the most clear-minded thinking person this side of the galaxy, because you most certainly are. You think of everything don't you?"

"Well, sometimes some things are essential enough to pay attention to and I consider this particularly important, in view of what I was able to extract from it," Jessica concluded.

"So, in spite of the little setback you had, there are no hard feelings then?"

Jessica shrugged her shoulders ruefully. "I'm not that type of person to deny what is truthful. I still do have strong feelings for Marcus; he knows that because I expressed the way I felt for him. But I'm a realist also, enough to know where the road ends. Besides, this proposed venture of mine has given me a new lease of life altogether. My dear, you just cannot imagine how good I feel about myself right now. It's as if I have wings."

"Good for you girl." Precilla echoed. "I'm so pleased to see you so committed and I really mean that."

"Thank you very much for coming on board. I feel great; this is a delightful place to be especially with your concurrence."

"So tell me, once you are there, would you reconnect with your old boyfriend Alan?" Precilla quizzed.

Jessica paused long and hard. "Let's just say he's not on the agenda this minute. I still think fondly of him occasionally, but I do not believe I could accommodate Mr Bray right now for very obvious reasons."

"Why ever not?" Precilla enquired curiously. "Now that the coast is clear, what's to stop you?"

Jessica offered a sombre smile to what she thought was a very complex question. "Alan was good for me several years ago; I was young and giddy then and very much up for the challenge. Now I'm not so sure. A lot has changed since."

"Like what for instance?" Precilla enquired.

"Let's just say I'm a little wiser now and I'm very pleased about that."

Precilla chuckled happily. "I hope you're not worried about the competition with his other ladies? As I see it, with your looks and personality, it's bound to be a no contest."

"Let's just say you're right about that." Jessica countered. "What do I stand to gain from that?"

"Oh come on girl, you are beginning to sound like a disillusioned old maid, when in fact you are a fantastic woman with brains. Alan would be only too pleased to continue where he left off."

"That's it," Jessica remarked. "I have been told as a child, not to build your house on shifting sand. Alan's lifestyle is hardly the kind that I could cope with. Thinking seriously about it, I know that is true. He has roving eyes and he is definitely not one for stability. That being so, I would suggest that I leave well alone."

"He's no Marcus is he?" Precilla asked teasingly.

Jessica merely shook her head negatively. She did not think the question merited a serious answer.

"Never mind," Precilla assured. "You're refined enough to have all the men falling over themselves to meet a sweet woman like you."

"Precilla," Jessica announced almost impatiently. "Men are not my first priority right now. That will come when I'm settled and not before. Do not worry your pretty head, I will find someone in due course."

Precilla giggled sheepishly. "It's silly of me to be so one track minded. I really should know better. I am sure you are not the type to be rushed."

"Exactly," Jessica reassured. "That time will come eventually. Besides, it may be an absolute surprise to you, if I tell you that Alan and I have never ever corresponded all the time I've been here – not once."

"Really?" An astonished Precilla asked. "Isn't that extraordinary? What was the reason for that?"

"It was multiple," Jessica informed. "Like I said before, Alan had no intention of coming here. He repeatedly echoed those sentiments. According to him, he would only leave his beautiful island for the USA. Since I was here, I was determined to pursue a career and generally getting on with my life, it would have made no sense to carry on with something that had no future. What is more; it would have been folly to jeopardise my position with Marcus who gave me an opportunity I would never have had otherwise."

Precilla smiled broadly. "As usual you are the most level-headed woman I know. That's all the more reason why I do not intend to lose your friendship, not ever."

"Nonsense young lady," Jessica informed. "That is not going to happen, we are friends for life; neither land nor water will diminish what we have built up. Quality friends are in short supply and ours is solid gold."

Precilla smiled pleasantly. "I know, I know, our friendship is built on solid rock. You are an inspiration with a personality to match. I am confident you are going to do well wherever you go. That I am certain of."

"Come here, you silly girl," Jessica replied with her arms outstretched in welcome to accommodate her very special friend. They embraced warmly. It was the epitome of loyalty and undiluted comradeship. A bond that they were both certain would stand the test of time.

# ALAN

The days slipped by slowly into weeks, with expectations running high in anticipation of things to come. Time was of the greatest essence in the life of Marcus, especially. A huge chunk of his existence took a hiding when Teresa walked out on him. The disaffection was almost unbearable, punctuated no doubt by the temporary loss of his children, Sara and Peter to the village, residing with his mother. That period ranked alarmingly high in his life, so far as challenges go. His sanity was tested to capacity in no uncertain manner, merely to survive. Those days were now coming to an end, much to his delight. Having endured the worst, he now looked forward to reuniting with his children once more. The waiting with each passing day accentuated his level of excitement and longing in expectation of their arrival.

Jessica also had a sense of thrill in the hope of meeting Sara and Peter in the flesh and even though her agenda was never the same as her over-jubilant friend, she thought her contributions – keeping in touch by communication – was indeed valid. Also, her efforts could not be dismissed lightly, in view of her concentrated attempts to keep in touch over a prolonged period of time. It was essential if nothing else that this created an urgent interest in meeting them. It was an opportunity of gaining intimacy and respect which increased to a rather unique understanding which ultimately benefited everyone. That made it a compelling factor in her robust quest to meet them. Once that had been achieved, it would then be plain sailing on her part to accelerate her own plans accordingly.

For now, this was a downward spiral so far as her interest in London was concerned. This period gave her a prevailing sense of peace and contentment. All that was needed now was to be patient, a quality she was convinced she possessed. She felt so good but resisted punching the air in jubilation; knowing her time had come to do what she wanted and to put in place her dreams and aspirations for a future that was delightful and one that would give her peace of mind. It was also an afternoon that ideally matched her mood with its vibrancy and lustre. The colourful evening sunshine in all its splendour appeared as if it was displaying an act of defiance against the gloom that was waiting to dominate what was left of the daylight. Reminding herself thoughtfully that her optimism as far as her aims were concerned was totally justified.

She sucked in the now permanent night air and smiled contentedly. It was also a period in her life when everything seemed so uplifting. Peace and tranquillity had prevailed in a seamless manner. She felt good about herself, enjoying, at last, a state of harmonious indulgence of which she was appreciative of and fervently hoped that this particular brand of satisfaction would long continue.

In the interim, things were happening that were completely out of her control. What should have been a period of utter bliss, changed course rapidly. In its place came a total departure that brought dark clouds of depression and pain, altering the entire dynamic of her carefully constructed plans. This was no ordinary event; it was what nightmares were made of, the kind that she could never have foreseen. Such life-changing circumstances are borne out of destruction and disenchantment. A train wreck if ever there was one; adversity the young woman could well have done without. As incidents go, this was monumental.

It was a fairly pleasant evening, with absolutely nothing to report. There was stillness in the air, even the trees stood motionless. Jessica had just finished supper and was never one to allow boredom to predominate, not when good books were around.

The sounding of the doorbell startled her. A slightly riled Jessica answered the door and was immediately engulfed in utter consternation. Confusion reigned supreme. This was a shock of immense magnitude. One which was about to be blown into a full-scale crisis, the kind she did not anticipate nor bargained for. Was this a dream, a total illusion? Could this be real? She shook her head vigorously as she tried to unravel from this catastrophe which was about to change events of her life for no good reason. Standing before her, baggage in hand and wearing a smile was none other than Alan Bray.

Suddenly this became the most surreal moment of her life, one she was convinced she would never ever have to experience again. Unbelievably, here was a man with whom no contact of any description was made since her arrival in London. Having time to review the situation over a long period, she concluded it was prudent not to keep in touch for very obvious reasons. For one his flamboyance was a huge factor; his insatiable appetite for the ladies; his restlessness and his absolute certainty that he would never set foot in London were grounds for her actions. Since her intentions were to remain in London and to advance her career substantially, she thought there was no future in pursuing a lost cause so far as Alan was concerned.

Jessica was quick to acknowledge her good fortune in meeting Marcus and was never prepared to disrupt a plan that was enhancing and very successful. She was very conscious of the fact that this was a grave error of judgement that she made by introducing Alan as her nephew. It was both naive and senseless; a deception that had undoubtedly come back to haunt her; one that was now her primary worry. Still in a state of complete disarray and trying to be as inaudible as possible, she whispered. "What the hell are you doing here?"

Alan standing tall and wearing his trademark grin was completely oblivious to the problem he was imposing on her. "Hello Jessica, be nice to me, I've come a long way to see you."

"Who on earth gave you this address?" She demanded.

"Your cousin Cleveland, he's making a big name for himself back home."

"You have no right to do this." She barked. "No right whatsoever."

"Look!" Alan explained. "I'm only here for a few days; I'm on my way to New York. I'm meeting Lorna Caleu – you may know the family. Anyway, I thought it would be nice to see you since I'm here. That's it."

"Alan, I'm not interested in your visit or anything else. This is totally outrageous."

He was taken aback by her outburst. He thought that his presence would be welcomed.

"Jessica, why are you so dismissive? Aren't you happy to see me?"

"No, I'm not." She insisted. "You shouldn't have come."

Suddenly, it dawned on Alan that his plans were out of line and he began to apologise.

"Never mind that." Jessica snapped. "Listen to me, and listen good; you are supposed to be my nephew, do you understand?"

With barely enough time to digest his new found relationship, the sound of approaching footsteps brought Marcus into the fray. It was obvious to everyone; he was heavily involved in the process of preparing his home before the arrival of his children. "Hello, Jessica." He called out as he focused squarely on Alan, if anything, with a degree of concern. "What seems to be the problem and how can I help?"

Jessica was in a state of nervous agitation and wearing a false smile, indicated by pointing to the stranger. "This is Alan – you know the picture on my mantle piece?"

After a period of reflection, Marcus nodded acknowledgment. He remembered the photograph well enough. "Oh I know, that's your nephew if my memory serves me right."

"Yes, that's correct." A heavily relieved Jessica responded. "He's only passing through and has decided to pay me an unexpected visit."

"Well," Marcus announced, scratching his head in quiet contemplation. "I'm all for family, but as you can see this place is in disarray.

"I can take it rough; it's only a few days," Alan announced.

Marcus rubbed his chin. "Look, I have a sofa in my study which is useable. I guess it can withstand a little inconvenience."

A beaming smile quickly engulfed Alan's face upon hearing the good news. Without hesitation, he gathered his cases and energetically entered the house. "Thank you for that. Like I said I am willing to adapt to any situation." He was quick to remark.

"That's settled for the time being," Marcus suggested, as he manoeuvred his way towards the study – the younger man following diligently.

"You have picked the wrong time to be here," Marcus announced. "I am afraid I will not be able to show you the sights of London. My hands are filled at the moment."

"Oh no, that will not be necessary." Alan was quick to reply.

Marcus engaged Alan quizzically, surprised by the remark. "Don't you want to see a little bit of the city now that you're here?"

"No, I have absolutely no such interest," Alan assured him.

Marcus turned to Jessica wearing a look of astonishment. "Isn't that the strangest thing? Your nephew comes to a wonderful city like London and not wanting to visit the many places of interest?"

Jessica smiled wearily. "I'm not surprised; Alan is that kind of a person. I don't believe he has one curious bone in his entire body; isn't that so Alan?"

Alan nodded vigorously in the affirmative. "That is correct Aunty Jessica. I do not care much for certain things. Unfortunately, that's the way I am."

Marcus opened the door to the study. "Well, this is it. I hope you find it comfortable."

Alan still smiling looked around approvingly. "This is very nice. I'm grateful for your hospitality; I can assure you I will be no trouble whatsoever."

Jessica breathed a heavy sigh of relief. For now anyway, the situation was incident free. She was bolstered by the fact also, that things might get better, due to the fortunate coincidence that it was the weekend of the annual Lodge convention that Marcus attends conscientiously in Birmingham. This one was a little different, due mainly to the overloaded schedule that he placed upon himself, in pursuit of getting his home properly adorned, in expectation of his children's imminent arrival.

Nevertheless, Jessica's fury for Alan's indiscretion was palpable. This farce was never supposed to have befallen her. Without a single word of warning, he had arrived, not only to destroy her peace of mind but also to bring into conflict, her well-laid plans; placing them into total disarray. The lie she told about Alan being her nephew certainly didn't help. She understood that only too well, she knew it was an act of dishonesty, but based upon the knowledge that Alan would never ever set foot in London, she thought in her view it was a pretty safe bet. Especially Alan's own insistence and bold prediction of that ever being possible. That he was now guilty of breaking his own golden rule, was selfish, cruel and unforgivable.

In spite of this unfortunate problem, Jessica was relatively optimistic, by virtue of Alan's stance of remaining anonymous; only leaving the study to engage in eating and washing. How times have changed. Alan was undoubtedly the personification of flamboyance and flair as she remembered him. Ducking and diving was a complete departure from the man she knew. However, she believed that there was a method to his madness and that he appeared to have a plan of action.

But Alan's nonconformist attitude became conspicuous and prompted attention from Marcus. Jessica did not mind at all for obvious reasons and was quite happy for it to remain that way, desperately counting the days to his departure. As for Marcus, he was far too busy to properly analyse Alan's peculiar ways, other than to dismiss them as strange. His blank refusal to grasp the opportunity of seeing the sights of London and his unusual habits indoors were noticeable for their oddity, but not enough for Marcus to dwell on, especially since his stay was only brief. However, it was a distraction Jessica could well have done without.

The convention kicked off in fine style. Marcus's mood, however, appeared rather sombre. His mind was fully occupied with matters totally unrelated to the events. Nevertheless, it was always an occasion he looked forward to and endeavoured as best as he possibly could to capture the mood of the moment. It was always fun reacquainting with old friends and colleagues occasionally, which very often made a huge difference in raising his spirits, but more especially his old boss, Gerald Carlson. Gerald was a man of distinction, a solid human being with a mountain of stories to tell. They were mostly rib-splitting ones. His natural ability to create laughter was uncanny. Everyone around was convinced that Gerald's tales were the direct result of an enormous and vivid imagination, coupled by a large degree of fabrication, which incidentally did not seem to bother anyone and only succeeded in making the man a complete entertainer. A little bit of Gerald's banter was enough to raise the spirits. He was a fine storyteller.

At the other end of the scale, Jessica endured what she considered a hectic weekend attending her patients as a midwife, which she found particularly demanding, but that was never a serious issue so far as she was concerned. She regarded her work as part and parcel of a profession which she enjoyed implicitly. Her conscientious nature and her desire to do what was necessary gave her the end product she sought and one that brought her satisfaction. That aside, she was heading home and happily so, after what she considered a very draining weekend. It was Sunday afternoon and she was looking forward to a period of relaxation which she thought was well deserved and thoroughly justified.

Pleased also that Marcus was out of town, easing the stress and anxiety that had surrounded her by the presence of her uninvited house guest, Alan. He was a source of great danger to her for every single moment he was around. Even his weird antics of being persona non grata did nothing to help the situation. Looking back, how she regretted her transgression for introducing him as her nephew. It was utter folly on her part and a blemish she thoroughly despised. She had always regarded herself as someone with integrity, someone who believed in honesty. To place herself on the periphery of being seen as a fraud and a liar was not how she wanted to be remembered. Therefore, her reputation rested purely on a relatively successful departure of Alan with nothing for her to answer for. All things being equal, and with fingers crossed, she hoped never to be found wanting again.

Before the house guest's unfortunate arrival her plans to depart from London were very much in place. She considered it imperative the chance of meeting Sara and Peter. Her involvement with them merited that meeting, after which her intentions were very clear. She would discretely leave Marcus and his children to reunite and to function without any distractions whatsoever. Her hope was for Alan's seamless departure, which carried no further problems or complications. Jessica's philosophy remained constant. She was sure she did not want the earth. Her aspirations were not impossible ones. She simply wanted a chance to do things differently and at her own behest. Her decisions were clear, she was homeward bound and that was her immediate objective. In the interim, her thoughts were primarily on matters less important, she was looking forward to a warm bath, a good meal and of course an excellent book. The thought of that brought a smile of contentment.

# SHOCK ENCOUNTER

Simultaneously in Birmingham, things had taken a complete departure from the original programme. Gerald Carlson's focus was on matters elsewhere. He had been nervously awaiting news about his granddaughter's condition, about her state of health and her newborn child. Receiving the news that mother and child were well, made Gerald wild with excitement. He was waiting a long time for this moment and now that it had happened, he was justifiably elated. Being a father of three children, this was his first and only grandchild. After several attempts, she had at last triumphed. It was a situation that moved Gerald to tears of joy and happiness. Being a complete family man, this news prompted a course of action far removed from the original undertaking in Birmingham. In a mode of urgency, he was heading home to be a part of this grand occasion and in a manner of speaking, cajoled Marcus into leaving the convention prematurely. He needed company and being the persuasive person that he normally was, it was difficult for Marcus not to oblige.

Initially, it was Gerald who gave Marcus his first opportunity as an engineer after leaving the Army. He regarded Marcus highly and a huge degree of fellowship existed between them, throughout their working life. Gerald reminded Marcus of his old friend and confidant, Sergeant Pearson. Gerald was very much his own man, never judgemental or cynical in any way whatsoever. He was forever ready to show compassion and kindness when it was necessary. Marcus himself did not mind leaving the convention early for very good reasons and in the circumstances; this was a good excuse for an early exit. Gerald was exceptionally keen to abort proceedings in order to join his family back in London to celebrate this momentous occasion. Leaving prematurely also was never a problem for Marcus since in its own way there was unfinished business that needed attention, before his own larger than life event – seeing his kids again – was accomplished. It would also be a great feeling to sleep in his own bed. That situation now agreed, the journey back to London had begun.

Back in London, it was late afternoon and as the last vestige of light drained away to give prominence to dusk, Jessica felt brimful of contentment. The quietness of the evening matched her mood and gave her a reason to be satisfied. She had achieved all the things she had hoped for and was now looking forward to indulging in her favourite pastime of a good book. She was very much in a submerged state of concentration when she was suddenly interrupted by a knock on the door. "Come in." She called out, regretting the intrusion but automatically knowing it was Alan. The door was pushed open slowly and equally slowly entered Alan. He was quite aware of the fact that Marcus was out of town, giving him a glorious chance – perhaps the only one – to have a conversation with Jessica without any obstructions or interference.

This was a totally different creature to the one that was elusive and awkwardly evasive, who kept out of harm's way for good reasons. But knowing that the coast was clear, he was now more assured and confident than he was earlier. Standing in the doorway, wearing a T-shirt that accentuated his physique, he somehow appeared taller than she remembered. He was also wearing a smile so huge; it was capable of charming the proverbial wicked witch, let alone Jessica. Her anger was still very much intact, having not forgiven him for turning up as he did, totally without a hint of warning, which ultimately left her in a precarious state of nervousness and guilt, a situation she never expected to be placed in. Seeing him in the flesh and with no imminent danger looming, she could not help having an extra flicker to her beating heart.

His infectious smile, a trademark of his, brought a ripple to her face, one she was very careful to conceal. Her immediate intentions were not to give Alan any kind of advantage. After all, he had placed her in a precarious position which she considered totally unacceptable. This intrusion, although inconvenient in its own way, gave her an opportunity to give vent to her feelings over his cavalier behaviour of leaving her in a state of panic and distress. Even though she was satisfied that she was free from any obligation to Marcus since that eventful evening which did not go as planned, she was nevertheless fighting for her reputation to remain intact and was certain she was not prepared to allow Alan to have her good name besmirched. "Hello Jessica," he announced. "It is so very nice to see you looking so wonderful," Alan remarked.

Jessica closed her book in an effort to concentrate on the man in front of her. It was many years since she last saw him and apart from what she considered a slightly more matured individual, not a great deal had changed.

"Hello, Alan." She replied again not wanting to show emotions of any kind whatsoever. "What on earth are you doing in London?"

"I came expressly to see you. It's been a long time since you abandoned me." Was his retort as he moved effortlessly across the floor and slowly sat at the foot of the bed, exuding a vibrant and effective body aroma that wafted inexorably into the open space with devastating consequences. It was as if he was on top of his game.

"Yes, I know." Jessica declared. "But circumstances dictated my reasons for not contacting you."

"That's funny, are you saying there was nothing there? What we had between us did not matter?"

"Alan!" Jessica responded. "That was then, this is now. I really have no intentions of racking up the past and if you must know, the experience I endured because of that relationship, is something I would not wish on my worst enemy."

Alan was taken aback. "I cannot remember ever treating you unkindly, how can you say that?"

"You did not, but it was as a result of me linking up with you, that I was simply dumped on a boat and sent to England."

Alan sighed heavily. "I know your parents did not want us to be connected in any way, but I can assure you, I cared enough about you to make a go of it. I sincerely want you to believe that."

Jessica contemplated for a while before answering, looking directly at Alan. "Don't make me laugh, you making a go of it? Are you saying you were serious enough to marry me?"

"Something like that. Like I said, I did care and now that I've seen you again after such a long time, I can see why."

Jessica chuckled. "Would you care to enlighten me why that is so?"

"Because you are even more beautiful now than when you left." He expressed.

"Flattery was always a huge part of your game plan. Wasn't it Alan?"

Alan chuckled boyishly. "That's not true. I'm very sincere about what I say; you can trust me on that."

There was no way of knowing how true Alan's remarks were, although he showed her amazing consideration in the brief relationship that existed between them. But deep down, the doubts remained. "What you're saying and you expect me to believe, is that you were prepared to quit being the person that you are; to halt your cavalier attitude and be prepared to settle with only one woman?"

"Yes, as strange as it may seem, that's undoubtedly what I had planned. My aim was to find someone that would make me truly happy and you fitted the bill perfectly."

"Isn't it true that men say things like that because it makes women feel good?" She questioned.

"No, no, no. I'm very serious about that. You could quite easily have changed my life completely. That's why I felt so bad when you left."

"Alan!" Jessica responded impatiently. "When I left Trinidad, you had a very dismal reputation. You had a string of ladies as long as my arm. That's why my parents would not sanction our relationship. You were famous for all the wrong reasons. Please do not try to impress me with this dubious rubbish. The truth is knowing you as I do; these sentiments are very hard to swallow."

"I'm so sorry you feel that way Jessica, but that's how I felt at the time."

Jessica appeared slightly more conciliatory. "What you are asking me to do is to take your word as your deed, am I correct Alan?"

"Look, Jessie, that's the way I see it. When you left Trinidad you left behind a broken man. You may not believe it but it was the worst period of my life. The truth is I did not give up hope, for three long years I remained believing that you would give me the chance to prove the way I felt about you. I waited for a sign or something tangible that I could hold onto, instead, all I got was silence. Have you any idea how that felt?"

"Isn't the reason fairly obvious?" Jessica countered. "Or am I going nuts? If my memory serves me right, we were miles apart. I was in London and you were in Trinidad. Once I was here I decided to do something worthwhile with my life. You, on the other hand, were never coming here. You had repeatedly announced to anyone that was prepared to listen that you would not set foot on English soil. That would never happen to you was your boast. Can you remember how adamant you were when you declared with great emphasis that London was perhaps the last place on earth that you would want to visit? So, can you quite comprehend the enormity, the heart-stopping shock I experienced when I saw you at the door? Tell me in your own words, Alan, how can I take what you say seriously?"

Alan grimaced embarrassingly. "What you say is true in some ways. You are correct about London and to be honest, the place was never on my list of places I wanted to see, but circumstances have changed. Anyway, I'm not here to lay down roots, I'm only passing through."

Jessica produced a curious expression. "And what are these circumstances if I may ask?"

"I'm on my way to New York. So you see – that can hardly count. It is not an excuse, it's a fact."

Jessica pulled another face. "Then let me take a wild guess. You are travelling via London because of a woman – would I be right in saying so?"

Alan giggled somewhat nervously. "As a matter of fact, you've got that spot on. It's hardly worth lying about it."

"Now that the truth is well established, do I have the privilege of knowing who the lucky young lady is?" She added sarcastically.

Alan hesitated momentarily. "Well, the young lady is coming from Yugoslavia. She has just qualified in accountancy and is heading off to the States."

"Surely this unfortunate young lady has a name!"

"Look, I'm sure you don't know her." He stammered.

"Try me." She teased. "Not that it matters, but she has a name I imagine."

"Her name is Lorna Caleu. Do you know her?"

Jessica gave the name her fullest attention and remembered a young girl with a family of that name. "I believe I know that family, although I am pretty vague about the lady in question. So – is she your girlfriend or your wife?"

Alan did not answer; he merely smiled and pointed to his nose. This was an indication that he thought that Jessica was prying. Jessica burst out laughing. She saw the funny side of this particular episode.

"Look, Alan, I do not want to know your business. As it happens, I knew it had to be a woman to get you off our beautiful island. Let's face it, you are a man of abundant charm and charm is what you use best, but it's not the criteria for getting on in life. You need something far more substantial, it would do you a power of good to understand that. So take my advice, the next time charm comes knocking, just say go away and exchange it for maturity. In other words dear Alan – grow up."

Alan attempted a weak unconvincing smile. "Thanks for the advice, but I think it's a bit unfair, you are basing your assessment of me at a time when I was young and perhaps irresponsible. That time has long gone; I'm a totally different man now."

"Okay, you may have a point and I do not want to be unfair to you. So the big question is; are you prepared to make a real go of Miss Caleu? Or are you going to seek another conquest when boredom sets in, as was always the case in the past."

Alan took a deep breath. He felt he was wrongly targeted, but accepted Jessica's criticism for his past excesses. "Why are you so hard on me Jessica? If I appeared to be a playboy in the past and that may have been a long time ago, I can assure you I am not that person anymore."

Jessica smiled pleasantly. "You know what they say; a leopard cannot change its spots."

"This one can and I do hope you stop trying to pin me to the wall."

"Alan." Jessica retorted impatiently. "When I left the island, you were renowned for your reputation. Everyone knew how notorious you were. Believe me; I did not make it up. That's why my parents were so set against you. You were famous for your numerous affairs and for all the wrong things you may have done. So you can plainly see why I cannot swallow what you say easily."

Alan grimaced. "I can see why you are so sceptical and who can blame you. However, let's try and lay the past to rest. The truth is, we cannot erase what has happened already. If we could I'm sure we would all be better people. Don't you think so?"

"Perhaps." She uttered scornfully. "But what I see in front of me is someone who cannot alter his ways. Everyone knows how much you love doing what you do. For instance, you barged in here like a bull in a China shop, creating havoc. Do you really care? I do not think so. You were just thinking about what was good for you, no matter how damaging it might be for anyone else. What you did by coming here unannounced is mean and unforgivable, but do you care? No not one little bit. Alan comes first and last and I'm afraid to say so, but I know you cannot change."

Alan for the first time appeared humble; he looked at Jessica with a huge degree of surprise. "So tell me what I'm supposed to do? Maybe I'm this way because of you. Should I have waited for you forever?"

Jessica's response was not forthcoming. She felt less inclined to rebuke him further; after all, there was hardly any merit in doing so. That interim period gave Alan an opportunity to regain his composure.

"I've heard a lot about myself, how about you? What is the attachment you have with Marcus? Is he your husband or just your fella?"

"He's neither of those things." She blurted out feeling somewhat aggrieved.

"Come on Jessica," Alan responded surprised. "Do you really expect me to believe that?"

"Believe what you like, I've no reason to lie to you."

"So what's wrong with him? Is he blind or is he just grazing in another pasture?"

"Whatever do you mean by that remark?" A slightly peeved Jessica asked. "Marcus is a real man like you or anyone else. He has fathered two wonderful children that are expected here anytime now. So be careful what you say."

"Tell me." He asked quizzically. ""What is behind this business? Of me being your nephew?"

"Alan." She barked angrily. "You have caused enough damage as it is; I have no intention of answering any more questions."

"Listen, I'm not in any way trying to ridicule or cast aspersions on Marcus, nothing of the sort. It's just that you're so gorgeous, any man should find you most irresistible."

"Is that a fact?" She responded warmly.

"Yes, it is. You were always a very sweet person, but you have truly blossomed into a fantastic woman since I saw you last."

Jessica was touched by the remark. Her smile was as wide as a barn door.

"Alan, are you still trying to flatter me?"

"No, I'm being honest." He exclaimed. "That's the truth. Anyone would be proud to associate with you. You're simply marvellous. That's the reason why I cannot understand the man's lack of interest."

"Some men are capable of controlling themselves and know how to behave. Marcus is a model human being; I have yet to come across anyone better." She explained.

"High praise," Alan interjected. "He must be because you are so adorable. I personally still find it difficult to resist you."

"That's because of who you are. You cannot help yourself falling for every pretty woman you see."

"Jessica, there is no denying I have faults. Sometimes I allow my heart to rule my head, but with you, it's very different. You were the exception from the first time I saw you. If you did not leave the island, who knows what might have been. I still believe it was very possible that you would have made an honest man out of me."

Jessica laughed out loudly. "Alan! You do have persuasive qualities. You are a charmer like I said before, and let's be real, in a day or two you'll probably be telling Lorna exactly what you're expressing to me right now."

"That's only because you left me in complete limbo. I had no way of knowing what had happened to you."

Alan reached out and touched Jessica's toes with gentle purpose. "You could well have been my wife and I want you to believe that."

Alan's presence was infectious to an alarming degree and she felt no apparent reason to discourage it. His aura generated a commanding sense of intoxication, the kind that provoked a state of sensuality and enchantment, not there before. It was an amazing mood change that brought on an incredible feeling of exhilaration, one which made her pulse race and quickened her heartbeat. Jessica immediately acknowledged a parallel feeling in proportion to the one she experienced with Marcus. Then, it was that elaborate and sophisticated plan of seduction she engineered on that memorable evening some months ago. It was to accomplish what she regarded as a way of winning his heart and securing a future of wonderful expectations. It was to have been a romantic climax and a fairytale ending of pure joy and happiness. She felt it was a golden opportunity to show him she really cared and to demonstrate her deep desire she felt for him. She also recalled her sense of euphoria; believing her plan was successful; that she had once and for all broken the shackles that kept them apart; only to find profound disappointment on a scale she could not have imagined.

With Alan, it was entirely different. He was his usual self. He was a man of supreme confidence who was purely in the mood for conquest come what may. Jessica by now realised she was not at her rational best. She was cosily relaxed and allowed herself to ignore the fine qualities she possessed to aimlessly drift, especially her judgement and her common sense, which incidentally became temporarily redundant. It is often said that in the life of everyone, there is a lax or unguarded moment that sometimes cannot be accounted for. That happened to be a Jessica moment. She allowed herself to be overwhelmed, a decision she lived to regret. Alan was now in her embrace. He kissed her tenderly on her cheek as if to test her resistance, then gradually their lips met. It was now obvious that Jessica decided not to offer any resistance towards Alan's amorous advances or to blunt his desires. He was very much in his element, moving favourably in the direction he craved. This for him was a day of triumph.

It seemed like a particularly long ride home, but Gerald being the man he was; the journey was in fact quite entertaining. His exceptional wit was key to his popularity which was very much on display and which made him an absolute joy to be with. It was midnight and Marcus was glad to be home, even if it was later than expected. He smiled contentedly, partly because of the rich vein of banter which he was able to share with Gerald. These jovial moments were especially uplifting and humorous, and left him in considerably good spirits.

Observing the light in Jessica's bedroom burning brightly, it gave him the indication that she was very much awake. It was not uncommon for her to be engrossed in a book until the wee hours of the morning with scant regard for time. Still very much in the mode of Gerald's humour, a sudden thought process emerged. He decided for the fun of it, to give her a complete surprise by his premature arrival and since she was not expecting him until the following day, his sudden appearance was bound to arouse and alarm her. After all, it was meant to be in good fun.

Approaching the front door, he opened it with the utmost caution possible and taking a deep breath, he proceeded as discretely as he could, using the opportunity to make a successful fist of his venture. The light in Jessica's room offered the assistance he needed for a clear and uninterrupted passage. His approach to the foot of the stairs had been manoeuvred without blemish and with the same caution, he progressed towards her room. He moved furtively towards his goal. The door of the room was ajar and instinctively he realised there was something sinister afoot. The whispers were now audible, giving him the unmistakable notion that there was suspicious intent ahead. Marcus immediately experienced a rapid mood change. Gone was the fun aspect that he had planned, in its place was a distinct attitude of belligerence. He looked around and being an old soldier, he decided to arm himself, in case he was confronted with hostility of one kind or another. He grabbed an old walking stick, a relic of his old friend Sergeant Pearson. It was left there all those years ago; in readiness of any untoward development. Taking another deep breath, Marcus was now ready to face whatever perils or adversities that may ensue. Needless to say, he was now full of negative emotions. His throat was dry; his palms were sweaty; his mouth was parched; his heart was pounding like a jackhammer.

Finally, he entered the room; a man agitated. His findings were as he imagined. Jessica and Alan were in bed and in the process of making love, much to his utter disgust. Marcus stood there for a moment in pure disbelief. It was as if he was in a trance. What he was witnessing left him totally mortified. This was no ordinary disaster, in his estimation; it was an appalling act of treachery. He considered this as a profound lack of respect and trust that had befallen him. A hideous nightmare that was unfolding in front of his very eyes. One he never ever expected to behold. It was undoubtedly a monumental error on Jessica's part. This situation was punctuated even more so, by the fact that Alan was her nephew. How on earth could she?

Overpowered by wrath, he raised the stick above his head as if to strike Alan a serious blow, but somehow common sense prevailed, enough for him to desist. Jessica looked up alarmingly and was plunged into absolute consternation by the sight of seeing Marcus standing there. Her volatile reaction triggered Alan's awareness, with very much the same intensity and in his eagerness to find safe sanctuary; he scrambled under the bed leaving Jessica to bear the brunt of any potential danger. Alan's rapid retreat, exasperated Jessica's embarrassment even further, exposing her nakedness and leaving her in disharmony and panic. Pulling the bedclothes up to cover her naked body was almost the final humiliation. She buried her face in her hands to hide the tears that followed uncontrollably, regretting the unfortunate misery that had come to haunt her.

Marcus was now in a state of complete indignation and outrage, fighting vigorously to maintain his control. He stood there motionless, confronted by an ordeal he found to be nauseous, uncomfortable and emphatically against the grain. This was a setback of enormous impact and most unpalatable. The kind he could well have done without. Consumed with an overpowering measure of disgust, frustration, disappointment and despair, constraints that were not easy to overcome, he somehow managed to draw on every sinew at his disposal and in the process was able to buy himself a modicum of calmness necessary to combat this alarming tragedy. Finding his voice at long last he blurted out. "You under the bed; whatever your name is; I'm giving you ten minutes to get out of my house, or I'll forcefully throw you out myself." He swiftly turned to exit the room, but as he reached the door he stopped, turned around and for the first time looked at Jessica. "And on your way out; take that slut with you." He announced. "And remember, I said ten minutes."

Marcus clambered down the stairs like a broken man. Events had moved so rapidly, it was almost too much to comprehend in so short a time. He poured himself a large whiskey and slumped into a chair, feeling drained and languid. It was as if the spectacle he had just witnessed, removed every ounce of energy he ever possessed. He took a huge swig of the contents in his glass and tried desperately to contemplate the events that had caused him so much bewilderment and distress, but nothing constructive came to mind, only sorrow and pain. The stillness of the moment was suddenly interrupted by Alan's hasty retreat. With luggage in hand, he scurried through the door and was gone. Marcus watched him go as he took another gulp, merely to ease the hurt that sadly persisted. The overwhelming quietness of the moment, coupled with the effect of the alcohol, brought an element of calm which changed the unbalanced condition that prevailed.

He drew breath as he waited patiently for Jessica to appear, as he was positive that she would. The liquor he imbibed was beginning to take a stronger hold, but even in this sodden state, he felt a tinge of good fortune, that Alan did not yield to the request of taking Jessica away with him. After all, there were questions to be asked and answers given in response to this calamitous situation that now existed.

VICTOR WALDRON

# DISILLUSIONED

It was an act of indiscretion that was purely the parting of ways and completely out of character with Jessica's manner and attitude. Her normal disposition was always correct which spoke volumes. To depart in such a fulsome way was baffling and contrary to her way of thinking as he remembered her. If only for his own ego, he needed to know that his judgement was accurate to say the very least. His special interest in Jessica was clearly obvious. He watched her develop from a timid and unsure person, to what he now regarded as someone of substance. She grew from a plain unassuming and reserved young lady, to a woman of exquisite beauty with an excellent personality. In his eyes, she was a thoroughly decent woman with impeccable qualities. How could he ever have been so wrong?

Marcus was now feeling the effects of the alcohol he so rapidly consumed, and although he was not completely intoxicated, he felt he was now driven by a parallel force of unimaginable proportions and in ways that were difficult to harness. He rubbed his eyes vigorously, trying as best he could to stay alert. The night was long and appeared longer by the extended interval of silence that was apparent. So he waited and just in the nick of time, he heard footsteps. Jessica ambled down the stairs, lowered her luggage and slowly but deliberately parked herself next to him.

The lull was deafening. It was as if one was waiting for the other to begin. Marcus's head still spinning like a top, decided it was time to, air his discontent. His voice was harsh and prickly, mostly as a result of the drink.

"How could you end up in bed with him? You're own flesh and blood! How despicable, have you no shame whatsoever?"

Jessica's response was low and almost inaudible. She seemed bereft of all energy. Her natural distress, her constant shedding of tears and the total humiliation of the evening, left her with no desire to confront this horrific situation that stood in her way. She cleared her throat and tried her level best to maintain her composure. "Marcus I'm so sorry. This should never have happened. You really do not have any idea just how bad I feel about this."

"You have not answered my question." He exploded. "Are you that desperate for a man, that you are having it off with your own family?"

Her answer was not immediate. She quite understood the way he felt in view of what had happened. "Marcus, please do not judge me harshly until you hear the truth."

"How am I to judge you? I went away for one weekend, only to find you using my home as a brothel, as for the truth, I'm not sure you are capable of that." He railed.

"Alan is not my nephew." She paused as if to give Marcus time to grasp the gravity of the situation. "He happens to be the person my parents sent me to London in order to get rid of."

Marcus stared at her in utter disbelief. By now his anger was manifestly more pronounced. "So you lied to me? Is that what you are saying? What kind of a human being are you? Why the subterfuge Jessica? I trusted you and you let me down badly."

"That, unfortunately, is the truth. I have no reason to lie anymore." Jessica replied in a most deflated manner.

Horrified by Jessica's admittance of guilt, Marcus began to realise the scale of the challenge. If nothing else, it was unique in scope and quite formidable in context. "Am I to understand that you have been deceiving me all these years?" He roared. "Pretending to be this wonderfully honest woman and at the same time having a clandestine relationship behind my back. Is that the kind of woman you are?"

"Look Marcus! I am ashamed of myself and I know how angry you must be right now." She confessed.

"Young lady." He stormed. "You do not know the half of it. I really must be losing it. I placed so much faith in you. I guess I had you on a pedestal that you do not deserve. How wrong can a man get?"

Jessica visibly winched. "I deserve to be trampled upon." She continued. "Alan came here unexpectedly only to destroy my credibility. He has brought me pain and humiliation, the kind I did not deserve."

"Are you trying to tell me you did not know he was coming here? Are you making me out to be a total fool?"

"Not at all; strange as it might seem, Marcus, that man was not supposed to be in London. He was adamant he would never set foot on this soil. That is why when you asked me about that picture – I lied. I did not know it would come back to haunt me."

Marcus was livid beyond all recognition. "One way or another where is the respect you've shown for me, or what I have done for you. Do you think I deserve this kind of betrayal?"

"You cannot understand how rotten I feel about this sordid mess. Worst still; I did it to you. I can well understand if you cannot forgive me for what happened." Was her limp retort.

Marcus was still plainly angry. "Just now, I'm not in a forgiving mood. You really can't imagine how totally upset I am." He bellowed.

Jessica frowned at her friend's fury. "You are as upset as I'm embarrassed. Please understand how ashamed I am at this moment."

"And so you should be." He declared harshly. "You have behaved like a common prostitute."

Jessica cringed visibly. It was not the kind of language she understood. "I really do not think I deserve to be called that!"

Marcus was deeply hurt by this act of indecent behaviour. He felt a sense of revulsion about this repugnant episode. This was a totally surreal experience that left him emotionally bruised and utterly frustrated.

"A man turns up at my door." He sneered. "Someone you know and to the best of my understanding, he was supposed to be family, only to find you in bed with him. How else do you expect me to react?"

"There's nothing I can do to change what has happened." She pleaded. "So I beg of you, please let us have a conversation."

"Conversation – Jessica? I'm beginning to lose my patience with you because you are trying to make a complete idiot of me. How on earth did he know where we lived if you did not inform him?"

"I did not invite him here." She responded calmly. "It was my cousin Cleveland who is now back in Trinidad. He would have told him where I lived. What kind of a person do you take me for?" She interjected.

"You tell me." He snarled. "So far, nothing seems to make a great deal of sense. He was your nephew one minute and then he was not. To tell you the honest truth, I really do not know whether it's a lie or not!"

For the first time, Jessica felt angry with his response. "Look, I did transgress and you are using it to make me out to be a bad person. There is no need to withhold the truth from you anymore. Alan was my boyfriend which my parents did not approve of. As a result, they put me on a boat to London and that is where I met you. You helped me to recover from that terrible ordeal, for which I am very grateful. You were patient with me throughout that journey; it is something that I will never forget."

She stopped momentarily, pushing back negative emotions, wiping away tears that flowed freely down her cheeks.

"London was not a place that I knew and what is more, I was not sure how I would ever cope. I was truly terrified. You held my hand and showed me the way. My very first experience – seeing where my cousin Cleveland lived sent shivers down my spine; being in that shabby rundown existence. That derelict house and that degrading atmosphere that I witnessed, not only opened my eyes, it made me shudder with fear. You could have left me there to my own devices but you did not. You brought me to your wonderful home and you welcomed me accordingly. This is the place I stayed until now. I must take this moment to place emphasis on what I'm about to say. Not once have I ever sent Alan a note, a message or a letter. That, Marcus, I swear is the solemn truth. The fear of me being in a city as large as this without the help and guidance you gave me; I do not believe I could have survived. Perhaps this is the reason why I lied to you. I simply did not want any complications. That is the entire story. I cannot be more honest than that."

Marcus took in a lung full of air, releasing it gradually. His demeanour demonstrated confusion and agitation in equal measure. "Jessica – what I saw tonight is too awful for me to contemplate. I hear what you are saying, but I am not sure how to take any of it. I am totally bewildered."

"Then let me tell you the way it is." She stressed. "From the moment we met on the *Aracassa*, I had no doubt in my mind that a sense of compatibility existed between us. I grew to care about you more than you will ever know. Alan means nothing to me and whether you believe it or not- he never will. At the moment he is on his way to New York with his wife, or his woman or whatever. When I came here I had enough time to think about him and decided that he was not the kind of man I wanted. Alan played the field and as they say, 'A leopard can never change its spots.' In my view that will never change. Tonight was just a horrible mistake. It was an unguarded moment that means nothing. If I imagined our relationship would have blossomed or taken roots when we made love I would never ever have allowed anything of that sort to happen if I was not rejected by you."

"Jessica, I am struggling to understand how your mind works. If Alan meant nothing to you, why do you allow yourself to go to those lengths with him? I find it difficult to buy your story."

"Look, it happened and there is nothing you or I can do about it. I admit I made a complete fool of myself that much I know. But, what I am certain of; Alan would never have succeeded had it not been for your actions. Marcus, please do not forget, you rejected me."

Marcus looked completely bemused by Jessica's comments and immediately felt a sense of guilt ignoring her, especially after that unforgettable evening that they spent together. He believed it may have been appropriate to explain his position more clearly in terms of what his intentions were, which obviously was to give his children all the attention they needed in order to settle.

Ignoring Jessica as he did, subsequent to that magical night showed a degree of callous indifference. Yet somehow conforming to her wishes would have been counterproductive to his ideals. "Jessica I did not reject you. Heaven forbids, that is not my way. But you know who I am and you are aware of what I stand for." He hesitated momentarily, "What happened between us – grand as it was – could have been a case of over-indulgence on that evening and sometimes that throws up accidents of one kind or another.

Jessica swallowed hard before speaking. Her voice trembling with emotions said, "Marcus that was no accident. I beg to differ. I initiated it! I did it because I really cared about you and hoped that our relationship would prosper. It was not easy to do what I did, but I gambled and lost. What I am saying is, I seduced you. It was my way of letting you know how I felt and that Marcus is the truth."

Marcus shuffled restlessly in his chair. He remembered that night with great fondness. It was exceptional in all its glory, but her ulterior motive in that instance, based on her confession, did not fit squarely with his plans. Her dimension of feelings for him, however, was far more than he imagined. He needed to respond and quickly. "Are you trying to justify what happened tonight? Or are you just trying to make me feel bad?"

"No, Marcus, I just wanted you to know the truth. I was well aware of your convictions as regards to our age difference. You have said often enough I was too young. I also know that you still believe that Teresa would return. What I tried to do was to break the shackle that existed and to hopefully change your way of thinking, but I was wrong. Marcus does not break away from his strong principles."

Although Marcus was not totally guilt-ridden, he nevertheless felt a tinge of conscience about that illustrious evening. It was enthralling in every sense. To assess it as euphoric was not in any way overstating it. Revisiting that fabulous occasion as she did, calmed his mood appreciably. "There are things in one's life that are not easy to change. I'm sorry for that and to be truthful I had no idea you cared that much."

"Would it have made a difference? I think not! You are just who you are." Jessica declared.

"Look!" He responded. "There are some things in life that you cannot change easily. I hope I did not lead you on and give you the wrong impression."

"It's not your fault Marcus, I took the blame. I misjudged the whole situation, but I would not change that evening for all the tea in China. That night when we made love, your body against mine – how can I express it – an experience of a lifetime! I'm struggling to know if it was not the best moment of my entire adulthood. It was so beautiful, so magnificent, it cannot be surpassed." Jessica chuckled sarcastically as she continued. "I envisaged a future of excellence that our lives together would be rosy and purposeful, I felt a symmetry that was difficult to explain, how wrong can a girl get. I must say however, rejection came quickly. The very next day I came down to earth with a vicious bump. Up went the shutters and as they say, that was that. But let me make it perfectly clear. It is only because you rejected my advances and I realised that there could be no future between us, which is why this unfortunate incident occurred. There was no way that I would have entertained Alan if our relationship were intact. That just happened on a careless whim. But let's not cry over spilt milk. I'm just not interested in playing the blame game."

"What do you expect me to say? Are you blaming me for what happened?" Marcus enquired.

"Nothing of the sort." She interjected. "Like I said, you gave me no reason to feel the way I do. I took a gamble and I failed miserably."

She got up slowly, picked up her luggage and sighed. "Before I go, I must tell you this. You are a good, decent man; the very best but for someone of your intellect, living a fantasy, hoping for some miracle that your ex-wife would return is an illusion too far. Take it from me: she is gone forever. She is as close to returning to you as I am to Mars. Get real Marcus and stop living a lie for your own sake and for your well-being? I am a woman and I know how a woman thinks." As she moved gingerly towards the door, she became fully aware of the fact that a genuine relationship, built on a solid foundation was about to collapse so dismally. It brought a moment of sadness that was difficult to comprehend. Reaching the street door, she opened it with a heavy heart and much sorrow.

Marcus followed her path with reciprocal feelings of distress and as she opened the door, he called out. "Jessica it would be better if you stayed the night."

Jessica turned to face Marcus squarely and attempted a weak smile, which her sullen expression and her sense of bewilderment did not allow.

"Thank you for your kind consideration, but I'll be alright." She said as she turned and walked towards the door. "Please do not think too badly of me. I'm only human."

Then she was gone.

His gaze at the closed door was that of a man in turmoil. The events of the evening had taken their toll. He stood up, emptied the contents of his glass and then hurled it at the closed door.

Throughout the following days, Marcus worked feverishly to nullify events of the past and to a large extent, he succeeded. There was much to do around his home in expectation of the imminent arrival of Sara and Peter. Being a man of extremely strong conviction, he and only he knew how to persist in what was necessary to accommodate his loved ones at the expense of all else. However, recognising the gulf that existed, now that his houseguest had departed, a conspicuous, almost eerie atmosphere was now prominent.

He was conscious of the change and needed to invest in disciplining himself in order to maintain normality and being a veteran in that department, he was able to do so with a modicum of success. But success is not always achieved unilaterally. There were unguarded moments when the inevitable would happen and even he was not immune to that reality. Ever so often, thoughts filtered in a direction he was not always willing to accommodate. Such as for example; the unfortunate incident he witnessed, which brought him anger and deep sadness. However, there were other times when his thought process would recall those occasions that were uplifting and memorable.

In her hasty retreat to leave, Jessica left items that were both essential and necessary for her personal use. He was also convinced that she would not be brave enough to return out of sheer embarrassment to a place that gave her so much pain. Equally, those items were reminders that dictated his thinking of her. He regarded those effects as an unnecessary distraction he could well do without. He felt he needed to commit to matters far more important, he believed it was imperative for him to take the initiative in getting her belongings to her, in order to save face. Doing so, he imagined would also rid him of a past which he was sure had gone forever.

Precilla, her most cherished friend and confidant would be the most obvious port of call. Precilla would know of her whereabouts, so he decided to investigate.

Precilla was pleased to hear his voice. "Hello Marcus, how are you?"

"I couldn't be better." He responded, trying as best he could to remain calm. "I'm working hard to get things ready for the kids."

"That's good to hear. I am aware of how much you are looking forward to it and I can't blame you."

"You bet." He assured her. "I just cannot wait. At the moment I can think of nothing else." He informed.

Precilla laughed out loud. "Just be patient Marcus. These few days will disappear before you know it."

---

"That's easy to say, but for me, it seems like an eternity."

"You sound like the proudest dad on this planet."

"Who says I'm not." He giggled. "When the time comes I'll be on top of the world."

"I'm so pleased for you." Precilla continued.

Marcus felt he had chit chatted enough. "Precilla, would you be in a position to give me any information about Jessica? I need to speak to her urgently."

"Jessica?" She echoed.

"Yes, your very good friend." He responded with a degree of surprise.

"You mean you don't know?" Precilla asked.

"Ah, what should I know?"

"Jessica's gone back to Trinidad, I thought you knew."

Marcus was totally shocked and shaken by the news. "I'm sorry, I had no idea."

"Jessica left a week ago for her hometown and she is not coming back."

Marcus pondered for a moment. He was thrown by the suddenness of her departure. "Is that a sound decision?" He heard himself say. "Why the haste?"

"Search me. I was hoping I could persuade her to change her mind. But she was having none of it."

Marcus sighed heavily. "Well, I can only wish her the very best of luck."

"Me too." Precilla mourned. "She is such a wonderful person, she deserves the very best."

"I agree totally. I wish her every good fortune. Take care Precilla. Goodbye, and I hope we will meet again soon." Marcus said as he placed the phone receiver down with a heavy heart.

Reflecting on the information received, Marcus was now sure that the curtain had come down on a friendship he never remotely imagined would have faded so abruptly. It melted away like salt in water. However, somewhere in the corner of his mind, he still regarded her as a very special human being, with a superb personality. The news of her departure was extraordinary.

He imagined her leaving would have been to his benefit that he would now be able to concentrate fully on matters more important to himself and his children. His primary objective now was to close the book on something that had run its course. However subconsciously and more to the point, the opposite was true, which was ironic.

Jessica had left a huge stamp on his otherwise solid character. Harbouring much regret that the parting of ways had been so unfortunate and concluding perhaps for the first time that she had meant more to him than he had cared to admit. It was now time for him to be constructive, to put his mind straight. Jessica was now gone for good and the reality must now be faced. Regarding what was in every sense the end to a chapter. In his lifetime he had overcome many obstacles and in doing so, reaped many benefits. He learned as a soldier to be disciplined in the face of adversity and understood fully this was not the time to weaken. There was no denying the fact that Jessica had clearly left a legacy. She was undoubtedly a formidable woman and what remained of her was an indelible footprint – a presence that he would find difficult to erase. However, for his own peace of mind, he needed to let go.

# THE NEW ARRIVALS

At long last, that great moment that Marcus was anticipating had arrived. The waiting was now over. The kids were back in his safe custody once more. Peter had grown to be tall and handsome. He was the product of parents that were not short of that particular quality. Sara was less vertical than her brother, but there was no mistaking her beauty. In many ways, her facial appearance was identical to her mother's, almost a true carbon copy. Nevertheless, that was where the comparison ended. Teresa's extroverted manner, her aggressive fervour and her direct approach to things, did not transcend in any way to Sara; who by contrast was gentle and amiable. For the benefit of a good healthy relationship, Marcus was very relieved to know that his daughter's general attributes were closer to his rather than her mother's.

Their arrival and subsequent adjustment to the general pace and conditions of the city impressed Marcus considerably, it was as if they had never been away. It was now left for him to fill that void that existed, to bring them back into the fold, to nurture them and to give them his maximum effort for a future he envisaged to be of the highest calibre. A prouder father could not be found anywhere. This was the moment he strived for if only to show his love and commitment that he was unable to give when they were far away and outside of his control.

Marcus was also overwhelmed by the role his mother, Mama G, played in substituting for their birth mother. Their conduct and natural demeanour were a true mark of her careful and considerable influence which mattered greatly by the way they enthused about her. Singing high praises for her kindness and humility, her sense of fun and her quiet authority. So much so, Marcus was left with the impression that sending them to the village was a wise decision. Endorsed by both of them and in a manner that showed how appreciative they were for the experience. Mama G was always a thoughtful old soul and did not leave Marcus out of the reckoning among other things, his quota of rum was quite substantial. He was positive that he would not be short of that particular commodity for a considerable length of time.

Peter, his son, was excellent company; he was a true conversationalist. He gave an absolutely noteworthy account of things in and around the village. He explained also how they took up the mantle – with the passing of Nanny May – of walking to church on a Sunday morning in the old traditional way; just as Mama G had always done in the past. In fact, it became normal to see her proudly taking her English grandchildren to worship. A journey she made without fail. It became a familiar site and from the outset and for some time afterwards, it had become a spectacle. Everyone wanted to hear the strange accent of these English kids.

The villagers thought they were different and as a result, they became a novelty to everyone. Peter, adorned with an easygoing temperament had become a huge favourite around the place and because of his good nature; everyone, especially the young ones who needed to be seen or to be associated with him. What was equally refreshing to hear and clearly extraordinary also was the excellent news of Nanny May's robust and genuine rapport with Peter. By the time he had arrived in the village, Nanny May had lost her vitality and much of her desire to indulge in activities of any significance. Even matters relating to the church were put on hold.

It was indeed clear to everyone that her race had been run, but there was something about Peter to which she was attracted. She admired the way he conducted himself and was always willing to reach out to the young man at any given opportunity. Peter showed extreme tolerance and patience in dealing with Nanny May and being so approachable also helped, especially when the topic of conversation was about his father Marcus.

Marcus found his Godmother's summary of his life far from inspiring. Listening to his son's account of how he was perceived by her was a sobering thought indeed.

On the other hand, his mother, someone he gave reverence to was totally different. Whatever the occasion she always stood by him, her love and devotion never wavered. In his estimation, that was all that mattered. But for what it was worth, he was satisfied that his Godmother's opinion was not an isolated case. Many of the villagers viewed him as something of an eccentric. As a result, leaving the village as he did at an early age was an opportune moment for him. In the grand scheme of things, breaking the mould of a legacy that was clearly negative and a bad reflection on his character, made him only too happy to depart.

Sipping rum and listening to Peter's narration of Marcus's youthful days according to Nanny May brought a wry smile to his face. Her analysis of him was clearly wide of the mark. He disliked her overzealous stance as seeing life in a selfish and uncompromising way, but he never disrespected her. In a strange and ironic twist, she did not care much for the father but doted and actually became a very good friend of the son. It was comforting to know that she could really care for someone after all.

The weeks flew by with alarming speed and for that period, Marcus utilised every available moment at his disposal, concentrating on Peter and Sara's welfare. His task was made easier by the reciprocal response he received in return. Their willingness and favourable reaction was excellent compensation for his efforts. Peter's passionate aim of becoming a doctor pleased his father considerably. Sara, much younger and less mature, was still in the stages of uncertainty. Nevertheless, both showed an ability to get ahead and it was evident that the help they received from their Grandmother was a huge benefit in advancing their academic cause. That fell naturally in the way Marcus anticipated it to be. He was prepared to be with them every step of the way in their endeavours, which meant reclaiming the role of a dutiful father, who felt a sense of guilt letting them out of his sight for so long and was now ready to do his level best in order to give them that much desired comfort and satisfaction he was positive they deserved. It was something a proud father would hope to accomplish and above anything else he wished that to be his crowning glory – his inexhaustible ambition.

Gradually, however, as time progressed, he was experiencing a degree of restlessness. He began to harbour a strange notion that something was amiss. Whatever it was did not readily come to mind as he expected. In the ensuing days, much of his discomfort had become a worry. It grated on him. He pondered this unease with some trepidation, doing his utmost to set it aside, but somehow it kept rumbling on. Since he was not aware of what the problem was and could not determine the scale of it, he wondered if it was real or imagined. This was the equivalent of a huge jigsaw puzzle with a vital piece missing. So alarming it became, it was beginning to give him serious cause for concern. He was more than satisfied that to the best of his ability, everything was in place that needed to be.

The children were here, safe as houses, they were healthy, happy and most satisfied, he himself was relatively at ease, why then was he so troubled? If only he knew. His sense of unease was now thoroughly unjustified. This was not something he could feel or touch and as a result, it began to take hold in the most alarming way. It had a momentum of its own, one that was gradually overwhelming in its dimension. His confidence was now slightly shattered by this obnoxious feeling in a manner that surprised him.

He always imagined that he was someone with the know-how and sensibility to overcome problems of one kind or another with the minimum of ease. Yet, here he was, finding himself in an untidy state of near paranoia. This matter, whatever it was, became a stumbling block that began to affect his mental equilibrium. Fear was now becoming a factor, a trait that was totally unfamiliar to him and one he needed to expel immediately. What was once considered a mere distraction initially, had now germinated into something of monumental proportions. So much so, he began to experience sleepless nights as a result.

It was one of those nights when the incredible happened; when the burden of grief that pursued him finally relented. It was a stormy night, accompanied by lashings of rain, thunder and lightning. Which by its sheer vehemence and fury, rendered sleep almost impossible. In this violent atmosphere, he twisted and turned restlessly as he listened to the claps of thunder and the heavy drops of rain against the window pane, not to forget the brightness of the light, when suddenly as if by magic, his mind began to clear.

Immediately and without warning the problem that so dominated his consciousness and the turbulence of it all, gradually began to be lifted. Marcus smiled ironically. He could not have imagined that something so insignificant, so minuscule, could have caused so much grief. At last the missing piece of that puzzle was now established, enabling him to breathe a huge sigh of relief. He sat up in bed in absolute joy and delight, wondering why this saga dominated his mind as long as it did without detection. This amazing drama relieved the simple fact that his children, Sara and Peter, were withholding information valid to his general peace of mind.

For almost five weeks since they were now in their new domain, functioning normally and peacefully with their father, they failed to convey the information they manifestly held from him. Neither of them at any time uttered a single word or asked any questions about Jessica's whereabouts. It seemed incredible for that to have happened without a valid reason. Jessica was a well-established person in their lives. There was a consistent flow of contact between them. The extent of their communication was considerable. She was someone whose preoccupation and general interest in them was remarkable in the very least. She was regarded as a friend and confidant in such a way that it would be impossible for them to behave as though she never existed.

Therefore, it was obvious to him that they were, by virtue of their behaviour, keeping information from him that he needed to know. He was particularly disappointed in their collective attempt of not shedding light on what was a deliberate effort not to make known what was clearly hidden knowledge of one kind or another. He hoped sincerely, mainly for the purposes of trust and good relationships, that their silence was wholly justified. What was required now, was a strategy which was both practical and sound, in order to retrieve the information they were withholding. After much consideration, he concluded if there was a weak link, it had to be Sara. Peter was the strong and positive kind, with the capability of handling situations like this adequately. Breaking him down would be too much like hard work. His best option, therefore, would be Sara.

Feeling a sense of relief from this niggling problem that was so overbearing and clearly worrisome, Marcus was now able to find truce in the notion that answers were vital in order to put right a situation that warranted clarity. Then and only then would he be able to get to the bottom of this intricate if not mysterious problem. He trusted his children implicitly, and he knew also, that their trust was reciprocal. Yet, he was positive that hidden somewhere, was a secret that needed to be unveiled for his own sanctity and peace of mind.

Considering the inclement conditions that were evident only a few hours ago, the morning appeared perfectly normal. The sun was shining brightly and the gloom of the night before was a faded past. Sara in her usual manner was first down to breakfast; she appeared relaxed and relatively cheerful as per usual.

"Good morning Daddy." She called out as she sat down.

"Good morning Sara," Marcus responded. "Did you sleep well?"

Sara smiled broadly. "I always do Daddy."

"So the heavy rain, thunder and lightning did not disturb your rest?"

"No, not at all, I had no idea it rained."

"It was an awful night." He assured her. "Anyone sleeping through that cannot be normal."

"I'm as normal as you can get." She giggled. "When I go to sleep Daddy, nothing disturbs me."

"That's the way it should be I guess." Marcus retorted. "The thing is! Not everyone is that fortunate, the storm kept me awake all night."

Marcus scrutinised Sara closely as she tucked into her breakfast. There was nothing to suggest that her natural demeanour was anything but normal. He was sure he did not want to give the impression that this was an interrogation. He figured it would be better considered as a mere conversation between father and daughter. That way much more could be accomplished.

"So tell me, my dear girl, how are you finding things around here since you are back? Are you adjusting well to the environment and to school?"

"Excellent Dad; I'm beginning to get the hang of things. I'm even making new friends."

"Splendid." He acknowledged readily. "If anything happens, whatever it might be, you would not hesitate to let me know, would you?"

"Everything is swell, Dad, what exactly did you have in mind?" She enquired.

"You can tell me anything whatsoever my dear. Please understand that your dad is always here for you. I do not expect you to withhold anything from me that I should know. I'm here to help in any way I can."

Sara looked at her father with a hint of suspicion. Worried that he might be seeking information she was not prepared to offer. "I would not do that Daddy if there's a problem I would come to you."

"Good girl. That's what I want to hear. You know, kids sometimes hide little secrets from their parents and very often it could lead to situations that everyone could easily regret. You understand don't you?"

Sara nodded her head affirmatively. But before she responded, her brother arrived at the table.

"Morning everyone," Peter remarked with a cheery smile.

"Good morning Peter," Marcus answered. "I take it that you slept well also, with no interruptions?"

"None that I know of Dad."

"That's simply amazing. All that bad weather that kept me awake the whole night through and neither of you were disturbed."

"Sleep is good Dad. That's why it was invented." Peter chuckled.

Marcus laughed loftily. "I swear I'll get used to your sense of humour one day Peter, but it will take some time."

"Time and patience are what I have plenty of." Peter giggled.

"I can't argue with that." His father admitted wearily as he turned his focus on Sara. "I was just explaining to your sister before you arrived, that if anything untoward should happen to either of you, I expect you both not to be afraid to tell me about it. As you already know, I'm the kind of dad who wants to be aware of everything about my kids, without exception, do you understand?"

Sara appeared uncomfortable about the way the conversation was going. She looked at her brother with a degree of circumspection. Knowing they were both guilty of a tiny little secret between them. Peter, on the other hand, a young man made of sterner stuff, did not appear ruffled.

"I fully understand what you are saying, Dad," Peter responded.

"You are both here now and it is my duty to give you two the best care I can possibly give." Marcus insisted. "What I want in return is for you folks to see me as a dad that you can be straight with – is that fair?"

They both nodded agreement.

"Well." He continued. "Is there anything you might want to say to me that I should know?"

Peter was still unmoved by his father's remarks. Sara, however, showed vulnerability to a high degree. Her chin began to drop to her chest as she under looked her brother. It was a sure sign of guilt; this was enough for Marcus to ratchet up the interrogation further.

"Like I said kids – let's be fair to one another. Just like I'm prepared to level with you, I do expect the same from both of you."

Peter was more forthcoming. "Dad, you must know we would not deceive you in any way whatsoever, we are your kids and what is more, we love you. However, you need to be more specific in what you are trying to extract from us. We want to help if we can."

Marcus paused momentarily, giving the impression that he was deliberately imposing serious scrutiny on his children. He was determined to extract the truth and making them aware of his intention which was his ultimate objective. It was obvious that they were made conscious of his suspicions. Based on simple logic, it would have been impossible considering the close affiliation they had developed with Jessica, not to be curious enough to ask the inevitable question of her whereabouts. "Kids, you know full well what I'm speaking about. It's about your Aunt Jessica."

Peter looked at Sara and she did likewise. At last their little secret was out. It was now a matter of being honest and to reveal what was indeed suppressed information. Peter sighed heavily. "Dad I have to be truthful. Both Sara and I made a promise not to reveal or ask any questions about Aunt Jessica and that's the gospel truth."

"Why ever not for heaven's sake and who in their right mind would ask you to do that?" A puzzled Marcus asked.

Peter shuffled restlessly in his chair. "We were told by Aunt Jessica herself."

Marcus sat there, looking at his children in total disbelief and shock. It was evident for a little while, he was dumbfounded and speechless. "Did I hear you clearly?" He enquired. Still suffering from the impact of what he just heard. They both shook their heads affirmatively. Sara was by far much more enthusiastic than her brother.

"I don't understand what you're telling me, Peter. Am I correct in thinking that Jessica in person instructed you in this matter?"

Again the agreement was unanimous between the children. It was then and only then that Marcus was beginning to comprehend the magnitude of what was being told to him. This for the first time had an authentic ring to it. He was hoping it was a prank of some kind, the type that could suddenly emerge as a huge joke. But by all appearances and judging by the seriousness of his children, it obviously was not.

Marcus was truly baffled and mesmerised by this news. He was listening to an account by his children that somehow did not tally with logic. His instincts try as he may, could not accept the conclusion that Jessica in actuality was not only in the village – a place where she knows nothing about – but she was able to instruct his children on matters he regarded as fundamental to him. The plausibility of it was not only perplexing but it was bordering on the ridiculous.

"So let me be clear about this; Jessie came to the village, am I correct?"

"Yes Dad, she came to the village three weeks before we left," Peter uttered.

Marcus listened intently. This mystery was still way beyond his comprehension. There was no tangible reason to doubt his son's credibility, so far as he knew. Peter was of a sound mind, he was not prone to telling imaginary tales, nor was he hallucinating – and since he himself was not in some kind of a coma, or having a bad dream, he found this information difficult to understand. Gathering himself as best he could; he was now ready for more.

"For starters, what was Jessica doing in the village and why?" He asked astonished.

"Dad, I did not ask her those questions. All I can tell you is that she was there. She told us who she was and we welcomed her."

"What on earth for?" Marcus questioned. "What brought her there and why?"

"Apparently and I can only guess that she wanted to see Sara and myself."

Marcus still not entirely convinced and needed to know more. "You mean she travelled to a country she knows nothing about, found our village which she has never been to, merely to say hello? Is that really credible?"

Peter shrugged his shoulders. "Maybe, I do not know. However, Mama G was convinced she was a Godsend."

"Why should Mama G think that?" Marcus questioned.

"As it happens, Mama G was not quite well. Aunt Jessica was very quick to recognise that there was a problem."

"And what was the problem?" Marcus asked anxiously.

"Mama G collapsed the day after Aunt Jessica arrived," Peter explained. "She was suffering from diabetes..."

"What!" Marcus interrupted. "My mother was ill and no one bothered to let me know about it. What the hell is going on?"

Peter maintained his calmness. "Well, as far as I know, Mama G is alright now Dad. It was a situation that Aunt Jessica handled swiftly. We took her to the hospital where she stayed for about eight days. She has now recovered fully and when we left she was in fine fettle."

Marcus's anger was now quite evident. Hearing of his mother's illness brought on a copious degree of stress. How insensitive of them not to have told him of something so important.

"You mean to tell me that my mother's illness is something I should not know about? How can you two justify keeping that a secret from me?"

"Like I said Dad, everything that had to be done to help Mama G, was taken care of by Aunt Jessica, no one could have done a better job."

"I really do not care how good she was." Marcus raged. "My mother's illness is important to me and I deserved to know about it."

"Dad." Peter declared solemnly. "Aunt Jessica assured us that she was taking care of communications with you. She begged us not to divulge any information until we heard from her. She told us that she took the responsibility of contacting you and we believed her. We trusted that she would not let us down."

It was hardly enough to heal Marcus's wrath, but the deed was already done and it was certainly not worth any further unnecessary distress.

"You two have been here over four weeks now and not once have I received any communication from the folks back there. Can you explain that?"

Peter again shrugged shoulders casually. "I cannot account for that, all I know is we kept our side of the bargain. Look, Dad, Aunt Jessica is not our biological mother, but she is someone who we admire, care for and respect. What she did for granny was outstanding, not to mention what she did for us. She asked us to conceal information from you until she was ready to instruct us otherwise. We agreed and I do not think it was too much to ask, considering the grand effort she made throughout her stay with us. Her contribution was immense."

Sara, who remained tacit throughout, continued to give nodding support to Peter when necessary.

Marcus sighed impatiently. "What was the state of your Grandmother when you left?"

For the first time, Peter was able to smile. "Dad, Mama G was fully recovered when we left. Aunt Jessica assured us that she would not leave until she was satisfied that Mama G was totally fit to carry on."

"And where is Jessica now?" Marcus enquired.

"We left her in the village. Take it from me Dad, Mama G is fine."

After this sudden and most alarming revelation; Marcus was left in a state of deep disaffection, His children's reticent manner regarding the specifics of his mother's ailment was most unsatisfactory. He contended to himself that there was a great deal more to it than met the eye. He also felt aggrieved and disappointed that his children did not show the loyalty he expected of them, preferring to give the benefit of doubt to, in reality, a stranger they only just met, rather than their own flesh and blood.

He thought it was now necessary, for a swift response to a delicate, but vital situation and concluded that the only solution to the problem was a home visit to see for himself the full extent of his mother's condition. Reflecting on the general state of play, Adel his sister came to mind. Could she have been part of this bizarre episode? Would she have known that her mother was unwell and kept it a secret also? Was she complicit in this inconceivable shamble?

Marcus picked up the phone and dialled Adel, who was quite pleased to hear from her brother. It was obvious her contact with Jessica was far more meaningful than he originally anticipated. Her answer to his question gave the game away in more ways than one.

"Hello Marcus, how are you?" She answered.

"I'm very well Adel, are you?" He questioned.

"I am fine thank you."

"Look, Adel, I've heard Mama G was very ill recently and I'm curious to know if you were aware of her ill health?"

Adel was not immediately forthcoming, which gave Marcus reasons to believe a conspiracy was afoot.

"Well! As a matter of fact, I was told she was not enjoying the best of health, but it was nothing to be alarmed about." She responded after a short pause.

"Adel." A furious Marcus retaliated. "What kind of games are you playing? Mama G was hospitalised and you kept it away from me? Are you some kind of monster? Our mother could have potentially been dying and you kept your mouth shut? You should know better than to keep something like that a secret from me. That's shameful of you."

"Can you stop shouting like a lunatic?" She retorted. "Mama G is far from death's door, why are you always making a mountain out of a molehill? Don't forget she is my mother also.

Do not think for one moment that you're the only one that cares." She reminded him.

"Care?" He responded. "Sometimes I don't think you know the meaning of the word. You should show a proper example and lead, not follow like some headless chicken. I expect you to be upfront about things that are of importance, especially concerning your own mother."

He slammed the receiver down in a rage. He was now absolutely in no doubt that there was a copious attempt of concealment in place, designed to shut him out of information to which he should have been privy. It appeared to be clearly specific; this journey to the village was now all the more imperative.

# FLYING HOME

Flying to his place of birth was a totally new experience for Marcus. Of all the things he aspired to, this was never in his order of priority. He hated flying. In his opinion, birds with their natural attributes of wings were far more adapted to this particular process. Humans were certainly not, therefore his position as far as this novel adventure was concerned, was not a valued accomplishment he was willing to undertake. However, he was mindful of the mission ahead and since necessity demanded a quick response to a situation he regarded as urgent – if not most imperative – this journey had become inevitable. The flight had a surprising element to it, far better than he had ever anticipated.

Soaring high in the sky, gave him a sense of calm he did not quite expect. It also brought about an expansive degree of reflective moments, relative to both past and present. Marcus allowed himself a warm smile as he relaxed in quiet contemplation. He recalled in particular, Jessica's feat of daring. Her transiting from a shy, introverted and extremely nervous individual, into someone who was capable of displaying a high level of commitment, in her pursuit of achieving her objective, whatever that might be. Not only was her sense of adventure something to be admired, her ability to make friends and to influence people were noted with the greatest of satisfaction. All of this registered a complete departure from the young woman he met on the SS Aracassa, that very late evening all those years ago. Then, she was bordering on the edge of despair. She represented a human wreck. She was vulnerable, timid and a

VICTOR WALDRON

frightened individual, incapable of facing up to the challenges that beset her. He also remembered the first day that she arrived in London and the hustle and bustle of Victoria Station.

But most importantly, the terror in her eyes of seeing the atrocious conditions in which her cousin Cleveland was living. She cringed in observing the dilapidated hovel he called home and dreaded the possibility that she may become a victim of that existence. Fortunately, her fears were put to rest by someone she would never be able to forget – that was himself. For someone to have emerged as she did, in such a creditable way, was most commendable. Much of what she did, however, was influenced in one way or another by him. He nurtured her in the best way he could and felt that gratitude of some kind must be given to him for making her into the person she had become. He accepted in no small measure, his input in aiding her development, if only for his own ego.

What had become a complete metamorphosis, without doubt, was his surprising and in its own way, remarkably pleasant preoccupation with Jessica which he found strangely comforting. That mode once belonged exclusively to Teresa. Since her abrupt departure and that most unfortunate and disconcerting incident – finding her in bed with Alan – Jessica had invaded his thoughts in ways he could hardly comprehend. Conversely, what was also extraordinary was the sudden reduction of that wholesale thought process that went Teresa's way. Now she seldom ever came to mind. He could hardly have imagined that such a thing was possible. This was a quantum leap if ever there was one.

He recalled how slavishly Teresa consumed his thoughts. The unrelenting and rigidly fixed feelings that possessed his life in almost every living moment of his adult years had come to an end. His love for Teresa was not an infatuation; it was true and honest on his part. Perhaps there was an element of obsession about it, but in his own way, he regarded it as something he was incapable of resisting. As challenges go, he was ready to climb the highest mountain or swim the deepest sea in his quest for Teresa's affection. Unfortunately, try as he may, he was unable to attain that objective. In many ways, he felt that would have been the crowning glory of all his ambitions. Alas, it was not to be. His was nothing more than an unfulfilled dream.

Sitting in rarefied conditions, high in the sky, with so much time to reflect and review situations generally, Marcus came to the ready conclusion that he was something of an enigma. His good fortune had given him the opportunities to erase the miserable thoughts of Teresa and all that she stood for when he met Jessica. It would have been difficult to conclude, even remotely, that the relationship would have developed in the way that it did. No one would have foreseen two strangers meeting by sheer chance, could have established such a good friendship in such a comprehensive way.

Convinced that fate played a hand in all of this, he was left wondering why. No one on this planet could argue that Jessica was not a person of impeccable attributes, the kind that Teresa was bereft of in so many ways. She constantly displayed qualities of kindness, maturity and grace. She was affable; she was loving and amazingly beautiful. He admired and appreciated in no uncertain way her fine personality. His attraction for her was more meaningful than he ever anticipated. He recognised her tremendous effervescence, especially that fabulous experience he remembered with the greatest of pleasure. It was one that was full of delight and incredible joy. It was an evening that was one of sheer ecstasy.

Yet, in all of this, there was a huge stumbling block that did not fit the criteria in terms of what he wanted. Jessica was nearly twenty years his junior and even though she possessed all the credentials necessary in a more than satisfactory manner, her age was a major factor against her. What he dearly wanted was someone to fill the gap that was left by Teresa. He grew weary of waiting for what he now believed would never happen. Teresa was gone forever. Marcus knew the time had come to renew his vows. He was ready once again to accommodate someone to share his future years. There was no doubt in his mind that he needed a good woman.

VICTOR WALDRON

What had emerged and remained paradoxical, however, was the notion that perhaps Jessica was someone he could accept as a prospective wife. There was absolutely no reason to argue against the qualities she possessed. Equally, it would be futile to deny her finer points. Again and again, Jessica appeared to be very much in Marcus's focus. It was also true that the way he felt about her, especially since her departure from his home, his thoughts about her had grown immeasurably. Yet, in spite of what she may have to offer, a major problem existed.

To accept Jessica as his wife, he would have gone against the very grain of his beliefs. He would be breaking a fundamental rule – a solemn vow – never to marry someone so young. Marcus pondered all the possibilities and decided it was prudent to dismiss them temporarily, concluding that nothing can be solved in haste. Whatever developed subsequently, it must be done wisely and with utmost care. This journey, however, in many ways was regarded as a leap of faith. It was merely to validate what was told to him by his children, which needed to be confirmed. There were many questions to be answered, then and only then would he be able to deal with the situation constructively.

It was morning. The gloom of the night was still self-evident as Marcus arrived in the village. It was shadowy and dark; with dogs barking in the background and insects still inhabiting the darkness, actively and distinctively before the spread of light. The silhouette of trees swaying hither and thither like ballerinas, accompanied by a swift and friendly breeze; that filtered robustly throughout the empty spaces creating an atmosphere that typified the uniqueness of what he remembered as a young man growing up in the village. That brought a pleasant smile to his face, as he sucked in a lung full of country air and for the first time he was able to observe the home where he was born.

Then, it was a very modest cottage of very little distinction, now it had been transformed into a substantial and homely place of residence. This was done for the benefit of his children's comfort and with equal consideration for his mother Mama G, who he felt was deserving of it. Ascending the steps, Marcus was full of nervous energy. His thoughts reflected on Jessica and wondered, with a degree of anxiety, what kind of reception he was to expect. His pounding heart and dry lips gave evidence to a strange sense of emotions that consumed him, in anticipation of what might eventually unfold. This undoubtedly was the climax to a journey of uncertainties, one that he felt imperative to make, merely to satisfy his quest for answers that in his opinion were in very short supply.

# REFLECTION

Marcus knocked on the door and waited with bated breath. The gloom of the morning was gradually giving way to daylight. Yet, the lights came on much to the surprise of Marcus, Mama G arrived at the door, reducing the impact he so anticipated and with it, the expectation he had hoped to engender. Mama G, agog by her son's sudden arrival, staggered backwards.

"Marcus?" She bellowed in surprise. "Boy, are you trying to give your old Mum a heart attack? Why did you not say you were coming?"

Marcus stood grinning lavishly. "Hello Mama G, I was hoping to give you a very pleasant surprise."

Mama G pushed open the door. "You have certainly done that. Come on in and let me hold you."

Still smiling he approached his mother with open arms as they embraced lovingly. His observation of his mother was enough to pay her a compliment. "Mama G you do look well. You have lost a bit of weight but it suits you."

Mama G looked up at her son and smiled. "Thank you my son, God has been good to me, I'm almost back to normal now."

Marcus nodded agreeably. "I'm happy you're doing well, but someone should have informed me of your illness. I was kept completely in the dark."

"Well my son, I'm sorry for that, but make no mistake, I was in good company."

"It's good to know you're okay." He expressed.

"So tell me son what about you? Are you keeping well?"

Marcus held his mother at arm's length. "As you can see my dear Mother I am as fit as a fiddle."

"That's good to know." She responded as she scrutinised Marcus thoroughly. "And how are my grandchildren?"

"Peter and Sara are keeping very well. They are getting used to the climate once more, but make no mistake, not a day passes without them speaking about you."

Mama G sat herself down slowly, her smile fading rapidly. "Marcus you cannot imagine how much I miss those kids. They were such a vital part of this home when they were here."

Marcus was quick to notice her sudden state of sadness. "I know how you feel, I can tell you with some confidence that they feel exactly the same way."

"I know, my son, they are lovely children."

"Mama G, I guess you know why I'm here. When I heard of your illness, I was very upset about it. Even Adel, who knew, kept the news from me. I found the entire situation unsatisfactory."

Mama G smiled contentedly. "My darling son, like I said and as you can see, I'm okay now. Thanks to that wonderful young friend of yours, Jessica. Boy, she is a miracle worker. She came to the house as a complete stranger and in no time at all, she was like family. It was as if we knew her all our lives. I had not seen anyone so committed. She showed compassion beyond her years. In my opinion, she is a living treasure, the kind that comes very rarely in anyone's life. She also had nothing but the highest of praise for you and as for the kids; it was if they were born for each other. They got on like a house on fire. Do you know what I think? You two would make a wonderful couple."

Marcus smiled sheepishly. "Mama I know the young lady very well. She is a delightful person; she also has extremely good qualities."

"You can say that again my son." His mother echoed happily. "When she arrived I was feeling jaded and lacking in energy. She noticed it immediately and just as quickly, she was able to tell me what was wrong."

"Well," Marcus assured his mother, "Jessica is a highly qualified young woman that much I can tell you."

"So, my son, what are you going to do about it? If I had a say in the matter, I would tell you not to let her out of your sight. She and those kids were hand in glove." Mama G stopped briefly and smiled a smile of contentment. "Your kids are very special, they are a delight to be with, boy – you should have seen them with me on a Sunday morning, sauntering leisurely to church. They took the place of your Godmother Nanny May – God bless her soul. You can't imagine how I felt, me and my two English grandchildren; believe me, it was a sight to behold; simply wonderful."

English grandchildren? Is that how the villagers saw them?" Marcus enquired.

"Yes, my son." She responded cheerfully. "The villagers loved to hear them speak, especially Peter, what a charmer. It's their accent that they could not get enough of."

"Quite unlike his dad eh Mama?"

"You were never switched on in that way, but you were a good boy. Your son, however, was a special attraction to the village. He is such a great character."

"Well, at least they were a good replacement for my Godmother."

"Of course." She responded, pausing slightly before she continued. "Poor girl she suddenly popped off."

"It was a shock to hear of Nanny May's demise, I know she was your best friend. It cannot have been easy for you." He reminded his mother.

"True my son." She remarked sadly. "But life is not forever, she is in a good place now." Mama G chuckled. "Strange as it might seem, she was very fond of your son Peter. She constantly kept looking out for him because he always made her laugh."

Marcus giggled. "Isn't that just odd, she loved Peter, but found his dad objectionable."

"Well Marcus, that's the way life is. Your Godmother did not dislike you; she merely wanted to keep you on the straight and narrow. She always felt you disregarded things that were important. In other words, she would have been much happier if you conformed to village ways, let's face it, you were a bit stubborn."

Marcus laughed out loud. "You know Mum I love you dearly. But you allowed Nanny May far too much scope over me."

"Son, it's an old custom." She confirmed. "Godparents have a duty to help bring up their Godchildren and that's all she was trying to do. She desperately wanted you to be a good lad."

Marcus was insistent. "Mama G, I was always a good lad, in spite of what she believed. The truth is; I was never going to be what she wanted me to be, I just could not conform to her wishes. The times I'd been clipped around the ears at church because I was not paying attention to that white priest, forever telling us how to be servile and passive and insisting that we remained meek and gentle. The truth is Mama G; I was never convinced about the sentiments of his sermons. I always wanted to be like those wealthy white folks, not remain hopeless and passive."

Mama G listened intently, with a solemn look. "Marcus you were different. The village did not suit you for whatever reason. You could not make friends and you cared very little for the community."

"On the contrary, I loved the village. What I did not care for was the attitude of the people. I wanted something more out of life and I was positive I was not going to get it here."

His mother nodded agreeably. "I know my son, you were always ambitious. Folks took that the wrong way."

"That is so true." He insisted. "I guess I was the most misunderstood person around. I simply had no choice but to escape."

"Well my son, I hope you did not feel too badly about your Godmother. She was not always that way. She turned to the church when her husband deserted her. As you know he went prospecting for gold and never came back."

"My dear Mother." He smiled broadly. "What is passed is passed. I hold no grudge for anyone. I have no axe to grind."

"Anyway; you've done remarkably well for yourself and I'm sure you'll be doing the same for those lovely children of yours. I cannot begin to tell you how much I miss them." His mother responded joyously.

"There's an answer to that problem Mother, come to London with me. There is nothing to lose and so much to gain."

"My boy!" She mused. "I've told you once; nothing would make me leave this village. That was before Sara and Peter came here. Now, I'm not so sure. I never imagined I could feel this way for those two kids, I guess old age brings on sentimentality. But I feel so lost without them."

"You're always the one for giving good advice to people. I think it would be good for you to listen to what I am about to say. You need your grandchildren and they need you. Peter never stops talking about you. They both would be delighted to have you in London."

Mama G appeared glum as she shifted restlessly in her seat. "Nothing would please me more than to see my wonderful grandchildren again, but uprooting myself at this stage of my life, would not come easily. I still see this village as the place that I want to be. Many things have changed over the years, most of it I would not consider as desirable. The British have gone now and so too have the village elders. Some are deceased, some following their siblings to other parts of the world – God knows where. Even the Malisons have all vacated the place. The village is now full of strangers who are not part of that strong bond that once existed, but it is still my home. Changing it for somewhere else would be against the normal grain of things. This house is now a palace compared to what it used to be and I am proud of you for giving me such a sumptuous place to live in. In my humble opinion, in spite of all the changes, there's no place as comfortable as home."

"Mama G you said it yourself, so many people have left, that is an indication that sometimes change can be good for you, especially in this instance. It was a worry to me that no one alerted me to your illness. It would make good sense to come to

London where I can keep my eye on you and much more, you will be cared for health-wise."

"How could that be?" Mama G asked in surprise. "Jessica was writing to you regularly."

"Not so Mama G. I heard of your illness in a roundabout way." This information given by Marcus seemed rather contrary to his mother's, who was told emphatically by Jessica that she was taking care of business and keeping Marcus abreast of the situation.

"Are you saying to me that the young lady was not telling us the truth?"

"Not at all." He responded. "What I'm saying is no correspondence of any kind was received by me. I guess I got a bit excited seeing Sara and Peter and may have taken my eyes off the ball, but I can assure you, no correspondence came to my home."

"Well Marcus, I'm baffled. Believe me, Jessica was sending letters to you and I can vouch for that. I saw her writing them with my own eyes."

Marcus was not about to argue with his mother about something that had no merit. There was a mystery of a sort that he needed to get to the bottom of. It was obvious to him that Jessica had influenced the situation with great skill and more importantly, with a good measure of success.

"Mama G." He responded wearily, "It's hardly worth crying over spilt milk, more to the point where exactly is Jessica now?"

Mama G smile was one of warmth. "The young lady is not here anymore, she went back to Trinidad a fortnight ago."

The news of Jessica's departure created something of an anticlimax and compounded his disappointment. It was as if she had become an elusive target. One that he was sure he needed to pursue.

"Mama G, have you any idea what Jessica came here for?"

Mama G giggled heartily. "She came to see Sara and Peter of course. She thought it would be a perfect opportunity to meet them before she went back to her homeland."

Marcus nodded approvingly. "I guess they were attached to her for a long time, but I imagine it has come to an end now."

Mama G studied her son's facial expression momentarily. Being old and wise she instantly observed that he seemed distracted and less than happy. "Marcus!" She asked warmly. "Is there something worrying you and can I help in some way? You look troubled."

His false smile betrayed him. "I'm okay – nothing that I cannot handle."

It was clear to his mother that he was somewhat troubled. "Marcus you are a remarkable young man, there is so much about you to be admired. From the day you left these shores as a very young man, until this day, I begged the Almighty to keep you safe and my prayers have been answered. Maybe I should not mention this, but you were the one amongst my children that I've always had a soft spot for, mainly for the way you are. I think you are bold, ambitious and different, you always knew what you wanted. Right now I can see you are bothered about something, is it to do with Jessica? And why did she leave London to go back to Trinidad, so unexpectedly? Did you fall out with her?"

Marcus was hesitant to give a definitive answer to his mother's question. Since he could not be sure what Jessica may have told her. "Mama G that's not a question I can answer easily. Maybe she had grown tired of the big city and wanted a change, who knows!"

"Did she not tell you? Could it be that she got tired of living in sin and decided to find someone who would appreciate her more?"

"Mama G." He frowned. "Are you assuming that Jessica and I were lovers?"

"Yes." His mother replied with some degree of assurance. "Are you telling me that such a sweet girl was living with you and you two were not connected in some way? Do you expect me to believe that there was nothing going on between you two?"

# A MOTHER'S WISDOM

Marcus was quite astonished to be told so emphatically by his mother about a relationship that in actuality did not exist. He knew his mother was not one for making accusations without proof. He therefore readily accepted that it was not difficult to imagine that man and woman living together equalled romance. Since he was positive beyond doubt that his mother was not one for making rash statements, it was obvious to him that this bit of information had Adel's stamp written all over it. The news brought a wide smile to his face. "Mama G, there is no romance between Jessica and myself, that is the truth."

"Marcus my son; what are you trying to hide from your mother?" She pleaded.

"Nothing whatsoever." He declared. "Look! I'm a big boy now and I have absolutely no reason to be telling stories that are not true. Would I be correct in saying that this rumour came from Adel?"

Mama G blushed in a way he had not witnessed before. She was not in the habit of naming names and she was not about to start now. "Do not blame your sister for anything. I personally cannot imagine such a smashing young woman with such striking looks, did not take your fancy."

Marcus nodded affirmatively. "You are right my Mother, she is a lovely girl and I would be lying if I said otherwise. But there is a story regarding our relationship that I have not told you about and I'm not prepared to keep it a secret from you anymore. After all, you are my mother and I'm sure you would understand."

Mama G's look of puzzlement was apparent. "So what is the story you want to tell?"

"Contrary to the belief you have, Jessica and I are genuinely good friends and believe it or not it is based on the solid respect we have for each other and nothing else."

Mama G sighed heavily. "My son, I'm about to go to my grave and in my lifetime, I've seen and heard it all, but something tells me, that it would be very hard not to be attracted to someone so sweet. So tell me, my son, how is that possible?"

"Well, Jessica was a victim of an experience that was most unfortunate. We met on my return journey to London after leaving Peter and Sara with you. It was compassion, not love that brought us together. When I met her she was a pathetic sight, a human wreck and perhaps as close to being suicidal as you could possibly get. She was placed on that boat against her will by her father who for his own selfish reasons, decided to send her to London." He stopped for a brief moment.

"It was apparently to avoid her having a relationship he did not approve of. She needed help – I mean, can you imagine putting a young woman on a journey like that? London is a huge city, one that is full of uncertainties, to place her in that position was totally heart wrenching. As you can imagine, Mama G, she was a desperate young woman, utterly out of control; it would have been inhuman to walk away. So I did my best to dispel her fears, to take her out of her misery and to deliver her safely in the custody of her cousin who was supposed to have met her. On board, we had time on our hands and as a result, we became friends to the extent that she knew exactly what kind of person I was among other things. In fact Mother, our discussions were very in-depth, largely because I anticipated, once she was in the safe hands of her cousin that as they say would be that. Unfortunately, she encountered more problems when she arrived in London. There was no one there to receive her, so being a man of my word, I went out of my way and took her to what should have been her final destination. Mama G, her cousin was in no fit state to accept her, it was terrible. He was living in the most appalling, substandard conditions imaginable. What was I supposed to do? Abandon her? That would have been an exercise in futility. It would have defeated the purpose completely. So I was left with no alternative, but to take her into custody and into my home. That my dear Mother is the entire story."

"That's very interesting son." Conceded Mama G. "But she is such a delightful girl; most men would find her irresistible."

"Mama G, she was not always so, I watched her grow and blossom into that radiantly beautiful woman. And yes I guess there were possibilities, but I remained strong. My dear Mother, I do admit to the fact that I did not have your religious fervour, but I'm a firm believer in marriage. That being the case, I'm afraid Jessica was completely out of the reckoning. I was not seeking a live-in partner. Jessica is almost twenty years my junior and when I decide to marry again, it would not be someone so young."

Mama G took a deep breath. "My son, I did not realise that you had such strong principles, but there is a danger that you can allow these beliefs to get in the way of progress – to dictate your life. Circumstances can change and when that happens, adjustments are sometimes necessary."

"I understand." He reasoned. "I'm not totally inflexible Mother, but what I have expressed to you are long-held views which I would find difficult to alter."

Mama G listened with intent. In her mind, she felt certain that her son had a secret desire for Jessica; in spite of his public utterances. The very same was true of Jessica, who displayed a remarkable degree of unpretentious yearning for his attention. In fact, it was not difficult to identify that she cared deeply. "Let me be truthful, son. What you did for Jessica was most becoming, but somehow what you've said has left me a bit sceptical. There is a gap in your story. I may be old but I'm not foolish. That young lady stayed with you all these years and suddenly decides to leave your home without a reason? Are you sure you're not holding back something from me?"

Marcus felt guilty, but he knew he could not divulge the true reason for Jessica's leaving. He realised his mother sensed there was something more to be said. Her sense of perception was most uncanny. "Mother, Jessica has a sound mind. She decided to exercise her choice in where she wanted to be. That was her decision, not mine."

Mama G studied Marcus carefully before confronting him. "Like I said, my son, her reason for coming was based on Sara and Peter, but in my eyes, it was more to do with you. That was evident by the things she said and the way she acted. Would I be wrong in thinking that my observations were correct?"

Marcus smiled wryly. "Mama G, I would never question your wisdom. Clearly, you are a woman of vision. But I am not certain why Jessica decided to leave."

"Then, if you think I'm right, remove the obstacles in the way and confront Jessica. In my mind, I think that is what you want to do."

Marcus was definitely in agreement with his mother's reckoning, in terms of his strong feelings towards Jessica. She had become a permanent fixture in his head in a way he did not expect since her departure from his home. It was as if that pent-up emotion that he kept under wraps had suddenly been released. However, it conflicted with a lifelong conviction which was difficult to abolish. In the grand scheme of things, a choice had to be made imperatively, one way or another.

"Mama G, I do hope you understand this is a decision I cannot take lightly. There is a lot to think about."

Mama G took a long look at Marcus. "My boy, I have little or no doubt about Jessica, do you know why? She is an angel, as you know; I am a person of faith. I truly believe in the power of prayer and my prayers were being answered. That is why I say to you, Jessica was heavenly sent. From the moment she arrived, she was able to tell me what my problems were. Although she spoke professionally, she never forgot to show tenderness and compassion towards me. When I collapsed, she was so understanding, she calmed my anxiety and assured me that I was not in any grave danger. I do not know too much about these things, but I believe if she was not here, my life would have been in serious danger. She administered her service with such care and attention, it was very impressive indeed. What I could not understand, was how a complete stranger, was able to display kindness and humanity in such abundance, especially towards a person she had only just met. It's nothing short of a miracle."

"Jessica is that sort of a person, although I'm not entirely sure she's an angel." He continued.

"Well, you may not think so, but I do. She took care of business from the moment she arrived. Her attention to detail was simply amazing even when I was in hospital. As for Peter and Sara, she mothered them as if they were her own. She was thorough and faultless."

"If nothing else Mama G, Jessica has certainly left her mark on you." He giggled.

"She is a good person." Mama G gushed. "A perfect gem and when someone like her comes along with the quality and goodness she possesses, it would be folly not to take advantage of it."

Marcus paused briefly, he was unclear what his mother meant by her statement. "Whatever do you mean by that Mama G? Jessica is not a trophy. She is a very intelligent young woman, who for all you know, may not even want to know me in that way."

"Marcus." His mother retorted. "I see things you may not see. Age gives you an insight and it's an advantage in many ways. Believe me when I say that Jessica cares deeply about you."

Marcus grinned lavishly. "Did you see that in your crystal ball? How can you be so sure?"

"Do not mock your mother, boy, I have eyes and I can see. For starters, you have done everything right in your life except Teresa. I warned you about that girl as I recall. You did not listen and you paid the price. And what was the result of that? You've had many years of unhappiness, which you could have avoided. My son this is not a rebuke. We all make mistakes, although that could have been prevented. So here is my advice – if you are interested in making your life joyous and fulfilling, go find

Jessica and tell her how you feel about her before someone snatches her from under your nose."

Marcus took a deep breath. "You did warn me about Teresa, but you really never understood my feelings for her, I sincerely loved that woman. Teresa was the prize I wanted; you have to understand me when I say it was all about love. If there was not so much prejudice in the world, maybe, just maybe, she would still have been my wife."

Mama G snared almost scornfully. "Understand the world you live in Marcus. Firstly – love comes from the heart. Teresa did not have that kind of love for you. Maybe she found true love when as you mentioned she met that white boy. Secondly, Teresa and her entire family did not see you as their equal. Whatever you may have achieved was invisible to them, because they knew your background. They were aware of where you came from and there was nothing you could do to stop them thinking that you married above your station. In other words, my son, in their eyes you did not come close to ever being accepted."

Marcus felt peeved. "My darling Mother let me say this. What I did in my life was notable in the eyes of white folks in London. I have achieved in one of the biggest Metropolises in the world and what I have attained, can be compared with anyone, anywhere. As a result of that, do you not think I'm qualified enough to be their equal? Are you still implying those people are better than us?"

"My son, I'm not in a position to make judgements on folks. I'm an ordinary woman, no more, no less. As you know society is what it is and I'm not sure that you or I can change that. Regretfully, I'm not in the best position to judge people. Heaven knows all my life I've worked in order to put food on the table for my family. Your dad was not well and could not contribute as we all hoped. So it was left to me to work in those people's homes, merely to provide for my family and to be honest, I'm not ashamed of that. I exchanged my efforts for wages, cleaning, washing, cooking is what I did. In my life, there was very little time to analyse anyone."

Marcus nodded approvingly. "Mother, you are absolutely correct. It was unwise of me to be so mindless. You have done wonders for us and we should all be very grateful for that. Anyway, Teresa and the like are memories of the past and rightly so."

Mama G took a serious look at her son. "My dear boy, we were poor, your dad and I, but we knew our responsibilities and tried to do our best in very difficult circumstances. We also knew our limitations."

"I know," Marcus responded. "And I appreciate everything that you and dad were able to do for us. It's a great pity that he was not able to live long enough to see his grandchildren."

His mother smiled pleasantly. "He no doubt would have been a proud man, but we are not here to question God's work. What I really want to know is; why are you so adamant about Jessica's age? Why does it matter so much?"

"Because that has been a long-standing established belief of mine. It is something that I solemnly believed in wholeheartedly."

Mama G looked directly at Marcus and shook her head negatively. "The way I see it, son, you are caught between two stools. You must either stick to your principles or listen to your heart. What will it be?"

"I really do not know Mum," he answered in a resigned manner. "It's a decision to which I shall have to give greater thought."

A surprised Mama G laughed out loud. "Come on Marcus! What am I hearing? Did you say 'tomorrow'? You of all people? Even as a small boy, you always wanted everything in a hurry. 'Tomorrow' was never in your vocabulary. What I'm saying to you, son, is that 'tomorrow' is a luxury you simply cannot afford. Leave that remark to the hesitant and the undecided type. You have a serious choice to make and you need to make it now."

He paused momentarily, gathering his thoughts before proceeding. "My dear Mother, I have learnt my lesson not to go against your expert advice. You always succeed in winning the argument anyway. I do promise from here on to process this matter in a positive way."

"You had better." Countered Mama G. "In my opinion, that girl is one of a kind; it would break my heart if you would allow her to slip through your fingers."

"Rest assured Mother, I would not want you to have a broken heart. But there is something that has bothered me over the years and if I can help it I would never ever want to be like that old man, I believe his name was Sidwell and his wife's name was Mertle. Do you remember them? She was an awful woman to that old man and I promised myself never to be in a position like him."

Mama G pondered for a while before recalling. "Yes, I remember old Sidwell and his wife. What about them?"

"He was an old man if my memory serves me right. She was half his age and what I found bewildering was her inconsiderate attitude and her bad behaviour towards that respectable old man. The thing is no one in the village seemed to care."

Mama G was somewhat hesitant. To the best of her recollection, Marcus was still a very young man. It was surprising to learn that her son, mentioning or having any knowledge of what was then known as the odd couple. "Son, what did you know about them? You were only a boy around ten or twelve. Surely, kids do not remember things like that?"

It was Marcus's turn to laugh out loud. "Not only do I remember them, but I hated that woman intensely."

"You were always way too mature for your age." Mama G chuckled. "How on earth were you able to recall something that happened so long ago?"

Marcus's remark was more hostile than expected. "That woman was making a mockery of that old man and no one in the village seemed to care."

Mama G laughed heartily. "I remember Mertle very well. The entire village knew what she was up to and it was not behind Harry's back. It was a marriage of convenience. All that old Sidwell wanted was for her to keep him tidy, look after his home, cook his meals and wash his clothes. That was the drill. Whatever she did outside of that mattered very little to him."

"Are you saying he agreed to that? Her abhorrent ways were acceptable?"

"Yes." His mother responded. "That was it, the marriage was not about love or romance, it was purely business. What I'm surprised about is that someone of your tender age would have noticed that."

"I did notice, but I guess I was too young to understand it."

"So, my son," Mama G pondered. "Could that be the reason why you believe that marriage to someone so young is bad for you?"

"Perhaps, it may have contributed to my thinking. What I do know, is that I hated her with a passion."

Mama G was sympathetic. "Marcus my dear son, why was that a problem for you? You are only a young man and you have so many wonderful years ahead of you. Try to make the very best of it while you can, make it count. After all, you only live once. The truth is Marcus I was not aware that Jessica was so young. She seemed so mature. However, her age should not be a factor if you really care about her. She is a beautiful person, both inside and out. Her qualities are exemplary and that can only be to your benefit. My boy, I'm your mother and what I saw of that young lady, I can tell you with confidence she cares deeply about you and your children. If you love her as I seem to think that you do, go find her and let her know how you feel about her. Do not be distracted by anything else."

Marcus nodded enthusiastically, and gave his mother the benefit of doubt; her long years and wisdom could not be ignored. "Mama G, I hear you. I will make this a priority above everything else."

"That's what I want to hear my boy, I think it's the best decision you will ever make. God's blessing."

Marcus gave the idea much thought. Something had changed subconsciously and even though it was not immediately apparent, he felt less burdened and appreciably relieved. The discussion with his mother was most revealing, both in terms of attitude and incisiveness. Doubts that clouded his powers of reasoning previously were beginning to subside. In its place, a clearer outlook prevailed. It gave him the capacity to tackle the situation with a greater degree of certainty.

By his own admission, he felt there was a need to be more conceptual, thus allowing his mind to evolve with relative progression and to be less dogmatic. He was now embarking on what he considered to be a taxing and elaborate challenge, one he was looking forward to, but with some trepidation; especially since it meant meeting up with Jessica once more. The acrimonious conclusion to their friendship was clearly an enormous stumbling block and in spite of his mother's assurance that this was a match made in heaven, his own reservation regarding the outcome was far from certain.

The following day Marcus felt he needed to go back to basics even if only for one last occasion. To assume his routine habit of visiting the seafront, in the manner he did as a young man all those years ago. Then, it was an important period of contemplation, of creating dreams that he felt mattered and one he derived a great deal of joy from. Sitting on the seawall and looking across the wide expanse of the vast ocean, gave him the inspiration to think big and locked into that vision of thought, he could allow his imagination to run wild, where there could be no limits to what he would be able to achieve. His principle thoughts and the things he hoped for was always the very same. He felt like every wish was achievable.

On reflection what he had achieved in his life was remarkable. He became a soldier in the British Army which he was proud of; he succeeded in becoming an engineer of repute. His General progress in most matters was exceptional. However the ultimate reward, that golden prize he yearned for, somehow eluded him. That dream sadly faded into oblivion. As he sat there in contemplation, he knew Teresa was now a faded memory and no more the focus of his life. He knew only too well that yesterday's dream belonged to the past. Time and events had moved swiftly on. A new chapter and fresh challenges were now beckoning. Could it be with someone like Jessica? What was significant and most impressionable, was how much the village had altered from what he remembered. It was as if the profile of the place had been substituted significantly. The element of familiarity no longer existed. He marvelled in an unbelievable way how inconspicuous he had become. He recalled vividly the exalted welcome he received as a returning soldier after the war. Then, he acquired celebrity status to a remarkable degree. Everyone, young and old, was falling over themselves to meet and greet him, mainly to express their appreciation for his act of bravery.

Two decades later, his presence, walking through the village did not impact on anyone. He contended rightly to himself and acknowledged that life was always in a state of flux and forever evolving. He accepted also that there was no time like the present. Perhaps his single regret was not being able to contact or communicate with the person he truly regarded as his friend, Martin Jules. Marcus held Martin in the highest esteem. He was both an inspiration and a mentor, who was partly responsible for giving him the opportunity of leaving the village. It was not unreasonable to imagine that perhaps in his quest for knowledge about him was both vague and largely unavailable. Local rumours indicated that he immigrated to the United States and had become a tutor in history. The authenticity of that was difficult to assess, however, it was good news that he did not remain in the village environment and stagnate or become just another statistic. In many ways, the news of his development gave Marcus reason to be happy. He hoped that, perhaps, one day their paths would cross.

The fierce wind blew aggressively across his face as he sat and reminisced, tempering the prevailing heat that once predominated. He looked up and clearly observed the fading sun bowing obediently to the might and power of the night and decided immediately to take refuge in the comfort of his mother's home. He was left with a feeling of mixed emotions, accepting with a huge degree of trepidation the grand paradox, that as man and boy, this place, this village that he loved so dearly, for reasons that were difficult to understand, folks have always regarded him rightly or wrongly as something of a stranger. He wondered long and hard what kind of legacy he would have left in the eyes of those who knew him. Would it be one of praise or one of ridicule? That judgement would forever be a matter of speculation, one he was sure would border more on the latter than the former. Since it was only a matter of conjecture, he was satisfied that the only thing that really counted was giving your best and allowing life and events to take care of itself.

# TRINIDAD

Climbing the steep hill of Maraval, Marcus realised the moment had come to confront Jessica for the first time since that unfortunate incident that fractured the relationship between them. In view of what had happened, he considered this meeting something of an acid test. The climb to the top of the hill was clearly challenging, leaving him time to speculate about this venture that could so easily go wrong. He acknowledged that this was a reunion with a difference and no doubt one that needed to be handled with precision and care; such was the delicate nature of it. Reaching the green door, Marcus felt excited and nervous in equal measure. It was the first occasion he had of meeting Jessica and her mother, after the prompt disconnect between them; that saw a flawless friendship degenerate into a shipwreck. Although the incident was still fresh in his mind, he did his level best to erase it from his thoughts. Whatever the outcome, he was determined not to make that a stumbling block.

He knocked and waited for what seemed like an eternity; before the door eventually opened. Standing tall and elegant at the entrance was Mary Wiss, Jessica's mother. She looked much younger than he imagined. She was a well-groomed woman with what seemed like an imposing personality. The grey hairs that were evident by her temples adorned her appearance and merely embellished qualities which she was fortunate to possess. There was no question of her beauty and it was not difficult to imagine where Jessica extracted her good looks.

Mary did not smile, but her pleasant features suggested that she was of an accommodating nature. Marcus shuffled around nervously, giving the indication of disappointment, primarily because of his expectation of seeing Jessica herself. Such contact would have given him much relief, especially in generating a surprise element to his visit. The impact which he felt was so vital to his approach was sadly lost as a result.

"Good morning," Marcus announced as he observed Mary's fixed gaze. "My name is Marcus Gullant..."

"I know," Mary interrupted. "My daughter has sent me many photographs of you. In a very strange way, I get the feeling that I know you, even though we have never met." Came her refreshing and friendly reply.

Marcus immediately felt relieved. His smile was consistent with his mood. "I must say I feel the same way. Jessica never stopped telling me what a wonderful person you are."

Mary appeared flattered and started fingering her already well-groomed hair as she offered a welcoming smile. "Please come on in." She moved aside to allow him entry. "Jessica has gone to the city on a business errand. I'm afraid you'll have to wait until she gets back or come back another time." She concluded.

"Okay, I'll wait' that will be fine." He informed. "At this moment time is what I have plenty of."

"You would have to excuse me for not entertaining you properly. I have a pressing duty to someone that I must fulfil. Failing to do so, would make her extremely unhappy. It's her wedding dress that needs adjusting and there is absolutely no time to waste." She informed.

Mary led Marcus towards the veranda, which overlooked a huge chunk of the immediate surroundings and beyond. She pointed to the padded seats that were placed neatly on the platform. "Since you may have some waiting to do, I suggest you will do well to relax here. It's really the coolest area at the moment."

Marcus was impressed by the scenery. It was a most picturesque sight to behold. "This is a truly delightful view. I bet you would not exchange this amazing landscape for anywhere else in the world."

Mary chuckled quietly as she offered Marcus a cool drink. "This place gives me a reason to live. When I cannot sleep at night I would come out here and be inspired. Take my word; it's a very satisfying experience."

The anticipation of waiting for Jessica's arrival carried a measure of anxiety, which Marcus struggled to contain. Subsequently, for what seemed an eternity, the waiting was over. Jessica had returned home from her appointment, to face the unexpected. Her mood was upbeat as a result of the positive end product she obtained from her mission. Her eagerness to relay her good news to her mother was somewhat overwhelming. "Hello Mother, I'm back and I can tell you the prospects are excellent."

"That's wonderful news, my dear," Mary replied, raising her voice considerably. "There's good news here also. Someone is patiently waiting for you on the veranda."

"Who might that be?" Jessica questioned.

"Go find out." Mary retorted. "It will put you out of your misery."

Jessica quickly turned and headed towards the veranda, her curiosity getting the better of her. Marcus hearing the conversation was equally jittery. The element of excitement coursing through his veins, gave ample evidence that this meeting was vital. It carried an abundance of expectations that was necessary for his future ideals. So much rested on a positive outcome and in that regard, failure was not an option.

Jessica came face to face with Marcus and stood there frozen in utter disbelief. It was as if she had seen a ghost. Being their first contact since that fateful and inauspicious parting of their ways and it was obvious that both parties suffered an element of attrition or guilt as a result. For Marcus however, this was a process of mending fences and subsequently extracting as favourable a result as he possibly could. He was quick to break the ice. "Hello Jessica, how are you?"

Jessica, regaining some measure of composure, gave a half-frozen smile which quickly faded. "I'm doing very well, as you can see." She replied.

It was very strange seeing Jessica for the first time after her departure. She looked awesome. Her striking features and general characteristics gave the impression of a matured young woman in every aspect. No more was she shackled by the condition of shyness. Her dainty and elegant posture was most appealing. It was evident also, that she was the beneficiary of the climatic conditions around her. Her healthy tan emphasised her appeal to a remarkable extent.

"You do look incredibly well." He announced.

"And so do you." She offered as she looked around for somewhere to sit. "Well, well." She muted. "I never thought I'd see you again."

"Ditto," Marcus replied. "But this is an important mission and it was imperative for me to bite the bullet. Anyway as they say 'mountains do not meet, but humans do'."

She made herself comfortable, sitting opposite him with her arms folded and her legs crossed; which gave the impression of extreme confidence. Her white blouse and light blue skirt, accentuated her immaculate figure to the fullest, sending shivers down his spine. "Have you been waiting long?" She asked.

"Not exactly, but I did not mind the wait. Although I must admit, it made me rather anxious." He responded.

"Well!" She continued. "I'm sorry to have kept you waiting, I've just returned from town. I was competing for a job and would you believe it, I was successful. I managed to outshine the opposition and landed the position. I start in ten days time, isn't that wonderful?"

"Yes Jessie, that's hardly surprising to me. You are a very clever young woman and a most capable one." He offered.

"It's such a relief." She uttered. "Now I can concentrate on making a success of this new venture."

"Glad to see you're so content." He uttered unconvincingly.

Jessica looked thoroughly at ease. Beads of perspiration became evident, flowing from her temple down to her cheeks, a direct result of the tropical heat, but somehow amazingly, it looked immeasurably attractive. She patted her forehead delicately as she pondered about his agenda. She suspected that it was for a good reason, but could not quite put her finger on it. Whatever it was, it most certainly was not anything to do with love or romance. Having been told repeatedly that she did not fit the bill, she was positive Marcus was not about to alter his unshaken beliefs. "Now what brings you to my neck of the woods?" She enquired.

"I came to thank you for saving my mother's life." He announced with a smile.

Jessica thought it funny. "Ha! I'm afraid that is a total exaggeration, nothing could be further from the truth."

"I can only convey to you what I've been told and, if I'm honest, you must be deserving of her praise. My mother is not one for handing out accolades."

"Well Marcus, it was good of your mother to think so highly of me, but I cannot remember doing anything out of the ordinary."

"Please Jessica." He pleaded. "Whatever you do, don't sell yourself short. Anything you have attempted, you've accomplished comprehensively."

Jessica raised her eyebrows wryly. "I really don't know if I deserve such fine compliments. Anyway, what is the story? Surely you did not travel all the way here to tell me how wonderful I am!"

"You are absolutely correct; there is more to my visit than that. But firstly I cannot help being intrigued by your visit to my country and my village. That was quite a sense of adventure for you. May I ask why you did that?"

"The simple answer is I went there to see your children."

"Of course, I should have thought of that. You were an important fixture in their lives and it was good of you to do that. The thing is, I did not believe you could do anything so daring, it was completely out of your comfort zone."

"How right you are, but sometimes it pays to function that way. Anyway, it was my only chance to get to see Sara and Peter in the flesh."

"That I quite understand. But while you were there, something happened that I regarded as most important. My mother fell ill and for some unknown reason, you or no one else took the time to inform me. Not even my own children. What was the mystery about?" Marcus enquired.

"There was no mystery. It was my doing and I'm afraid I'm guilty as charged. You see Marcus; I was faced with a conundrum, letting you know that your mother was ill or keeping it under wraps and dealing with it accordingly. I must confess, it would have been most embarrassing for me to have you there, just after the problem we have had and to be honest that would not have suited me, not in the very least. So I did what was required of me and left."

"But my mother told me you were writing letters to me, she was convinced of that. So where did they go?" He asked with some surprise.

Jessica laughed out loud. "Give me a moment, I have something for you." She hurried off and returned with a bundle of letters neatly tied with a blue ribbon. "These are your letters. I did not send them for fear that you would recognise that they were written by me and I could not take that risk. Let's set the record straight. I simply went there to see your children. Your mother's illness just happened to coincide with my visit. It was one of those strange things, no more, no less."

Marcus took a deep breath. In view of his intentions, he was left to eat a huge chunk of humble pie. In all of this, it was prudent of him to keep a lid on the situation. "I guess fate has played a big part in all of this. The simple truth is, I'm very grateful for what you've done to help. I'm amazed to see how things just fell into place. It was a coincidence that you left London, only to rescue my mother from certain doom."

"Nothing so dramatic." She giggled. "Your mother is a very strong woman, providing she manages her illness, she is likely to outlive the both of us."

"That's a possibility." He agreed. "What took me by surprise was the news of your decision to leave London. What on earth made you want to do that?"

"There was nothing left for me to do there. All my future plans had disappeared and what I was hoping for did not materialise. Hence my decision to leave for pastures new, which seemed appealing."

"On the contrary, I tend to disagree. I think your prospects would be a whole lot better there than anywhere else."

She shook her head negatively. "My prospects had been trampled into the mud. In other words, my race was well and truly run. Like you Marcus, I have made choices, so coming back home and starting afresh, made sense to me."

"Come on Jessica." He appealed. "You have everything to live for. You are young, you are bright and what is more, you have the quality to succeed in a place that has far more prospects than here."

"You may well be right, but what I hoped would be my ultimate dream, simply did not go according to plan. What I needed was a totally new challenge."

"I'm trying as best as I can to follow, but how can someone like you, with so much to give, take such a stance?" He questioned.

Jessica gave him a rueful smile. "Not everyone aims for the stars. My own dreams are pretty modest. You can say I'm not as ambitious as some, but take my word for it, I know what I want." Was her assured reply.

"Well! Since we are on that subject, would it be too much to ask, what exactly do you hope to achieve by running away?"

"Let's start from the beginning. The facts are Marcus, that night when we made love; I was hoping that it would be the start of something big for both of us. It was an earnest attempt on my part, to develop a relationship that would give both of us enduring happiness. Heaven knows how much I wanted it to succeed. As it turned out, I got the answer loud and clear the very next day. You made it distinctly obvious that no such relationship was possible." She paused briefly.

"You were in the process of having your children back with you and your interest was taken up fully with their welfare. Such rejection is rather difficult to digest for a woman like me. What I actually did Marcus; I unknowingly exposed myself to that indignity. So, I got up from the floor, brushed myself off and decided to take another option. That was for me to leave London for good – to set myself new and realistic goals, to change my life completely."

She composed herself, before continuing. "In the interim, my main objective was to see your delightful children before I left. I had so much fun communicating with them over the years; it would have been an utter shame not to be able to meet them in the flesh. After which, it was my intention to leave discreetly and allow you and your children to bond without distraction. The error I made was to let you know how I felt about you. It was a judgment call that failed, the onus was mine completely. You never encouraged it, if you are anything, you are consistent. You have never once wavered from your beliefs and a person should be defined by their principles. It is something I truly admire. Sadly my plans went awry when Alan arrived and managed to put a huge spanner in the works."

"Jessica," Marcus pleaded. "Let's not get too involved with that particular subject. That's not why I'm here. The least said about that the better."

"That may well be so." She countered. "But Alan is not a figment of my imagination. He was the person you accused me of having a clandestine relationship with and please do not forget also, he was the very reason why I had to leave your home."

"I'm well aware of that, but I was hoping you don't dig too deeply into what I regard as unimportant matters at this juncture." He pleaded.

"Well, it's important to me. Alan was the principle reason why our relationship came to an abrupt end, have you forgotten?"

"How can one forget such a thing?" Marcus admitted. "However, my motto is to find a way forward and not linger on things that are not conducive to progress."

"It may not be helpful in any way, but I can assure you it was the worst nightmare imaginable for me. It was an experience I did not enjoy in the least and it was then also, that I decided that coming back to Trinidad was my best option."

Marcus nodded sympathetically. "I do understand. It was hardly a moment I care to recall with any degree of pleasure myself. What I'd really like to know, however, was when the decision was taken to travel to my village?"

"That was never a prescribed plan." She admitted readily. "It actually came out of the blue. I realised it was my only chance of seeing Peter and Sara. Failing that, I was positive the opportunity would be lost forever. So, I threw caution to the wind and decided to have a go. It was extraordinary, however, how smoothly it all went. The thing is, no sooner did I get there and quite by coincidence, I realised that your mother had health issues that needed urgent attention, which I was only too pleased to assist with."

Marcus puffed out his cheeks impatiently, but knowing full well he was skating on thin ice, he knew he needed to remain cautious. "Having gone out of your way to get there, would it not have been better to inform me? That way we could have worked together to solve the problem? After all, she is my mother."

"I beg to differ," Jessica argued. "I'm a qualified midwife. I am quite capable if I might add. I was able to identify the problem and dealt with it accordingly. Besides, I myself was dealing with a very raw and emotional problem, which having you there would not have helped me in any way."

"Look, Jessica, I was not questioning your fine qualities or your professional skills, I was just thinking that two heads are far better than one."

"Point taken," She admitted. "But you must remember the situation was a delicate one, which I'm sure you would agree. I was not soliciting attention in any shape or form. I surely did not want you to think that I was trying to attract or influence your opinion, one way or another. So I dealt with the problem as best I could and if I may add what I did for your mother I would have done for anyone else because that's the way I am."

Marcus giggled lavishly. "That is why my mother is so impressed. Just imagine, she had never met you before and you were able to be there for her in her time of need, rendering the kind of assistance that was pivotal to her recovery. No wonder she thinks you're an angel."

"An angel did you say?" Jessica asked ruefully. "Me an angel? You can attest to the fact that I am nothing of the sort."

Marcus was quick to reassure her. "That's not the way my mother saw you. The way she assesses you, left no doubt in my mind, that you don't need wings to be considered an amazing person, because you certainly are."

Jessica appeared moved and altogether more conciliatory. "Well, considering the way we parted, it's very kind of you to think I'm amazing."

"But you are," He insisted. "What you've done for my family is nothing short of remarkable. You are an outstanding person and we all appreciate it immensely."

Jessica smiled warmly. "What I did for your family, pales into insignificance, compared to what you did for me. Let's not forget when we met on my journey to London, I was inconsolable. You changed that. You also made me a solid promise to deliver me safely and you kept it. You cannot imagine how fortunate I felt meeting someone like you. You gave me the full benefit of your hospitality and accommodated me as though you knew me your whole life. Perhaps that is the reason why I became so attracted to you. It was difficult to restrain myself from someone like you who possessed so much charm and such an infectious manner. You kept me in London for an indefinite period as a friend. So, if you are in the business of handing out praises. Mine has come a long way second."

"In my mother's, eyes that is not so. She has emphasised that you are the most amazing human being she has ever encountered." He assured her.

"Well, I can say the same about you. The generosity you showed towards me cannot be ever overstated. However, Marcus, I have seen the other side of you. To be called a slut, a liar and a cheat is not something anyone wants on their resume. I can assure you that for a woman to be seen as such in anyone's eyes is a difficult pill to swallow. I've always tried as best I can, to be honest, perhaps that is why my first transgression got me into a situation that I'm thoroughly ashamed of. It is a stain on my character, which I'm afraid I'm not sure if I will be able to erase."

He looked bemused and embarrassed. "What can I say, other than to tell you that I'm sorry. Sometimes things said in haste almost always come back to haunt you. As for the other matter that you stated, I did not really reject you, if you think so, it was most definitely not my intention. The kids coming back placed a priority over everything else. Look, I had a great deal of time to think about what happened between us and as they say, hindsight is a marvellous quality. I was silly not to have taken the opportunity that was placed before me. You have to believe me, Jessie, when I tell you that so much has changed since then. I have learned some hard lessons and not before time. I have come to fully appreciate you and what you stand for. It is imperative that you understand that."

"People change, I can agree with that. All the same, some things are difficult to accept."

Marcus tried to seize the moment. "I was informed that your dad left your Mum. Mama G told me about the incident. That must have been horrendous for you to take..."

"That is a very confidential matter," She interrupted. "It was not something I am prepared to discuss with you. It is personal to me. However, my mother needs no sympathy. She is a very resilient woman, who can take care of herself. My mother had to put up with my dad's indiscretions over a long period of time. He was not an easy man to deal with. That situation may have contributed in a small way to my returning home, but it was not my principal reason. I needed something different, as I was clutching at straws and feeling unsettled. I was aspiring towards a new venture; the kind that would stimulate me. This new job that I'm starting gives me hope, a measure of expectation and a new focus. I can now get on with the rest of my life the way I want to and that pleases me no end." Jessica remarked proudly.

Marcus's disappointment was clearly visible. The frown on his face betrayed his feeling in a very obvious way. However, he nodded approval. "Great news, I'm happy for you now that you have found peace of mind. Normally I would readily congratulate you on your new venture, however as things stand, your accomplishment does not bode well with what I have in mind. As you may gather, I'm here on an important mission. One that is vital to our future."

Jessica smiled warmly. "Whatever that might be, I sincerely hope that you are able to achieve it." She stopped briefly in contemplation before adding. "How strange life can be from one moment to another. When I left London, I felt completely empty. I was almost bereft of any feeling. It was truly a traumatic experience, none more so than when you questioned my honesty. That was awful mainly because I saw no merit in being untruthful to you. I could not help but feel that there was an element of doubt in your mind as to what I told you and I felt totally disillusioned that you did not believe me. As a result, your attitude left a cloud hanging over me. Which I can assure you left me with a sense of discontentment. It was all the more reason why I had to leave London." Jessica looked up and smiled warmly as she faced him. "I am now in a completely different place. I feel grand. My life has taken on a new perspective and right now I am prepared to do everything possible to keep it that way."

Marcus exhaled slowly behind a vapid exterior. He was convinced Jessica had a valid argument which she expressed with genuine conviction. He had also, come to realise that this mission of his was no picnic. In a strange way, he momentarily began to question his mother's wisdom, in believing it would be easy travelling here and trying to restore that wonderful friendship that was fractured by the regrettable incident that happened not so long ago.

"I understand your sentiments completely and I cannot dispute any of the things you said. I admit the attitude I demonstrated in London was bordering on the bombastic. I really thought I knew all the answers. How wrong can one be? I hope you can find a way to forgive me for my actions. In a strange way, you have helped me to see the light and more than that, you have brought me to my senses. To be frank I'm here on a damage limitation exercise. I dearly need your help and your patience and I am positive that you are a very forgiving person." He expressed passionately.

Jessica sighed heavily. "Marcus, you should know that it is not in my nature to hold grudges."

"That's all the more reason why my mother and I think that you are so amazing." He gushed.

"It seems to me, Marcus, that someone wants to make me feel better than I should all of a sudden." She indicated.

"Not at all." He suggested. "My reason for coming here can only be explained positively. It's true my mother insisted that I come to thank you for your kind deeds, but even without her prompting, I would not have missed this opportunity of seeing you once again. With regards to that unpleasant experience we both shared, I can assure you that I have totally erased it from my mind. What I am here to tell you is of the greatest importance to me and similarly, I sincerely hope that it would also be for you. I thought when my children returned it would have given me all the joy and satisfaction that I needed. Peter and Sara did bring a massive degree of comfort, which served me well, but I was quick to realise that there was an emptiness that existed in me. There was a lack of fulfilment that I really could not explain, in the end; it occurred to me that your absence was the reason for it. What I found out Jessica is that you are the one that I really want."

Jessica's astonishment was real. "Hold on a second, where has this all come from? Have you lost your mind? Is this some practical joke?

"This is no joke, Jessica. Since you departed London, you've left a huge gulf in my life that I've found impossible to fill."

"But, Marcus," Jessica responded cautiously. "This is all too much for me to take in so suddenly. I know you and I happen to be aware of these sentiments which are preserved for Teresa and not me. You've told me time and time again that I could never be part of your plans because of my age. Again I ask, what has come over you?"

"Jessica, things have changed in a comprehensive way. I am no more a slave to the dictates of Teresa. She has been the bane of my life. Most of my adulthood has been caught up with her one way or another. It felt like she owned my soul. The whole thing had become an addiction – a drug, which until now I was never able to liberate myself from." He paused momentarily. "And you know what's so bad about it? I allowed it to happen. I invented and reinvented ways of why she should return. The thing is I was always hoping for a miracle. It was a simple case of allowing my heart to rule my head. Do you want to know what was so funny also? The evening when you told me she was never coming back, the penny dropped and reality kicked in. You can say I've learned the hard lessons that you cannot own anyone. But you can love someone and that is such a beautiful thing."

"I'm so glad you are seeing things with such clarity; I hope you are officially free of that obsession. It was entirely up to you to change gear and you did not. You caused your own affliction and you cannot blame anyone else but yourself." She insisted.

Marcus had a resigned look on his face. "You sound so much like my mother. She was always one for wise words. She always warned me about Teresa, but I did not listen. Unfortunately, I paid a very high price. She kept insisting that love should be mutual and ours most certainly was not."

"Well, that should be a welcome relief for you. It's all behind you now. You should have listened to your mother. She's quite a woman, make no mistake about that."

"You are so right." He lamented. "Mama G saw the pitfalls and alerted me accordingly, but I pressed on regardless. I needed to prove a point. After all, what is a man without an ego, especially an untarnished one? It was the time when I thought I knew all the answers to every problem. It so happens that I can now see the folly of my ways."

Jessica nodded approval. "Yes, sometimes we tend to think we are superior to our parents in our way of thinking, forgetting that they have seen it all before."

"You are so correct," He agreed. "Mama G is a canny old fox and I've learned to respect her views. For instance, she has insisted that you are the brightest star on this galaxy and I'm not about to dispute her opinion other than to say, you have certainly left your mark on her and that sentiment goes for me also."

"Oh, how sweet." She countered. "Would I be correct in thinking that you are here on your mother's influence? Why do I get the feeling that you are on some mission, conducted purely on the strength of your mother's advice?"

Marcus giggled nervously. "Come on Jessica, you should know I'm my own man. I am here on my own volition, please believe me."

"So why is it that everything you say, sounds remarkably like a message from your dear mother?"

"Because I think it's good to know how impressed my mother feels about you. Correct me if I'm wrong; are her compliments about you out of order?"

"No Marcus I certainly don't have any quarrel with that. However, it seems such a waste of journey for you, only to let me know how your mother feels about me."

"Look, my mother's sentiments are partly why I am here and it would be wrong of me not to tell you that she encouraged me to make this visit. But I must emphasise, that one way or another, this trip would have been made based on the way I feel about you. This is not about Mama G; it's about me and my feelings for you. What is more, it is vital and most important that you are aware of it."

Jessica's look was one of incredulity. "This is unreal. What is this? Am I just hallucinating here? Or will I wake up from a dream, only to find out that it was nothing more than just that – a dream. Are you saying that my age is no longer a factor?"

"This is no dream, Jessica. It is as real as it gets. I have made mistakes in my life and letting you go may have been my biggest. I simply want to correct that." He assured her.

Jessica still shocked and surprised responded. "Where is all this coming from? I've lived with you for many years and for that entire period; you took no notice of me. I am also aware of how dogmatic you are, especially where women are concerned. You've expressed time and again why someone of my age could never be considered as the significant other in your life, not even remotely, based on those lofty principles of yours. What has changed so suddenly and why?"

"It's a question I ask myself repeatedly so many times, the answers do not readily come to mind. What is so fascinating however is the way I see you now and how different it feels being with you."

Jessica took a deep breath. "Marcus, it's all so confusing and difficult to fathom. There were times when I thought you did not even find me attractive."

She paused momentarily. "Look, I even made the ultimate sacrifice of sleeping with you, letting you know what I wanted and how I felt about you. And what did I get? A total rebuff and now all of a sudden, here you are, expressing compliments I find difficult to comprehend."

"Yes, Jessie that's right, things have altered considerably. You can say I was like an ostrich with my head buried deeply in the sand. But I knew instinctively when you were gone, that I must have been insane not to realise how strongly I felt about you. The notion I had of you being too young is clearly not compatible with the way I feel now. So I expressed that to my mother and she assisted me in removing the scales from my eyes. I'm now able to see clearly what I've been missing all along. How stupid of me. Now I dearly want to correct my mistakes."

"Aha!" Jessica responded immediately. "This is not about you it seems. This is about your mother. You are reacting to your mother's wishes, I should have known."

"Nothing of the sort." He assured her. "I arrived in the village brimful of love for you. All my mother did was help guide me in the direction I was heading for anyway. Look, Jessie, I'm here to let you know how much I care. If at all you feel the same way. I would gladly ask you to be my wife."

Jessica maintained a solemn look. What should have been a joyous moment suddenly appeared challenging. "Look, Marcus, I have decided with a lot of care and effort to change course. That meant investing a great deal of time and energy into what I want my future to be. Believe me that did not come very easily. What I did was to set myself simple goals, which meant looking straight ahead. So what did I do? I have trimmed my sails, adjusted my life accordingly and in so doing began to think differently. I have secured a job which will commence in ten days time here in my own environment, which appeals to me. The job offers me prospects which I'm only too happy to accept. Are you asking me to sacrifice those things for a proposal that has come completely out of the blue? I do not know if I can wrap my emotions around what you are offering right now. I care about you, but I do have a mind and I'm trying to make it up, please do not try to complicate matters, I beg of you." She urged.

"Jessica, I'm not about to sell you something you do not want. That is not why I'm here. This means so much to me, please understand that. If you let me I would like us to share a life of happiness together. I do know you care and we have so much in common. I believe we have a mutual love; let's make it count. If your answer is 'yes', I guarantee that you will never regret it." He pleaded wholeheartedly.

Jessica's stare was fixed and unyielding. "Marcus I always try my very best to maintain a measured existence that is suitable for me. No thrills or frills. As you well know my idea of excitement is reading a good book and it may interest you to know, that's how I like it. I really do not believe in extremes. Only a few minutes ago I was contemplating how best I was able to tackle the complexity of my new life and now a few minutes later, I'm being proposed to. This transition is breathtakingly surreal. It is more than my poor heart is able to withstand. I'm still at a loss to know, what has happened to your creed? What has happened to that solid doctrine of yours, never to deviate from your lifelong principles; of ever getting attached to someone as young as me? Have you suddenly become a victim of the tropical heat? Did it dissolve all you stood for? Or are you having a midlife crisis with this dramatic change of heart?"

Marcus giggled nervously. "It's because I've found it fundamentally important to do so. There is a saying that maturity teaches wisdom and who am I to disagree. Everything in life requires a thought process, the kind that is necessary to evaluate our very existence. I am not exempt from that quality. So I've decided in the light of reason to think again, to give consideration to this fixed opinion of mine and found to my utter astonishment that my principles were not beneficial to me in any shape or form, or to my future for that matter. In view of that, I have decided to depart from an attitude of sterility to a more enduring and hopefully far-reaching philosophy. Our happiness depends on that. I have come to truly believe that there are greater rewards in that approach, than being the way I was. I envisage great things ahead for us in the not too distant horizon. Our future depends on it."

Jessica's deportment became more amenable. The smile she offered was now one of great satisfaction. It was obvious Marcus was committed to change. "Welcome to this side of good reason. I am happy to know that you have adopted a degree of pragmatism in your thinking. That can only be good for you." She expressed.

"Jessica," Marcus retorted. "One cannot remain naive forever. I have learned my lesson and I am so pleased to be able to make you understand that."

She exhaled deeply. "I follow your meaning and I am glad that you are more flexible in your long-held views. I guess I can live with that."

"I sincerely hope so," Marcus contended, feeling a sense of relief. "You cannot imagine how amazing it is to rid myself of that noose around my neck. For the first time, I can safely say, I can go to bed and sleep without that recurring theme floating around in my head as if it was a permanent fixture. Perhaps looking back, it was nothing more than my own ego and sheer stupidity for encouraging it. I only became fully conscious of my feelings towards you, when you departed. It dawned on me in a massive way, the huge gulf you left behind. It became almost unbearable. "

Jessica was still somewhat mystified by Marcus's sudden turnaround, offered a faint smile. "It's so strange to hear these words coming from your mouth. Are you quite sure that you have overcome that obsession that you had for Teresa? Has it really come to an end?"

"Oh yes, that is for sure. Teresa's manipulative ways have had the better of me for far too long. As of now, after a very long time, I have a sense of joy that has returned into my life and it's a great feeling. Besides, you cannot imagine how much Sara and Peter are waiting to have you in their world again. You have given them something that is so unique and so wonderful. Something their natural birth mother couldn't provide."

Jessica's eyes lit up. The thought of seeing the kids once more was an exciting prospect. "Marcus I have to tell you that they are remarkable children, I would be delighted to see them again."

"Good," He declared. "Now that we have removed the huge obstacle in our way, we can now go forward in glorious harmony."

Jessica's smile was most inviting. It was quite obvious that the wind of opportunity was blowing in her direction. That visit to the village which she made, was strictly on a whim, merely to satisfy her curiosity of meeting Sara and Peter, but nothing remotely indicated to her of an end product so rewarding. As was suggested by Marcus, fate had played a remarkable hand in bringing them together. So far as she was concerned, it was undoubtedly a wish come true. A turn of events beyond her wildest dreams and she was not about to throw this wonderful prize away. "Marcus what can I say? Right now I'm a completely satisfied person. I love this environment. I am with my mother whose company I cherish with all my heart. I feel a sense of belonging here. Can you give me a tangible reason for leaving all of this?" Jessica enquired.

"Jessica," Marcus pleaded. "There is no greater gift in this world than love. It is what all mankind strives for. The fact is you and I have it in abundance. Let us use it to give our lives that happiness we deserve."

Jessica's pause was long and deliberate. It was as if she still did not believe that this was reality. "Marcus, are you positive this is what you want?"

Marcus's reply was swift. "Jessica, I was never more positive about anything in my life than I am now."

Jessica bowed her head momentarily, her emotions getting the better of her. Tears were trickling slowly down her cheeks. Marcus reached out and gently touched her shoulder. "Jessie this is not an occasion for sadness."

She lifted her head and smiled. It was one of sheer joy and contentment. "These tears are not about sadness Marcus. Somehow I never imagined that this day would come."

"Well." He demanded. "Sometimes we cannot foretell what the future holds. I can only say that this was meant to be."

Wiping the tears from her cheeks with the back of her hand she smiled broadly. "Well at least I would be seeing two of my favourite people once again and that would be a delightful prospect."

"Oh yes," Marcus replied gleefully. "Sara and Peter just can't wait to see you again."

Still smiling she declared. "No, I was referring to Mama G and Precilla."

Marcus was almost taken aback by Jessica's comment but was quick to see the funny side of her humour. "That's why I care so much about you. That was a Jessica special. "

Just then, Mary Wiss appeared, wearing a look of satisfaction. "Jessica, lunch is ready and I do hope your friend Marcus will join us for a bite."

Marcus rapidly rose to his feet and nodded approval. "Thank you very much – may I call you Mother Wiss?"

"Of course you can, I see no reason why not." Smiling pleasantly as she led the way towards the table.

Marcus turned his attention to Jessica, with a beaming smile across his face as he took her hand and trudged slowly towards lunch, behind Mary. "I sincerely hope I've got this right." He whispered.

"What?" She asked.

"I will be having my first meal with my new family."

Jessica looked up and giggled happily.

Marcus reciprocated.


### THE END